DARK INTELLIGENCE

DARK INTELLIGENCE

TRANSFORMATION, BOOK ONE

NEAL ASHER

NIGHT SHADE BOOKS
NEW YORK

Night Shade books may be purchased in bulk at special discounts for sales promotion, corporate gifts, fund-raising, or educational purposes. Special editions can also be created to specifications. For details, contact the Special Sales Department, Night Shade Books, 307 West 36th Street, 11th Floor, New York, NY 10018 or info@skyhorsepublishing.com.

Night Shade Books® is a registered trademark of Skyhorse Publishing, Inc.®, a Delaware corporation.

Visit our website at www.nightshadebooks.com.

10 9 8 7 6 5 4 3 2 1

Library of Congress Cataloging-in-Publication Data is available on file.

ISBN: 978-1-59780-824-8

Cover illustration by Jon Sullivan
Cover design by Claudia Noble

Printed in the United States of America

Caroline Asher
10/7/59—21/1/14
They say time heals.
No, it just wears away pain.
It grinds everything to dust.

ACKNOWLEDGEMENTS

Many thanks to those who have helped bring this novel to your e-reader, smart phone, computer screen and to that old-fashioned mass of wood pulp called a book. At Macmillan these include Julie Crisp, Louise Buckley, Ali Blackburn, Ellie Wood, Jessica Cuthbert-Smith, Sophie Portas, Rob Cox, Neil Lang, James Long and others whose names I simply don't know. Further thanks go to Jon Sullivan for his eye-catching cover images, Bella Pagan for her copious structural and character notes and Peter Lavery for again wielding his "scary pencil." And, as always, thank you, Caroline, for putting up with a husband who's often a number of light years away.

1

THORVALD SPEAR

I woke in crisp white cotton sheets to the sound of skylarks, with the sun beaming through a window somewhere nearby. I gazed up at a lighting panel inset in the pale blue ceiling and smelled comforting lavender with a slight acrid undertone of antiseptic. I could also detect the distant promise of coffee. I felt really good and, after a deep, relaxing breath, sat up to look around. The arched window at one end of the room gave a view of mown lawns scattered with perfect springtime trees. Gentle puffy clouds neatly decorated the sky, with just the stark lines of a single-cargo grav-barge crossing it for contrast. Within the room stood a chair, and side table with a mirror above it. The small touch panel in a bottom corner indicated that it also served as a screen. Next to the bed my clothes lay neatly folded on another wooden chair: including my favourite jeans, ersatz rock-climbing boots and enviro-shirt.

I whipped the sheet back and got out of bed. Nothing ached, nothing hurt and I felt fit. It then occurred to me to wonder, vaguely, why I might have expected otherwise. I headed over to an open side door into the en-suite, glanced at the toilet but felt no need to use it, then went over to the sink and peered at myself in the cabinet mirror above. No stubble, but then I'd had permanent depilation years ago. I opened the cabinet and took out a small brushbot, inserted it into my mouth and waited while it traversed round my teeth, cleaning them perfectly. Took it out and dropped it into its sanitizer, then went back into my room to dress.

Vera, as her name-tag declared, arrived just as I was closing the stick-seam on my shirt.

"Oh, you're awake," she said, placing a tray on the side table. I walked over, the pungent smells of coffee and toast eliciting something close to euphoria. I picked up the coffee and sipped, finding it as good as it smelled, and studied Vera. She was beautiful, her complexion flawless and the balance of her features perfect. She wore a nurse's uniform of white and navy blue, a silver crab pendant at her throat, and sensible shoes.

Crab.

My mind keyed onto that and I rose to a slightly higher level of consciousness, where I found I wasn't quite so comfortable.

"He'll be waiting for you on the veranda when you're ready," she said, then turned to go.

"Wait," I said.

She turned back and gazed at me expectantly, but I couldn't find the words to express my unease.

"It's nothing," I finished.

She departed.

The toast with its butter and marmalade was, like the coffee, the best I've ever had. I finished both with relish, then headed for the door. I turned left into a carpeted corridor, then right into a clean decorously appointed sitting room—seemingly translated from centuries in the past. A glass sculpture on a nearby bookcase caught my eye; something insec-tile squatted there, with hints of light in its depths. It made me as uneasy as that crab pendant and my awareness rose to yet another level. I pushed open paned glass doors and stepped onto a wooden veranda, replaying the moments I had experienced from waking, wondering at their perfection. Then, as I saw the figure sitting at an ornate iron table on the veranda, the confines of my mind began to expand.

Sylac . . .

Of course everything was perfect; *too perfect.* I had no doubt I was Thorvald Spear and that if I concentrated I could remember much of my past. But it bothered me that my recent past wasn't clear and that I felt no inclination to remember it. I walked over to Dr Sylac, pulled out one of the heavy chairs and sat down, and studied him for a second. He was dressed in an old-time safari suit, a thin, shaven-headed man with an acerbic twist to his mouth and black eyes. This was completely wrong, because at that moment I had a clear recollection of how he'd looked last time I saw him. The extra cybernetic arm with its surgical tool-head no longer protruded from below his right, human, arm. His skull was now unblemished—not laced with scars and the nubs of data interfaces, all ready to plug into a half-helmet augmentation.

"Interesting scenario," I said, waving a hand at our surroundings.

"I wondered how quickly you would notice," he replied. "You were always the brightest of my . . . associates."

"All too perfect," I added, "until now."

"Standard resurrection package," he said dismissively. "They create a virtuality to ease one back into existence with the minimum of trauma."

"So why are *you* here, then?" I asked.

"They took me out of storage. A reduction in my sentence was promised if I worked on you." He shrugged. "It seemed like a good deal—I get to return to corporeal form and I've been moved up the Soulbank queue."

"Soulbank queue?"

"Oh yes, after your time." Sylac paused for a second then continued, "It's where the dead are stored, either awaiting their chance of resurrection in a new body or leapfrogging through the ages. Some criminals are kept here too . . ."

So Sylac's dodgy games with human augmentation had finally caught up with him. It quite surprised me that the AIs had bothered to store his mind. Some of the things he had done should have resulted in a permanent death sentence.

"But it's noticeable," he continued, "how you haven't asked how and why you're here."

I stared at him, first realizing that he was part of the process of easing me back into existence, then understanding that his words were a key made to unlock my memories. The war, I remembered. After many years of working in adaptogenics, nanotech and multiple biological disciplines, I'd formed a partnership with Sylac. This was during the first years of the prador/human war—when humans and our AI overlords discovered we weren't alone in the universe. And our nearest neighbours were vicious alien killers.

Upon realizing that Sylac was leading me into experimental and illegal territory, I'd said my goodbyes and joined up. My extensive knowledge and skillset were highly regarded by the AIs, the artificial intelligences running the war. In fact, I'd been very highly *regarded* by them before the war, as they'd wanted to know how my brain worked. Intelligence was something that could be measured and, in some forms, perfectly copied into artificial minds . . . up to a point. But for some, IQ ceased to be measurable and genius blurred into madness. They called me a genius, but I didn't like that. I always felt that what they'd seen in me was just another immeasurable facet of human mentality—will power.

After both real-time and uploaded combat training, I went into bioweapons and bio-espionage. The AIs tried to keep me away from the front, but I went there anyway. I remembered the desperate fighting, my first encounter with the prador, first attempts at interrogating the creatures and the increasing sophistication of our techniques thereafter. Then things became vague again.

"Are we still losing?" I asked.

"The war ended over a century ago," he replied.

So, a moment of deliberate shock to shake things free in my mind. Even though I recognized it as such, I still felt panic and confusion.

"It ended about twenty years after you died," he added.

I closed my eyes and tried to recall more, but the detail remained hazy and I just couldn't nail anything down. This was frustrating because clarity of thought had never been a problem for me before. I tried to figure it out, wondering if whatever had been done to enable me to handle revival shock was also interfering with my thinking.

"My implant," I finally realized, opening my eyes. I'd died, and someone with my background couldn't fail to understand what that meant. Sylac had implanted a certain piece of hardware in my skull, and the "me" who was drawing these conclusions was a recording of my original self.

"They call them memplants or memcrystals now," he said conversationally. "Yours was the first of many I developed. I sometimes think they're why I'm still alive. The AIs must have weighed my research on the scales of life and death, and my augmentations resulted in more lives saved than lost. Or maybe it's that sticky area concerning the definitions of murder and manslaughter, especially when the supposed victim is a willing participant. The AIs would have us believe that if you kill a sentient being, a true death sentence—the utter erasure of you from existence—is automatic. I know otherwise, because there are many like me in storage. And there are many kept there who have committed murder." He gazed musingly at the parkland beyond the veranda. "Of course it's much easier to sentence someone to true death when they're not useful . . ."

"We won?" I asked, still trying to get my thoughts in order.

"Debatable," he replied. "We were winning, but the prador king was usurped. The new king, apparently not so xenocidal, decided that fighting us was no longer a good idea. They retreated but we didn't have the resources to go after them and finish the job."

"My memplant," I asked, "where was it found?"

He glanced at me. "Someone who knew my work recognized it. It was set in a brooch in a jeweller's window, which was an interesting outcome." He paused, studying me, then reached out to tap my skull. "It'll be back in place when they truly resurrect you, as there are difficulties involved in copying that technology across to something more modern."

Truly resurrect . . .

I filed that away for later and made another attempt to think clearly. The memplant Sylac had fitted inside my skull was a ruby. It was a decent size too, being as long as two joints of my little finger. So it being used for jewellery seemed surreal but made sense, although this particular ruby was rather more than it seemed. The quantum computing lattice interlaced throughout its crystal structure gave it that bit extra that allowed me to live.

"They couldn't trace its source beyond the shop in which it was found, though there was speculation that it was picked up by salvagers out in the Graveyard—"

"Graveyard?" I interrupted, feeling like an idiot.

"A no-man's-land between our Polity and the Prador Kingdom."

"Ah."

"The Polity, that human and AI dominion spanning thousands of star systems, had been shocked out of its complacency upon first encountering the prador. The alien monsters that resembled giant fiddler crabs had been unremittingly hostile and genocidal.

"Your memplant had been damaged before it was recognized for what it was, and the forensic AI that first studied it only made basic repairs. Otherwise, it could have lost the data it contained." He lifted his hand from the table and stabbed that bony finger at me again. "That data being you."

"So they got some expert advice," I suggested.

"Absolutely." He nodded. "It also seems that they *felt*," he sneered at the word, "that you were owed a life for your service during the war."

"So what now?" I asked.

"A body awaits you, tank-grown from a sample of your own DNA, stored by wartime Polity medical."

"Then it's time for me to start my life again."

"I envy you, but I don't envy you trying to incorporate your memories. You don't have full access at the moment."

"What do you mean?"

"I can tell they're not clear—as I said, the memplant was damaged, almost certainly by the intrusion of search fibres from a prador spider thrall. Not even the AIs can work out how you died. But they, and I, uncovered enough to know that it's all very ugly." He turned to gaze at me again. "You can, if you wish, decide to edit those memories out."

My immediate reaction was distaste. They'd started using memory editing during the war and, even though it turned battle-stressed and highly traumatized people back into useful soldiers, I hadn't liked it. It was a cop-out, reneging on responsibility, going through life with blinkers on.

"I want all my memories," I said, which was enough to trigger what had been hidden until now.

A chaotic montage of horror returned, delivered through a tsunami of fire.

THE WAR: PANARCHIA

The reality of the war was scribing itself across the sky of Panarchia in brighter text every night. In the beginning it had competition from the accretion disc of Layden's Sink, a bright oval lighting up half the sky. Perhaps a century hence this black hole would suck down this whole planetary system. Yet now, even that formed a dull backdrop against which Polity and prador forces tore each other apart.

"Close your visor, soldier," said Captain Gideon.

I touched a control on my combat suit's helmet, and its visor slid silently closed. I needed the light amplification now, anyway. And, during the night here, given the hostile local wildlife, you maintained suit integrity or you stayed in your tent. General Berners said the octupals, or the "fucking molluscs" as he described them, were an alien import. Yet it struck me that they had burgeoned very nicely thank you, in an environment supposedly not their own. As Gideon settled beside me, I scanned the emplacements around us, uncomfortable with our exposed position, then dropped my gaze to the sheet of solidified lava beneath our feet. This was dotted with small pools where large gas bubbles had burst and looked like a slice of cherry chocolate cake in the twilight. Already some octupals were crawling from those pools, ready to set off on their nightly hunt for prey and for mates—though sometimes they made little distinction between the two. And already I'd heard swearing from some of Gideon's troops who, like me, had forgotten to close their visors.

"You ever seen a real octopus?" asked Gideon.

"Yes," I replied, returning my attention to the body of the captured prador first-child—one of the vicious children of our enemy. It was sprawled before me beside the foxhole it had made in the rock here. Its legs, manipulator arms and claws were stacked in a pile a few paces away, behind our big autogun. I now had its carapace open, hinged aside on gristle like the lid of a waste bin. I continued sorting through the offal inside, pulling aside various glutinous items to finally expose its main ganglion, or brain. This sat inside a ring-shaped chalky case. Picking up my surgical hammer, I hit hard, cracking open the case. The first-child hissed and bubbled and I felt the stubs where we had cut off its mandibles knocking pathetically against my leg. Still, even knowing what a creature like this would do to me were it mobile, I hated what I was doing.

"Where?" asked Gideon.

"Where what?"

"Where did you see an octopus?"

"In an aquarium on Earth."

"Never been there," he said dismissively. "Never wanted to go there."

I guessed he was trying to distract himself and, with anyone else, I would have assumed he didn't want to think too much about what I was doing. However, he and the rest of his men had been fighting the prador for a long time and had ceased to have any squeamishness about bio-espionage. When the enemy's inclination was to both kill and eat you, you tended to toss away any human rules of engagement. I wished I could.

Finally having broken away enough of the ganglion casing, I selected an interrogation implant from my steadily dwindling supply—a chunk of hardware that looked like a steel door wedge—and stabbed it into the required spot. The prador jerked under me, hissed and bubbled some more and squirted green blood from its leg sockets.

I turned away, feeling small impacts on my suit, and noted a nearby octupal shooting poisonous darts at me. It had decided it wanted to either eat or fuck me. Light stabbed through the twilight and the octupal exploded like a microwaved egg. One of our mosquito guns moved on, its camouskin rippling.

"They don't look much different," I said.

"What?"

I gestured to the steaming octupal remains nearby. "These look just like terran octopuses, though the ones on Earth live in water and some varieties grow larger."

"Do they shoot poisonous darts?" Gideon asked.

I shook my head. "They don't have tri-helical DNA and three eyes either."

Gideon snorted then turned back to look at the prador. "How long before you can get some answers?"

"A few minutes, but I'm not hopeful."

Gideon looked back the way we had come, towards the mountains, which were now silhouetted against the furthest rim of Layden's Sink. The eight thousand or so remaining men of Berners' division were encamped there and fortifying. If the prador already on this world moved against us, there was no doubt that we would be screwed, and fast. But the hundred thousand or more prador surrounding us had just spread out and dug in and were simply waiting. Berners reckoned they were awaiting the result of the space battle raging above. This sometimes turned the night to day, or shook the ground when some leviathan piece of wreckage came down. It was also close enough that passing Polity attack ships could help us out, sending down ceramic shrapnel daisy-cutters to shred the dispersed prador forces. Berners further pronounced that whichever side ended up controlling near space, owned this world and could quickly dispose of the opposing forces on the ground from orbit. But I didn't agree.

The prador had already been bombed by Polity ships, yet Berners' division, whose location the prador certainly knew, had not been touched in retaliation. I suspected a complicated game of strategy. Maybe the prador were keeping us alive in the hope that the Polity would make a rash rescue attempt, putting the AIs at a tactical disadvantage. It was, I felt, a strange strategy to use when you were fighting Polity battle AIs, but seemed to be the only explanation that fitted. I was now hoping for confirmation from this first-child, or at least some explanation.

"It's not right," said Gideon.

I turned to him, thinking he was having similar thoughts. Instead, he was staring up at the accretion disc.

"What's not right?"

"Y'know," he continued, "in another life I was an astrophysicist."

"What?" Now I was getting confused.

He pointed up at the accretion disc. "It's been described as a Kerr black hole because of the massive spin and other readings that indicate a Kerr ring, but there are irregularities." He lowered his hand and looked at me. "Its electrical charge is just too massive—thought impossible in something naturally formed."

"But evidently not impossible."

An icon blinked up in my visor as the interrogation implant made its connections: a small cartoon crab with a speech bubble issuing from its mandibles. We had more pressing matters in hand than out-there theoretical physics. It was my contention that to appreciate the wonder of the universe, one must first remain alive.

"We're in," I said. Then, "What's your name?"

"Floost," the prador replied.

Of course the creature was not replying to me directly. I'd flooded its brain with a network of nanoscopic tendrils, and these were similar in design to the connection routine of a standard human cerebral augmentation. That device had broken the barriers between the fleshy human brain and computing, but this one had a coercive element that standard augs lacked. And the data-feed routed back through a translation program. The upshot was that Floost couldn't refuse to answer. However, the prador could give perfectly true but misleading replies.

"Why have you not attacked the human forces on this world?" I asked.

"Because Father ordered us not to."

"Why did your father order you not to attack us?"

"Because you would be destroyed."

"Why does your father not want us to be destroyed?"

"Because he was ordered not to destroy you."

I realized then that this first-child had been coached in how to respond should it be captured and interrogated in this manner. This was going to get a bit laborious.

"Why was he ordered not to destroy us?"

"Because of the tactical advantages."

"We've got movement," said Gideon, gazing out towards our emplacements.

I glanced over and saw the big autogun swinging its barrel across, then beginning to heave its weight off the ground on lizard-like metal legs.

"Twenty-four targets closing," someone stated over com. "One first-child and the rest seconds—two of them implant tanks."

Implant tanks, great. As if the prador children weren't sufficiently bad in their natural form, their fathers transplanted their brains into heavily armed and armoured war machines.

"Fuckit," said Gideon. "Get your data, Thorvald."

"Why would not destroying us be a tactical advantage?" I asked.

"Accruing assets is advantageous."

"How are we assets?" I managed to ask just before Gatling cannons started thundering. Our force-fields took the strain, their powerful hard-fields appearing in the darkness, gleaming periodically like torch beams falling on glass. Tank shells next ignited the night, followed by a particle cannon beam in royal blue. A shock wave picked me up and deposited me on my back and, as I fell, I glimpsed the burning wreckage of a hardfield generator and projector tumbling past, leaving a trail of glowing molten metal on the stone.

"Covered retreat to the canyon," said Gideon calmly. "Tic mines all the way."

I only just heard the prador's reply over this, and it simply didn't make any sense, then. "You will serve us," it had said.

"We've gotta go," said Gideon, tossing a tic mine into the opened-up first-child even as I struggled to my feet.

I grabbed up my equipment and threw it into my backpack. I didn't bother with the interrogation implant because the things were single use. The rockscape was now constantly lit by pulse-rifle fire, the glaring stabs of beam weapons and the dance of glowing hard force-fields. Our mosquito guns were spitting fire, while our big gun was steadily backing away. Our remaining hardfield generators were now up off the ground and retreating on grav, their cooling fins already cherry red. About a mile beyond their defensive perimeter the prador were advancing behind their own layered hardfields. I could make out a big first-child firing a Gatling cannon. This was attached to one claw and it had a particle cannon attached to the other. Second-children half its size were firing the prador equivalent of our pulse-guns, or staggered along under the load of hard-field generators. The two implant tanks rolled along on treads with side turrets firing shrapnel rounds, while their top turrets coloured the night green with high-intensity lasers.

I watched the troops pulling back behind, firing occasionally and dropping tic mines in selected pools. These last devices behaved just like the insects they were named for. Upon detecting nearby enemy movement, they leapt from concealment and attached themselves. They then detonated their copper-head planar load, to punch through armour. As I retreated after Gideon, I saw one of our troops just fragment into a cloud—seemingly composed of nothing but scraps of camo-cloth.

"Move it!" Gideon bellowed. "We can't hold this!"

The troops broke into a run and within minutes we reached the edge of the canyon and began scrambling down to the riverbed. As we reached it, all our autoguns and shield generators entrenched themselves above to cover our retreat.

"Full assist," Gideon ordered.

I hit the control on my wrist panel and felt my movements become easier, smoother. Soon I was running android-fast with the others, back towards the mountains. Behind us the battle continued. I heard a massive detonation and, glancing back, saw that our big autogun was gone.

"Damp down assist," said Gideon, sounding puzzled. "They're not following."

That, I felt, must have something to do with us being "assets" or "resources" but it still made no sense to me. As I cut down on suit assist, splashing through the shallow pools that were all that remained of the river's flow, I realized that the sky was lighter. Now that Layden's Sink was out of sight behind the mountains, I could see that the night was nearly over.

"Hey, looks like we've got visitors!" someone commented.

We all paused and gazed up above the peaks. High above Berners' division, a Polity destroyer hung in the pale sky. I felt something relaxing inside me. Every other visit by a Polity vessel had been a quick in-and-out job, sowing destruction amidst the enemy behind us. Maybe now the fleet was making a concerted effort to get us out.

"Why a destroyer and not a transport?" asked Gideon.

"Maybe just cover until they can get something bigger down," I suggested. "If they're moving something in to get us out, they know the prador down here will react."

Then a particle beam stabbed down from the destroyer, blue coherent lightning reaching down here and there in the mountains, giant flash-bulbs going off where it touched. The symphony of destruction reached us shortly afterwards, complemented by the shuddering of the ground.

"What the fuck?" I wasn't sure whether it was me or someone else who said that. But even as the beam winked out, I knew that our division's outlying guard posts had just been annihilated.

Did I actually see what happened next or did imagination fill in the details for me? Black objects hurtled down from the destroyer—one of them visible only half a mile or so ahead. Then the ship peeled away, igniting a fusion drive to hurl itself back upwards. Bright light flashed, and my visor went protectively opaque for a few seconds. As vision returned I saw, in nightmare slow motion, mountains heaving and crumbling, their broken stone turning to black silhouettes that dissolved in a torrent of fire.

"They've killed us," said Gideon.

The fire rolled down and swept us away.

THE WAR: A BELATED PRELUDE

The miners of Talus push a runcible transfer gate, enmeshed in hardfields, into the giant planet's core. Here, they prompt thousands of tons of nickel-iron to squirt through underspace, via the gate, to a distant location. Meanwhile, a hundred light years away, the autodozers on plan-etoid HD43 shove mounds of ore into mobile furnaces. These metals are rare on some worlds, but here on Talus they are easily field-filtered, refined and transmitted. HD43's orbit is perturbed by a strip-mined loss of mass, which runs a mile deep all around the planetoid as it is gradu-ally peeled like an onion. Silica sand billows into a runcible gate on the planet Fracan, where a desert is being vacuumed away to bedrock. Old Jupiter swirls with new storms as its resources too are stripped, but by gas miners feeding like whales. In the Asteroid Belt combined crusher and smelting plants select asteroids, as if choosing the best candidates from a vast chocolate box. Materials gate through nowhere from numerous locations, becoming non-existent, and arrive. And these invisible transit routes converge at a point on the edge of chaos: factory station Room 101.

Resembling a giant harmonica, discarded by a leviathan eater of worlds, Room 101 sits on the edge of a binary star system. The station is eighty miles long, thirty miles wide and fifteen deep. The square holes running along either side of it are exits from enormous final-fitting bays. One of these is spewing attack ships like a glittering shoal of herring, which eddy up into a holding formation. Drives then ignite upon orders received, and they shoot away. At a slower pace, another exit is birthing the huge lozenge of an interface dreadnought. Another seems to be producing smoke, which only under magnification reveals itself to be swarms of insectile war drones. Some of these head over to piggyback on the attack ships, while others gather on the hull of the dreadnought. Still others, those of a more vicious format, head off on lone missions of destruction.

Inside the station, the sarcophagus-shaped framework of a nascent destroyer shifts a hundred feet down a construction tunnel eight miles long. Into the space it occupied, white-hot ceramal stress girders now stab like converging energy beams. Then these are twisted and deformed over hardfields which glitter like naphtha crystals. The skeleton of another destroyer takes shape and is moved on after its fellow, cooling to red in sections as directed gas flows temper it. From the tunnel walls, structures like telescopic skyscrapers extend and engage in hexagonal gaps in the ship's structure. A third such device moves up the massive lump of a three-throat fusion engine, hinges it up into place, then extends constructor tentacles like steel tubeworms. These commence welding, bolting and riveting at frenetic speed.

Fuel pipes and tanks, skeins of superconductor, optics and all the apparatus of the ship's system come next—some of it preprepared to unpack itself. The constructor tentacles are now ready to proceed inside, rapidly filling out the destroyer's guts. A main railgun slides up like an arriving train as the tentacles withdraw. The skinless vessel is turned and the railgun inserted like a skewer piercing the mouth of a fish. The conglomerate chunks of solid-state lasers are riveted in all around. The loading carousel of the railgun clicks round, as its mechanism is tested, then racking is woven behind it. This is filled with both inert missiles and CTDs—contra-terrene devices—because nothing says "gigadeath" quite so effectively as those flasks of anti-matter. A particle cannon arrives like a gatecrasher and is inserted just before the destroyer is shifted on, two more rising skyscrapers coming up to pin the next bug in this procession.

Next, another lump of hardware arrives: two torpedo-like cylinders linked by optics. These are trailing s-con cables and sprouting brackets and heat vanes like fins, a distortion around them causing weird lensing effects as they're inserted into the ship. Constructor tentacles bolt them into place and now small maintenance robots unpack themselves, moving in to connect other hardware.

A fusion reactor fires, powering up computers, which in turn run diagnostics that feed back to the constructors. A solid-state laser is removed and sent tumbling away—to be snatched up by scavenger bots crawling across the walls like car-sized brass cockroaches. Then another is inserted. Next come the tubes of dropshafts and large blocky objects, whose only identifiers are the airlocks and shaft connections on their outsides. They are inserted and connected throughout the ship, like a bubble-metal lymphatic system. And it's time for furnishings, suites, supplies and the other paraphernalia of human existence to be installed inside. Diamond-shaped scales of composite armour begin to arrive, as impact foam expands to fill the remaining inner cavities.

Constructors lay down the heat-patterned ceramal, which they weld and polish to a gleaming mirror finish. Space doors are installed over an empty shuttle bay. Inside a last remaining cavity, two objects like old petrol engine valves part slightly in readiness. The all-important crystal arrives as the final hull plates are being welded in place. It sits inside a shock-absorbing package a yard square, but this prize already hides faults due to hurried manufacture. The crystal is a gleaming chunk two feet long, a foot wide and half that deep—laminated diamond and nano-tubes form its quantum-entangled processing interfaces. Even its microscopic structures possess a complexity which is beyond that of the rest of the ship. A constructor arm like a tumorous snake strips it of its packaging, revealing its gleam through an enclosing grey support frame like a dragon's claw, and inserts it. Lastly, as the valve ends close down to clamp it in place, the last hull plates are welded shut and polished.

And the fractured mind of a destroyer wakes.

You are the war-mind Clovis, trapped in a mile-wide scale of wreckage falling into the chromosphere of a green sun. In the remaining sealed corridors around you, the humans are charred bones and oily smoke. Your Golem androids have seized up and your escape tube is blocked by the wreckage of a prador second-child kamikaze. When the salvage crab-robot snatches you from the fire you are indifferent, because you accepted the inevitability of oblivion long ago . . .

You are the assassin drone named Sharp's Committee, Sharpy for short. Your limbs are all edged weapons honed at the atomic level, your wing cases giant scalpel blades and your sting can punch even through laminar armour to inject any of the large collection of agonizing poisons you have created. You have sliced away the limbs of a prador first-child—one of the adolescents of that vicious race—and it screams and bubbles as nano-machines eat its mind and upload a symphony of data to you. You love your job of creating terror, because it satisfies your utter hatred of your victims . . .

You are dreadnought AI Vishnu 12, so numbered because that is a name chosen by many of your kind. In the five-mile-long lozenge that is your body, you contain weapons capable of destroying the world below. But you are mathematically precise in their use because of the higher purpose you serve, the knowledge of those aims and your adherence to duty. But the world is now fully occupied by the prador enemy and the fate of the humans trapped below is foregone. Your railguns punch anti-matter warheads down into the planet's core, while you set out to accomplish your next task. So you travel ahead of a growing cloud of white-hot gas, laced with a cooler web of magma . . .

You are not fully tested and may not even be viable. You are version 707: composed from the parts of wartime survivors. The crystal you reside in has its fault, the quantum processes of your mind cannot, by their nature, be predicted, and time is short. You are newborn from the furnace and about to enter Hell. And in time you will, for reasons others will find obscure, name yourself Penny Royal . . .

2

SPEAR

The second time I woke was in an amniotic tank, breathing through a tube and with the unmistakable feel of things attached to and penetrating my skull. I opened my eyes to a blur as I felt a metal grid slide up beneath me, hoisting me up and out of the liquid under harsh bright lights. It swung me to one side of the tank, then lowered me down again. Cold metal clamps took hold of my head, but this evoked a recently returned memory which I hadn't yet examined closely, so I struggled.

"Remain still," said a calm and slightly prissy voice.

I obeyed but felt the skin crawling on my back, as those cold fingers removed what had to be the modern version of upload optics and neurochemical conversion nodes stuck into my skull. My vision cleared in time to see the metal hand of a Golem android retract out of sight. The clamps opened and I immediately sat up, then just as immediately felt sick and dizzy.

"Take it slowly," said the Golem, turning back to me.

During the war the Golem had been the standard android manufactured in the Polity, and perhaps it still was now. Its ceramal motorized chassis, or skeleton, was usually concealed under syntheflesh and syntheskin—and it ran an AI mind in crystal. This one also looked like Vera from the virtuality where I'd experienced my first waking from . . . death. She was clad in a monofilament overall and, while I watched, she pulled a syntheskin glove back over her metal hand. She sealed it around her wrist, joining it invisibly to the skin of her arm, then pressed it home in various places, doubtless to reconnect its nerve network. I noted humanizing imperfections I had not seen in the virtuality: a slight asymmetry, an ersatz scar and messy tied-back hair that looked as if it needed a wash. The Golem of my time had always looked utterly perfect and had never quite blended in.

I rolled off the metal grid and stood up, aching from head to foot and feeling very weak. We were in a room that I later learned was the delivery end of mechanized resurrection. I looked around, a strong feeling of déjà vu arising as I watched the grid rise up again on its telescopic poles.

"Where am I?" I asked.

"Chamber R12 in the Krong Tower, London, Earth."

The name "Krong" nibbled at memory but almost in panic I decided not to pursue it. However, despite the familiarity of this chamber, I just knew I had never been here before, or in any place remotely like it.

"What now?" I asked.

She stabbed a thumb towards a door at the other end of the room. "You can clean up through there, where clothes are provided, along with a wristcom linked to an Earth Central submind. It will tell you everything you need to know. Thereafter . . ." She shrugged. "What you do next is entirely up to you, since you're a free citizen of the Polity."

"Really?" I wondered if the AIs had finally understood the workings of a mind like mine, in the past century, and I was to be left alone. It then occurred to me that even if they hadn't, they'd probably made a copy to examine at their leisure.

"Really," Vera affirmed.

"Thank you," I said, but she was already turning towards another tank. It was sliding into place with another of the resurrected moving sluggishly inside.

I trudged out of the room, trying to accept all I'd been told, but deliberately avoiding my most recently returned memories. They felt wrong, disjointed, like the recollection of some nightmarish pub crawl and exhibited a similar cringe factor. I didn't want to touch them yet because they hurt. Instead, I concentrated on the simply amazing facts of the now. The memplant Sylac had developed had allowed me to circumvent death. I was now in a clone body, whereas, for over a century, I had resided in a chunk of ruby netted with quantum computing. Maybe my corpse had rotted away completely somewhere, or my memplant had been separated from it by whatever incident had killed me—perhaps I'd been shot in the head. Perhaps the implant had been deliberately removed at the point of death. I just didn't know. Then it had found its way to someone who decided to turn it into jewellery, and I was thankful that person had not decided to cut the jewel. Finally, recently, it had been found and returned to Earth.

Over a century . . .

How much had changed? I wondered, as I surveyed the room Vera had indicated. Set in one wall were eight tall cupboards, each with a stick-on LCD label showing a name. I stared at it, that familiarity impinging again. But I felt out of kilter because my name on one cabinet, which was completely right, felt absolutely wrong. As I opened it, I tried to dismiss the feeling that I was interfering with someone else's property. These odd reactions had to be some sort of hangover from the drastic process I had just undergone. Glancing along the cabinets on either side, I also surmised I was just part of the batch being resurrected today, though perhaps the only one from such a distant time.

Inside hung clothing much like the kind I had worn so long ago. I suspected this had been made specifically for me, for I doubted fashions would be the same now. I turned away from this to wander through a door in the other wall, finding the washing facilities while briefly wondering how I had been sure they were there. I took a shower and scrubbed myself until the tank's clamminess had left my skin, returned to dress, and took up the wristcom.

"Thorvald Spear," it said as I strapped it on.

"I haven't noticed any vast changes in technology," I said, to test the intelligence of the submind speaking through it.

"The development curve flatlined before the war," it replied indifferently, "rose during the war—mainly for weapons, medical and spaceship tech—and settled to a steady but slow climb afterwards."

"One would suppose someone is keeping things slow," I suggested.

"One would suppose that necessary to allow slow organic creatures to keep up."

I decided I liked this particular submind. "What's your name?"

"You can call me Bob."

"So where now, Bob?"

"Outside, to where an aircab is waiting for you. It'll take you to a hotel where I have booked you a room. I'll stay with you while you adjust, but thereafter it's up to you. Left out of the door, through the door at the end then right to the dropshaft. Next go down, then out through the lobby."

"How do I pay?" I asked.

"Earth Central's paying, but you've no worries about funds."

"How so?"

"You receive backpay up to the moment of your resurrection—that's been standard for all soldiers whose memplants were discovered late. In your case it means you're filthy rich."

The dropshaft was my first encounter with change. For, though they were introduced aboard spaceships during the war, Earth buildings had still used stairs and elevators. I hesitated at the yawning gap then, following Bob's instructions, pressed the touch screen to select lobby and stepped in. I doubted they had resurrected me only to watch me plummet to a mangled death. The irised gravity field took hold of me and I descended gently, stepping out into an area decorated with large planetary scenes. The street outside was wide, with miles-tall buildings all around me, the sky a narrow blue river directly above. The driver was my next encounter with the future. There had been nothing but autocabs here last time, so was a need for drivers a step back? He wore a skin-tight blue bodysuit, his skin scaly and his eyes those of a snake. He grinned at me, exposing a viper's fangs. "Where to?"

"The Auton," Bob replied.

The aircab was decidedly retro—looked like a groundcar from centuries before I was born and even had wheels. As he took us into the air, whisking me through canyons of buildings, the driver tried some conversational gambits that left me confused. I had no idea what a "hooper match" or a "gabbleduck" might be, let alone "Jain tech" or "haiman" and yet felt further confusion at a sense of familiarity with such terms. I wondered when this feeling would go, for I had felt this déjà vu a few times now. However, I certainly understood what a Dyson Sphere was and knew, despite Bob's talk of flatlines, that I was probably due for some shocks. The driver subsided in obvious frustration. I later learned that people drove cabs for social interaction and interest, rather than financial gain. I probably wasn't his best fare that day.

London had changed: I recognized some buildings, but they were dwarfed by new structures that must have been close to two miles high. I spotted Elizabeth Tower and Westminster in a semicircle of parkland by the river. But there was no sign of the shimmershields, the "soft" force-fields that had protected these buildings from the depredations of tourism in my time. I subsequently learned that every part of them had been nano-coated with chain glass, so tourists had been allowed back. Finally the cab brought me down onto a high airpark platform extending, amidst many of the same, on a stalk from the side of a building resembling a mile-high scalpel blade. From there a dropshaft conveyed me into the plush interior of a lounge-bar.

A wide panoramic window ran along one side, facing a long bar, behind which stood a silver-skinned humanoid who might have been Golem or human. Mockwood lattices separated seating areas around the walls, while in the middle rested comfortable sofas and low tables. The place was crowded with both human forms and figures that weren't so familiar.

"Your room is 1034," said Bob. "If you have any enquiries, just ask, or you can use the console there. It will take me three seconds to respond from now on because I'm off to deal with some other matters."

"What other matters?" I asked, suspecting that Bob had already guessed my intention to make use of the bar.

"Personal," the submind replied briefly.

"Okay—you said *everything* is paid for?"

"Yes, until you find your feet. We done for now?"

"We're done."

I walked over to the bar and as I passed one of the low sofas a black-haired woman stood up. I glanced at her curiously, noting her pointy ears, sharp teeth and feline shape to her face. She was wearing very little: a skin-hugging lizardskin top that might as well have been sprayed on and khaki knee-shorts of a loose meta-material. This shifted transparent diamond-shaped areas over its surface, and the ensemble was coupled with slightly antediluvian red high-heeled shoes. I later learned her kind were called catadapts and as such, she had only altered herself so far— she hadn't, for example, opted for body hair. Everything she had done to herself emphasized her sexuality. I found her appearance grabbing at my gut and my groin and just wasn't ready for the intensity of the effect. She glanced at me and smiled knowingly. I nodded an acknowledgement and continued to the bar, blushing like a teenager. That the feeling of déjà vu was kicking in strongly didn't ameliorate my embarrassment.

"I'll have a large brandy," I said to the silver-skinned humanoid, expecting him to ask me what kind. Instead he turned back to the long rack, selecting a bottle of Hennessy and poured me a healthy measure into a cognac balloon. He held it in his hand for a moment then placed it on the bar, the glass warmed. Noting his lack of obvious augmentation, I guessed that he must be a Golem. And presumably one who had downloaded data on me. Second thoughts then occurred, because it had been a hundred years and I just didn't know enough.

"Thanks." I breathed in the fumes then sipped—the taste and sensation more intense than I remembered. I took another sip, contemplating the effect of the catadapt woman, then wondered about the body I now occupied. Like many soldiers during the war, I'd made many alterations to how I functioned. I'd numbed my ability to feel pain, sped up my reaction times and strength and altered my tolerance to certain performance-enhancing compounds, though I'd drawn the line at physical augmentation, or boosting. Also, because it wasn't that helpful during combat or bio-espionage operations, I'd tuned down my libido. Did this body have a suite of nano-machines or whatever other methods of adjustment they used now? Almost certainly, but they must be back at their base setting. I heaved myself up onto a stool.

"I have a question," I asked to my bracelet. After a short delay Bob was back: "What?"

"Does this body contain a nanosuite?"

"Yes, though somewhat more advanced than you were used to."

"Where can I get it returned?"

"Things have changed in that respect—Duckam has something for you."

A moment later the silver barman was back in front of me.

"Duckam?"

He dipped his head in acknowledgement and placed a transparent bracelet on the bar before me. The thing was paper thin and about an inch wide. I picked it up and studied it closely.

"What is this?"

"A nascuff," Duckam replied, then shot away again to serve someone at the other end of the bar.

Miniature controls were visible all the way around it, and when I hovered a finger over one it expanded to displace the others. Testing each control in turn, I found all the functional adjustments to the nanosuite I had known, along with a few others that left me puzzled. I put it on my right wrist, whereupon it closed up, seemingly bonding to my skin, and turned red. I quickly found the control, with sliding scales governing all aspects of the human sex drive, and stared at them.

"Now that would be a shame," purred a voice at my shoulder.

I turned to watch her as she slid onto a stool beside me. Duckam was there opposite her in an instant, placing some green concoction in a tall glass before her. She sipped, licked her lips, rattled little jewelled claws on the bar. Déjà vu returned hard, reflecting encounters like this seemingly to infinity. I shook my head to try and dispel it, focusing on her.

"You're just out of Krong Tower?" she queried.

"I am," I replied, "and finding my responses a little unnerving with my nanosuite at its base setting."

"Best place for it to be," she replied, holding up a wrist enclosed with another nascuff. Its colour was red too.

Glancing at other patrons of the bar I asked, "What does blue mean?"

"It means boring." She downed her drink. "I take it you have a room here?"

"Shouldn't we at least have a short period of 'getting to know you'?" It annoyed me that my voice was unsteady and that it seemed incendiaries were going off in my body. My instinct was to force utter self-control because deep inside I felt an urgency I could not define and knew there was something I had to do . . .

"We could," the catadapt replied. "You could talk about a war that ended twenty years before I was born and I could talk about runcible culture, lost art and the Klein patterns of Tirple Glasser."

The war, I thought, *something about the war . . .*

I had to let it go. My mind wasn't working properly and I was without vital information.

"I was always *fascinated* by Tirple Glasser," I said, and drained my glass. The war could wait. It had, after all, waited a hundred years.

She slid off her stool. "And I always found the war *so* interesting."

I pushed through the door into room 1034 with her tongue in my mouth and one of her legs wrapped round me. By the time I'd located the bed she'd kicked off her shoes and had both her legs round me. I staggered over and dropped her on the bed and began pulling off my clothes. Her clothing was much easier. A touch at her waist, and her top sucked into a nodule there, which she detached and tossed on the floor. Her breasts relaxed and shifted invitingly. Another touch and her shorts rolled up into a tube around her waist which she also whipped away and tossed on the floor. She flung herself back and began wriggling against the bed, rubbing her fingers between her legs, licking her lips like a porn star. My inner sophisticate and cynic stifled a bark of laughter, but the rest of me wasn't paying attention.

"I have to get my apology in now," I said tightly.

She grinned at me, exposing long canines, rolled over onto her knees and stuck her arse out. I climbed on the bed behind, knocked her knees out wider apart to bring her down to the right level, grabbed her hips and pulled her onto me while shoving as deep inside as I could get. I guess she had time to emit a couple of porn star moans but not much more than that.

Her name was Sheil Glasser—daughter of the famous Tirple Glasser I'd never heard of. We talked for a bit and had another drink from the autobar in my room. I then tuned some things down on my nascuff and the ensuing hour was very enjoyable, though tempered by that urgency deep within me, still undefined, and some guilt on her part. I found out why a little later: she was one of five women who had learned through the AI net of my resurrection and had competed to be the first to nail me. So this was how some entertained themselves in peacetime human society. She just got lucky by putting herself in the right hotel. I should have realized she knew more about me than she should have when she mentioned the war. I didn't mind. Hell, why should I? She screwed without guilt thereafter and suggested inviting her friends over. I drew the line there, because despite other adjustments to my cuff I was getting tired—perhaps some after-effect of resurrection—and anyway, I was kind of old-fashioned about stuff like that. She kissed me on the forehead at some point while I was dozing—an act I found curiously disturbing.

I woke to daylight and was briefly reminded of my preresurrection interlude in the virtual hospital. Then I sat upright, wondering what time of the day it might be. After getting off the bed I eyed the wrinkled and stained sheets with something approaching shame, then bundled them up and tossed them on the floor. Silly really, since they would probably be dealt with by a robot. While I showered, things began to slot into place in my mind and I really started to think beyond the immediate. And that undefined urgency I had felt had gained a name.

"You there, Bob?" I asked my com bracelet.

"Always," he replied after a short delay.

I moved to sit at the room console, the mirror above it immediately switching to screen mode, with holographic controls springing into being on the surface below. I paused then, not sure how to pursue my enquiries, but decided to be direct.

"What do you know about an AI called Penny Royal?"

The moment I said the words, my encounter with Sheil Glasser slid somewhere into the back of my mind. A footnote, a brief sojourn of no consequence. My past loomed around me, ready to sweep recent pleasures aside and determine my future. A longer delay ensued before Bob replied succinctly, "A search should give you everything permissible. I suggest you get up to date."

Did Bob know my history, and had he guessed my intentions? I wanted to ask more, but decided I really needed more data before I set out on my course. It was one that seemed almost inevitable—a quest for vengeance. I needed to work out not just how to kill a rogue AI, but one that had long been on a Polity blacklist. I sat back, hand straying to the holographic controls then dropping away again. Further memories nagged at me now with hints of horror. And I knew, deep in my gut, that facing them was going to be no easy task . . .

THE WAR: PANARCHIA

I woke in complete darkness, suspended upside down, my body feeling as if it had been fed through a rolling mill. My mouth was dry but the stuff that came out of my suit spigot tasted of piss. My face was sore and painful, probably from a flash-burn my visor hadn't been enough to prevent. I didn't want to move, because I knew I must be feeling just the edge of my true injuries. That I was alive at all—after standing on the edge of a multiple CTD strike in the megaton range—stretched credibility.

I realized I was swaying and that I could hear sounds of movement, even though all my suit electronics appeared burned out. What had happened? Well, a Polity destroyer had come in and bombed Berners' division to oblivion . . . I had to leave that one alone—could make no sense of it. The blast wave and firestorm had picked me up and now I was . . . hanging upside down. Maybe I'd been thrown into a tree? No, because there weren't any trees here on Panarchia. Well, at least not in our region.

Something thumped against my ankle, accompanied by a high-pitched whining, and after a moment that ankle felt cold. Next, the whining started on my other ankle and was followed by a sharp pain; I jerked, then something clamped around my neck, stretching me while the whining continued down one leg. I felt my suit falling away and realized someone was cutting me out of it. The material and armour were stripped in turn from my legs, hips and torso and roughly pulled from my arms. Then, with blurred vision, I watched a line of light scribing down my visor. The whining rattled cicada-like in my eardrums, continued over my scalp and moved down behind—then my helmet split in two and went clattering to the ground. I blinked to restore my vision, then wished I hadn't.

A second-child close up is no pleasant sight, and this one was a particularly ugly example of the prador species. Its carapace was a dirty custard yellow, heavily scarred and shell-welded, with those marks fading to an interesting mixture of green and purple. One of its palp eyes was missing and had been replaced by a motion detector. This was riveted to its visual turret beside the other palp, which looked burned and blind. The crescent of eyes below, actually on the front of the turret, were clean ruby behind a protective eye shield. This it shifted up away on its turret with one crusty claw lined with armour glass blades, before scuttling back from me. It then whipped its squashed pear of a body around on just five crablike legs.

Now focusing beyond it, I saw the first-child. It was twice the size of its smaller relative, coloured purple and yellow and had all its parts. These were complemented with attachment points for its weapons, which were stacked on the ground nearby, being worked over by another second-child. I scanned further and spotted three more second-children, various mounds of equipment and a row of four naked human corpses. I didn't recognize any of them, since they were all burned red raw. Turning my head slightly, I found I was hanging from a pole. This extended from a partially dismantled implant tank, with its other end attached to another pole imbedded in the rock ground. Further along the horizontal pole hung two other people, who were still alive. The one right next to me was Gideon, the one further along I didn't recognize, because even though alive he didn't have a face.

I knew how this would go now and, by the expression on his face, so did Gideon. We would be interrogated over a long period and, even if we answered all the questions they posed, we would still be tortured to death. We would probably see bits of our bodies being eaten by the creatures before us. But, if we were lucky, one of them might get over-excited during the process and kill us quickly.

The second-child swiftly moved to one side, obviously cringing as the first-child now advanced. This creature loomed over us. It inspected me closely, prodded with a claw like an industrial chisel, which knocked the wind out of me. Seemingly satisfied it moved on to Gideon and gave him the same treatment. Obviously not as damaged as I felt, Gideon swung up from the waist and made a grab for one of its palp eyes, trying to inflict at least some injury. The prador's claw came up fast, snipped and Gideon yelled, blood squirting from his wrist as his hand thudded to the ground. The first-child moved on to the last in the row and began prodding, eliciting a horrible keening noise. Meanwhile the ugly second-child moved in behind, rose on its back legs and caught Gideon's arms in its claws as it extended manipulator hands from its underside. Something went snap and Gideon screamed again as it stepped back, a metal band clamped into the forearm above his damaged wrist. They didn't want any of us bleeding to death, not yet.

The first-child continued prodding the faceless soldier at the end, setting him swinging. Then, obviously coming to a decision, it snipped twice and severed both his ankles, catching him as he fell then tossing him behind. A few bubbling clicks of prador speech ensued and all the second-children closed in. His shrieks didn't last long as they were eager for this morsel. In a matter of seconds, he was in pieces and disappearing with a gristly crunching into prador mandibles.

The first-child moved back to study Gideon and me, then it bubbled and a human voice issued from a translator, shell-welded below its mandibles.

"Father comes," it stated. "Testing is required."

"Fuck your legless father and fuck you!" Gideon shouted.

He was a brave man, I knew that, but I also knew he was trying to hurry his own end.

The pole jerked and I glanced across to see a second-child, still chewing merrily, sliding it off the tank. We crashed down and the next thing I knew, a second-child had hold of me and was dragging me across the rock. I didn't fight like Gideon, but the result was the same. We both ended up face down on the ground, with metal clamps holding down our legs and arms. Having been suspended for so long this was a relief to me, but I couldn't understand why it had been done.

An hour passed, maybe more, and I'd just managed to gain enough movement in my neck to watch events around me. The prador did not touch us again. One of the second-children tried snacking on a corpse and had its carapace cracked open for its trouble. It crouched off to one side, hissing and bubbling, leaking green blood. Such was simple prador discipline and it wasn't enough to kill it.

Finally something approached across the rockscape—a rough prador grav-effect transport resembling a short, fat cargo ship. A wind blew across us, carrying ash and a spray of water from the surrounding pools, and the ship's shadow fell over us as it slowed and settled. The deep thrumming of its engines vibrated through the ground for a long time, then slowly died away. Next, a huge ramp hinged down, bringing with it a cold gust of sea-smell and putrefaction. Two first-children came scuttling down carrying two heavy, oddly shaped metal frames. The father followed, hovering on grav-engines. The creature was massive, with a fifteen-foot carapace, and prosthetic claws fashioned of brassy metal extended towards the front of its body. Two remaining legs on one side were obviously paralysed and on the point of dropping off. I noted four hexagonal boxes, shell-welded along below its mandibles, one of which was also prosthetic. I wondered what the hell they were. Speculation soon fled my mind when I saw what came down the ramp next.

Four human beings walked down: three men and one woman. They were big and heavily muscled, their skin mottled with strange blue rings as if they'd suffered some sort of alien pox. All three were naked except for weapons harnesses and they were heavily armed. They also carried assorted items of equipment and, when I saw that some of it was Polity medical tech, I felt a horrible intimation of what might happen next.

"Fucking traitors," Gideon managed, but his voice was hoarse and weak now and probably intended for my ears only.

The prador father slid in to loom over us, so close I could feel the effect of his grav-engines alternately trying to shove me into the ground and peel me from it. He settled then, his first-children inserting the frames under each side of his body. Thus supported above the ground, he was all nicely positioned to watch the show.

The four humans, who until then had been standing unnaturally still, now jerked into motion. They headed straight for Gideon and gathered round him. He kept swearing, even as they hooked him up to a combined plasma and drug feed, used a Polity diagnosticer on him and injected various drugs. He fell silent and limp when they placed nerve blockers on several parts of his spine. Now I was truly puzzled. They'd numbed him—so preventing him from feeling any pain.

Then they started cutting.

It was quick, efficient, as if a practised butcher was preparing meat. They peeled first skin, then flesh from the back of his head and neck, then used bone saws to cut his skull, then levered off a section to expose his brain. They cut away sections of his neck vertebrae and inserted thin but flexible blades and made incisions into his lower back. Various fluids were now injected at some points. I heard an acid hissing and watched Gideon's legs shivering. Next came a sucking crunch and the blue woman held up something globular and bloody, trailing a tail, then tossed it to one side. As it hit the ground, I realized they'd just extracted his brain and a large portion of his spinal cord. It made no sense. They'd killed him under anaesthetic. Surely they'd discarded the one part of him that might be useful to them?

Meanwhile, the prador father, just like a film-goer tucking into the popcorn, was chomping down chunks of human flesh—fed to him by one of the second-children. I wondered if I'd died and been consigned to some thoroughly insane adjunct of Hell. Then I turned back to Gideon and saw that they hadn't finished with him.

A ribbed glassy tube went down into his neck where his spinal cord had been. Before it was all the way in, they attached a squat metal cylinder to the end, which immediately began to extend sharp metal spines. This they pushed inside his skull. The next stage was to put back the skull they'd removed, using a Polity bone-welder to fix it, then a cell-welder to close up his opened flesh. I just stared, horrified and baffled.

Bubbling clicks issued from the father. I looked at the monster and saw one of the first-children present him with another hexagonal item, like the ones bonded to his shell, which he accepted while munching on his grisly snacks. When I looked back at Gideon, one of the men was pulling out the metal staples that had held him to the stone—an almost impossible feat of strength. I wondered what they would do with his body next, even as the woman came over to me with the plasma feed and diagnosticer. Maybe that thing they'd inserted imparted some special flavour beloved of the father here? I watched the woman as she squatted beside me, hoping to die as easily as Gideon, then returned my attention to the man himself.

Gideon jerked, jerked again, then abruptly heaved himself up onto his hands and knees. Or, rather, knees and one hand. I realized then what I'd been stubbornly refusing to see up to this point. They'd implanted control hardware in him. But surely his body couldn't survive such trauma? Then I looked at the woman as she hooked up my plasma feed, and wondered.

Gideon stood up, his pose quite unnatural, and took a couple of shuffling steps. Glancing at the prador father I saw he still held that hexagonal device—like the four attached to his carapace—and made the connection with the four humans here. My ex-comrade heaved a breath before taking a lurching step and falling flat on his face. The four blue-skinned humans and all the prador, except for the father, now froze. Gideon jerked and spasmed on the ground for a little while, then shiny metal spikes protruded from his skull for a moment before retracting. Next, with a crunch, his skull popped open, breaking its bone welds, and the device inside shot out. It was still attached to its glassy tube, like some strange sprouting thistle. The prador father discarded the hexagonal object, and in one huge prosthetic claw snatched up the second-child that had been feeding him, and chopped it in half. The two halves hit the ground running but, only having legs along one side, could only manage a perverse circular dance which spread gore over the rock.

I remembered Gideon trying to remote-start a damaged mosquito gun. He tossed aside the control unit before bawling out the person responsible for the damage. This was similar, but thoroughly, grotesquely, magnified.

About me, the humans were in motion again. They injected me, which hurt, but the result was an artificial euphoria and comforting indifference. Any moment now the nerve blockers would go on and it would all be over. It didn't matter—nothing mattered any more. But there were no nerve blockers, and I screamed when they cut into the back of my neck and returned rapidly to hard reality. I saw the thing they brought over. It looked like a chrome spider with a cylindrical body—I felt it digging in and screamed some more.

Whether it was unconsciousness or the loss of my ability to act in any way that stopped me screaming, I don't know. All I do know is that the blackness was welcome.

3

SPEAR

It didn't take me long to familiarize myself with modern methods of using the AI net, despite my thinking still lacking clarity. On occasions my mind did function as it should and, in one of those moments, I created a sub-AI informational bloodhound and dispatched it on a search. While I awaited its results, I turned my attention to more prosaic tasks.

With feelings of déjà vu, of *familiarity*, recurring with annoying regularity, I skimmed reports on the after-effects of resurrection. I discovered that some people did experience this, along with a huge range of other mental problems. But linking these conditions to a specific cause was apparently a grey area. They might stem from the shock of dying, the shock of finding oneself alive or from feeling alienated by seemingly sudden transitions between places and times. Or death and resurrection might not be the cause at all. Considering what Sylac had told me, I surmised that my admittedly small problem might be due to the damage to my memplant and its subsequent forensic reconstruction. I suspected the feelings would fade with time and turned to other matters.

It took me just a few minutes to find out that anyone I'd cared about was either dead or untraceable. There were a few acquaintances I could contact but no one I could call friend—most of them had died on Panarchia. My mother died after the war and my father chose to upload to a portion of the Soulbank where people could live virtual lives. My elder brother had seemingly discovered a need for suicidal pursuits early—at the age of a hundred-and-fifty—and disappeared on a world called Spatterjay. After spending a fascinating time studying the history and biology of Spatterjay—the evil that Jay Hoop and his band of pirates had committed there, the viral immortality imparted by the leech, and the fascinating and dangerous Old Captains—I turned to the data my virtual bloodhound had been accruing. All other research felt like a mere duty in comparison.

Penny Royal.

It seemed, that even after more than a hundred years, the murderous AI was still around.

Penny Royal had controlled the destroyer that bombed Panarchia, murdering over eight thousand troops with "friendly" fire. Directly after that event, the AI went black. To the general grunt this meant it went off the radar and was never heard from again, but if you worked in bio-espionage it meant something else entirely. The AIs couldn't keep knowledge of Penny Royal's actions secret, because you might come across their results. I soon learned that when an AI went black, this aptly described the colour of its soul, were such a thing to exist. When something as powerful as Penny Royal turns into a sociopath, the results can be . . . unimaginable.

After Panarchia, I remember the first time I saw one of the rogue AI's victims. There had been a battle on one of Rhoder's moons. Afterwards, I was called in to examine a bunker on our base's perimeter. The bunker contained a particle cannon, stripped of computerized controls as EM and computer viral warfare had been fierce at that time. For a while there, humans had been without any AI assistance at all.

The cannon sat in an armoured pillbox, its polished square-section barrel protruding through a full-sphere traversal port in the domed ceiling. The cannon's lower section looked like an old Earth weapon from one of the World Wars fused with an array of chain-glass-sealed ultra-capacitors. Except, when I arrived, the gunner himself had become a disturbing part of the mix.

Although gun and gunner had been amalgamated, the gunner was still alive. His head had been linked to the gun's targeting laser and optical sights, and was only connected to his body via extended artificial electrochemical nerves and blood vessels. His hands and feet had been directly spliced into the relay board that controlled the thing's hydraulics. His heart could still supply oxygenated blood but, because his liver, kidneys and other organs were missing, he was dying. He died when we tried to remove him but, via a voice synthesizer, he managed to describe the black-spined AI monstrosity that had remade him.

I never made the connection then. Later, I read a report of a similar incident on another world and it was filed under the heading *Rogue or Black AIs*, with a subheading of *Penny Royal*. That report further revealed that it was Penny Royal who had incinerated my friends and comrades on Panarchia. The AI had not disappeared into the void, and had not suicided as so many such rogue AIs did. I could still find it, and I could kill it. The need for payback back then was a driving force—a feeling I only resisted because, well, I had a war to fight. And now I didn't want to resist it at all. Not just because Penny Royal wiped out Berners' division, but because of what had happened to me afterwards. I blamed Penny Royal directly for my fate at the claws of the prador, for that spider thrall and for all I'd lost.

THE WAR: UNDER THE THRALL

The humans with blue rings on their skin were tough. Maybe that hue denoted a nanonic sub-system that repaired their bodies, for time and again I saw them damaged and recover. They'd be cut by a sharp carapace edge or chewed on by one of the ship lice, but they bled hardly at all and healed up ridiculously fast. I received similar injuries, and the glue my prador second-child handler sprayed on my wounds only stopped the bleeding. This was why I was dying. The pain, which the device in the back of my neck didn't block, drove me into a fugue and weakened me in ways the thing could not control. When we arrived on yet another world, I knew for certain I hadn't got much longer. Once away from the prador ship's stink, another smell became distinct, and I recognized gangrene.

Pain is difficult to remember for, if we truly remembered it as a direct experience, we would go mad. Intellectually I know that my suffering at that time was terrible, that because of the spider thrall's rigid control I was only able to scream somewhere deep inside. But the mind has its defences and, through the prism of memory, I only remember a dull indifference.

First- and second-children went ahead to secure the area before the prador father-captain left the landing craft, accompanied by human thrall slaves like me. Beyond the ramp lay dank, thick jungle that had been cut down by laser and hammered flat by the passage of many feet to make a path to the encampment. I didn't then know why we were here, only later learning that this was one of the subplots of the war. Two prador fathers were meeting on neutral ground to hammer out an alliance against another prador faction. Even while conducting all-out war against another race, these creatures were still scrabbling for power and killing each other.

I walked behind the father-captain with three other thralled humans. We were all armed, including the second-children pacing along on either side of us. As were those lying ahead, plus the father-captain's first-children. I understand now that allowing so many first-children to live was unusual—one of the exigencies of war. After all, they were closest to maturity of all the offspring, so the most likely to challenge their adult kin. It took about an hour to reach the clearing and, perfectly on time, the other father-captain arrived from the other side. By then I was shaking and failing to make all the movements my thrall required. I was very weak and it was a relief to know I couldn't manage the return journey, so would end up as food for my masters. I was contemplating my brief future just as the mine went off.

Across the clearing the other father-captain rose on a massive blast, its under-carapace tearing free and its children tumbling away around it. The ground bucked and debris rained down all around me. I saw another adult prador come down and bounce into nearby jungle, a great mass of its guts ripped loose. I staggered, but my thrall righted me in time to see a missile streak from the jungle. It hit my father-captain in his face, punching through to detonate inside. He exploded into large fragments, each one a chunk of heavy carapace attached to a tail of steaming green entrails. One of these fragments struck me in the chest, knocking me flat on my back. I just lay there, doing nothing as no further instructions arrived through my thrall. Then came the sudden shock. I could move! I could actually move myself.

I reached up and shoved the messy debris away, but even that left me exhausted. Now small arms were firing. The nearby second-children were strafing the jungle, though I could see no sign of targets. First-children were cutting swathes through the same jungle with particle beams, trying to rid the attackers of cover. I looked at my human fellows, who had similarly been knocked to the ground by the blast.

"It's not controlling us anymore," I said, my voice rusty from lack of use.

No response; two of them just lay there staring blankly at the sky, while the third was face down, apparently trying to inhale mud. It was obviously too noisy for them to hear me, but they would realize soon enough they were free.

"We can . . . escape," I added and slowly tried to roll over so I could crawl away.

The air was filling with smoke and flinders of wood, yet as I tried to crawl I saw a strange thing. Right ahead of me the ground moved, then a hatch of woven vegetation hinged up and aside. Something crawled out, something practically invisible but for vague distortions and the movement of crushed vegetation. It approached and I looked up, at last able, making out a man-shaped figure in the smoke. It removed its mask to reveal a face and squatted down in front of me.

Chameleoncloth, I thought.

"Spider thrall?" he enquired.

I managed a grunt of agreement. Though I wasn't sure what he meant, the thing they had put in the back of my neck did resemble a spider.

"Just stay there—it's as safe as anywhere." He closed his mask and moved away.

I tried to keep track of him as he approached a nearby second-child, slapped something against its carapace, then moved on. Then I lost track of him as that something exploded, tearing the prador in half. All around me I could hear similar detonations and smoking chunks of my captors were flying in every direction.

Sticky mines, I thought, and other memories nibbled at my mind.

All around now issued the panicked hissing and mandible clattering of the prador, further explosions, then the sawing crackle of laser carbines. I turned my face to the ground and just breathed and, I think, lost consciousness for a while. When I came to, the noise level had dropped and the air was clearer. The explosions were more distant now and I could no longer hear the prador.

"They're no good," said a voice nearby. "Take DNA samples and then burn them."

A hand came down on my shoulder and turned me over gently.

"Spider thrall?" a second voice wondered. "Never seen that in anyone not a hooper."

"They don't live long," said the first voice. "Doc's on his way."

The first speaker now shimmered into existence and I realized that my first assumption had been partially wrong. They weren't just using chameleoncloth but were also using chameleonware. This man wore fatigues that colour-matched the smoky orange sky behind him, but didn't conceal him as well as before. He hit some control at his belt and his fatigues switched to some prestored setting: the yellows and browns of desert fatigues. He pulled his mask aside and shoved back his hood, stripping off his gloves to reveal a left hand made of gleaming ceramal. Of course I recognized him, despite his close-cropped beard. Only someone completely cut off in some backwater, without net access, could have failed to do so. Before me stood Jebel U-cap Krong, a hero of the Polity. Here stood the man whose favoured method of killing the enemy was to slap sticky mines directly onto their carapaces. Here was someone the prador feared and, judging by the devastation all around me, rightly so.

From somewhere distant came the sounds of two further massive explosions.

"There went their landing craft," said the one crouching beside my three fellows. He was snipping pieces of flesh from their ears, placing these in sample bottles. I watched him until I realized someone else was beside me, who proceeded to heave me upright as I groaned in pain.

"Can't use a neural blocker," said the one I presumed to be "Doc" as he pressed something against my throat.

"We need to move fast," said Krong. "That dreadnought up there isn't going to hold off for much longer."

Doc turned to look at him, and gave a slight negative shake of his head. It was something I'd seen on other battlefields. I'll do what I can for him but, no chance.

A hissing sound was immediately followed by blessed numbness. Doc used a diagnosticer on me, inputting its data into a drug manufactory and injecting the results. While he did this, I watched the ear-sampler drag the other three bodies into a heap, inserting a device underneath. As he walked away this ignited—a slow-burn thermic grenade—and soon the three were lost in hot white flames and oily smoke.

"No," I managed.

"Don't concern yourself," said Doc. "They weren't alive." Then he injected something else and the world started to fade. I felt sure it wouldn't be coming back.

A century or more later, I learned when reading about Spatterjay why one of Krong's troops had burned the three thralled hoopers on that jungle world. The hoopers were humans made inhumanly tough by a virus found on Spatterjay—their infection enforced by the pirate Jay Hoop, who thereafter sold them to the prador. Unlike me, they had received full thralls, which meant complete removal of brain and part of the spinal cord. And unlike Captain Gideon, they had survived the process, but just as mobile meat.

4

SPEAR

Those who died with memplants in their skulls and were subsequently uploaded to Soulbank usually had a plan. There was often a contract detailing what they wanted to happen next: they had prepared. Some plumped for insertion into a virtual world, to live out eternity in fictions of their choosing. Many chose resurrection in AI crystal placed in a Golem chassis. Others wanted to inhabit drone bodies, ships and even static planetary AIs. But most chose revival in bodies cloned from their own DNA. Being one of the earliest recipients of a memplant, I had chosen none of these because none of these options were available. A clone body had been selected for me as the least traumatic option.

I had wondered why I hadn't felt panicked, displaced and completely out of my depth, until, while still struggling to find Penny Royal's location, I briefly studied resurrection methods. All of those returning to life were buffered. They walked out of the resurrection chamber with their negative reactions tuned down, fight-or-flight responses hamstrung, and with a gene turned off in their brains to make them youthfully malleable so they learned quickly. I also noted that, as well as my nanosuite being at its base setting, this genetic fix must have contributed to my reaction to

Sheil Glasser. My mind, as well as being youthfully malleable, had been youthfully libidinous. Again, this was something that helped integration: the sexual act being something rooted right down in the reptile brain.

Usually this buffering lasted for a couple of months, gradually declining towards the end, by which time most people had reintegrated and could move on. Perhaps it explained my problems with déjà vu. I don't know. According to Bob, I was a special case, since I had been dead for so long, and the buffering would only come up for reassessment after two months.

No way.

I spent four days in the hotel room, alternately researching Penny Royal and my new body's nanosuite. Sheil paid me a few more visits, but I fear I did not give her too much attention. On her last visit she told me she wasn't coming back. That I was obsessive, distracted and becoming a bore. I made adjustments to my nascuff as she went out the door, whereupon the device turned blue and became a deterrent to those seeking a physical relationship. With the distraction of sex suppressed, I felt I could think more clearly, and coldly. Though in truth that might have been more about how I *expected* my mind to work, and so was an illusion. However, a few hours later, I felt I understood my nanosuite and the deeper architecture of the nascuff's controls. I manipulated them, found the tweaks that had been put in place and realized that my body had been generating an excess of its own narcotics. I turned the adjustments off but left the genetic fix in place, because now I did need to learn.

Clarity returned as the coughing engine that was my brain accelerated.

Money first. Within a few minutes I found my account, learned how to access it from any location and worked out how much I had. A minute later I was shopping for an upgrade, an augmentation to be precise. And since I was now very rich, I wanted the best on the market. Studying the stats of the best aug available I noted a reference to gridlinks—computing hardware installed against the inside of the skull. This aug was the closest you could get to the same level of function as a gridlink without a lengthy recovery time, and my need to be after Penny Royal wouldn't wait. A few minutes later and I was out of the hotel room, heading off to be fitted. I noted wryly that the aug was named "Sylac ChromeSnake 47."

Half an hour later I was sitting in a chair in an aseptic room with an autodoc poised over me. The thing was specialized for the procedure. No humans were involved. Perhaps this wasn't a job where you got to meet interesting people. The aug was cold against my skull as the bone-anchors went in with a crunch, and the connection routine followed. I ignored the instructions package surfacing in my mind and engaged on an almost instinctive level. The aug had been made to accommodate varying levels of intelligence and it responded perfectly. I felt a joy at the ramping up of mental function as I overrode the block on net connection. Just minutes into the fitting, I began uploading data on my interests, updating myself on augmentation, nanotech, adaptogenics and thousands of branches of biology. This ability to integrate knowledge rapidly was of course precisely the reason AIs took an interest in me, over a century ago.

While all this was occurring, lights began flashing on my wristcom. I peered at them, not really sure what they might mean.

"This is too soon!" Bob exclaimed from the device.

I simply reached over and turned off the wristcom, even as I mentally made purchases of increased memory and processing for my aug. A moment later, I updated myself on what was known about the prador and our history with them since the war. I also collected from my hotel data store everything I had gathered on Penny Royal, now setting my aug to update constantly, or at least when netlinks were available. This last required uploading a quasi-AI search engine to sort rumour and legend from hard fact.

The fitting finally completed and the autodoc withdrawing, I realized I now had all the essentials for my quest. I possessed money and the aug on my skull was constantly updating my knowledge-base. But most importantly my determination to hunt down and destroy Penny Royal remained. There was no reason to return to my hotel, for I was finally ready to leave Earth. Even as I went out of the aug fitting room, I abandoned Bob, leaving the wristcom on the chair.

Once the fitting room was behind me, I trudged the high-towered streets, looking for a taxi to take me to the nearest runcible. En route, I used my aug to book a four-jump transit—the first one from Earth to the main interstellar runcible on the Moon. From there, I chose a world halfway across the Polity, then a newly built outlink station which sat on the Line dividing the Polity from the Graveyard. I felt excited and determined but knew that, despite everything I had uploaded and integrated so easily, I would have to be cautious. Such an expansion of knowledge and the ability to process it could easily lead to overconfidence. I had to remember that such options were available, sometimes within constraints, to everyone. Though, admittedly, I was confident of the workings of my mind. It was just that the content needed a major update.

During a flight in a driverless aircab, my mind worked overtime and soon after I was walking towards the shimmering meniscus of a London runcible. These instantaneous matter transmitters enabled the massive spread of humanity throughout a large portion of the galaxy. But this device had also been the reason for our near-defeat by the prador, because our spaceship technology had been so behind theirs. During my allotted slot I stepped through, and felt no transition as I stepped out into the massive interstellar runcible complex on the Moon. I was still uploading and integrating knowledge, fascinated by new research and new takes on the old. I sought out the eclectic and the prosaic, selecting what would be of most use to me.

When I finally arrived on Outlink Station Par Avion, I booked a room in a local metrotel and spent time refining those plans made throughout the journey. I now needed to finesse the physical preparations required to enact them. From the data I'd accrued on Penny Royal, I had found a valuable lead. Because of her particular connections, I felt sure this woman would know the location of the AI, or at least would have some information about it. This woman could also get me to a particular abandoned spaceship. This vessel would be a further source of needed data—and my main weapon. I then learned, upon checking the lie of the Graveyard, that the ship was conveniently within it. But now I needed to ensure I knew everything about the woman. I needed to understand her perfectly, to be able to predict how she would act. And I also needed to understand her unique condition.

This last required, in addition to everything else I had loaded, all available information on creatures called hooders. These were hostile alien creatures resembling centipedes the size of monorail trains. They were also the devolved descendants of war machines, or biomechs. These had an interesting heritage, being made by one of three extinct alien races that had spanned the galaxy before humans even appeared on the scene.

I also had to get data on some of the more esoteric research in adaptogenics, and information on a field of human adaptation which was new to me: haimans. My driver from Krong Tower had mentioned them. It turned out that they took augmentation right up to its present limit. Haimans were human cyborgs with highly expanded sensoriums and mentalities. This took them as close as a human mind could get to computing, just a spit away from AI.

All this extra research did slightly extend my stay on Par Avion. But I could feel my mind climbing towards a zenith I had known before and didn't begrudge the time. Also, the woman was dangerous. If you're going to play with fire, you should know the location of the extinguisher.

ISOBEL SATOMI TRANSFORMED

Landing coordinates arrived, and Isobel Satomi gazed at them for a long time, before staring out through the cockpit screen at the black planetoid looming out there. Was she doing the right thing?

Why did anyone make a deal with the devil? Desperation, pursuit of power and wealth . . . Or perhaps a mistaken confidence in one's ability to avoid pitfalls, to take something worthwhile from that deal and not be, as some would have it, "royally screwed." Some managed to achieve this, it was rumoured. Janger had his vengeance on the father-captain responsible for killing his family and returned to the Polity. It cost him his massive personal fortune, but he got what he wanted. Jean Fraser had her dead child restored to life from its fifty-year-old mummified corpse. And Mr Pace, of course, became all but indestructible—defeated his enemies and established himself as the premier crime lord.

Isobel considered her deal worth the risk. And, really, if she didn't go for it, she would probably end up dead at the hands of Copellian or one of his killers. Mr Pace encouraged infighting between lower echelon crime lords like herself and Copellian—it kept them at heel. Copellian had been several rungs of the ladder below her just a few years earlier, but had now become a serious threat to her. His power and reach were expanding rapidly and his killers and contacts were everywhere—and the bounty on her head increased every day. Running was one option, but not a good one. She might survive if she headed into prador territory, but if she did she'd be beating the odds. Prador rules also applied to humans there: they were either predators or prey. She could also head for the Polity, but it was likely she'd be picked up by AI surveillance, whereupon Earth Central Security would be after her as well as Copellian's people. And ECS's AIs, assassin drones, monitors and agents tended to be even less forgiving than the crime lord's killers. She could run elsewhere, but no, she had too much invested here. She had to stay.

As instructed, she took her smallest shuttle—a vessel not much larger than a gravcar—down to the surface. She landed it near the edge of a crater where sparkling grey and silver dust had spilled like river sediment from gaps in the rim. New coordinates now appeared on her com-screen and she uploaded them to a guidance program in her suit, before pulling on and dogging down her helmet. Isobel then voided her shuttle of air, creating a brief mist all around, opened the single circular door beside her and stepped out into darkness. Her visor then shifted to the same maximum light amplification as her cockpit screen, revealing her surroundings, then blinked up a guide arrow for her. She followed this across rock strewn with flat hexagonal crystals like coins, finally arriving at the elliptical entrance to a cave.

The opening, as she understood it, was one of many such entrances to Penny Royal's domain. This wormed throughout the crust of the planetoid like the burrows of bark beetles. As she stepped inside, she spotted something poking up from a hollow in the rock—an appendage like an eyeball, impaled on a thin, curved thorn of metal. Whether it was part of the rogue AI itself or just part of its security system she had no idea, but the thing gave her the creeps.

Ten metres into the cave she came to a ceramal bulkhead with inset airlock, but this wasn't the main focus of her attention. Either side of the bulkhead, trapped in snakes of stone that had liquefied and flowed around them in a Medusa tangle, were space-suited figures. She walked up to the first, noting the old design of the suit, and peered into the visor. Light-amp wasn't high enough so she reached up and clicked on her suit light.The face inside was female, the eyes open and the expression slightly puzzled. No sign of decay, no sign that this woman was either dead or alive. Feeling further doubts about coming here, Isobel turned to the airlock, remembering a recent conversation with Trent—an employee who had been with her from the start.

"So it's dangerous, lethal even, but all I have to lose is my life," she had said, when he had argued against her coming here.

"No," he had replied. "Get on the wrong side of Penny Royal—and I've yet to know if there's a right one—and dying will be the least of your problems."

"Yes, but Mr Pace got what he wanted . . ."

Trent had frowned in puzzlement. "I'm not so sure Mr Pace is happy with what he is."

She had no idea what Trent was on about. Mr Pace was wealthy beyond measure and simply could not be killed. She had dismissed Trent in irritation. He hadn't understood.

The outer airlock door opened automatically as she approached. She stepped inside and it slammed shut, like a trap. Isobel tried to stay calm and checked the atmosphere reading as the lock pressurized: high in inert gases but still breathable. As the inner door opened, she stepped through, immediately undogging her helmet, then hanging it from her utility belt. Now that she was inside, she felt that she had taken an irrevocable step, and that the time for precautions was over.

The cave smelled of metal, with a hint of putrefaction and hot electronics. She advanced, then halted abruptly when a figure stepped into view. The skeletal Golem, wearing a silver face, gestured for her to follow as a ribbed umbilicus attached at its waist reeled it in. It led her through a triangular cave where she had to duck to avoid hitting her head, around a mummified human corpse seemingly pinned to the floor by a metre-long chunk of I-beam, then into a circular chamber. The place seemed like a junkyard for spaceship hardware—including fusion reactors and a whole ecology of robots. Except much of this stuff was actually connected and powered up, nestled in a web of s-con and optic cables. In the centre rested a sphere of more apparent junk, impaled on a mass of black spines. The tubing attached to the Golem originated from this sphere and reeled it right in. Here, it seemingly faded from view, but for its face. Then the sphere rotated, bringing that face to centre on her.

Penny Royal.

Isobel had heard many descriptions of this rogue AI. That it was a collection of interlinked Golem, or a steel octopus, or perhaps a spiny black flower on a strangler fig. It had even been depicted as a glittering cloud of crystal shards. Every description had been from someone who had actually encountered the AI, and had been verified either by aug-interrogation or from other accounts. She'd soon realized that Penny Royal did not maintain a single form, or perhaps it disguised its true form. Why it would do so was a puzzle, since there was very little in the Graveyard that could cause it harm.

"You want?" said the Golem.

Penny Royal, it seemed, did not engage in small talk.

"I want to be a haiman," she replied.

The thugs at his beck and call, his ships and his contacts were not why Copellian was winning. It was his facility with data and planning. He'd installed the latest Polity aug tech within both himself and his lieutenants, and apparently they were now all mentally interlinked. As a result, his operations were always tight, always perfect, and he had grown in power until he felt safe enough to start attacking her. He'd also publicly announced a contract on her. In essence, he was smarter than her, and that had to change.

"You want to be more powerful and dangerous than Copellian?"

"I do," she replied, unsurprised that Penny Royal knew why she was here. "And I have a half-ton of prador diamond slate up in my main ship to pay for that."

"Yes," said Penny Royal.

"Can you make me into a haiman?"

"You want to be the predator and him the prey?"

"Damned right I do," Isobel replied, feeling slightly bemused by the odd way this exchange was going and Penny Royal's strange intonation. She decided to affirm her aims: "I want to rip the flesh from his fucking bones!"

"Ah," said the black AI, and Isobel wondered if she had overstepped in some way.

"Shall I get my people to bring that diamond slate down?" she asked.

"You will be satisfied," the AI replied.

It expanded, then came apart. The seeming junk of its outer structure spread to reveal hard-edged blackness and a sinuous, tentacular movement. She began moving backwards as it advanced and turned into a wave of intricate movement, silver and black. She halted and waited. Too late to back out now. The wave fell on her.

When the agony came she thought it was her punishment for dealing with the devil, especially when she was so powerful and precise afterwards, her haiman augmentations raising her to a mentality she hadn't even imagined. That the visible hardware on her body wasn't metallic but organic she just accepted.

Taking apart Copellian's operation was simplicity itself after this encounter, so much so that she deliberately complicated it to make it more interesting. The man's downfall was protracted and humiliating, but he cheated her at the end by taking his own life before she could capture him. Isobel Satomi became a legend in the Graveyard—but her legend soon grew in unexpected ways. It became apparent that what she'd bought from Penny Royal was still changing her, and she joined the ranks of the damned.

ISOBEL

This area of town was pretty much safe for Isobel, since large parts of her organization were established in the city, but it was a good idea to take precautions. While she waited outside the Crab Chowder, once her favourite bar, Trent and Gabriel went in first. When entering public places like this, she always liked to have her men in position first. They were much less recognizable than she was and, despite their often-violent tendencies, had fewer enemies.

"*Okay, I got him located*," Trent auged her, also sending a feed from inside the bar. He'd laid a frame over a man sitting at one of the tables, along with the facial recognition confirmation.

"Can't see anyone we might have a problem with," said Gabriel over his comunit. "But we're positioned to cover you now."

"The people I'm concerned about wouldn't be as easy to see," she replied, then pushed open the door and entered.

As she stepped inside, she opened out the petals of the sensory cowl behind her head. She located weapons both visible and concealed, plus implanted hardware and augs. She also sought out those hidden behind the surrounding walls to see if they had acquired any weapons since her last external inspection. The situation looked okay so she relaxed a little. As always when entering this place, her attention strayed to a glass crab sculpture, sitting in a niche carved into one wall. The thing was made of rose and blood-red glass and always gave her the creeps, even more so because there were intricacies within that she couldn't quite fathom—even with her augmented senses. She would have liked to have had the thing scrapped but it was a gift from the indestructible Mr Pace, the Graveyard's highest crime lord. Shuddering, she dragged her attention away from the thing and closed her cowl. As usual, she found herself having to fight the knotty muscles growing from the bases of its chitin petals where they had sprouted from the back of her neck.

Whenever she entered a room, conversation died. The speed of its death depended on the attention those within were paying to their surroundings. In the Chowder, where some drank heavily, it died a slow death. She paused, running a fingertip over the row of hard spiky growths protruding along her jawbone. Then she touched one of the pits forming below her eyes, before realizing what she was doing and abruptly snatching her hand down again.

She shrugged to herself, concealed within the padded suit she wore to hide her other bodily changes, and slowly headed over to the client, or mark, at the table. As she walked, she concentrated on trying to prevent her cybermotors from conflicting with the new ropy muscles enwrapping her dissolving bones. Finally halting to stand over him, she rested one hand on the gas-system pulse-gun at her hip.

"Thorvald Spear?" she asked.

He auged his ident to her, along with limited permissions, from a state-of-the-art silver snake behind his ear, then replied, "I am. Won't you take a seat?"

His tone was mild and his demeanour convivial, but his aug security was tighter than an airlock seal. She detected a hard wariness in him, and was that twist to his mouth a hint of disapproval? He certainly knew who she was. He probably knew there were arrest warrants out for her covering kidnapping and murder, and he probably knew those words didn't sufficiently detail her crimes. But he had no right to judge her—he didn't know her past. There were prador in the Kingdom who still wanted human slaves and she supplied them. So what? It was a hard universe. She thought about her present acquisitions languishing in one of her warehouses. In another five days, the Spatterjay virus should have toughened them up sufficiently for coring and thralling. Then they would be ready to be sold to the prador. Still focused on this Thorvald Spear, something dark twisted inside her and urged her towards violence, to attack. But, as always, she managed to suppress it. However, she did decide that he would join those due for coring, unless his reason for seeing her turned out to be profitable.

She pulled out a chair and sat down, wincing as her backside settled on the grainy kelp wood, then again as she attempted to relax back. The bone loss in her spine and the growth of chitin plates over her body hurt.

"Would you like a drink?" he asked.

"Just water," she replied.

She'd tried self-medicating with alcohol and soon learned that method of relaxation didn't work well with cybermotor conflicts. It had led to torn muscles and further damage to her weakened spine.

He held up a finger and a vending tray slid through the air to hover above their table. It looked like a maple leaf, but with a jointed arm extending from the stalk and terminating in a three-fingered prehensile hand.

"Water for my companion, and another rum for me." He picked up his glass, drained the dregs and passed it up. The tray plucked it away and held it down on its upper surface as it shot away.

"Those who require my services usually come to me," she stated.

"But I piqued your curiosity?" he suggested.

She dipped her head in acknowledgement, though his message had first stimulated her avarice and belatedly aroused her curiosity. He was out of the Polity, so probably an easy mark, and he apparently had a profitable venture for her. When he'd added that he could also help her with her "problem," which was now public knowledge, her inner predator was roused.

"So you want to charter the *Moray Firth*?" Isobel enquired.

"I do."

"Expensive."

He acknowledged that with a slow nod.

"So what for?" she asked, wanting to get his first proposal out of the way and move on to her "problem." It was likely that he was lying, so she could then attack him.

"I have the probable location of an abandoned Polity destroyer," he replied. "I wish you to take me to where I can first acquire some . . . necessities, and then I'd like you to take me to it."

She stared at him calculatingly. A Polity destroyer. How likely was that? Being AI-controlled, such ships usually managed to make it home or call for help unless completely trashed. Either he was an idiot with too much time and money on his hands, or he was something else . . . Isobel opened her sensory cowl again, noted Trent and Gabriel becoming more alert as a result, and once more scanned her surroundings. Bounty hunter seeking her reward? It was possible, but then why the request to meet here, in what was essentially a domain she controlled? Surely he knew her reputation.

"Both the destroyer and the necessities I mentioned are on the far side of the Graveyard, right on the edge of the Prador Kingdom," he added.

She continued to stare at him for a long moment, then said, "The likelihood of anyone finding an abandoned, as opposed to completely trashed, Polity destroyer is slightly remote, don't you think?"

The tray returned with the drinks and, while it was putting them on the table, Spear took a small case out of his pocket and placed it in front of him.

"Well," he continued as the tray departed, "if it's not there, I will still pay you the full cost of the job." He opened the case and slid it across to her.

She peered down at it, searching with her cowl for poisons or a nano attack, but the six etched sapphires were all the case contained. She carefully reached over and picked up one to hold it close to her eye, linking to its microputer through the close-focus scanner in her artificial pupil. The sapphire was good and, if the other five contained the same amount of credit, there was enough here to pay for a complete refurbishment of the *Moray Firth*'s primary fusion reactor. She found avarice beginning to win the battle amongst her internal conflicts.

"This is a down-payment, of course," he said, "to cover your expenses. There is a netlink to Galaxy Bank here, where you can check on my credit rating."

She put the sapphire down. "If, as you say, you know the location of a salvageable abandoned Polity destroyer, you will also be aware that you'll need an AI to fly it."

"Which is why the location of those necessities I mentioned is a place called the Rock Pool."

"Shell people," she stated, without the rancour she had once felt for that kind.

"Yes, shell people."

"I'll have to think about that." She paused, "But you also offered help . . ."

He pointed down at the etched sapphires. "Net data on me is limited, so I've loaded a private file on me to the transaction memory of sapphire T782. I think you will find it interesting. You'll also see that the balance of the payment could involve something more valuable to you than money."

Still watching him, she reached down and ran her fingers over the sapphires, sensors in her fingertips identifying the correct jewel. Leaning her elbow on the table, she held the sapphire to her eye, accessing its memory right away. She already knew from her own research that this guy was old, he'd fought in the prador/human war, but there was little beyond that. This file filled in more detail which, after a security scan, she loaded directly to her mind.

"Polity bio-espionage?" she said disbelievingly.

"That's the one that leaps out," he said, "but check the others."

She took a few moments to get it all, then, with slow control, placed the jewel back in its case. Yes, he had worked in bio-espionage during the war, but the more interesting stuff was before then. He'd worked in numerous sciences and had even spent time in partnership with the infamous Dr Sylac. Then there was the other data: a report from a forensic AI on his mental stats. A lot of them were at the top of known scales, while others were listed as non-applicable, which meant the AIs had found no sensible way of measuring them. Something long-suppressed rose up inside her then—hope. To undo what Penny Royal had done required a level of skill beyond anything in the Graveyard. Certainly Polity AIs could have done something for her, but considering her history their first inclination would be to dissect and study her. And if that didn't kill her, they would execute the death sentence on her directly afterwards.

"You have a nerve conflict problem I can probably deal with immediately," he stated. "But that's almost certainly the least of your problems. Your haiman installations are overloading your human body, so you need base-level nanonic upgrade. You'll require secondary cyber-immune micro-factories inside your bones, to generate nano-machines which can constantly repair the damage."

"And you can do this?" she asked, trying to stamp on her bitter disappointment at the way he was deliberately circumventing her *real* problem.

"You've seen my CV," he said. "I specialized in surgical adaptation and adaptogenics before I trained under Sylac in cerebral augmentation."

"You have no idea," she replied, considering killing him right then and walking out.

"You mean about the change you're undergoing?" He gave a brief mirthless smile. "I understand that very well, Isobel."

"Oh really?"

"Oh really," he replied. "I know exactly what Penny Royal did to you, because I've seen similar . . . changes before."

He reached up and began scratching at the back of his neck, then snatched his hand down with a flash of irritation.

"Okay," she said, "we have a deal."

If he couldn't help out with her immediate problem, then she would add him to one of her cargoes—core him and thrall him and sell him to the prador. If he was lying about his ability to deal with her other problem, she would probably take her time with the coring, but the end result would be the same. In fact, even if he was telling no lies at all, his destiny was set now. After all, a working or at least salvageable Polity destroyer was worth a great deal of money, so she wasn't likely to let him just fly off in such an item.

SPEAR

The *Moray Firth* was an old Polity attack ship that had been stripped of its weapons and put up for auction after its onboard AI decided to move on. This AI had apparently acquired a drone shell fashioned in the shape of a giant barracuda. It was loaded with state-of-the-art weaponry and other tech, including a U-space drive, and was last spotted heading determinedly towards the galactic core. Nobody knew why.

The main body of the *Moray Firth* looked like a chunk of metal, one that had been sliced off at an angle from rectangular bar-stock. Two nacelles extended from either side of its flat rear end, in which clustered the throats of fusers. Lastly, a fat weapons turret sat on its top surface—just behind an up-slanting nose akin to the front of a twentieth-century troop-landing craft. With my hover trunk trailing behind me, I mounted the side ramp into its cargo bay, at the top of which stood one of Isobel's heavies, Trent. I studied him closely, recognizing him from the Crab Chowder. He stood a head taller than me and probably weighed twice as much. His head was an odd shape, decidedly pointed on top, which was emphasized by his black bristly Mohican. His irises were pure white and he wore a purple sapphire dangling from his left ear, with a Miltech Standard aug nestled behind it. His clothing consisted of a long crocodile-skin coat over dated businesswear and heavy toe-tector boots. I knew at once that he wasn't physically boosted or augmented, but a heavy-worlder with the genetic mods that implied.

"Origin-world Tranter, I would guess," I said as I approached him. "Probably the HG-92 series adaptogen . . . Sobel line?"

He just stared at me long and hard, reaching up to toy with that earring, but then had to acknowledge my words with a nod before gesturing me inside. He led me down a carpeted corridor that wouldn't have looked out of place inside a chateau. The exterior of the *Moray Firth* might have looked plain and utilitarian, but the interior was luxurious. This was clearly Isobel Satomi's personal ship—she had others she used to conduct her despicable trade with the prador.

My cabin was lavish too, and quite large, but I knew I wouldn't enjoy it for long unless I fulfilled the first part of our contract.

"She wants to see you now," said Trent, "in our medical bay."

"I need some equipment first."

Again the nod.

My trunk settled on the kelp-wood floor as I took out my key, programmed it and sent the required signal. Rather than the top of the trunk, the side of it opened to extend a drawer. I dipped down and took out all I needed. Here was my microbot factory, the Syban diagnosticer interlink (there was a whole series of technical names that related directly to my old boss "Sylac") and a selection of other medical tools purchased at Par Avion. It was unlikely that Isobel would have these aboard her ship. As I packed them into an ersatz nineteenth-century doctor's bag, I felt the ship move. We were on our way—there would be no turning back now.

Trent led me through further luxuriously appointed corridors to a dropshaft, which led to the deck below. Here the corridors were tile and brushed metal, aseptic and rigorously cleaned by beetlebots. The medical bay was equally as clean, very neat, and did contain some equipment you wouldn't expect to find out here in the Graveyard. Isobel waited beside a surgical chair that could convert into a table. Her right arm was quivering and she probably hadn't sat down because it would be too painful for her to do so. She took a step towards me, her hands clenching and unclenching. Seemingly with an effort of will, she forced herself to stop and gestured a dismissal at Trent, who departed with alacrity.

"You understand," she said immediately, "the penalties for non-payment?"

I glanced up at the ceiling, where a saucer-shaped security drone hung like a lethal light fitting. I presumed its polished throat contained some sort of stunner, tracking me as I walked into the room.

"I'm not stupid," I replied, putting my bag down on a nearby work surface. "If you could get into the chair?"

"Should I undress?" she asked bluntly.

"Yes," I replied, it being my practice, back when I worked with Sylac, never to be wholly reliant on remote diagnostic tools. She grimaced and began stripping off her padded clothing, while I walked over to inspect her autodoc.

The thing was a typical Polity design. A nightmare chrome bug that extended on a heavy jointed arm from a movable pedestal—although the bug was presently folded down against the pedestal with its surgical cutlery in sanitizer niches. I went round to its other side to study the manual console, which came on as soon as I stood before it. It wasn't reacting to me, however. Isobel had turned it on, ensuring I knew that through her haiman augmentations she was deep inside the equipment and would be watching my every move. I worked the touch-board and called up the stats for its integral diagnosticer. As I'd thought: it was modern but not up to haiman standards. I retrieved my Syban interlink, which was a cube of hardware covered with data and sample ports. Next, I opened up a cover on the pedestal, extracted the old diagnosticer core and plugged in the Syban in its place. It would take a while to boot up properly, so I walked around the column to inspect Isobel.

"Interesting," she said. "Very advanced."

She was obviously studying the Syban interlink even as it booted up.

"You received haiman augmentations from Penny Royal . . . well, sort of," I said, "but your medical tech here only extends to limited human upgrades, like augs."

She now sat in the chair, breathing heavily—perhaps in pain or exhaustion or as a result of some internal conflict. The look she threw at me carried a simple message: show any sign of disgust and you're dead. There was also something of an appeal there, buried deep. She wanted sympathy, but it mustn't be overt and there definitely mustn't be pity.

Her body looked bruised and it probably was, but the discoloration wasn't all due to that. Her breasts, which must have at one time been full, were now flaccid sacs. Like her face, her torso was now longer than normal, and its width was unnaturally even. I also noticed her legs were short. As I studied her, it was a good thing my nascuff was operating to suppress certain basic human drives. What I was seeing before me might otherwise have elicited disgust or even horror, which if evident, would certainly have been dangerous here. But I now saw her as no more than an interesting specimen.

I held up my hands. "I'm going to examine you now."

Her sensory cowl opened and I could see metallic movement in the pupil of one of her eyes as she inspected my hands. After a moment, she nodded. I reached out and used the small touch-plate on the side of the chair to tilt it back and raise the footrest, slowly turning it into a surgical table. When it finally locked, I probed around her collarbone to at least get that initial contact out of the way. She flinched, then relaxed as I began counting ribs.

Knives . . .

Just for an instant I found myself in darkness, with swirling obsidian and metallic movement all around me, and then came pain. I jerked my hand away and it faded. I immediately realized this fragment of memory was related to the feelings of déjà vu which I had been experiencing from the moment I boarded this ship. Perhaps this was something to do with my time under the spider thrall? No, it didn't feel like that. I tried to dismiss speculation because I really didn't need it right now.

"I have eighteen now," she said, "and two more are growing." I nodded, not trusting myself to speak for a moment.

I really hadn't needed to count by feel because, growing from her ribs, I could see prominent thorn-like growths protruding from her sides, with chitin plates spreading around them. And the ribs themselves now reached nearly all the way down to her pelvis. I noticed that the ribs at the top of her torso were much wider and flatter than usual and that the top two were overlapping. I wondered how long it would be before her skin started dying—it was already starting to look unhealthy, though no lesions had yet appeared.

Her arms had shortened too and her shoulders were positioning higher while her neck was thickening. There was no chitin on either her arms or legs and, in both cases, the digits were shrinking. She was down one toe on each foot, and the little finger on each of her hands was a stub. I guessed both sets of limbs were to be dispensed with.

"Could you show me your back?" I asked.

She tried to heave herself over but struggled, and after a hesitation I helped her, and this time nothing arose in my mind from touching her. I counted the neat row of vaguely rectangular plates of chitin down her spine and noted a spiky nub of a tail protruding from its base, then let her rest back.

"You were already making efforts to turn yourself into a haiman before you visited Penny Royal," I stated.

Her eyes narrowed in suspicion. "How do you know that?"

I waved a dismissive hand. "It's obvious. What did you have done?"

She assessed me a moment longer before replying, "Joint cyber-motors, twinned sub-AI augs and a sensor band. I had the augs and band removed when I bought black-market gridlink hardware, which failed after two months. The people who sold it to me are all in the Kingdom now—I didn't thrall them but sold them as flesh breeders."

She paused, studying me for a reaction. "They probably ended up being eaten long ago."

I reached over and keyed on the autodoc, which folded its insectile head out from the pedestal. It started running through the test routine for its multiple surgical limbs, which rather made it look as if it was preparing for a tasty snack.

"Just relax," I said as I shifted it over above her face. The thought was there to run something quick and final through its programming, maybe have it cut through her spine and clamp her carotids. But despite my time in bio-espionage, I was no killer. However, it was good that she'd reminded me of what she was, because for a moment there I had started to feel sympathetic.

The doc sampled and scanned her from head to foot and I viewed the scan images and data after it had slid back to a holding position over her stomach.

"The thing about Penny Royal," I said, "is that, should you ask, it might grant you the ability to leap over tall buildings. But it might neglect to inform you that your landing will be terminal."

"I know that," said Isobel.

I busied myself with my microbot factory—relaying the scan results from the autodoc and on their basis making a selection of preprepared microbots. I eventually brought over a blood shunt containing them in solution.

"What's that?" she asked.

"You understand that your cybermotors are in conflict with your changing body?"

"Of course."

"You could have countered that with your gridlink or your augs, but you don't have them. The haiman parts of you that Penny Royal installed don't even speak the same language as those motors, so cannot access them. To Penny Royal that didn't matter. How much you suffered during your transformation was irrelevant to it." I paused, watching her. "You didn't just ask to be turned into a haiman, did you?"

"Do you think I haven't thought about that constantly?"

"And?"

"I said I wanted to rip the flesh from someone's bones," she replied. "And Penny Royal asked me if I wanted to be the predator and my enemy the prey. I said yes."

I winced: the words that had damned her.

"Your cybermotors are sealed and encoded. My microbots will access them, whereupon I can reprogram them. Turn them off, in fact."

"I don't want them turned off," she spat, running her fingers down the thorns protruding from her side, "I want this turned off!"

"I can do that, but I will not do it now," I replied. "Our deal was that I alleviate your immediate cybermotor problem. I will reverse what Penny Royal did to you when I have my ship."

She really wanted to kill me then and I knew that once she had what she wanted from me she would attempt to do so. She nodded at the blood shunt. "Put that over on the deep scanner."

I walked over and placed the shunt on the flat plate of a deep-spectrum nanoscope, which powered up immediately. The screen above began riffling through cross sections of the device, then finally paused before expanding one of the microbots into visibility. It was an electro-chem device and up close it looked like an earth-moving machine made out of a child's building blocks. She next scanned a wide selection of these, very fast, then checked their carrier fluid for nanobots. As she finished her inspection my microbot factory beeped, lights flashing on it momentarily. Not only had she scanned the machines I would be putting into her body, but she was checking the program they would be running. After maybe twenty minutes, while I wandered round the room, inspecting the equipment, she was finally finished.

Her paranoia was perfectly as expected, and too late. She'd scanned my hands before I touched her, but, as with her scan of the blood shunt, her focus had been on microscopic mechanisms. She hadn't anticipated biological attack. Anyway, the prions had oozed out of my pores shortly *after* her scan and were now entering her body. Here they could multiply and spread to nerve-tech interfaces throughout, and to various portions of her spinal cord. There they would make primary protein folds in preparation for the tertiary fold, which in turn would lead to targeted prion cascades. I could then initiate these with a range of infrasound pulses at frequencies to which they had been sensitized.

"Continue," she said flatly.

I collected the blood shunt and placed it against her forearm, where it numbed her nerves before making its connection to a vein. I walked back round to the console and used the Syban software to access the process, so I could track it through the autodoc's diagnostic sensors. The autodoc simultaneously rose to a metre above her body for better coverage. The microbots quickly spread from her arm throughout her bloodstream, penetrating her flesh and coagulating around the nubs of cybermotors sitting in her every joint. These included all those down her spine, and in her fingers, toes and jaw. They next began penetrating electrochem interfaces, radio ports and sonar receivers. All I got was babble at first, but the Syban soon started to make sense of it, finally cracking the coding and listing a number of options. I ignored all the sub-options available and chose the one at the very top, turning off all her cybermotors.

Isobel emitted a sigh, and relaxed on the table.

"Better?" I enquired, now switching back to her original diagnosis. From that, I sent a formulation based on her nervous system to a drug manufactory on the work surface behind me.

"Yes, better," she replied, raising her head.

She did look a lot more relaxed and a lot less like someone suffering an illness. But the downside was that her added alertness suddenly seemed more alien, predatory and dangerous. She appeared more as she was: someone undergoing a major physical change. Isobel raised her head to look at me and I noticed that the pits below her eyes appeared more indented and the thorns protruding along her jawbone were already longer. As I turned to the drug manufactory, I thought it a good idea not to inform her that her transformation would be speeding up, now that she was no longer fighting her cybermotors. I eventually returned with a plain old syringe containing a slow-release drug implant.

"Why that?" she asked, still suspicious. "Why a painkiller?" She had obviously been watching the manufactory closely.

"As you have obviously just discovered," I said. "I may have fixed your cybermotor problem, but there will still be pain. This is afferant-nerve specific so will not hamper you."

She gave a sharp nod of agreement and I injected the implant above her groin.

"Are we agreed that I've fulfilled the initial part of our deal?" I asked.

She sat upright. "We're agreed."

Then she screamed.

Trent crashed through the door and, before I could say a word, kicked my legs out from under me and delivered a numbing punch to my kidneys as I went down. He had the barrel of a pulse-gun in my face before I could draw a breath, one heavy-worlder hand around my throat. Then he looked up at Isobel.

"The fuck?" he said.

He too had now seen the demonic red eye that had opened below Isobel's right-hand human eye. I wondered what horror this had enabled her to see, to make her scream like that. Perhaps her future, as she changed into a predator—something that could rip the flesh from people's bones. I wondered what she would see as her face grew longer, and as more eyes opened, and while she made her steady transformation from a human being into a hooder.

5

SPEAR

Beside Isobel and me, Trent and Gabriel were the only people aboard. Then again, should the second-child prador ganglion that served as this ship's mind be considered a person? I supposed so, even though it was a crippled thing that wouldn't make it through the latest iteration of the Turing Test. So make that five people aboard. I wasn't surprised that there were so few. I knew that Isobel Satomi's organization was big and that crime lords such as her usually had large entourages. But Isobel had fallen into a trap that heavy augmentation laid for many: she believed she didn't need so many people around her. Instead, she relied on her own expanded power and control.

"My name is Trent, and you already guessed that my last name is Sobel," said Trent. "How did you know?"

As I made my selection from the autochef menu and it was delivered out of a slot, I thought about Isobel's one-time boss, Mr Pace. He had also been a recipient of Penny Royal's attentions and had gone the same route, living a completely solitary existence walled in by wealth and power. I had considered using him to get me to the Polity destroyer and as a source of the other information I required—uniquely possessed by just a few. But I saw no way I could gain control of him, studying what little data there was on the changes he had undergone. It also seemed he was even more homicidal than Isobel.

Picking up my tray of food, I made my way back to Trent and Gabriel.

"I worked with some of the early adaptogens," I said. "The HG-92 series used in the Sobel line had certain easily identifiable side-effects."

He reached up self-consciously and touched his Mohican.

"Like what?" he challenged.

I sat down. "Like white eyes." Of course, I'd been getting feelings of déjà vu around Trent, but the reason for that was plain, and one I was about to reveal to him.

"Anything else?"

"Probably your pointy head," Gabriel interjected.

Trent glared at him for a moment, before returning his attention to me.

"However," I continued, "the main reason I plumped for that particular adaptogen is that facially, you could be Fellander Sobel's twin. You even sound like him."

Fellander Sobel used adaptogens to alter himself genetically so he could survive on a high gravity world. His traits were then inherited by his many children, but how many children they had in turn I had no idea. My interest had been limited and had waned when I joined Sylac, then a war and over a century of death got in the way.

"You met him?"

"I injected him with HG-92," I replied.

Trent stared at me dumbfounded and reached up to toy with that purple sapphire earring. I surmised that the jewel held some significance for him, because he always reached for it in moments of stress. Struggling for something else to say, he stabbed a finger at Gabriel. "What about him?"

I gobbled down some noodles and megaprawn while I studied Gabriel. He was another big lump of a man, but in his case his bulk was due to boosting. His muscle mass had been doubled and, judging by how pumped he looked, increased in density. This inclined me to think that he'd also had some bone lamination and joint reinforcing done, since that kind of muscle could snap normal human bones. He didn't have a visible aug and his skin was an unnatural pink, his eyes were pale blue and his neatly cut hair was blond. He wore the cut-off top of an acceleration suit which he'd turned into a jacket, an iridescent T-shirt, jeans and light rock-climbing footwear. But there were other more subtle clues about his past.

"Tharsis City, probably . . . or one of the Chryse hydroponics towns." I looked up at his face. "I'm guessing you got your tattoos removed here in the Graveyard. No Polity cosmetic surgeon would have been allowed to make such a mess of it."

The Graveyard, that no-man's-land lying between the Polity and the Kingdom, was a place lacking expertise. I'd learned that those working at the technological and scientific frontiers generally stayed in the Polity where better resources were available. This fact was my way in, my way to get to Isobel. However, the stuff about tattoo removal was just an educated guess. Martian tattooists employed a self-replicating ink that sometimes ran deep enough to penetrate bone, so problems with their removal seemed likely in such a place.

He grimaced in annoyance and reached up to touch his face. The blotching was just about visible, covering the pattern of a Mars man's facial tattoos.

"Tharsis City," he grunted.

"Hah! Gotcha!" said Trent.

We were all getting along famously and, as I took my flask out of my pocket and poured some of the contents into a small cup, I wondered if they took part in the coring of human beings. Or maybe they left that chore to thugs of a lesser station. Our conversation progressed to my wartime anecdotes and of course they wanted to try some real Earth whisky. They were still professional too, running personal toxin scanners over their drinks before trying them. It did them no good. They got their dose of prions from the outside of their glasses as I carefully held them while pouring in the precious liquid. This was just to make sure, since they should already have been infiltrated. They would only have needed to touch something I'd touched recently, as these prions had two hours of active life once outside my body. And I had been issuing them from my palms since my examination of Isobel.

*

A journey of some weeks ensued, to get us to our first destination in the Graveyard. I needed to find a particular sort of mind to control that abandoned Polity destroyer. I chafed at this because I wanted to get to Penny Royal *now*. However, I couldn't speed up interstellar travel, and I couldn't go up against something as dangerous as a black AI without the requisite preparations.

The planet had been contemptuously named the Rock Pool by spacers who travelled here, and it had been adopted with a kind twisted pride by its semi-human residents. Upon our arrival, I found myself speculating on the way humans changed themselves and were changed during their spread beyond Earth. Trent Sobel's ancestors had altered themselves to adapt to a new environment, while Isobel Satomi's pursuit of power had been turned against her by an insane godlike intelligence. For others the reasons for their changes were more obscure.

I'd learned more about the people of this world during the journey here. It seemed these were humans who admired the prador and took their admiration to extreme limits. So I shouldn't have been so surprised at my reaction to my first shellman sighting, the human mimicry of the prador form. I immediately analysed the feeling. Why did I feel such a visceral repulsion here when, in the Polity, I'd seen an adapted and enhanced take on forms much more bizarre than this? Why hadn't I had a similar reaction to Isobel's ongoing changes?

It was first, I realized, because in my own terms I'd been fighting the prador just a few months back. I also knew that the outer form of shellmen was an expression of their ugliness within. Admittedly, Isobel's appearance was the same in that respect, but hers wasn't through choice. Here, before me, was one of those who hated humanity and now worshipped, with close to religious zeal, a race that applied laws of selection to its children by eating the ones that weren't suitable. But that wasn't all. The prador were a race without conscience or empathy; vicious monsters whose predation extended beyond necessity into cruelty. They were creatures that surgically converted their children into biological mechanisms, ruthlessly exterminated rivals and would still, given the chance, exterminate rival humanity. They were, I felt, as close to irredeemably evil as you could realistically get.

Second thoughts occurred and I smiled, not realizing I had reached up to my neck to scratch the psychosomatic itch there. Next, I remembered the cold metal legs of a spider thrall digging into my flesh and I considered that my opinion of the prador might not be a balanced one.

"You're Spear?" grated the shellman.

"I am Thorvald Spear, yes," I replied, reaching up to take off my breather mask.

Though he was a foot shorter than me, the shellman was wider and bulkier. His carapace extended a few feet on either side of his back. And this was tipped forward forty-five degrees as if he was labouring under the weight of a heavy iron shield. However, the carapace was supported by the man's ribs, which extended out to its edges, enclosing his organs up against it. He had two pairs of arthropod legs supporting him and human arms extended about a foot down from where they should be. A heavy crab claw curled in from the buried right shoulder and a narrow claw, rather like that of a langoustine, extended from the left. From the front he looked as if he might fall, but didn't because of a horseshoe crab tail that poked out behind to balance him. His vaguely humanoid head rose up on a ribbed neck, but his human eyes extended on palps from the top of his skull. A crescent of ruby eyes was embedded where those human eyes should have been, and he possessed the mouthparts of a dragonfly.

It was a non-Polity surgical amalgam job, and not a very good one—judging by the rashes of acne pustules on the man's human parts where they joined his prador components. The man was definitely suffering an allergic reaction due to a failure in immune system reprogramming.

"And what's your name?" I enquired.

"Vrit," the shellman replied.

I spotted a human mouth, which was revealed each time Vrit parted his mandibles to speak. The man might well have radically changed his body and adopted a prador name, but he hadn't gone all the way. Why was that? Why did these people, who supposedly loved the prador and everything those creatures represented, not look more like the prador? Certainly the techniques were available. I grimaced briefly as I realized the answer lay in my first thoughts on spotting this man. The changes they made to themselves were a visible statement about what they didn't want to be, and that statement would be lost if they completely assumed the guise of their gods. It was all about self-hatred—and a denial of humanity.

"You've got payment?" Vrit asked, eyeing my hover trunk as it settled behind me.

The Graveyard was supposed to be a lawless buffer zone where neither Prador Kingdom nor Polity ventured. But in reality, both sides did venture here, and many Graveyard worlds had representatives from both species. However, they weren't here to do more than keep an eye on each other and look after their own interests. This world, like any within the border, was one you visited at your own risk. I knew things could get a little . . . difficult when bargaining with shellmen, for they tended to look after their own and hold normal humans in contempt. This was why, though declining Isobel's offer to have Trent and Gabriel accompany me, I had ensured I could summon them in an instant.

"I'm ready to negotiate," I replied vaguely, stepping forwards. Apparently inadvertently, I allowed my jacket to fall open to expose the gas-system pulse-gun at my hip. I felt like a fraud but, unfortunately, the threat of violence is often the only way to stop violence.

Vrit stepped back sharply, his palp eyes seeking something across the flat obsidian floor—the dock stone apparently extending into this reception building. I noted how he flinched as he moved, certainly experiencing pain related to the crappy postoperative work on him. Then I followed the direction of his gaze, taking in the mounds of cargo crates, busy auto-handlers and the mix of shell people and Polity citizens. There, perambulating along beside a glass wall, I saw a prador. The great crablike monstrosity had a Gatling cannon affixed along the edge of one claw, with ammunition feeds trailing to a magazine fixed to its underside. It was also completely clad in a form of armour I didn't recognize—a bluegreen metal that seemed to create more bulk than the usual brassy kind. I also couldn't tell whether it was a first- or second-child, because its size lay somewhere between the two. I stared at the thing and wondered why, despite my recent thinking, I felt no visceral hatred of its kind.

"So where do you have it?" I asked, bringing my attention back to the shellman.

Vrit was still staring at the prador, almost seeming to cringe a little. He snapped his attention back to me. "A barge." He indicated the wide oval doors at the back of the building.

"Shall we?" I waved a hand vaguely.

Vrit studied me warily for a moment, then turned and set out at a fast scuttle towards the exit. There were no customs inspections here, just a few safety protocols. Vrit put on his mask before opening a door made for humans, in the centre of the main prador door, and stepped into a short exit tunnel. I put my mask back on and followed. Bright pink sunlight glared at the end of this tunnel and soon I could hear the sea again. I could also smell something utterly putrid—which even penetrated my mask—as I had during my walk from the *Moray Firth* to the reception building.

I paused at the exit to gaze along a black stone shore scattered with stilt houses in the process of marching on stalk legs to oblivion in the wine-coloured waves. This was as close as the shell people could get to the deep-water prador enclave here. This enclave was apparently the home of a disparate group of prador, who had chosen to disobey their king's order to return to the Kingdom at the end of the war. Beyond that, all I knew was that they were ruled over by one father-captain and that they had established trade links throughout the Graveyard and into both the Polity and the Kingdom. Also, surprisingly for prador, they showed no inclination to come ashore and slaughter everyone.

I also knew that I had never stood here before, but felt on some deep level that I had. These feelings of familiarity were now so much a part of many of my new experiences that I'd almost accepted them. In fact, I suspected I might feel bereft without them. But what came next I just couldn't accept, because it was too definite, too shocking.

I was standing there holding a breather mask in my new claw, wondering if the shore wind would bring in another of those gusts of hydrogen sulphide. These were becoming frequent, down to new volcanic activity far out under the ocean. I felt strong and armoured against the world with my growing carapace, and I felt a deep kinship with and almost religious love of the prador in their ships under that ocean. The necessity for the mask irritated me, though even the superior prador were as affected by that gas as weak humans. I began to walk, slowly, because my human component felt sick and exhausted. It felt like a gangrenous limb or diseased skin—something to be excised or shed to expose my purity within . . .

"Are you coming?" asked Vrit, now crouched as if ready to flee or attack.

What the hell was that? I remembered what I had felt when I touched Isobel for the first time. And though I questioned how wrong it had felt, I had accepted it as some fragment of my past arising in my mind. I could not accept this. I had never been here and I had certainly never been a shellman. This was someone else's memory, hard and clear in my mind.

"Yes, I'm coming," I replied, straightening up. "Lead on."

Vrit headed to the right across the same black rock as the ground-down and polished dock stone. But here it was whorled and pitted, scattered with baroque clinging shellfish. After checking to ensure my hover trunk could deal with the uneven surface, I followed him down to a jetty poking out into the sea, a large covered barge moored beside it. I noted a small cargo platform with a rear cargo crane on caterpillar treads standing behind it, and felt a small relaxing of tension. Vrit would not have gone to the trouble to have such an unwieldy device brought if he intended some betrayal . . . probably. At the foot of the jetty, I turned to look back at the port building and could just see the upper hull and weapons turret of the *Moray Firth* on the other side. I had no doubt that Isobel was watching me at that moment, though I did wonder what she was seeing now that a second hooder eye had opened on her face, which itself had grown longer and now bore some resemblance to an Easter Island statue.

"Come, come." Vrit had already scrambled across onto a small area of clear deck and was now gesturing to me from the barge with his heavy claw.

I crossed the short ramp, stepping onto the deck as Vrit opened the wide door into the barge's interior. Lights immediately came on inside and I ducked in after him, stepping down yet another ramp into tatty living quarters. As I waited for my hover trunk to catch up, I noted the rubbish scattered on a single desk—analgesic patches, an auto-dispensary and a scattering of air injectors.

"You know," I said, as I watched my trunk enter the quarters with almost pernickety distaste, "if you don't get proper treatment you'll either get steadily worse and die, or at some point go into anaphylactic shock and die from that."

Vrit turned sharply. "What's it to you?"

I shrugged. "I don't like to see suffering. It's obvious to me that your human half is reacting to the rest of you." I paused, then added, "I might be able to help you there."

Vrit removed his mask, then parted his dragonfly mandible to show a sneering mouth. "It's reacting because it's weak, and I don't need any human help." He turned away and pushed through the plastic curtains, calling back, "Rather it is the true me rejecting the human."

I watched the curtains for a moment longer, realizing how that rogue memory had impelled me to offer help. But, even though I was sure the memory hadn't been Vrit's, it should have warned me help would not be accepted. Closing my eyes for a second, I wondered what I should do about that memory, but without something like a Polity forensic AI to investigate it, there was nothing I could do. I just had to live with it and continue towards my goals. These experiences only fazed me for a moment and, as in this case, they even provided potentially useful information.

Removing my own mask, I followed the shellman through and looked around. The area beyond the curtains was packed with jury-rigged equipment for testing and repairing computer hardware. This was a mixture of human and prador technology, webbed together with optics and s-con cables, the power being supplied by a stacked capacitor charge tower. At the far end, on an airplast pallet, stood the prador cryopod. The sphere of brassy metal was a metre across, trailing cables and optics to the nearby equipment. Inset in its upper surface were quadrant windows lit by an internal green light. I shivered, not because the thing was chilling the air, but because of the suffering it implied. The prador brain the pod contained would not have willingly left its original body. Once Vrit stood aside and gestured to the thing, I walked over and peered in through one of the windows.

The prador second-child ganglion sat inside in a cube of water ice, a coiled length of organic matter. It lay blurred behind odd crystalline structures that seemed to have grown from it into the surrounding ice. It was almost lost under its numerous plugs, interfaces and skeins of optics that in turn exited the cube to connect to various black-box hardware units. This object rested between two splayed-end columns and I pondered on their similarity to the supports within Polity spaceships for AI crystals. I reached out and rested a hand on the sphere, almost in apology. Though I was not to blame for the events that had resulted in the thing before me, in purchasing it I might be encouraging their repetition.

"What's it from?" I asked.

"Prador kamikaze—made a solstan year before the end of the war and never used." Vrit bowed towards the sea almost obsequiously. "Father-Captain Sverl, the ruler of our world, has been trading his limited supply for Polity tech."

Prador kamikazes, just like their Japanese namesakes, had been used during the war. The only real difference was that they flew in space and carried far more in the way of destructive potential.

"What kind of Polity tech?" I asked, immediately suspicious of this Sverl's motives.

Vrit gave an odd crippled shrug. "This one, along with some other items, was to trade for a picoscope, gene-sequencing nanobots and one or two other expensive items."

The first he'd mentioned was expensive enough. I'd considered acquiring a picoscope—something that just hadn't existed a hundred years ago. How amazing would it be to see sub-nanoscopic structures and to a limited extent manipulate them? What dissuaded me was my struggle to grasp how the damned thing worked—it having been developed by AI and involving U-space tech. In addition, I couldn't justify the huge expense with respect to my goals.

I turned back to my trunk, which had now settled down in the middle of the floor as if prudishly trying to distance itself from the surrounding mess. I stepped over and touched my fingertips against the upper surface, whereupon a half-lid hinged silently open to reveal neatly packed Polity computer hardware. I made my selection and stepped back to the prador cryopod, pulling an optic cable from the end of an oval processing unit, and searched for ports in the brassy metal.

"Do you want to hear it talk?" asked Vrit, as I finally found a port and plugged in the optic.

I glanced at him. "You've hooked in a translator?"

"Of course," said Vrit, scratching at one of his rashes with dirty human fingernails.

"Then why not?" It would do no harm, but I preferred my own methods of checking to ensure the second-child ganglion was viable. I peered at data appearing on my comp-unit's small screen and wiped a hand across it to expand it into a flat holodisplay. Then I waved the display up into the air beside me, where it hung running diagnostic code.

"Pilot," said Vrit. "Status report."

A voice, quite obviously tweaked to make it sound less human, spoke from a stalk speaker which sprouted from a console on a nearby work surface.

"I am fully functional," it said. "System ports 43 to 78 and 80 to 125 are disconnected. Port 79 is running a Polity-format diagnostic. New instruction: allow. Internal battery is at 40%. External source inadequate for maintenance level. Status of U-calculus nil—engine parameters unavailable. Status of—"

"End report," Vrit ordered, then turned back to me. "Do you want to ask it anything?"

"Will it respond?"

"It will now," Vrit replied, stabbing a finger down on a touch panel.

I nodded, then turned so I could address the cryopod directly, even though I knew that the microphones were probably over in that console. Something there about respect, I guess, and pity. "Tell me, prador second-child, what is your name?"

A sizzling sound issued from the stalk speaker, then I recognized the bubbling hiss of prador language, followed by confused tense clicks. Its name was something like "Vffloiotsht" but it obviously didn't know whether to add the clicks for "I am" or "I was" after its name.

"I will call you Flute," said I. "Henceforth that is your name."

"Primary instruction confirm?" the second-child suggested.

I glanced at Vrit, who gave a crabbish shrug.

"Confirm," I said.

"Of course," said Vrit, "it doesn't matter to me what you call it . . . when you've paid for it."

I was satisfied with everything my own hardware was showing me. Inside that cryopod there was indeed the surgically excised brain of a prador second-child, held in organic stasis but adapted to run electro-optics. The Polity AIs had claimed that spaceships could only navigate U-space with an AI aboard to make the necessary calculations. But they no longer bothered to quell the rumours that this was a lie—because otherwise how had the prador, a race without AIs, managed to travel in that same continuum? It turned out they adapted their own children for that purpose, and the surgical procedure was usually carried out without anaesthetic, either as punishment or simply for entertainment.

I stepped back over to my trunk and tapped the second half-lid so that it hinged open. Inside rested a chunk of a nacreous layered glassy substance.

"I believe five pounds of prador diamond slate was the agreed price," I suggested.

Vrit was over by the trunk in a moment, clicking his langoustine claw across the layers, mandibles wide and human mouth pursed pensively.

"I only take a small percentage," he said. "I am privileged to act as an agent for the father-captain."

I swung back to gaze at the cryopod, uncomfortable with this purchase; bothered by the morality of it. However, it was what was required if you wanted to travel through interstellar space without too many Polity AIs noticing. And it was certainly the kind of thing you needed if you intended to reactivate a Polity destroyer that had, essentially, lost its own mind. And you needed a Polity destroyer if you intended to attack a black AI in its own lair.

THE WAR: DURANA

I gazed back along the tunnel through the vegetation at the bluebarbs and twizzle vines, the lurking pumpkin cycads and offler weed. The only similarity between the vegetation here and anything terran was the fact that it grew upwards. Nothing had real photosynthesizing leaves, probably because the intensity of the sunlight here didn't require them. This world's version of chlorophyll contained in their structure supplied all the energy they needed. The twizzle vines were just pale blue corkscrews that draped over everything. The bluebarbs, though resembling twenty-foot-tall rhubarb dipped in blue printer's ink, were a variety of fungus. And the cycads could hardly be described as either plant or fungus. They built sugars via induction shifts in the planet's magnetic field. They also occasionally pulled up their roots and perambulated on a slug-like foot to a better position, after having drained the soil below of minerals. The offler weed was a particularly aggressive slime mould.

"You okay?" asked Krong.

I glanced across at this hero of the Polity and wondered how much longer he would survive. Certainly he was a man driven by his hatred of the prador and a firm loyalty to his perception of everything the Polity stood for. But his methods revealed inconsistencies. Slapping a sticky-bomb on the carapace of a prador, when you could have taken it out at a distance with a missile launcher, wasn't the most logical way to fight them. Jebel U-cap Krong and his comrades in this squad were all adrenalin junkies. I suspected the AIs allowed him to continue because of some arcane calculation concerning the advantageous publicity he produced. In their war for survival, the AIs and humanity needed their heroes.

"I'll be okay," I replied, "just so long as one of our prador friends is intact."

"We'll try our best." He grinned and moved away.

Durana was a world swamped in deep plant growth—a jungle world, if you will. It provided just the kind of preferred hunting ground for Jebel U-cap Krong and his squad of prador-killers. Their techniques did not work well where there was less concealment and, so Jebel told me, they were assigned to those environments where they could do the most damage. Before Durana they'd been on a desert planet, concealing themselves like trapdoor spiders in caustic white sand. Their goal was to ambush the prador who were installing a titanic ground-based railgun, until one of the new Polity dreadnoughts had spoiled their fun.

After a two-hour warning, it dropped a chemical reactor bomb that caused a chain reaction in the desert. This sank the gun emplacement into a lake—a glutinous syrup of something like caustic soda. I'd been with them for that one and the two before. These were the ice moon, where we used boring machines, coming up below the prador like rising sharks. Next was the H3 station on a gas giant, where we used motorized mono-cloth ornithopters, dropping on them from concealing fogs.

I spent four months aboard an Earth Central Security hospital ship recovering from my stint with the prador. The physical harm was dealt with in two weeks, but the other damage took longer. The mind-tech assigned to me kept insisting that my recovery would be sped up by a little memory editing, but I refused that. It seemed essential that I retain the horror as a driver to my need for vengeance. I healed the old way—learning to live with what had happened to me—and when I shipped out I was functional, if a little twitchy. ECS gave me bio-weapons scut work—first developing some nasty viruses and flesh-eating fungal spores—a chore I found less abhorrent than usual. Then afterwards they eased me back into bio-espionage. I began with extracting data from prador corpses and from second-child ganglions surviving in wrecked prador ships or drones. Or I retrieved information from their baroque computer systems. Once I'd proved that I wasn't going to run away screaming at the mere sight of the enemy, they moved me up to captive prador. During this time, the prisoners from a crashed prador dreadnought provided information about Penny Royal. It was becoming an obsession for me, though not to ECS. Shortly after that, I was considered fit for more active service and was allowed to respond to U-cap Krong's request for me. He needed a bio-espionage expert and I fitted the bill. I guess my psych profile after my experiences with the prador was just right too.

"Okay, we're clear," someone called. "Let's move on."

The target here was a prador mining operation. Deep under this jungle was a layer of rare metal that they used in their armour—a metal that had only recently been added to the human periodic table. I had to wonder if the suggested names for it, Ucapium or Krongium, had something to do with our presence here. Those running military PR wouldn't have been above that.

Our mission was to set up an ambush, then capture a prador—preferably a first-child—whereupon my speciality would come into play. And my main specialism, now more than ever, was the extraction of information from these minds. By whatever means necessary. After that, the data gathered should allow our companion for this assignment to penetrate the mining complex. I glanced over at said companion. The assassin drone had its chameleonware tuned down, so it was just about visible against the jungle backdrop. It looked vaguely like a large thick-bodied cobra, but it had four limbs folded below the spread of its hood and a long thin ovipositor extending from its tail.

I was told its appearance mimicked a particularly nasty prador parasite—one that laid its eggs inside them, which then hatched into larvae that ate out their insides. It was also a parasite the prador had wiped out long ago. However, somehow its genome had been resurrected by forensic AIs, and this drone now carried thousands of fresh eggs, ready to be implanted, inside its armoured skin. The drone was here on the usual mission the Polity assigned to its kind: that of spreading terror amongst the prador. We were here because intelligence had revealed that the mining operation was about to be closed down. So the four father-captains, along with their thousands of children, were soon to be recalled to the prador home world. If the timings were right, the eggs the drone injected would begin hatching out when they arrived. It was a particularly nasty biological weapon, so much so that it even made some of Jebel's troops a little uncomfortable. I was conflicted. I thought it a horrible weapon too. But, having been a prador captive, I felt a lot less sympathetic while simultaneously disliking this change in my attitude.

We moved on through the jungle, carefully, switching to full chameleonware when we came upon the first crushed-down trails left by prador patrols. There were ten in Krong's squad, but two had come here a month earlier to reconnoitre. As we drew closer to the mining complex, as yet concealed behind jungle, these two reappeared. I moved over to Krong as he headed forwards to brief them.

"The tracks you see are from punishment patrols," said the first scout, a woman who looked as if she should still be at school. "They don't expect a ground attack here, but send out those guilty of minor infractions not punishable by the usual methods."

The usual prador punishments ranged from a cracked carapace, up to being dismembered and eaten alive by its father. Some were, of course, surgically dismembered, their ganglions being used as the prador version of ship or drone minds.

"Irregular?" Krong asked.

"Nope, regular as clockwork."

"So you have a place prepared?"

"I do."

"Why are they a punishment?" I interjected. "The patrols, I mean."

She turned towards me. "The offler weed." She gestured to a nearby patch of the stuff that the assassin drone was examining. The gooey blue mass, which I already knew could move as fast as a fried egg sliding out of a greased pan, had frozen. And, becoming aware of threat, it was now extruding a bristling coat of spines.

"The spores lodge in prador joints and grow there," she continued. "To remove these before returning to the complex, they have to spray themselves with a solution of hydrochloric acid. You can hear them yelling every time."

Nice. I decided to collect a sample for dispatch to Bio-weapons.

It took us an hour to reach the ambush point. Here, the two who had been in place for a month had already dug a number of hidey-holes. Mine was set well back from the trail and I wasn't allowed to come out until after the squad had dealt with the patrol. This was apparently due within the hour. Lugging my equipment over, I gazed askance at the eel-like worms poking their thorned heads out of the disturbed soil, then climbed down inside. I pulled the lid over, then inserted my periscope bead up through it, shunting the feed to my visor display.

By the time I had a clear above-ground view, the rest of the squad was completely concealed.

"We've got them spotted," Jebel informed us all through comlinks and augs. "They should be here in forty minutes."

It was a long uncomfortable forty minutes, during which I had to shut down my visor display, switch over to light amplification and brush thorny-headed eels off my battledress. Then, later, a creature like a foot-long stick insect crawled up my leg. Eventually the prador came into sight: three second-children to the fore, followed by two first-children and then another four second-children. The leading second-children drew right opposite me before it all kicked off. I saw one of them pause and tilt its nose down, its palp eyes bent forwards as if to try and see underneath itself, then the sticky-mine there exploded. A moment after that one of the second two exploded, then two at the rear went, and one of the first-children went down with all its legs sheared off one side. The air filled with Gatling cannon fire and the stabs of particle beams, blue-barbs toppled all around and clumps of vegetation dropped in smoking lumps. I reached up and flipped the lid off my hole, anxious to be out of it.

The assassin drone, probably wanting to ratchet up the terror, shut down its chameleonware as it clung to the uninjured first-child, stabbing its ovipositor in at the point where the prador's legs joined its body. I could not see the point of this until the first-child, bubbling and hissing like a boiling kettle, also began to steam. It ran, but not far. Its legs began to fall off and it went down like a flying saucer crash-landing, its insides boiling out of leg holes and around the rim of its carapace. I realized the drone had not injected eggs but hydrofluoric acid. Surviving prador ran into the jungle, with Jebel's squad in hot pursuit. I hauled my equipment out of my hole and climbed out after it. The prador with the missing legs was obviously for me.

Stupidity, inattention, a failure to completely process the dangers—that's how it happens. I didn't realize I hadn't turned on my chameleon-ware until the first-child swung up a claw, with a Gatling cannon attached. I didn't hear it fire, only saw the flash and felt something like a speeding train slam into me. I flew backwards, bounced, oddly light, and came down on my back. I couldn't breathe and already things were turning black. Consciousness lasted long enough for me to see that everything below the middle of my chest was missing, including my arms beyond the elbows.

Then I died . . . I think. Chronologically, these should have been my last memories of the war. Yet, the earlier firestorm from the anti-matter blasts on Panarchia felt somehow more real. But one must never allow emotion to overrule logic, surely?

SPEAR

Months of travel had taken us deep into the Graveyard now, the world called the Rock Pool far behind us and the Prador Kingdom uncomfortably close. And, sitting in orbit was my Polity destroyer, above the world whose coordinates I retrieved from a prador mind long ago. The thing looked like a giant sarcophagus and, as Trent and I jetted over, I tried not to think about that. I concentrated on inspecting the vessel for damage.

I had inserted a memory sliver into this suit before donning it, to make sure I had full control of it via my aug. But I couldn't really close the suit's camera feed back to the *Moray Firth*. With Trent accompanying me, it wouldn't have made much difference if I had. Isobel was going to learn the history of this destroyer and she wasn't going to like it at all. What I did next would depend on how she reacted. Upon reaching the destroyer, Trent manually opened the airlock and we stepped through. I kept a close eye on the man, who was carrying a heavy laser carbine. I was more than ready to send the infrasound activation over suit radio, to start the prion cascade in his body.

The inside of the abandoned ship was thoroughly familiar, yet I had never set foot inside before that moment. I looked down at scratch marks on the floor beside the airlock and just knew they had been caused by a maintenance robot, scrabbling for purchase during heavy acceleration. Suddenly my attitude to this déjà vu flipped over and I became intensely annoyed with it. Would I never again experience the joy of new discoveries, new sights, sounds and smells? Was this the feeling that drove older Polity citizens like my brother to suicidal pursuits, in search of some small fragment of new experience?

The interior of the old ship wasn't airless, but the pressure was very low. I felt a visceral certainty that something horrible had happened here, and this extended beyond my knowledge of what *had* happened. Undeniable proof of this presented itself the moment we rounded the first corner. We found the first body in the corridor leading to the "ship's cortex," the globular chamber toward the nose of the ship.

"One of the crew," I stated.

"What the fuck happened to him?" Trent asked, pointing his weapon at the corpse. "Some sort of U-space screw-up?"

Whether this had been a "him" or a "her" was debatable, I felt. Difficult to sex a desiccated corpse still clad in a blue and green shipsuit. Especially when it was partially buried in a wall that had frozen, apparently partway through a transformation into a nest of adders. Gazing at the corpse, I felt my skin crawling and my space suit seemingly tightening around me. I turned away in a flash of terror. I definitely did not want this person's memories.

"This looks like a nano- and micro-machine matter transformation," I said, knowing perfectly well that it was exactly that.

"Triggered by the ship's repair systems?" Isobel asked from the *Moray Firth*, currently matching the Polity destroyer's course around a Graveyard green-belt world which had yet to acquire any human name.

Yes, the ship's repair systems, breeding constantly and controlled by something that might just give nightmares to a standard planetary AI.

"So, tell me more about how you located this," Isobel asked, obviously rattled by what she'd seen through our suit feeds.

"Like I said before," I explained. "I used a specialized search of a captured prador database. This ship was dead when they found it and lined it up for salvage, but they never got round to that before the war ended."

It was as close to the truth as I wanted to venture. I had used a specialized search of a database, after Panarchia and during my rehabilitation, before joining Krong. But I used the term "database" loosely as it had actually been the mind of a first-child, extracted from the wreckage of a prador dreadnought. Before that, the search teams had brought me the remains of the prador captain to examine, taken from that same dreadnought. Here I found glass worms wound through his major ganglion, and the internal ceramic mouth he had been impelled to use to feed on his own organs. And even before I opened up the first-child's mind, I had some dark intimation of what I'd found.

The child had been filled with delight that its beloved father-captain had found an abandoned Polity destroyer. They had docked and proceeded to assay it to see whether it could be adapted for prador use or should be cut up for salvage. Of course father had been delighted—such a find would add to his prestige and his personal fortune. Daddy's delight lasted until the horrific killings started. The culprit was a Polity assassin drone picked up from the destroyer, they were sure . . . then the killing stopped and the prador captain ordered his ship undocked and fled.

The child's memories stopped there, giving no reason why the dreadnought had subsequently crashed on a human-occupied world. When I found out the destroyer's Polity name and serial number in the child's mind I recorded them, then went on to record its location. But I reported none of these. After Panarchia, my personal quest for vengeance had steered me away from authority and towards personal satisfaction. I didn't know or care where this would lead, such was my need. When the first-child was then taken away for "humane disposal," the knowledge died with it. I knew then that the prador dreadnought had certainly picked up something from that other ship. But it hadn't been anywhere near as pleasant as an assassin drone.

We found another dead crewman just outside the narrow tunnel leading to the ship's cortex. This one had obviously decided on positive action in response to the developing threat. The desiccated corpse was pinned to the ceiling, a pulse-rifle having been driven through its gut. However, closer inspection revealed a blending of pulse-rifle and shipsuit, as if the stock and butt of the weapon had grown from the victim. After seeing that, I looked away quickly, because I didn't want Isobel, or Trent, to study the corpse too closely. As I ducked into the tunnel I wondered how long it had taken the victim to die, then had to accept that I'd probably never know. The thing that had exited through this tunnel set no limits on the suffering of its victims.

The ship's cortex was packed with machinery. A skeletal Golem rested with its back against the wall nearest the door, its android legs missing. Metallic tentacles wound from its pelvis, crossing the floor to plug into a socket in the opposite wall. Below its wrists, its hands branched into micro-manipulators which were scattered with silvery nubs like small steel berries. I recognized these as nano-manipulator heads. Its eyes were gone and in their place was something that looked ridiculously like ancient binoculars. I moved on in and round so I could keep Trent in sight.

Other maintenance robots were crammed into the area, some still in their original form, others converted in weird fashions. I paused to study a series of hand-sized beetle-bots, arrayed like the tines of a rake along a bar at the end of a long jointed arm. Though I could not fathom the specific purposes of the robots and the Golem, I guessed their overall task: they had been here to change a static object into something very dangerous and mobile.

"Looks like the ship's AI was shattered," Isobel observed.

Yes, there were flakes of AI crystal scattered all about the area, but nowhere near enough. I moved on to the central clamp—two columns terminating in flat plates extending from floor and ceiling, leaving a gap a foot wide between. Here was where the ship's AI should have been. I eyed the gap for a moment, then an object lying over beside the wall drew my attention. Something cold crept up my vertebrae as I walked over to study it.

Here lay a black spine a metre and a half long, the width of an arm at its base and tapering to a needle point. It was pentagonal in cross section with corners I *knew* to be of atomic sharpness. A ribbed tentacle extended from its base, with a tentacle junction box a hand-breadth down it and a metre of tentacle beyond that—torn off at the end with optics and esoteric electronics protruding. Gazing at the thing, I felt a weird sense of connection as well as the usual familiarity. And neither sensation had anything to do with the numerous descriptions of these that I'd heard. I stepped back, feeling very uncomfortable—worse than I'd ever felt before with this déjà vu, this *connection*. There was some truth here I simply didn't want to know about, or just couldn't allow myself to know about.

"There's no AI here," said Isobel, her voice hollow. "Or at least not all of it."

"No," I replied. Of course there wasn't.

"You had better start talking, and quickly," she said. "That was a piece of Penny Royal back there. What the hell was it doing here, and what the hell is your interest?"

"The destroyer is called *Puling Child*," I explained, because the time for concealment was past. "An amusing reference to a substance called pulegone which can cause babies to be aborted. It can be derived from a terran herb."

"That's all very interesting," said Isobel acidly. "Now why don't you cut to the dramatic climax you're obviously leading up to."

"The herb concerned," I continued, "is pennyroyal, which, incidentally, is the name of the AI that controlled this ship. Penny Royal did not come here, but came *from* here."

"Fuck," said Isobel vehemently. Then because she couldn't find anything else to add, "Fuck."

6

ISOBEL

Isobel watched Spear and Trent returning from the destroyer. Then, after trying to force herself to breathe evenly and calm down, she spoke to Trent privately, "I'm opening the space doors to the hold. Come in through there."

"You think he's been playing us?" Trent asked.

Playing us? He brought us to the birthplace of Penny Royal—I don't think playing anywhere near covers what happened! She paused, used her haiman augmentation to replay the last few seconds, to be sure she hadn't said that out loud.

"I do, and if I need to do something about that, I don't want to make a mess in our living quarters."

Ersatz toughness, when she wanted to scream hysterically. Or was it? She now recognized the growing predator inside her, and it wanted to tear Spear apart. It wanted to tear *everything* apart.

"Okay, I'll tell him we're going to move his second-child mind straight away."

"You do that."

Isobel swallowed an odd metallic taste in her mouth and sat back, using her augmentations to tune out the perpetually re-engaging input from her three hooder eyes as she gaped at the image of the destroyer on her screen. Her instinct was to have Trent and Gabriel glue Spear to the deck. They could then work him over for a few hours before using a cut aug on him, to wring every last scrap of information out of his skull. But she wasn't sure if that instinct was wholly her own. She had to focus on the fact that the man offered a cure, and she should do nothing until either he had given her what she wanted or she found out that he could not.

She reached up and touched her long cheek with quivering fingers. Her head was now twice as tall as a normal human's, and she could feel another red eye due to open in one of her developing eye pits. The protrusions, which had run up her jaw, now ran up the sides of her face and were longer. Some had acquired a joint, and the swelling towards their ends promised to blossom into a hooder manipulator. Her sensory cowl was still open and had been for a month, when she found she could no longer close it up. Further petals had also sprouted from the sides of her neck. Her arms and legs were shorter too, though she had lost no height because her body had grown longer. She was monstrous and just could not go on like this, surely . . .

She returned her attention to the screen, her extra eyes switching to infrared and ultraviolet, which was unhelpful for a screen formatted for human eyes. Again she tuned them out—the fight to do so just a little bit more difficult each time. She switched to a cam in the hold which showed, amidst crates of trade goods, where the second-child mind had been stowed. Trent and Spear's survey of the *Puling Child* had rendered the results Spear had expected, though of course he hadn't told the truth about why he had expected them. The destroyer was powered down but the fusion reactors could be restarted at any time. All it needed was the second-child's mind to be installed and it would be ready to fly . . . that was presupposing Penny Royal hadn't left any nasty surprises. She found herself shuddering uncontrollably.

As Trent and Spear entered the hold, the grav-plates powered up slowly, bringing them down to the floor as the space doors closed. A gale blew in there for a second as the hold filled with air, then Spear removed his helmet and placed it down on a nearby crate. Trent had moved back from Spear, his carbine casually pointed towards the man's stomach.

"Gabriel," said Isobel, standing up and heading unsteadily for the exit. He joined her on the way down and, sensing her mood, drew his pulse-gun. He also had one of those neat cattle prod devices used on Cheyne III to drive dark otters away from boats. Isobel hoped he would not be finding a use for it soon; hoped Spear would be true to his word.

"Penny Royal," she stated flatly as she stepped into the hold, determined not to show him both her desperation and her growing need for violence.

Spear turned towards her, looking annoyingly calm.

"Penny Royal," he said, with a slow nod.

"Why are we here?"

"Truth?"

"If you value your skin." Yes, maybe she'd take that, if he reneged . . .

"I was one of the few survivors left on Panarchia, after a division of eight thousand men was CTD-bombed from orbit by that ship," he stabbed a thumb towards the space doors. "I intend to track down and kill the mind that controlled it—Penny Royal."

Isobel stared at him, finding herself flicking to a wider spectrum view as panic tightened her torso. Maybe he wasn't playing them. Maybe he was simply insane.

"That explains nothing," she said, fighting to return her vision to normal.

"I need a ship to hunt Penny Royal down—it's not something that can be done through the runcible network," he explained. "I knew where Penny Royal's destroyer was and it seemed the best option. There may also be clues aboard to help me in my search."

"That still doesn't explain why you came to me," she said tightly.

"I needed someone familiar with the Graveyard . . ."

"Still not good enough, Thorvald Spear."

"Okay." He shrugged in defeat. "As well as being able to get me here, you can also give me the location of Penny Royal's base—that planetoid. You went there, and it's not a place I can find on any Polity database."

She stared at him for a moment, her enhanced mind flicking through this new information, and realized his error. He'd come out of resurrection intent on going after Penny Royal right away. He'd therefore searched for information through the Polity AI net, where the position of Penny Royal's planetoid had been suppressed. Just as subsequent information had also been suppressed: about Penny Royal's encounter with something dangerous and alien while in the Graveyard. Then the AI's near-destruction, and its rescue by a Polity drone called Amistad who took it to the planet Masada. How naive were the citizens of the Polity, to think their AIs revealed everything. She could tell him, but it was not her custom to give away information for free.

"And why should I?"

"Money?" he suggested.

She stared at him for a long time, trying to understand what the emissions coming from him might mean—she could pick them up with her additional hooder senses. They could perhaps be parsed for truth. She realized her stare had gone on for an uncomfortably long time when Gabriel started fidgeting and throwing worried looks her way.

"That will have to be another transaction," she said tersely. "But right now you have what you want."

"I will have what I want when my ship mind—" he gestured to the sphere containing the second-child "—is installed."

"That will be done when you deal with this." She indicated her own body with a hand that was becoming increasingly unusable.

"No, you get the mind over there first," he replied with that irritating calm. "You can keep Trent or Gabriel with me at all times. Once it's in place I will complete our . . . initial transaction."

She suddenly knew he was lying. He was trying to keep her hooked while he got that destroyer running. He was obviously technically adept, so probably had some plan to escape in it before completing his part of the deal. All that stuff about hunting down and killing Penny Royal had to be a lie because it was based on yet another lie. Anyone who knew anything about Penny Royal knew about the incident when it turned black. There had been no human survivors of the bombing of Panarchia.

"You seem to be under the illusion that you have some power here," she said, now considering losses and gains. There was no cure for her here, but she was about to acquire a Polity destroyer—a very expensive item indeed. The money she could make from it in a Graveyard auction should be enough to lure somebody top-flight out of the Polity—someone who really could deal with her problem. Meanwhile her inner predator raised its head and opened its eyes.

"Okay." He nodded, gazing at her.

She immediately understood he knew she'd seen through him. Perhaps she *was* reading something beyond the human visual spectrum, to receive this insight so clearly?

"*If he moves a muscle, burn off his feet,*" she auged to Trent, then glanced at the heavy-worlder when he didn't respond.

"You want some more truth?" Spear asked.

"*Trent?*"

Something was wrong.

"You, Isobel Satomi, are a murderous bitch," Spear continued, "and I can think of no punishment, other than you being cored and given to the prador, more appropriate than what's happening to you now. When it comes to adaptogenics and augmentation I know my stuff. But I'm barely shaping stone axe heads while Penny Royal is making Tenkian robot weapons. I could no more cure you than a witchdoctor could cure brain cancer."

"Bring him down!" Isobel spat, horrible delight arising now that she knew nothing barred her from attacking him.

Neither Trent nor Gabriel moved a muscle and then, just like an unbalanced sculpture, Trent fell flat on his face. Somehow Spear had got to them and she had to act now. She damned herself for not having a security drone installed down here in the hold, or something else as lethal that she could access with her augmentations. She would have to deal with him herself, right away. She took a step forwards, reaching down for her own pulse-gun, but it suddenly felt as if she was wading through treacle. Her hand reached the butt of her gun, closed round it, then stalled. In panic she cast about for some other option. Maybe she could get maintenance robots into the hold . . .

Even as she mentally reached out for those robots her connection to the hardware all around her began fizzing. She managed to get some robots on the move, then everything dissolved in static. Spear stepped over to her, reached out with one finger and prodded her chest. She went over like a felled tree, flat on her back.

SPEAR

As I gazed down at Isobel, I seriously considered just leaving her there while I opened the hold doors to transport my ship mind over to the destroyer. I did, after all, have a dangerous AI to hunt down. But I could not overcome the after-effects of my war; I couldn't take human life so casually. I opened the hold airlock doors, noting a couple of maintenance robots in the corridor outside. She had probably summoned them just as the prion cascade shut down the nerves linking her to her internal modem nodes. They didn't react to me, so I guessed she hadn't had enough time to instruct them further.

I quickly dragged her out of the hold then into a nearby storeroom, laying her in a recovery position so she wouldn't choke on her tongue. Then I went back for Trent and Gabriel. These two, weighing twice as much as her, were more difficult to move. At one point during the sweaty procedure, I considered heading for the bridge and shutting down the grav-plates. But soon they were lying beside her, the three of them like a row of parentheses. I closed the door on them, then used Trent's carbine to turn the electronic lock into slag, so the door could only be opened manually and from the outside.

Next I crossed the ship to enter the hold space on the other side, where I'd already ascertained they kept their EVA tools. What I required was clamped to one wall: a pulpit zero-gravity handler. The thing was named for its resemblance to a church pulpit, from which you controlled three large mechanical arms, powered up by laminar power storage underneath the platform on which you stood. Two of the arms extended from the top of the pulpit whilst a third came out from below. Each had four alternative sets of manipulators that I could revolve into position. Luckily the grav in this hold was off, so I opened the space doors, detached the device from the wall and climbed into it. After it powered up, I used its chemical steering thrusters to take it out into vacuum. It was easy enough for me to operate, being an ancient piece of machinery that had probably seen service during the war. I had never used such a device before, but of course *felt* as if I had.

Accustoming myself to the controls, I took it round the ship to the first hold. I entered, selected the required manipulators and picked up my new ship mind, Flute. Steering was sluggish with the extra mass, but I found a targeting program I could run, set a course for the destroyer and put the pulpit on automatic. As it slowly took me over, I inspected the damage the ship had received. Though it was intact, it had obviously taken a pounding during that fatal conflict above Panarchia. I wondered what had impelled Penny Royal to abandon it and board that prador dreadnought. And then the AI had made that dreadnought crash, surely leaving itself without U-space transport? Certainly, going black, it wouldn't have wanted a vessel as easily identifiable as its original shell. But why hadn't it taken full control of the prador ship? And how had it travelled from the world it crashed on to . . . elsewhere. It was a puzzle. Unless, of course, you realized that Penny Royal had at that point turned into the AI equivalent of a raving lunatic.

The pulpit decelerated to a perfect stop just out from the loading port. I climbed out and propelled myself over, struggled for half an hour with the port's manual controls, then we were in. Five hours later I had Flute inside the ship's cortex, had raided a ship's store for the required optical and s-con cables and connectors and returned to the *Moray Firth* for more equipment. It was then a bit of a business to insert Flute's case into the space designed for the ship's AI and hook it up, but I eventually did so.

"Wake up, Flute," I said out loud, also auging the instruction through to it.

"I am fully functional," it said at once.

"Status?"

"All system ports are connected, data loading. Internal battery is at 22%. External source has nil input. Status of U-calculus is loading—engine parameters on standby, but nil charge—"

"Do you have the fusion reactor data stream?" I interrupted.

"Acquiring," it replied, then, "I do not recognize parameters."

"Access data upload," I instructed, auging through and transmitting blueprints and stats for the destroyer. It had taken me less than five minutes to upload these from the Polity net. It took Flute over ten minutes to absorb and store all this.

"I recognize parameters—running diagnostics now." Then after a pause, "This may take some time."

I just stood there staring at Flute's case, as if searching for some recognizable expression. No, I must have been imagining that hint of irony in its voice.

"How long until you complete a full ship's diagnostic checks, and then how long until you can start up the reactor?"

"Forty hours for diagnostics. Unknown time for acquisition of maintenance control and unknown time for necessary maintenance," it replied, then added, "So I've no idea."

There it was again, but right at that moment my concern was that "forty hours." I knew that after a hundred years such delays were almost irrelevant, but I chafed at them. Perhaps I also felt that way because I knew there were more to come. I had acquired a ship and installed a mind for it. I now needed to ensure I had full control of that ship, its weapons and, of course, I had to find the target for those weapons.

"Very well," I replied, not sure if I wanted to wait that long before returning to the ship. And, as I turned to leave the ship's cortex, I had the creepy feeling that I was being closely inspected.

ISOBEL

Before he came back, she felt the grav-plates cut out and knew that he must intend to move her. Precisely twelve minutes later he entered the storeroom, heaved her up off the floor and propelled her through the ship to her own cabin. There he installed her in a form-mould chair. Grav came back on shortly afterwards, which meant he had now penetrated her ship's systems. She should have put in more security. She realized that she had been foolish to rely on her own perpetual control.

"I am allowing you to speak now," he said, pulling over a second chair and sitting down in front of her. "But that's all you can do."

"I need a drink," was the first thing she said, noting that he looked exhausted.

"By and by," he said, waving a dismissive hand, and she damned herself for giving him even that little bit of leverage. "I can't find the location of Penny Royal's planetoid in your astrogation logs."

"That's because the coordinates aren't there."

"Tell me the coordinates."

"What did you do to me?"

"Targeted prion nerve-blocking," he replied. "You're paralysed and you can't access anything mentally, since I've also shut down all cerebral connections to your modem nodes." He tapped his aug. "I control a selection of prion cascades through here—simple infrasound signals set them running and others set them in reverse."

She felt a creeping horror at how she had let someone so dangerous aboard her ship. Though everything she knew about him described someone highly capable with augmentation and adaptation, the expertise he had demonstrated was orders of magnitude higher. This was getting into AI territory. She felt a surge of frustration, understanding that anyone capable of curing her would be dangerous to have around and she should have taken greater precautions. Yet he claimed Penny Royal's work was beyond him . . .

Next, frowning, he continued, "After my own experiences with a spider thrall it's not something I like doing, but you're just too dangerous, Isobel. Now, tell me the coordinates of Penny Royal's planetoid."

"Why should I?" Let him push for a little while for this useless information before she gave it to him. He would head for Penny Royal's planetoid and find it empty. He might then spend time in the Graveyard searching for the AI, which would give her more time to hunt him down and kill him.

"Because if you do, you get to live," he replied.

"I'm supposed to believe that after your little speech about me being cored and given to the prador?"

"You don't have much in the way of choices."

"Go to hell."

The next moment she couldn't breathe, couldn't even fight to breathe, was just suffocating. This went on for a minute then abruptly stopped, leaving her gasping.

"Are you sure you want to die?" he asked.

As she fought to regain her breath she studied him, all her eyes open, and realized she was reading more about him now—that her hooder eyes *had* given her a deeper insight into human reactions. Was that because she was seeing all other beings wholly as prey? She understood now that keeping her imprisoned in this way was unpleasant to him and that shutting down her breathing had caused him actual pain. She found herself analysing this coldly. Had she been captured by any of her Graveyard enemies, she could be certain of death. But the outcome was not so certain with Spear.

"So if I tell you, what will you do?" she asked.

"I'll leave you paralysed until I have the destroyer running," he replied. "Then I'll instruct all the prion cascades to reverse, which should take a number of hours. By then I'll be gone."

"You're lying," she said, then silently cursed herself for speaking before thinking. Anyway, he hadn't lied to her, he had just omitted something.

"What makes you say so?"

"I don't believe that's all you'll do."

He stared at her for a long moment, obviously tired and irritated. "Okay," he began, "I will do precisely as I said, but I will also degauss your U-space drive Calabi-Yau frames before I depart. I calculate that it will take you at least six months to recalibrate them. By which time I will have visited Penny Royal's planetoid, completed my business there and, if successful, will have returned to the Polity."

There was still something not quite truthful there. She told him some coordinates.

"Now you're lying," he said.

"No I'm not."

"I'm monitoring you very closely, Isobel." He reached up and tapped his aug again. "We've known the mental processes involved in lying for centuries now. Tell me the coordinates of that planetoid and you get a drink and get to sleep on your bed. Lie to me again and I'll just leave you here to die while I take your ship apart. Is that clear?"

"They're shifting coordinates," she replied, because she knew he fully intended to carry through his threat, no matter how much it pained him, and because him finding the planetoid didn't matter at all really. "The planetoid is a wanderer between suns but its course is mapped. On the shelf behind you, do you see the ammonite fossil? The vector coordinates are recorded in the pyrite crystals inside—there's an electrocarbon microport in the centre of the spiral." That was how the coordinates of the planetoid had been delivered to her after she'd made her queries. Why were they recorded in that manner, in that object? It was foolish to expect logic from something so deranged. Though in retrospect she wished she'd extrapolated that derangement from the object, rather than from its source.

He walked over to pick up the fossil, and weighed it in his hand for a moment. "Thank you, Isobel." Crossing the room, he picked up a water bottle and held it to her mouth.

After she drained it, he put the bottle aside, stooped down to pick her up like a child and took her over to her bed. Carefully he laid her down and arranged her comfortably on her side.

"Sleep well, Isobel," he said.

She tried to fight it but it swamped her. The last thing she heard was her door closing.

SPEAR

After putting Isobel to bed I did the same for Trent and Gabriel, then for myself. Six hours of sleep later and I was rested, then I hurriedly showered and dressed. Heading directly to a small onboard lab, I ran a scan of the ammonite fossil to ensure accessing it as Isobel had described wouldn't destroy the data it contained. The scan revealed no evidence that it was manufactured at all, which showed the intricacy and precision of Penny Royal's work. The optic port was standard—no traps. However, the scan also showed pyrite crystals within that weren't connected to the optic data port, and it became evident very quickly that these contained quantum computing. Relevant? I didn't know.

Next, plugging into the port, I accessed the fossil and found vector coordinates. These traced the position of Penny Royal's planetoid for the next four thousand years, beyond which the accuracy of the predictions declined by two per cent per year. I loaded the coordinates to my aug, then sat in a chair, feeling frustrated. I had just under thirty hours before Flute finished its diagnostic of the destroyer, so what could I do with myself in the meantime? I decided to investigate those disconnected pyrite crystals in case they contained data pertinent to my target. I set to work, hoping to burn up that thirty-hour wait.

First I needed to make connections, so I used a braided diamond drill to bore holes into what appeared to be junctions in the individual crystals concerned. Then I inserted carbon whiskers tipped with interface glue. This took hours of work. I connected the other ends of the whiskers to an electro-optic converter. Lastly, isolating some of the ship's computing, I plugged it into that. This rendered rubbish at first, but applying translation and sorting programs slowly began to make sense of it. Over a period of an hour, the programs first affirmed that there was no recognizable text, then it became clear that a quarter of the material stored comprised holographic files. The rest, thus far, had yet to be identified. Now, finally admitting that this task could occupy me no longer, I asked my aug to alert me if anything further was identified, then headed down to the cargo bay.

As I walked, I decided that, though I'd made some assessment of the *Puling Child*, Isobel's *Moray Firth* might still offer valuable resources for a time. I'd long decided I'd rename the destroyer once I'd taken control. Penny Royal's ship had been a newbuild when it fought over Panarchia, but there was no telling how much its resources had been depleted by the war. I could wait for Flute to give me the full list in twenty hours, but I could also do some checking myself. I'd procrastinated for long enough. I donned a space suit, collected some tools, along with a laser carbine, and headed over.

The area of the ship once occupied by the human crew consisted of four cabins and a refectory branching off a corridor behind the small bridge. Shafts for access to many areas of the ship were also available, including a small shuttle bay and its attached hold. One such shaft led to the weapons systems in the nose, with a side-branch to the ship's cortex. I started my investigations with the bridge—immediately finding another long-dead crewmember still inside.

This was the woman Coral Stader—the ship's resident AI expert. Her head of long curly red hair identified her before I needed to do any scanning. It was a grotesque sight, that hair above a mummified hollow-eyed face. It didn't require a close visual inspection to identify what had killed her. Her acceleration chair seemed to have sprouted like a plant and wrapped its material around her—one vine of some metal-plastic composite having grown in or out through her mouth. I made a closer inspection through a magnifying glass—this being a square "glass" employing metamaterials. It had quantum computing in the handle, and was capable of magnifying to somewhere between the microscopic and nanoscopic. I immediately identified millions of somnolent microbots and smaller masses that might have been nanobots. The ship had to be crawling with them and, once Flute had full control, I would have to order their dissolution since I didn't know what programming was still in place in them.

The consoles and screens before the four seats abruptly came on, as did all the lights. I was momentarily blinded before the light amplification in my visor tuned down the glare. I saw that the screens were now scrolling code related to the diagnostics Flute was running. I thought it suspicious timing until Flute spoke from the PA system.

"Do you require any assistance, Thorvald Spear?" it asked.

Obviously it had powered up this area so as to dutifully ask that question. It was easy to get a little paranoid aboard a ship like this.

"Do you have any access to the ship's autolog?" I asked.

This was a piece of sub-AI computing that automatically recorded all the ship's actions and all events which took place inside it. It was a hangover from pre-Quiet War days, when humans rightly distrusted AIs. I suspected that during the prador/human war it had more to do with AIs distrusting AIs.

"Fragmentary data only," Flute replied. "Some internal video and some astrogation data, but that's all."

"Figures," I replied, now studying the four seats here.

Along with the two men and the woman there had also been a Golem android—standard crew complement for such vessels during that period of the war. The Golem was almost certainly the one I had seen in the ship's cortex. It must have been taken over by Penny Royal and turned into a tool. I considered the spine that still lay in the ship's cortex and understood that the rogue AI had undergone its main transformation there. There it had turned itself into its current nightmarish form or forms—an evil mega-scale offspring of a black-spined sea urchin and a silver octopus.

As I headed out of the bridge to the refectory, Flute announced, "I can now restore grav-plate function in the human areas."

"You're sure?" I asked. Though the grav-plates below my feet weren't made to produce anything more than about two Earth gravities, I didn't want any fluctuations. One of those at the wrong time could still leave me with broken bones.

"Only a mere ninety-eight per cent sure," Flute replied.

I'd always had the impression that prador second-child ship minds had poor conversational abilities, little above that of a broken chatter toy. But Flute was venturing into the complex territory of drone sarcasm. No matter, that the grav-plates could be powered up meant we were getting somewhere, and I was that much closer to continuing my quest.

"Okay," I stepped into the refectory and braced myself. "Power them up."

My weight increased gradually, as things fell to the deck—a cup containing the tar-like remains of coffee, a palm-top, a plate and various objects that looked like dehydrated food. I just about heard the noise they made, carried by the thin remaining atmosphere. As if reading my mind, Flute spoke up again.

"I can also restore the air supply," it said.

"I don't think so," I replied, noting that what looked like a stain on one wall was slowly shifting like some shadowy slug. The light must be power-ing up nanobots capable of photo-activation and I really didn't fancy the idea of breathing them in. "I would rather you concentrated on finishing your diagnostic and also pulse-wipe all onboard nano- and microbots. Do you have any of the larger maintenance robots running?"

"Certainly," Flute replied.

"Sanitizers and surface maintenance?"

"All are available."

"Then I'd be happier if you got on that now. I want a clean sweep of all nano- and microbots. Plus auto-manufacture of them must shut down until we can be utterly sure of what we're making."

"As you wish," Flute replied, then quickly added, "May I ask a question?"

"You just did."

"Another one, then."

"Go ahead," I replied, stepping back into the corridor leading to the four cabins and feeling a little worried about my ship's mind.

"Why am I serving a human?" it asked.

"Because, through an intermediary, I bought you from the prador and you have since been programmed to obey me, and me alone."

"But we are enemies," said Flute.

That gave me pause. Flute must have undergone the traumatic loss of its body during the war to end up as a kamikaze mind. But had it been somnolent since then? Its apparently enhanced verbal dexterity would indicate otherwise.

"The war ended a century ago," I tried.

After a pause Flute replied, "The new king ended the war."

"So it did," I said. "Now I would like to ask you a question." I waited but Flute remained silent, so I continued, "You are unlike any other second-child mind I've encountered. You have nuances of speech and responses unexpected in such a mind. Do you have any explanation as to why that is?"

Again a pause, then a tentative, "I am old."

"You have been active since being placed in that shell?"

"Father activated us after the war."

Interesting.

"Your father?"

"Father-Captain Sverl. He allowed us sensory access and he spoke to us."

Even more interesting. This didn't sound like the behaviour of any prador father-captain I'd heard of before. Second-child minds were considered disposable assets to them—no more important than sub-AI computing might be to a Polity citizen. It had also always been the case, as I understood it, that such a mind possessed a very limited ability to learn. Certainly such could acquire data, but what they did with it supposedly didn't change them very much.

"After your encasement, did this Sverl make any further physical alterations to you?"

"Our limited conversation annoyed him," Flute stated.

"And?"

"He gave us additional processing to improve it."

I shut my eyes and immediately started checking my aug for my initial scans of Flute. In a moment, I saw what I had missed at first—just a few decimal points. Flute's processing space wasn't in the usual gigabyte range but extended into the terabytes. This Sverl had made Flute much like some of the early human cyborgs. It was a flash-frozen but electrically active organic brain, which also allowed additional processing, the ability to learn and grow that AI crystal possessed.

"Well, I'm glad he did," I lied.

"Thank you," Flute replied, which was of course also a strange thing to come from the mind of a prador second-child. I would definitely have to run more checks and tests to be sure I had not bought myself a prador Trojan horse.

The first cabin was open, and a glance inside at the spartan furnishings and lack of a bed told me straight away that this one belonged to the Golem. Why it had required a cabin at all was puzzling, since it was made before humans could upload to a Golem chassis and so perhaps require human "space." The other three doors were locked and I felt no inclination to ask Flute to open them, sure that the moment I stepped inside I would remember occupying them. As I pressed on the last one, a hatch opened at the end of the corridor and a maintenance robot emerged. The thing resembled the carapace of a two-foot-long blue beetle, mounted on a hovercraft cushion. It immediately moved to one side, tilted up to reveal glittering convolutions on its underside and attached itself to the wall. With a low humming, it proceeded to motor along it. I watched for a moment, seeing the mottled grey of the wall turning to pure white behind it. It was obviously killing off the micro-culture of bots there and removing them—a process that would involve a lot more than simple suction.

When it was about five feet along its perfectly straight path, more robots followed it out of the hatch. These were mobile black hemispheres the size of half-apples; white plastic centipedes; multi-limbed small-repair creations similar to mantids, spiders and shield bugs—all gleaming like polished chrome. Still feeling somewhat wary, I turned away, heading back to the bridge and the ship's cortex. I wanted to inspect the object I'd seen lying on the floor near Flute—perhaps just as deeply as that ammonite fossil aboard the *Moray Firth*.

Once again, I saw the other dead crewmembers in the tunnel and once again felt my skin crawling.

"Flute," I said, as I approached the ship's cortex. "I want you to remove the three corpses, pulse-wipe any bots on or in them, seal them in mono-cloth and store them. I presume there's a refrigerated area?"

"Certainly," Flute replied. "There is a zero-store for food items, bio-electronics and casualties."

"Put them there, but first scan them for memplants."

"I have already scanned them—they have none."

I had considered ejecting them straight out of a waste lock but, even after all this time, there might still be someone around who cared enough to know what had happened to them. They might still merit some sort of ceremonial disposal. If not that, then I could hand them over to the Polity so that certain boxes could be ticked and files closed. Whatever—I just didn't want them giving me that hollow-eyed glare every time I walked past.

The ship's cortex was tidier now. Flute had obviously had robots in here vacuuming up all the crystal and other debris, and disassembling some of the tools Penny Royal had made. However, the Golem had only been moved back and rested against one wall. The spine—that long piece of dark glass with its sinister attached tentacle—had been decidedly left alone. It still lay on the floor where last I'd seen it and, while most of the floor had been polished to a gleam, the area around and underneath it had been left strictly alone too.

"Flute, why haven't you moved this object and cleaned this area of floor?" I asked, pointing down at the thing.

After a long pause Flute replied, "I do not understand it."

"What do you mean?"

"It is in either an active or pre-active state, like the bots aboard this ship, and scanning reveals quantum computing and picotech processes. It may be dangerous, so I was planning to ask you for instructions on how to proceed."

I peered down at the thing, then squatted to inspect it more closely. Why, I have no idea, because I wouldn't be seeing any picotech. While I was in that position I caught a flicker of movement out of the corner of one eye. Something was moving towards me, fast. I turned just as the Golem, on the end of the thick tentacle that had replaced it from the waist down, reached me. Its altered hand struck my space suit helmet hard, lifting me up off the floor and depositing me on my back. My suit immediately reported a leak and I realized two things at once. The helmet had just saved my life and, were it not for the Golem's lack of legs, I still wouldn't have made it. Had the Golem been able to brace itself against the floor, the full force of its blow would have smashed open both my helmet and my head.

Propelled away from me by the force of its blow, the Golem slowed to a stop in mid-air, swaying at the end of its tentacle, its head swinging from right to left. That strange binocular device that had replaced its eyes had perhaps left it blind in the human spectrum. It was probably for very close work: microscopic, maybe even nanoscopic. With its head movements it appeared to be trying to locate me by sound. Any moment now it would hear me breathing, or even detect the beat of my heart. I had to respond or I was dead.

I wouldn't be able to reach the exit before it got to me and, really, there was no knowing how long its tentacle could extend. It might even be able to get some way out of the ship's cortex. I wasn't armed, because quite stupidly I'd left the laser carbine in the human bridge area along with the various tools I'd brought. In the end I only had one option and it probably wouldn't work. In that moment I was glad they'd reinserted my memplant on Earth, because this situation was bad, very bad. The chances of an unarmed human surviving a homicidal Golem attack were remote.

The Golem abruptly froze, then slowly revolved to face me. It shifted its head from side to side, then up and down, to centre on me completely and began opening and closing its branched hands. This was it. I had to act now. I rolled and grabbed, then lifted and levelled Penny Royal's discarded spine, and braced its base against the floor. The Golem came down on me like a hammer, as I'd hoped, just as I aimed the spine's tip straight at its chest where its crystal should reside.

The impact through the spine dented the floor underneath me. The Golem's hands swung in and grabbed, one tearing the visor from my helmet and the other coming down on my shoulder, which I felt break like a snail under heel. Then the spine was snatched from my hands, the Golem shooting straight upwards to slam into the ceiling at the full extension of its tentacle, the spine right through its chest. I had no idea how the spine was made, to punch through ceramal like that, but was grateful for it. I rolled, put a hand down to push myself upright and headed for the exit, noting the bloody handprint I'd left on the floor. Checking my gauntlets, I saw that they'd been sliced to ribbons and the hands underneath weren't much better. Then I glanced back from the exit.

The Golem was groping along the ceiling as if searching for something by feel. I headed out of there, not waiting to see if it would expire. I had problems enough. My hands and shoulder were starting to hurt badly, and my suit was pumping its air straight out of its visor hole in an effort to keep me alive. My face felt bloated already by the drop in air pressure. Out in the corridor I kept going, starting to stumble, and clamped down on the urge to vomit. Finally reaching the human bridge, I realized I wouldn't even be able to pick up the laser carbine.

"Flute," I said. The suit radio responded with a series of buzzes, but I could just hear a voice.

"Flute," I said again and this time I could just hear the words, distant and tinny, and realized I was hearing them from the PA system through the thin air.

"I am restoring air supply," the ship mind told me.

Great, I thought, but wondered if it was Flute who had just tried to kill me, especially after what I'd learned about the second-child mind. Surely the Golem was merely a tool—an extension of the mind that previously occupied Flute's position?

"I need medical attention," I said.

"I have initiated an autodoc in cabin one," Flute replied.

Did I want to subject myself to the attentions of an autodoc that Flute could control?

"What happened . . . with the Golem?" I asked.

"I don't know," Flute replied. "It was powered down until just before it attacked. It bypassed the shutdown, but I do not understand why it attacked. I have just physically cut its power supply and, since its own has been removed, it is now inanimate."

Did I believe that? What were my options? I could probably struggle out of my suit and use a spare suit from one of the crew, but even that was risky. Firstly, any suit I found here would be a century old and possibly faulty. Secondly, if Flute was out to kill me, my donning such a suit would be a perfect opportunity. If it had sent that Golem against me, then it could easily reprogram a suit to either shut down its air, to alter the mix, or even to take command of its joints if it was a powered version. I realized I had to trust it. The actions of that Golem probably had more to do with Penny Royal than a second-child mind programmed for loyalty to me.

I stumbled through to the cabins, noting the door to one of them, previously closed, was now open. The moment I stepped inside, the door quickly closed behind me, which upped my paranoia but was probably so air pressure could be raised quickly within. The autodoc was a crawler—not pedestal mounted. It had come out of an aseptic store in the wall and was now down on the floor below it. I recognized it as the kind usually deployed on battlefields to search out survivors amidst casualties. It consisted of two linked beetle-like sections, a sensor head with antennae, pheromone sniffers, and short- and long-range eyes.

"Can you remove your suit?" Flute enquired.

I tried, but my hands had frozen up. "No."

"Lie down on the bed," my ship mind instructed.

I did as bid, slowly, my shoulder agonizing now. I heard the autodoc scuttling, then felt the weight of its front section rest against the edge of the bed beside me. Glancing over, I caught a look at its underside: the polished insectile legs, the folded surgical cutlery, the peeking bone-welder like the head of a micro-wire sprayer. It was all so familiar, but that I put down to the sure knowledge that I had been in this position before.

"It would be better if you were rendered unconscious," Flute observed, its voice more distinct now that the air was improving.

"Okay," I said. I would just have to trust the mind and, if I woke up, that trust would be justified.

The autodoc advanced to rest over my collarbone on my uninjured side. Something buzzed and tugged as it penetrated my suit. Numbness spread at that point and I felt the pressure of an object being inserted. This item made contact, input the correct signals, and turned me off like a light.

7

I didn't quite know where or when I was when I opened my eyes. I couldn't decide whether I would find myself lying in that resurrection cage on Earth, or coming back to lucidity after one of my "bad" periods while under the spider thrall. Or I could find myself again waking in that Polity hospital station after Panarchia, realizing the nightmare was over. But then memory began to kick in again and I lay still, frightened for a moment to move. Finally I tried to sit up and found that easy enough. I was naked, the autodoc was nowhere in sight and the sheet I lay on was bloody. Some splinters of bone lay on the bed beside me, neatly lined up. I checked my hands first, seeing the thin threadlike scars characteristic of an older style of autodoc. It had used fast cell-welding, which confirmed it was a battle-field design. Clenching and unclenching them, I found they worked fine, though they did feel tender. Whether this was due to damage still needing to heal or my body's memory of pain I couldn't say. Next checking my shoulder I found similar scarring there, and it was stiff and painful.

Okay, I was awake and alive, which proved that Flute had not tried to kill me. After all, it could certainly have finished the job through the autodoc.

"Flute," I said. "I need clothing and I need a space suit." My own space suit was crumpled on the floor with the remains of my clothing, and all were bloody.

"The cabin you currently occupy has clothing that may still be suitable," Flute replied. "I have begun diagnostic tests on the space suits in storage—thus far they only seem to require their power supplies recharging and air bottles refilling."

"Good."

I swung my legs off the bed, stood and peeled off sticky sheets and walked over to a sanitary unit and checked to see if it would work. It did and I stepped into the shower to scrub away the blood. It was too late now for me to worry about bot infection from the ship's water. Opening a cupboard, I checked through the men's clothing there. Some of it was highly degraded—one shirt just ripped in two as I pulled it out—but there were other garments there made from more rugged materials. I ended up clad in chameleoncloth combat trousers locked on some dark rocky landscape setting and a T-shirt. This started running some ancient black-and-white film the moment my body heat set its integral electronics running.

I tramped out of the cabin to the corridor and thence to the tube leading to the airlock. A door beside that revealed racked space suits hanging inside, with lights flickering on their various bits of computer hardware.

"Let me know when they're ready," I said.

"Minutes only," Flute replied.

Only then did I think to check the time through my aug and found that we were now beyond the predicted forty hours for Flute's diagnostic checks. First I was annoyed at the lost time, but then cheered at the thought that I could just have been waiting around for the diagnostic check to end. Despite the shitty circumstances that had left me unconscious, I could now *move*.

"So what *is* the condition of this ship?" I asked, closing the door and heading off towards the ship's cortex.

"All human-accessible areas have been deep cleaned of micro- and nanobots. Full deep cleaning of the rest of the ship will take many months since some disassembly will be required. U-space and fusion drives are functional, the reactor is stable, weapons systems are functional but depleted. It will be necessary to take on materials for in-ship manufacturing, as some components will need replacing and some items are in need of resupply."

"We can travel, though?"

"Yes."

"What needs replacing?"

"Railgun missiles and warheads. There are no CTDs left. There are also no solid-state laser assemblies and high-temperature fabricated components for the reactor and fusion drive. Some of these items I can make but these would be better supplied from a military depot."

Heading back toward the ship's cortex, I knew for sure I needed weapons. Without them, what the hell was I going to do when I found Penny Royal? Use strong language? I also realized by Flute's use of "military depot" that it was still thinking in terms of war supply and demand. It didn't seem likely that I could roll up at some ECS military base and select CTDs like tasty snacks from a buffet.

"Which items can you make?" I asked, pausing in the corridor and noting that the corpses were gone. The areas of wall and ceiling where they had been were now pristine.

"Simple railgun missiles can be smelted from debris or asteroid iron using lasers and hardfield moulding. High-temperature components can be made in the same way, but with higher energy demands. Solid-state laser assemblies can be built by nanobot, but that is a lengthy process. CTDs cannot be made with the resources available to this ship."

Of course, these ships were made so they could resupply most of their own needs. As for the CTDs, it was understandable that running up a chunk of anti-matter might be stretching things. I would have to check to see if Isobel had anything like that secreted away aboard her ship, and there were other options to try.

"What about fusion and fission bombs?"

"It will be possible to make them if the correct ores can be obtained."

I walked up the tunnel into the ship's cortex and paused at the entrance, feeling reluctant to enter. But then, dipping my head in for a look around, I saw that any danger from the Golem had been completely eliminated.

A mid-sized maintenance robot had cut off its arms, detached its torso from that tentacle and was now detaching the tentacle from its wall socket. I studied the robot for a moment then returned my attention to the Golem. It was still impaled on Penny Royal's spine. My next step—to get to the source of that spine—was overdue. It was time for me to leave. However, first I had to deal with Isobel Satomi . . .

ISOBEL

Everything within her mind was accessible, but nothing outside it worked. At first she had struggled endlessly to try and regain control of her body or reach out to her ship's systems, but she could affect nothing at all. However, straining against her invisible bonds seemed to accelerate other processes in her body. Although she could not move her arms and legs, she found she could now move the hooder manipulators growing out of her face. She could also flex her cowl and see out of yet another newly opened hooder eye. Her connection to these from the predatory part of her consciousness was also so much firmer, which only increased her overall panic. In the end, she deliberately put her mind into a state of semi-consciousness, woken when the door to her cabin opened once again.

"Isobel," said Spear. He squatted down beside her bed and peered into her face. She tried to reply but this time he was not allowing her to speak. "Looks like your changes are accelerating, but then that's probably because they're no longer fighting your body." He stood up and paced. "This is how the situation stands with you: I have set in reverse the prion cascades in your body, and those in Trent and Gabriel. You'll all be mobile again in a day or so, but I will be long gone by then. I have helped myself to various items from your vessel, including your surprising collection of CTDs. I have also disabled your U-space drive, but in ways you just won't be able to repair. It will take you approximately four years to reach the nearest place where you can get that drive repaired. By then either Penny

Royal or I will be dead. If by any chance it is I who survives, I'll have returned to the Polity and will be far beyond your reach."

After a long pause he again squatted down to gaze into her face. "I was once subject to a spider thrall, Isobel, so doing what I did to you and your men did not come easy to me. However, considering what you have done, you're lucky I didn't decide to shove you all out of an airlock." He was lost for words for a moment, his attention wandering, then he remembered something. "Oh yes, there's another factor we should consider. You won't be in any condition to come after me in four years, because by then your arms and legs will be gone. You'll be crawling on your belly and cutting up food with those things growing out of your face. I don't know if whatever remains of you by that time will even be interested in me—if you'll even remember me. Goodbye Isobel." He stood up and left.

Isobel just lay there screaming silently, then bleeding when one of her facial manipulators, which had now sprouted an object like a scalpel, sliced across her nose. Eventually she managed some self-control and shut herself down—timing a period of unconsciousness to last for two days.

Hiatus . . .

Isobel Satomi opened her many eyes and the effect was something like the sensory enhancement of her cowl, but with the visual feed coming from different parts of the electromagnetic spectrum. The input went into different mental partitions, and she was able to make selections from these on the basis of need. That need was human at that moment and so everything in the human visual spectrum opened to her. However, she knew at once that her human eyes no longer existed. She rolled onto her back then sat up, but even that action was different. She found herself peeling up from the bed, her spine as supple as a snake's and paused at a mid-point when her upper body was essentially upright. However, it was curving up from the midpoint of her long torso, which had now grown by at least another six inches.

Next, sitting all the way up with her weight coming down on her buttocks, she could feel a large lump down there and knew that her tail had grown by the same amount as her torso. She swung her legs off the bed and tried to stand, but her feet felt all wrong and she started to fall forwards. The prions had not worn off completely, because nothing was working properly. She felt a moment of panic when she realized she wasn't putting out her hands to break her fall, tried to turn her face to stop it smashing into the floor and just couldn't move her neck at all, then halted her fall just a few inches from the floor . . . but not with her hands.

Creeping horror worked its way up her hard flexible spine. She tried to turn to look back down along the length of her body but still couldn't move her neck. Something else moved instead, her spine twisting just below her neck at an angle impossible for a human body. Something crunched horribly as if her shoulder blade was dislocating, and now she could see her body. Five hard, insectile legs had torn their way free of her padded clothing to rest upon the floor; thick centipede legs terminating in feet that consisted of rearward-pointing curved hooks. She could feel those legs and she could move them. She felt a sense of irritation with the hard floor below, with a need for soft rhizome-layered ground to dig those hooks into, and thus propel her forwards. She screamed—abruptly folding the legs in to try and hide them—and dropped, smashing her damaged nose against the floor.

"Isobel! Isobel!"

Someone was hammering at the door. She had to get control of herself and she couldn't let them see her like this. It would be hard enough to dominate them when they learned just how long it would take them to return to civilization.

"I'm okay," she called then, realizing how odd her mouth felt, wondered how long it would be before she lost the power of human speech. "Go check if that destroyer is still out there, then give me a report over intercom." She paused, trying to think of other make-work tasks for Trent and Gabriel while she made herself presentable, but finished with, "I'll join you on the bridge in an hour."

She could hear muttering out there, then listened more intently and, as words became clear, her inner predator awoke.

"She's getting more erratic," said Gabriel. "I bet she just sprouted another fucking leg or eye. It's gonna be time to move on."

"Let's just head for the bridge," said Trent.

"The destroyer's gone," said Gabriel, his voice getting fainter as they moved away. "He told us that anyway." Then after a pause. "I've had enough of this."

"Have you got prion paralysis in your brain?" Trent enquired mildly.

Isobel now realized she didn't have to use her substantially increased hearing to continue eavesdropping. She linked into the ship's system, listened in through microphones, and peered through pin cams, just in time to capture Trent pointing to his ear then up towards the ceiling. Trent knew she was listening and wasn't going to say anything that might offend her. She listened avidly anyway, finding herself rising back up onto her insect legs and turning. She wanted to go after the two of them. She wanted to get hold of them and . . .

Isobel fought the predator and her new legs closed up again, but this time she turned her head as she hit the floor. She had to retain control and so deliberately cut the sound and image feeds from Trent and Gabriel's location. There was no point listening to them anymore, she told herself, because they wouldn't be saying anything damning now. Instead, she forced herself to link to other ship's instruments and saw that the destroyer had indeed gone. Spear had also been as good as his word and had disabled the U-space drive. He hadn't actually broken anything, but he had destabilized energy balances in the Calabi-Yau frames—which was something that would require shipyard retuning to put right. Isobel swore, and concentrated on her immediate problems.

She found herself not only fighting to use her arms, hands and legs, but fighting to *want* to use them—as if her body didn't consider them relevant any more. At length the predator in her subsided and she did want to stand up again, like a human. But now that felt as if she were trying to move parts of her body that just weren't there—or as if she was trying to twitch her nose when she simply didn't possess that ability. She was getting very little feedback or sensation at all. Finally, feeling as if she wanted to cry, she had to admit defeat and run searches using her haiman hardware. They located the nerves for her human limbs and programs deep in storage to fire them up, and then link them back to her mind. As these began to load, sensation returned and she remembered how to move her limbs. The software for such an exercise, if you could call it that, had been wiped from her mind.

Managing to get her hands underneath her, she tried to push herself up, but her spine bent into a ridiculous curve again. She straightened it, positioned her knees under her, then stood, tottering unsteadily. However, with every movement and the subsequent feedback from that movement she became more sure. It was also noteworthy that her predatory urge was now all but somnolent. She understood the connection then, and the separation—the more she transformed into a hooder, the harder it would be to fight that *irrational* predator. Penny Royal's transformation of her apparently went deeper than the physical. As a human she had always been a predator, but now she felt that predatory part of her human self separating out into her hooder part. Meanwhile, what remained of her human part, or even humanity, grew weaker and more difficult to maintain.

She moved over to her large cabin screen and, gazing at the blank slab of nanofabric, remembered how in times past she'd had it on the mirror setting. At one time she'd been a beautiful woman. Now it was mostly like this: blank grey. First preparing herself for the undoubted shock, she turned it on with a mental twitch.

Isobel gazed at her reflected image for a long time. Her head was now twice as long as normal, cylindrical, and possessed three pairs of red eyes evenly spaced down its length—her own human eyes now having changed into hooder eyes. The lower set of eyes was positioned just above her mouth and below her nose. Her mouth was now narrower, with a pronounced harelip above. The nose was smaller, melting into her face. She reached up to run a hand over the bald dome of her skull, then reached down to each shoulder, scooping out the tangled mass of her own hair to discard it. Her sensory cowl had grown wider and sprouted more petals. It now extended out to the width of her shoulders, and, reaching back, she felt how it had attached itself to the back of her long head. Feeling along the cowl's base on either side, she noted that her jacket had ripped—this to accommodate the lower petals of the cowl, which were now attached to her shrinking shoulders.

She stared. She had expected to feel disgust, horror, fear or anger but all those were dispelled by the sight before her. She had passed some stage in her development. Previously she had perceived herself as a deformed human. Now she was something else; now she was hardly human at all.

With slow care she undressed, her clothing snagging on hard pieces of carapace and insectile legs. Her body was now a long column, her breasts sunk away and her nipples and her belly button fading. The legs below were like those of a dwarf, short and bowed, and her feet were toeless stumps. Gazing at that smooth column with its neatly folded legs, scales of carapace protruding in a neat dorsal line behind them, her perceptual change came home to her. For now she saw her human legs as the deformity and the rest as somehow . . . right.

Still she stared, feeling suddenly completely cold. She reached up to the ugliness that was her human mouth and almost negligently pulled out one of her loose teeth, to cup it in the palm of a hand. She stared at the bloody tooth, framed by a hand which only possessed two fingers and a thumb. A sensation rippled through her and her spiky tail twitched as the predator stirred. A huge need set the manipulators arrayed down each side of her face rippling. She quickly turned away, discarding the tooth.

Selecting the right clothing was a trial. Her usual trousers and blouses just wouldn't do. In the end, heavy-world support boots and a long dress of rippling nacre over a padded jacket were the only things that made her look remotely human. Exiting her cabin, she headed straight for the ship's refectory, knowing that lightly cooked vegetables and chicken weaves just wouldn't do either. She hoped that Trent and Gabriel had remained on the bridge, knowing that they would.

CAPTAIN BLITE

Blite gazed at the metre-wide plastic cube sitting on the labouring sled. The contents of the box were heavier than anything that size had any right to be, and the necessity of having to use a grav-sled worried him greatly.

Although it was shielded, there were some watchers here who might see through even that. Masada was a dangerous planet for this kind of operation now it had acquired an AI warden. Wardens in themselves were bad enough, but this one had been a war drone before its upgrade—a slightly psychotic robot fashioned in the shape of a giant steel scorpion. And, as if that wasn't bad enough, its sidekick was rumoured to be something even stranger and more dangerous . . .

"I'm sure something's following us," said Ikbal.

Blite paused to gaze back across the landscape of flute grasses rippling in the evening breeze. It was bright out tonight because Calypse, this system's inevitable gas giant, was on the horizon, while one of the numerous moons of this world was speeding along above. He could see nothing in the flute grasses, no gabbleducks or siluroynes, no hooders and no sign of what Ikbal really feared.

"I'll say it once and no more," said Blite, "and you'd better listen good, Ikbal." He knew he could make no more threat than that. Ikbal had been with him a long time and was well aware of just how far he could be pushed.

"There is no black AI haunting this fucking bog," he continued. "This Amistad, even if he was a crazy war drone, would not allow such a thing to exist here. The Polity simply would not allow it."

"Those Tidy Squad guys seemed pretty certain," said Martina, pacing along behind the grav-sled and controlling it with a remote.

Blite glared at her, then realized that in this light she probably couldn't see his face through his breather mask. He sighed, took a deep breath and tilted his head back to gaze up at the nebula. Like some sculpture fashioned of glass, it spread across the dark aubergine sky. The sight calmed him, as did the sight of the space port's foam-stone raft when he lowered his gaze. It was now just a mile ahead.

"Look," he said, "this place is supposed to have had every kind of shit thrown at it, ever since the Theocracy ruled here." He held up a gauntleted hand and began counting off on his fingers. "We're told it's had revolution—fomented by Polity agents—it's also had some psychopath arrive in a Polity dreadnought blasting the fuck out of everything. Dragon dumped on them here too and left dracomen." He lost the thread for a moment.

They had actually seen a dracoman working on the landing platform shortly after they landed. The things were lizard-like humanoids, based on an old human idea of what dinosaurs would have evolved into but for the intercession of a large meteorite. And it was a verifiable fact that they were also created by the entity called Dragon—a giant alien biomech that looked nothing like the name it had given itself. The presence of dracomen here somewhat undermined the point he had been intending to make about the plausibility of anything those Tidy Squad members had said.

"Jain tech's supposedly been let loose here," he continued doggedly, then had to pause again when he realized he was running out of fingers. He lowered his hand. "It's also been attacked by some alien machine, a hooder that was apparently an ancient war machine and an *artist* defeated that. And apparently one of the 'dead' races is now living here. And do you know what all this tells me?" When there was no reply he continued, "It tells me that this is the perfect place for rumours and conspiracy theories. It tells me that the best thing to do is disbelieve at least half of what you're told and reserve judgement on the rest. It tells me you got to use your noodle." He stabbed a finger against his head a little too hard. "It tells me to think twice when I'm told that the Polity has forgiven the black AI Penny Royal and absolved all its sins. Especially when it's supposedly working here like some security drone, in the service of a fucking warden! And it tells me you really need to shove the face of the one telling you this stuff into the nearest table, repeatedly, until the shit stops coming out of it!"

After a short pause, while Blite stood there panting and wondering where his momentary calm had gone, Brondohohan spoke quietly from the darkness to one side.

"Which was, as I recollect," he said, "precisely what you did."

"Of course some of the stories are true," added Greer from over the other side of the trail.

Getting ready to start shouting, Blite squinted at the heavy-worlder woman. But he could see her pointing at the box sitting on their grav-sled and realized she had a point. At least one of the stories about alien technology was true, because that thing in there seemed to be the real deal.

If it hadn't been, they wouldn't have been here trying to retrieve it. If it wasn't, their buyers in the Separatist movement wouldn't have been so interested.

"Come on, let's keep up the pace," he said, realizing they'd slowed to a dawdle, then checked his com-plate for positioning. Chont and Haber were to the rear, with Brondohohan and Greer on each side. Then Ikbal and he were by the sled, Martina controlling it. They were good, and soon they would reach the edge of the space port. He shouldn't have allowed the fears of his crew to distract him, but he also shouldn't get complacent now that they only had a little distance to go before reaching his ship. Sure, they wouldn't have to go through port security, which was a relief. This world's enterprising brand of homegrown terrorists, the Tidy Squad, had bored a smuggler's tunnel through the port's foam-stone raft. But there was still a chance of them being spotted. They still might have to fight their way back to the ship, or even abandon their acquisition and run.

Trudging on through the Masadan evening, Blite wondered which of the stories about this place he really believed. Though he considered the one about the ancient alien machine and the hooder dubious, there were none he could definitively discount. He understood himself enough to know that his angry response to that Tidy Squad idiot glooming on about Penny Royal had two sources. He didn't want his crew spooked and, tough as they were, that was just the kind of thing to get under their skins. He also didn't want to believe it himself, because Penny Royal was already under his skin. Blite shivered.

He still clearly remembered that operation twenty-eight solstan years ago. He supplied some thralls and control units smuggled out of Spatterjay to some *collector* on the edge of the Graveyard. The buyer had apparently been a rich Polity citizen, keen to add to his collection of wartime memorabilia. Only, when Blite and his crew delivered the items, it turned out that the buyer was a front for some nascent coring operation in the Graveyard itself. Shortly after the buy, the heads of this were meeting someone who would repair and activate what they really wanted: working prador thrall technology.

The buy was going bad, quickly, because the shits involved had decided that their large amounts of weaponry gave them a bargaining advantage.

It was all about to turn into a nasty firefight when the other side's repairman turned up, and then it turned into a complete nightmare. The meet had been in a valley on a heavy gravity world, where plants grew ironhard and close to the ground, and where most humans wore motorized suits. Blite had looked up as he prepared to open fire and order the thrall tech they had come with to be blown up. On the ridge above, a metal flower had bloomed. A giant black thistle-head atop a stalk of braided silver snakes. He stared at it in shock as, like a slow black explosion, it came apart. Its individual spikes turned as they sped away to point down into the valley, all settling to hang still in the air—a wall of daggers woven through with silver lace.

"Penny Royal!" one of the opposition called, gazing at Blite with a superior smile.

Blite immediately wondered about the possibility of surviving what was about to happen here; if he left this valley alive, he would be glad to do so. He knew about Penny Royal. However, it seemed the opposition did not for, like so many fools, they had obviously struck some sort of bargain with the devil.

The second shout of that name came filled with panic, as the wall of knives suddenly swept down. Pulse-fire and the snap and crackle of laser carbines filled the valley. The light in the sky went out, then a discharge like pink lightning left one motorized suit belching fire and smoke. Something picked up Blite and deposited him on his back, his bones crunching. A massive explosion followed and dust rolled through. Blite lay there for maybe an hour as the firing stuttered to a halt, as the screaming died away and the dust settled. Finally heaving himself to his feet, he went to take a look around.

The eight heavily armed thugs who had accompanied the buyers were out of their suits, gasping in the poisonous air. They were naked, crawling along the ground, the tops of their skulls missing, each with a prador thrall in place in the emptied cavity inside. Two of the buyers had survived as well. Their bodies were melded at the waist and they scuttled on all eight of their limbs like a prador, hexagonal control units sprouting from their skins like technological pustules. They no longer looked sane, drooling, with eyes rolling. Blite walked away, realizing that Penny

Royal had done what they wanted. The rogue AI had made the thralls and control units work. The problem with Penny Royal, as any sensible Graveyard trader knew, was that it often did a lot more of what the recipient *didn't* want. Back at his shuttle, he found two of his six-man crew waiting for him. There were no life-signs from the other four suits and, after much indecision, he went back to look for them. All he found were four empty suits, coated inside with a black tar-like substance.

"You okay, boss?"

Blite snapped out of his reverie and glanced at Martina, who was watching him with concern.

"Fine," he said, realizing that the space port raft lay directly ahead. He had lost himself in memory for rather longer than he had supposed. He shivered again and checked their surroundings, suddenly feeling that coming here had been his worst idea in twenty-eight years. He called up a map on his com-plate, then pointed off to the right, towards the smugglers' tunnel. After he'd returned his plate to his pocket, he drew his flak gun.

"Pick up the pace," he instructed, "and stay alert."

Not that there was anything they could possibly do if that nightmare came for them.

They began pushing through standing flute grasses, leaving the previous trail, which had probably been made by some of the local fauna. His obvious anxiety spread and his crew closed in, checking wrist-mounted motion sensors and heat signature scanners. Blite found himself breathing heavily—getting spooked—and when they pushed out into an open area beside the foam-stone raft, he gazed warily at the dark mouth of the tunnel, partially concealed by a hatch of woven flute grass. He really didn't want to go in there, but no other choices were viable. Up above, the tough ceramic razor-mesh fence was loaded with sensors, punctuated by autogun towers and scattered with smaller security drones. Just climbing up onto the raft would result in capture, let alone approaching the fence.

"Come on." He headed over to the tunnel, the skin on his back crawling and his stomach tight. He reached the hatch before the others and dragged it aside, ramped up the light amplification in his visor, then looked through the sights of his gun into the tunnel. Nothing there and no sign anything had been there, either. He could only see the footprints they'd made when they used this tunnel four days ago. He led the way in, abruptly glad to be in this enclosed space. If anything came for him, it could only come from ahead or behind. Glancing back he saw that all his crew were in, the grav-sled wobbling as it adjusted to the curved foam-stone floor. A few hundred feet further in, he even considered blowing the tunnel behind them, but decided he was being irrational. Anyway, that wouldn't stop the likes of Penny Royal, supposing the AI was even here.

Finally they reached steps leading to the surface of the foam-stone landing field. The grav-sled hesitated, then levitated in fits and starts as if reluctant to make the climb. They then stepped out into the shadowy framework supporting fuel silos, before making their way across a hundred feet of landing field to *The Rose*. Gazing at his squat vessel, which some had compared to an iron mosque, Blite felt his tension beginning to ease. He used his plate to signal the cargo hold ramp to lower and they all entered that way. As the ramp closed up, Blite let out a slow breath. It had been silly to get so spooked.

"Let's get out of here," he said, pulling off his mask the moment the hold's atmosphere light switched to green. "Leven," he continued. "Are we clear to lift?"

Their ship's mind replied through the intercom. "I requested clearance as soon as I saw you coming in. We've got a window in five minutes—AG only, no chemical thrusters."

"Take us up as soon as you can," Blite replied, following the others through the airlock to the main ship.

When *The Rose* began to ascend, Blite was secured in one of the chairs on the bridge, gazing across the space port through the chain-glass screen. He supposed the stricture on their launch method might be due to the wildlife. The Tidy Squad had advised that it wasn't a good idea to use lights out in the flute grasses, so perhaps the glare of chemical thrusters might attract unwanted attention to the space port. Soon they were high enough to see beyond the port to the flute grass wildlands, then to chequerboards of sqerm ponds and the fortified town they'd recently visited. Within half an hour, the edge of the main continent had resolved, the rim of the world closing in. Blite spotted a satellite like a set of church organ pipes, and guessed it was some sort of Polity weapon.

"We're clear for secondary drive," said Leven.

"Take us out."

A few minutes later the fusion drive kicked in and they were leaving Masada behind them. Blite felt a further relaxing of tension. He decided then and there that he had no intention of returning to this place while rumours of black AIs abounded.

"Captain, I'm getting some weird readings from the hold," said Martina from a neighbouring bridge seat.

"That's to be expected—it's alien technology," he replied.

"I know, but these are different readings."

Blite unstrapped himself. "Okay, let's take a look."

He and Martina made their way down to the hold, Martina picking up some diagnostic tools on the way. He wasn't too worried about the chunk of technology he'd brought aboard. It wasn't Jain built—just a piece of some other alien tech with some strange variable mass readings. These indicated it might be something that messed with the Higgs field in ways they hadn't seen before. However, the readings from it were weak and it was very doubtful it had enough oomph to reach much further than a few feet around it. The most likely reason for the change in readings was some induction effect from the ship's systems, feeding it just an erg more power.

Ducking in after Martina, he peered at the cube-shaped box. He began to wonder if it might be better, and safer, to sell it to a collector rather than the Separatists. They would probably just end up destroying it in an attempt to extract some lethal advantage, whereas a collector would be a lot more careful and methodical.

Studying one of her sensors, Martina began, "This is really odd. I'm getting hardfield and—" A loud noise interrupted her.

It sounded like a sword being drawn from a metal sheath, only hugely amplified, and the air all around them pulsed. The plastic box on the sled suddenly parted, dividing through the middle. The two halves shot away to thump against the walls, then dropped to the floor. Blite stared at the exposed contents. The compressed laminar lump of silvery metal and black glass had changed shape. In a way that was difficult to define, it was moving. Then it really *moved*. One layer of glass sprang upright and fanned like the head of a tubeworm, one made of knives and shadow. Below it, the rest of the mass began to unfold in seemingly impossible ways—long spines extending and silver snakes unravelling—the whole thing expanding, growing, multiplying.

Blite felt sick with terror, and with a sense of inevitability, as the thing rose above him. He found himself down on his knees, all his energy draining away. He saw Martina had dropped her devices, saw them falling to the floor in slow motion. She was then back up against the wall, mouth open, horrified. And he watched as, in all its glorious, terrifying magnificence, the black AI Penny Royal continued to unfold itself to occupy their hold.

"Hello, Blite," it whispered.

8

AMISTAD

Over a decade ago, Amistad, the scorpion drone, had been technically upgraded to the status of planetary AI, but more recently politically
downgraded to his current position of planetary warden, so now had time
and processing power to spare. Poised upon the viewing platform of his
tower, he gazed inwardly at a perfectly recorded memory of the time
before he took up this chalice. Penny Royal had been on the point of
dissolution when Amistad found its remains, isolated in its roaming planetoid, and began examining them. This had been the ultimate find for the
drone in his long exploration of madness and brilliance, for Penny Royal
was the apex of both. It was an AI psychopath, or perhaps a schizophrenic,
or perhaps something else for which a term had yet to be invented. Its
technical abilities lay some way beyond those of Polity AI designs—even
the slightly mad forensic AIs or the ones who had retreated into esoteric
mathematical realms. Study of those remains soon revealed that Penny
Royal had fractured sometime in the far past, its various parts containing different states of consciousness. In that respect it was much like
Mr Crane, another being Amistad and Polity AIs were anxious to study,
but this "brass man" had disappeared long ago. It had vanished with the

Polity agent who had been either its nemesis or victim—the details were unclear.

Further study revealed that Penny Royal had compartmentalized its evil, locating it in a state of consciousness Amistad had labelled Eight. Admittedly, the lines of division were difficult to distinguish. Called to serve here, on Masada, Amistad had decided to separate out that eighth state and raise the rest back to functionality. Amistad was mainly driven by curiosity because, although he'd been able to map Penny Royal's madness, he couldn't fathom its brilliance. Other Polity AIs had allowed this, for they were curious too. What had made this creature and how could it do the things it did—could it return to the fold and still retain its uniqueness?

Amistad was slowly coming to the conclusion that the whole exercise had been a huge mistake. He had resurrected and now unleashed something terrible indeed.

The eighth state was the key. Amistad had managed to isolate it physically from the rest of Penny Royal, secreting it in a container on the bottom of the ocean. However, he had never fully understood it. Without it, Penny Royal had remained functional, brilliant, and had served well enough. But, on discovering that the eighth state still existed, the AI had retrieved it and then apparently destroyed it. There was the rub. Amistad was beginning to doubt the veracity of those events and so studied its memory:

"You lied," Penny Royal whispered, swinging towards Amistad an array of spines unnervingly like icicle eyes.

"Is that so unusual?" Amistad replied, edging round, up to the caldera rim just ten metres away, still contemplating how to take Penny Royal down because he was sure the AI must have by now reincorporated its eighth state of consciousness—its madness. Taking a quick peek over the edge, the drone decided the magma down there was plenty hot, but it would probably take everything in his armoury to keep Penny Royal in it for long enough . . .

"Am angry . . . concerned."

The Amistad of the present realized he should have paid more attention, right from the moment he rebuilt Penny Royal. The black AI had been playing him, grooming him for something like the diorama on the edge of that caldera.

"*Why did you keep it?*" *Penny Royal asked.*

"*Scientific interest,*" *Amistad replied.*

The spines abruptly surged closer, extending on necks of plaited tentacle. Did Penny Royal want a physical fight here and some Holmes and Moriarty ending in the fire below? Amistad targeted the rock below, where the AI had rooted itself, selected a chemical missile and loaded it.

"*Interest is finished,*" *said Penny Royal.*

The black AI shifted, spines rippling, slid to one side to reveal what it had been squatting over. There lay the armoured sphere that contained Eight, unopened.

And there, right there, an assumption he had been led into. Penny Royal had played the part of the slightly unstable but generally good little artificial intelligence. Even its speech patterns had been part of it. The AI had showed itself quite capable of taking apart and putting back together a human being, even at the atomic level, and yet it couldn't manage more than a limited vocabulary? Amistad could now see how the performance had been designed around Amistad's own mind. Penny Royal had played on his arrogance, on his belief that he could cure such a creature. It had presented a believable persona of an autistic intelligence trying to come to terms with its new self.

Amistad examined this memory of the confrontation much more closely, running through the different EM spectrums, focusing on the sphere itself rather than on his greatest concern at the time—an AI that might try to kill him. And there it was: an even pattern of heat spots on the sphere's armour that showed up in infrared. The ceramal surface in that area showed a different crystalline pattern from the rest. Some sort of physical connection had been made. Amistad reckoned on a nano-fibre penetration to facilitate upload. He played the rest of the memory through.

Like some child's model of a hand, four spines folded out on corded tentacle, swung to one side, paused for a moment, then swung back, slapping into the sphere. It tumbled over the edge, bounced on the slope below, then splashed into boiling magma. It wouldn't be destroyed, not yet; it would take ages for the heat to do any damage. Amistad shifted right to the edge, almost went over, rocks dislodged and tumbling down, but then scrabbled back. What did he really want that thing for? Was he keeping it because of his attraction to madness—a prime sample for some collection? A missile spat down, hit with a sharp detonation like some massive fuse blowing. The side of the sphere peeled open on arc fire and it turned over, began to sink.

For a moment Amistad thought he had fired the missile himself, but no, Penny Royal had just killed part of itself.

"We have things to do," said the AI.

"Quite," Amistad agreed. "Quite right."

No, Amistad now understood perfectly. Penny Royal had not destroyed its eighth state. The AI probably hadn't had time to copy the vast repository of evil that the sphere had contained, so had undoubtedly uploaded it. In obliterating the physical object, Penny Royal had just been removing the evidence of that act. But what to do? Penny Royal was gone now, had smuggled itself off-world, and Amistad had responsibilities here . . .

"Do nothing," a voice replied.

In a microsecond Amistad traced it to his own internal U-space transceiver, and a microsecond later identified the source: Earth Central.

"I thought you didn't listen to my private thoughts," he said.

"I don't," Earth Central replied.

The implications of that were quite simple. After Amistad's report that Penny Royal had gone missing, Earth Central had ascertained, down to the second, when the drone might consider dropping his tenure as AI warden. It was frightening in some ways and reassuring in others. Amistad understood that, despite his upgrade, he was still a long way down the food chain from the likes of the Polity's de facto ruler.

"But something must be done," Amistad tried.

"Do you think for one moment that you would be the prime mover in this matter? That you would be allowed to dictate next steps regarding something as dangerous, and as precious as Penny Royal? A quorum of four minds has been analysing every scrap of data available, and . . . events move to a resolution."

"What resolution?"

A long, in AI terms, pause ensued.

"Within the next two years—and the quorum can be no more accurate than that—you will receive a visit from a human who will in himself be part of the answer. You must also desist from any intervention in subsequent events."

"Can you elaborate on that?"

"No," Earth Central replied.

Amistad pondered the words. He felt, in his steel heart, that more had been said in the long pause before them. Though a quorum of minds might be analysing Penny Royal's actions, including its abrupt departure from Masada, he was sure those minds were no closer to answers than Amistad himself. He was sure that Earth Central had not elaborated, simply because it could not.

BLITE

Blite waited to be turned into something monstrous, waited to be sliced into a million pieces and then reassembled, or waited to die. He knelt with his head bowed, chilled to the heart of his being, terrified. He heard the airlock open and looked round to see Martina poised beside it. With a nod of her head she indicated their way out of the hold, but he remained where he was.

"You go," he said.

Without any further ado she ducked out, closing the door behind her. What was the point? They had nowhere to run . . . then he thought of a possibility. Penny Royal had just let her go, so maybe it would let him go too. Maybe they could all get to the shuttle and abandon ship . . .

Just then Penny Royal shifted as if sensing his thoughts. He looked up at it, then slowly climbed to his feet. All he could do was try to escape. As he began turning towards the airlock, a weird twisting sensation worked its way from his feet, through his body, then out of the top of his head. Other people had different responses, but this was the sensation he had every time his ship dropped into U-space. He hadn't ordered this and his ship's mind—previously a Golem that had decided it wanted to view the universe from a different perspective—wouldn't have accepted orders from his crew. He just knew Penny Royal had taken control of the ship and, as a consequence, removed the possibility of a shuttle escape. So, instead of continuing to the airlock, he turned back to the AI. Oddly, with hope now dispelled, he felt his terror fading.

Penny Royal was beautiful he realized: the absolute quintessence of sharp lethality. A demon utterly without relation to the human form. Now, in one of those mind-deceiving transformations, it had spread into something resembling a peacock's tail fashioned of black daggers. It could definitely change the size and shape of its body too. Only a few minutes ago, the black glassy objects had been long spines yet were now flat blades. The lacework of silver that bonded them was also nothing like the thick silver tentacles it had used to raise itself from the grav-sled.

"Hello Penny Royal," he said.

Damn it, he might be about to be chopped into pieces, or whatever. But he was now ashamed of his initial reaction—he would face the devil and swear at it as it tore into him.

"You will be paid," said the AI, its voice not issuing from one point but seeming to coagulate out of the air all around, while also echoing in his aug.

"Paid," Blite repeated. "I want nothing from you."

"You will take me, to the Graveyard. Far side," said the AI. "Payment."

Something folded out of the peacock tail to seemingly peck at the floor. It looked like the head of a silver bird at the end of a long silver neck, with sharp, black beak. For a second Blite thought this was it, it was going to start on him now. But the beak just touched the floor by his feet, depositing some objects, after which the whole bird-head retracted. Blite remained very still for a few seconds, then slowly tilted his head to peer downwards. Four rubies rested on the floor, cylindrical, each the size of the last two joints of his little finger. Rubies in and of themselves were relatively worthless—if he ever had a use for them, he could make them himself with some of the equipment aboard this ship.

However, the particular shape of these and the shadowy web-works they contained made him suspect that they were more than simple jewels.

"Memplants," he said. "The Polity gives a reward for every one of these handed in. It is substantial, but it's hardly enough to pay for a jaunt to the other side of the Graveyard."

"First payment," said the AI.

A moment later, Blite found himself experiencing a vivid flashback to events many years past, powerless to stop the memories overtaking him.

He was sitting on the bridge of his ship, gazing at a vid on his tablet, which had been taken on a world called Amber. In the vid, he was sitting in a bar with all of his old crew. While on the bridge, he was remembering the four he had just lost. His throat tight, he quickly closed the file...

... and found himself on his knees in his hold and back in the present, gasping and nauseated. The four rubies lay in front of his face. He just stared, then after a moment reached out and swept them all up in his fist.

"Why are you here?" he managed, his voice hoarse as he stood.

"Transcendence," Penny Royal replied.

Blite turned away and headed for the airlock. It meant nothing. Penny Royal could be playing with him, just prolonging his torment in the same way any psychotic killer might. He opened the airlock, progressed through, then headed towards the bridge. But perhaps if he could divine the truth about what he held in his hand... was there some way he could find out if Penny Royal had truly given back his four crewmen, lives it had taken away so many years ago?

"Captain?"

Blite looked up to see Brondohohan, Ikbal and Greer waiting in the corridor ahead of him, all three heavily armed and standing behind a tripod-mounted proton cannon. He was quite stunned at how they had moved the thing out of stores and set it up so fast. But of course they had plenty of motivation. Beyond them stood Martina, and then Chont and Haber rushed up carrying yet more weapons. Blite felt proud, but recognized the futility of the defence. Penny Royal didn't have to come up this corridor to get them and, as he well recollected, such armaments had little effect on the AI.

"Penny Royal," he said, "there wasn't any Separatist buyer for those thralls, was there?"

Again a memory surfaced, its clarity as painful as a knife, yet it wasn't one of his memories.

He saw a man standing on a jetty, shooting a pulse-gun into an iron-coloured sea. The man was screaming curses as he emptied his weapon, then he turned to look back down the jetty. The thing disintegrated, starting from a point by the shore, falling into dust. When the destruction reached him, he just dissolved into a bloody fog.

Then Blite was back. He'd managed to stay upright this time but still felt sick. Was that the Separatist? Was that a yes or a no?

"Why us?"

Now it was a memory of his own.

He put down a bet on the fight between a dwarf-form lion and some hideous alien insect. He won because, unexpectedly, the lion managed to bite through the back of its opponent's ridged neck.

"How did you know?" someone asked.

"Just lucky, I guess," he replied.

So that was it: a sarcastic comment from the AI. They were just lucky. Back in the present and feeling even more nauseated, Blite asked, "Are you going to stay in the hold?"

No memory this time; just cryptic words coalescing out of the air. "I must connect all of me."

Blite moved forwards to stand directly before his crew. "We're taking it to the other side of the Graveyard, apparently. We have no choice."

"Do you trust it?" Ikbal asked, his face pale with fear.

"Not in the slightest, which is why I want you to take a welder back there and seal shut the hold airlock." Ikbal didn't much like that idea, but bobbed his head in agreement. "Brond . . ." The man watched him expectantly. "I hope the shuttle is well stocked and fully fuelled. We need to be prepared for . . . eventualities." Blite winced, feeling that was too obvious. He considered sending a message to all his crew by aug, but knew that would be no more secure than speaking.

Brondohohan nodded an acknowledgement and the others exchanged knowing looks. If they tried to use the shuttle while in U-space there was no telling what would happen to them. Theories varied. They might just drop back into realspace or they might do so travelling at a fraction below light speed—a velocity impossible to counter with the shuttle's engines. They might end up trapped in U-space for eternity, or they might wash up in the real through one of those rumoured U-space maelstroms. As far as Blite knew, no one had found any of the shuttles that had attempted such a thing, though there were stories of strangely distorted wrecks containing the inside-out remains of human beings. However, when they arrived at their destination they just might be able to escape, so they had to be ready.

ISOBEL

It was getting more and more difficult for Isobel to stand up. Her feet were almost gone, the bones in her legs were now ridiculously bowed and they were growing shorter at an increasing rate—almost as if her body was sucking them inside. She had considered knocking off the ship's gravity, making some excuse about conserving power, but knew that wouldn't wash. Both Trent and Gabriel were aware that energy wasn't the issue and that their problem was a lack of material resources—mainly propellant for the fusion drive. They would recognize such an action as an admission of debility from her. However, there was another solution.

Munching on a chunk of bloody synthesized steak, she opened a door into a storeroom just ahead of the hold. She was always hungry now, always eating—and she tried to control her urge to use the manipulators down each side of her face to take it apart and feed it into her mouth. Taking a step inside, she studied the racks of supplies. Here were pulse-rifles and other armaments, a grav-scooter and a selection of grav-sleds. She also spotted a proton cannon still in its original boxes, yet to be assembled, and a heap of prador armour. She'd stripped that off a drifting

prador corpse that had probably died during the war. She found it difficult to move further into the room and in the end relented, relinquishing
the steak to her facial manipulators. That way she could use the remains
of both hands for support.

Eventually she found a suitcase on one of the shelves. Inside, neatly
packaged in foam, lay a grav-harness. Leaving it where it was for the
moment, she deliberately sped up her snack, for when she consigned
food to these manipulators, they ran on some unconscious program
that involved carefully slicing off layers of meat. Once the last scrap had
vanished into her mouth, now triangular in its steady transformation into
a vertical slot, she stripped off her dress, then her padded jacket. She had
no concerns about Trent or Gabriel coming across her like this—they
tended to know where she was and avoided her.

Now naked, she found the sight of her twisted little legs even more
detestable. The neat armoured torso seemed so much more right, as it
blended into her extended head and sensory cowl. She studied her arms
and hands. She had lost two fingers from each hand and her arms were
shorter and more bowed, but they weren't disappearing at the same rate as
her legs. She suspected this was something to do with usage. Aboard this
ship she really didn't do much walking around—spending a lot of time
in her acceleration chair in the bridge or on her bed in her cabin—but
she did use her hands a lot. But that would change. Gabriel had already
come upon her unannounced, finding her operating a touch-board with
her facial manipulators. She also suspected that her legs would disappear
even more quickly once she made use of the grav-harness.

She pulled the thing out of the suitcase and shrugged it on over what
remained of her shoulders. She closed the belt around her, above where
her waist had been, between a pair of insectile legs, and then found she
had to open everything up to its full extension to get the leg straps to
reach. It was necessary to position the belt further down, between another
set of her hooder legs. The main control hung loose on her chest and she
tightened the straps. They were still at the extension she had required
last time she used this thing, when she had breasts. The grav-lift itself
came both from this unit and from the nanofactured Higgs fabric in the
harness itself.

Next she hit the power-up tab, began to increase the lift on a touch-bar then realized the last time she had used this she had not even been a haiman—just a slightly augmented human. Dropping her hand, she immediately linked through to the harness's controls and used her mind to operate them. The thing tightened about her, as if attached to an invisible hoist positioned above. She took the control all the way up until her feet came up off the ground, noting how much heavier she was now—nearly twice her previous weight. In fact she was now as heavy as Trent or Gabriel. This massive weight gain wasn't surprising. She had recently grasped that, despite her shrunken legs, she now stood taller than the two men. It also appeared that everything she ate was converted into hooder flesh and armour, for she couldn't remember the last time she had taken a shit.

She then adjusted the lift down again so her boots were resting on the floor, and picked up her jacket. Suddenly, she sensed a powerful smell and at first didn't know what it was. She went utterly still, all senses stretched to their maximum. After a moment she identified tobacco smoke: Gabriel down here enjoying one of his disgusting cigars. She had told him again and again not to smoke aboard her ship, yet he continued to disobey her. In the past this had been mildly irritating but right now it made her livid. He was also walking down the corridor towards her and any moment now would be opposite the door—he would see her, naked, just wearing this grav-harness. Suddenly she'd had enough. She was spending far too much time concealing her changes from them. Wasn't she their boss? Shouldn't they just obey her orders and keep their obvious abhorrence of her to themselves?

In a moment he was there and glanced inside, startled. She saw him all across the hooder spectrum. She saw right into him; saw the pulse of his blood through his veins, saw his bones, and the distinction between fat and muscle. He just didn't look like Gabriel to her; he looked like prey.

"Isobel!" he managed, but she was already on the move.

Part of it was unconscious, but a much larger part, her predator, knew what it was doing. She shut off the harness completely and dropped, her hooder legs clattering against the floor. Skidding against the roughened metal, they propelled her forwards, then up at forty-five degrees. Her face slammed into his, her hooder legs clamping to his body, her full weight slamming him back against the wall. He tried to shove her away but she twisted and he couldn't keep his footing, falling sideways. Even as he fell, her manipulators dug into his face, slicing neatly round his cheeks and taking them away. This exposed his back teeth on either side, then he was down on his back with her on top of him. She tried to close her cowl around his head and couldn't manage it, but still her manipulators sliced and levered. He kicked and struggled underneath her but just couldn't get away. Then, by the time she had taken off his face, he grew still.

Her senses told her he was dead and she couldn't understand why, until she backed up a little and saw the blood pooled all around. Her insectile legs had hit him so hard they had penetrated, and one had gone through his ribcage and into his heart.

"I knew it. Fucking hell. I knew it."

She looked round to see Trent at the end of the corridor, gazing at her in horror. Then he drew the gas-system pulse-gun he had taken to carrying all the time. Calculations ran through her brain. She was sure she could get to him before he managed to kill her. She could tell him she'd punished Gabriel for his continued infringement of her rules. However, he might not accept that having your face eaten off was suitable punishment for smoking aboard her ship. But mostly, she just wanted to be alone with her prey. Mostly, she just wanted to finish her meal. Suddenly she moved, manipulators hooking in through Gabriel's eye sockets, legs engaging with the floor again as she dragged him towards the storeroom. Trent fired, on automatic, pulses of white-hot ionized gas slamming into her. Two punched into her right arm, two more entered her side, then a further two slammed into one of her human legs. But she did not release Gabriel. As she went through the door she used her augmentations to order it shut, and locked.

The pain hit next and she shrieked, but it was no human sound. She lay shivering over Gabriel, something twisting inside her. Looking down at her side, she saw just two sooty marks where he had hit her there. However, her right arm, which had felt on fire, now abruptly went numb. Almost without thinking, she dipped towards that shoulder and began cutting. She sliced a circle around it, probing inside to sever ligaments and tendons so fast it was done before she had a chance to feel horrified. The arm dropped to the floor with a thud, but there was no blood. Nothing bled from the arm or from her shoulder joint which, even as she gazed at it, began to film over with something glassy.

"If you come out of there, Isobel, you're dead."

It was Trent, speaking to her through the intercom. Managing to return her thought processes to something approaching humanity, she wondered why he hadn't tried to pursue her inside. After a moment of consideration she realized the reason was obvious. First, he didn't want to rush in after something like her; secondly, he knew about the weapons this room contained. Isobel dismissed him from her thoughts. She would leave when she was ready to do so. She might have lost one of her human arms but these manipulators were very precise, and she had so many options. She could find a way to use these weapons, and she was stronger than him, much stronger.

Next, coiling round, Isobel began to cut away her damaged and now numb leg. She decided then she would remove both of them. They were no use to her any more.

SPEAR

Though I disliked the delay, it was necessary for us to make one stopover on our route to Penny Royal's planetoid. The *Puling Child*—I had yet to think of a new name for the destroyer—was depleted of weapons and I was on the way to confront a very dangerous AI. It is a simple fact that you don't go hunting a lion with an empty rifle. It was two weeks' travel to the stopover, and I spent the time sleeping for six hours then working for twenty, stopping only to tend to human needs. My body didn't require sleep but I did use it to stabilize my thinking, and with everything that had occurred I felt I needed that.

With plenty of robot assistance and plenty of time, I stripped out the cabins, moved walls and built equipment. Near the end of those two weeks, I had one large workshop and laboratory, containing all the facilities I would need. I had rid myself of the refectory and moved the food synthesizer in there. I enlarged the bridge, lined the walls and ceiling with screen fabric and set a single acceleration chair in the middle of the floor, partially surrounded by a horseshoe console. I found this setup less claustrophobic than the previous arrangement and it gave me a better field of view for dealing with Penny Royal—I wanted all the advantages possible. Upon arrival at our first destination I sat in the chair and turned on the screen fabric. This immediately created the illusion that I was now sitting in that chair on a bridge floor open to vacuum.

The sun here was a glaring blue giant of about fifty solar masses. From my perspective, it looked about ten times the size of Sol as seen from the surface of Earth. Here the lack of air wouldn't have killed me, had I actually been exposed in open vacuum. This close to the star, with it putting out twenty thousand times the luminosity of Sol, I would've been turned to ash in a second.

"Do you have a target for our raw materials?" I asked, impatient to get this done and be on the way to Penny Royal's planetoid.

In response Flute put a cross-hairs scope circle over to the left of the sun and magnified. I suddenly felt I was rushing towards that point and found myself gripping the arms of my chair. A globular red mass drew into view.

"Fifteen tons of nickel-chrome iron," Flute explained. "The asteroid is highly refined, having out-gased its impurities while being melted every time at its perihelion. It is currently just below melting point, so little energy will be required to form it."

While I watched, the image grew larger and larger as we drew closer, then it adjusted back as Flute dropped the magnification. I felt the fusion engine fire up briefly to slow us, then steering thrusters kicked in to position us very close to this mass.

"What about the ship's cooling mechanisms?" I asked.

"Thermal converters are at full operation," Flute replied. "I will not need to use refrigeration lasers or plasma expulsion for five hours, which should give me enough time to manufacture forty standard railgun missiles."

I was about to say "proceed" but Flute wasn't waiting. Already I could see flat spots appearing on either side of the asteroid as Flute clamped it in hardfields. A moment later a third hardfield began peeling off shavings, which it propelled slowly towards the ship in a neat line. These soon began to glow more intensely as Flute hit them with anti-personnel lasers, before rolling them between further hardfields into neat cylinders, their ends snipped off as if by invisible cigar cutters.

I could have sat there watching the railgun missiles being manufactured for hours, but I needed to do something first. This need pushed me out of my seat and had me heading for my laboratory-cum-workshop. The entire setup here was for one purpose. If I was to confront Penny Royal, I needed more than just this ship and a new stock of weapons. I had to have knowledge of the AI, understanding, *intelligence*, and two items I had moved here might provide these.

I'd taken a nanoscope, nanofactor and various other items from Isobel's ship. From these, I'd fashioned a variety of other devices and installed them here on work surfaces around the walls. I'd set up contained computing and hung more nanobot-woven screen fabric across one wall, and even installed a hologram-projector. I'd rigged a couple of ship's robots for specialized tasks—one now dangled from the ceiling like a multi-fingered grab and one was mounted on a movable pedestal. The latter was ready for the object presently clamped in a frame on the central table. I walked over and studied it.

The Golem torso still had Penny Royal's discarded spine through its chest. I stepped back, folding my arms, then auged through to take control of the machines in this room. First I brought over the pedestal robot, which opened out its two larger arms and closed heavy serrated clamps on either side of the Golem's chest. It then readied its smaller arms on the rails down its front, reaching in to close neoprene-faced clamps about the base of the black spine, avoiding the sharp edges, then it slowly pulled. I metered the amount of resistance in my mind, watching it build then release as with a horrible screech the spine came free.

Releasing its larger serrated clamps, the robot backed up to retract the spine fully and there I paused it, stepping over to examine the thing it held. Again I felt that weird connectedness to this piece of Penny Royal, that odd familiarity. And though I didn't like the feelings I experienced being this close to the thing, I gave it a thorough visual inspection. The damned thing wasn't damaged at all. Even the point was still so sharp it was difficult to see where it ended and where air began. I stepped back and ordered the robot to consign it to a glass cylinder in the corner of the room, sealing it in and surrounding it with inert gas. I would have to give it a closer examination in the future, if only to find out what the hell it was made of, but right now my main interest was the Golem.

The pentagonal hole punched through the android's chest was as neat as if it was part of the thing's manufacture. The only materials that could cut through such ceramal were high-compression nanofactured diamond tool bits, or the slugs for portable railguns used to penetrate prador armour. Penny Royal must have been very busy with what had been state-of-the-art manufacturing, back when it transformed itself from a ship's crystal AI to a thing like a giant sea urchin. The smaller exit hole in the Golem's back had five neat petals of ceramal ringing it. Again, they looked so even that they could have been made by a machine. I stepped back, now summoning the robot hanging from the ceiling; it descended like a nightmare chandelier.

First I ran a scan and, as the results loaded to my aug for my inspection, I experienced a cold sweat. The spine had gone in underneath the Golem's crystal and merely scored grooves in its lower surface. It had also nicked the s-con cable that supplied power to its servo motors, but that should not have been enough to stop it. I just didn't know why I was still alive. I glanced over at the spine in its glass cylinder, puzzled, suspicious.

Giving the robot further instructions had it dismantling and removing the remains of one of the Golem's arms. Afterwards it inserted a thin, ribbed worm of a tentacle which terminated in a small claw and an interface plug. This sought out and found the Golem's sensory feed inside its chest, disconnecting it. We were nearly there, as it next found the main socket for direct uploads and downloads, plugging in and forging connections for both power and the necessary frequencies of coherent light. Then the moment I'd been waiting for, when everything came alive in there. And, ensuring there was no way the Golem could make its own connection and do something like seizing control of my robots, I lastly connected it up to my hologram projector—its projection point set out over the floor.

The air fizzed as a white cylinder as tall as me was projected in the centre of the room. A rainbow rippled from its top to its bottom, then blinked out. After a moment the rainbow traversed the white cylinder again, but now it carved away its whiteness to reveal a sculpture inside. A man-sized Oscar appeared, seemingly fashioned of liquid mercury. It had reverted to an industry projection used in Golem manufacture. This was worrying, because it meant its android source had no conception of its own physical appearance, so might contain no useful data at all. I watched it for a while but it did nothing further, so I decided to prod.

"Hello Daleen," I said.

The Oscar opened its eyes and they were midnight black, which certainly wasn't in the industry handbook. Its arms separated from its body, it raised one leg, then as it tried to throw itself at me the projection broke up. It briefly became a fractured morass, the kind of images seen through a nanoscope during nanofacture. After a moment the cylinder went white again, before again revealing the Oscar. I eyed it while running through data gathered directly from the Golem's mind. I could find no response to language prompts, which made me think this Golem had been completely wiped. However, if it had been wiped, I could see no reason why it would have tried to kill me. Again taking care not to let anything out, I selected a language package from a file on my aug and sent it to the Golem. The response this time was different. Instead of opening its eyes it opened its mouth and screamed before breaking up again.

Two hours later, after numerous screams and attempts at attacking me, I finally felt I was getting somewhere. It opened its eyes, didn't immediately attempt an attack, then opened its mouth and licked its lips with a silver tongue.

"Hello Daleen," I tried again.

It stared at me for about ten seconds, then something appeared in the air down by its waist. I recognized a nanobot type used in heavy gravity manufacture—they were used to build stuff on the surfaces of dead stars. Then this object fragmented and disappeared.

"Not real," said Daleen the Golem clearly, then closed its mouth.

"Why did you try to kill me?" I asked.

"You . . . destroyed."

"Destroyed?" I was puzzled. "I must be destroyed, or I destroyed something?"

Daleen looked at me with an expression I could only style as contempt and the Oscar began to change. It took on the colours of human skin, grew hair from its scalp and formed recognizable features. After a moment a naked man stood before me, which was wrong, because Daleen's chosen external form had been female. He was the same height as me with well-defined muscles but these weren't as prominent as some-one who had been boosted—more like the physique of a swimmer. The skin tone was pale Asiatic and he had a Roman nose below pale green eyes, above a mouth with a slight twist as if he found something secretly amusing. His brown hair was long and slightly curly with streaks of grey in it. I considered this image for a moment and decided I must run a check on my body's standard suite of nanobots and retroviral biotech, because my hair shouldn't have been turning grey like that. The image was, of course, me.

"I presume you're making some sort of point," I said, "but I fail to see it."

"It doesn't know," said Daleen, abruptly seeming panicked, then simply froze.

I tried for a further hour to get more responses from the Golem, but it was just refusing to communicate. In the end I shut down the hologram and shifted Daleen's torso from the central table to one of the worktops. I then instated a direct connection from the Golem to the hologram projec-tor. It would come back on again the moment Daleen did want to talk, if ever. I then went back to the bridge to check on Flute's progress.

Flute had manufactured thirty railgun missiles. Did I really need any more? I had anti-personnel lasers, a working particle cannon and CTDs stolen from Isobel. If these weren't enough to kill a black AI, then a few extra railgun missiles weren't going to make much difference, surely? Then I reconsidered.

"Flute," I said. "I want you to ensure a full stock of railgun missiles, so we will stay here until that is done—if necessary shift us away from the sun for cooling."

"That would be over eight hundred missiles," Flute replied.

"No matter. I also want you to scan this system for radioactives." I paused, then continued, "You said we are capable of making fission bombs, but what about fusion bombs?"

"They can be made."

"Hardfield containment fusion? Multi-megaton range?"

"Yes—it may be possible to make a fusion bomb ranging into the hundreds of megatons. That is if we use a kiloton-range CTD as the detonating package and hardfield-contained deuterium in the outer shell."

I certainly had the weapons to kill a black AI, but they might not be enough to root it out of the tunnels in its home. Better then to ensure those tunnels ceased to exist.

9

BLITE

The journey had felt interminable and there was absolutely no doubt for either Blite or his crew that something . . . dangerous and strange was aboard *The Rose*. Blite had heard tales of weird supernatural goings-on aboard some ships, but had never believed them. He always considered such stories irrational when there were so many other logical explanations available. And there was so much in present technology that could be mistaken for the supernatural. He still didn't believe the legends, but he now knew how it felt to be aboard a haunted ship.

For twenty hours after Penny Royal revealed itself in the hold, they'd made preparations for escape once *The Rose* returned to realspace. All the time they were doing this, the tension grew with the expectation that the AI would grow bored with toying with them and come after them. Finally, after a further ten hours of waiting, discussion, argument and unbearable tension, Blite decided it was time to go to bed. He just couldn't maintain such a level of fear. Sleep brought nightmares: replays of that encounter all those years ago, but now it contained novel twists. These involved a screaming crowd of partially dismembered people and a deeprooted terror of a CTD blast that Blite just knew was about to incinerate them all. Despite the nightmares he woke rested and energetic, but then just a few hours of wakefulness drained him.

The sounds of the ship were not the same as they had been, the difference akin to rapping a rotten log rather than a healthy tree. Everything around him felt less substantial, less reliable. Checking cams in the hold, all he could see were black and silver kaleidoscope-like images. These did nothing to explain the extra power drains there, nor the rise in temperature. Then other things began to happen. Ship's diagnostics began reporting faults which, before they could even be inspected, vanished. The ship shuddered once—something that shouldn't be possible in U-space—and which could only be a source of terror to those experiencing it. After that, Blite talked to his ship mind.

"Leven," he said, "what the hell was that?"

The Golem mind Leven took his time replying. He probably had no more control over this ship now than Blite himself.

"Penny Royal," he said leadenly.

"What did it do?"

"It's playing with the Calabi-Yau frames and other components in the drive pod. It seems to be recalibrating the drive."

"What?" Blite called up cam views into the engine shell, where earlier he had sent Chont and Haber to run some tests—just to keep them busy. Kaleidoscope images again. Trying other cameras, he found the very married couple on the other side of the bulkhead door leading into the engine shell. They were standing facing each other—not talking.

"Everything okay down there?" he asked through the intercom. They both turned simultaneously to look up at the nearest cam, then simultaneously said, "Everything is fine."

"I want you to go back in and check again," Blite ordered.

After a few minutes of watching them trying to open the bulkhead door and failing, he said, "Okay, leave it."

If Penny Royal didn't want them in there, they wouldn't be getting in. It also turned out that everything wasn't in fact fine with either Chont or Haber. Over the ensuing days, this previously inseparable man and woman spent a great deal of effort trying to avoid each other, then finally stopped sharing a cabin. Haber moved her things into one of the passenger cabins.

Brondohohan was next. Shortly after Leven had informed Blite that U-space drive efficiency had increased by eight per cent, the big man said, matter-of-factly, "My brother visited me last night."

Greer was ever a woman to point out the obvious. Her speech was as blunt as her heavy-worlder features, and she replied, "Last I heard you had only one brother and he was toast ten years ago."

Brondohohan and his brother were initiated in artificial wombs some eighty years apart—the brother sometime before the war and Brond himself sometime after. His brother—Mandohohan—Blite recollected, had reached that stage of life in which boredom became the greatest threat. He'd tried one of the most dangerous sports available: surfing pyroclastic flows.

He hadn't been very good at it.

"Nevertheless," said Brond. "It was my brother."

Next it was Greer's turn. It took four of them to subdue her and stop her trying to rearrange her face with a commando knife. Finally, drugged to the eyeballs and strapped to a gurney in the medical bay, she admitted that she didn't want to be a heavy-worlder any more—she wanted to be beautiful. When Blite asked her how trying to cut off her own face might help, she'd just given him a very puzzled look. While she was still there, undergoing some sort of treatment involving drugs and lights that the autodoc had dragged out of its memory bank, Ikbal began his muttering. He didn't know he was doing it until he was told. And when he tried to stop himself, he started on the scratching and pulling out pieces of his white hair. But it was when Martina entered Blite's cabin, naked, and demanded he "fuck her hard" that Blite decided enough was enough. Martina had been a lesbian ever since he had known her—her dislike for heterosexual sex almost morbid.

Blite left her sleeping on his bed, a knock-out drug patch stuck to her neck, and headed to one of the ship's stores to pick up a small atomic shear. He made his way back to the hold airlock, then carved out Ikbal's welding job with the shear's force-blade. It took him mere minutes and he wondered why he'd thought it would in any way stop what lay on the other side. There was no doubt that tools like this were part of Penny Royal's body. Soon he was inside the airlock. Noting that the air in the hold was still good, he opened the inner lock door and stepped through.

Once inside, Blite just stood there with his mouth hanging open. The back wall of the hold, along with most of another wall, was missing. Somehow their materials had been converted into organic-looking pillars and crossbeams. From where he was standing, he could see all the way to the U-space drive. Notable too, were clumps of hardware that had sprouted from the ship's structure like puffballs, interlinked by a mycelium of optics and bright silver s-con wires. Penny Royal was where Blite had last seen it. But now it lay right down on the deck in simple black sea-urchin form—if such a creature could measure ten feet across.

"What have you done to my fucking ship!" Blite roared. Then, remembering just what he was shouting at, along with his own intention to abandon ship as soon as possible, he felt foolish. "What have you done?"

Some spines twitched towards him but otherwise there was no response. He moved further in, right up to those spines, but felt decidedly vulnerable. With his skin crawling, he stepped back. He walked over to one of the puffball objects, pressed a hand against it and found it solid, also noting small lights gleaming in deep recesses in the surface. There were occasional holes through to packed and highly complex tech. He turned and sat down on it.

"I want you to leave my crew alone," he said.

Again that twitch of spines, then a silvery tentacle extruded from underneath the AI and rose up into a two-foot-high spike. While he watched, the end of the spike, just below the point, swelled into a small sphere which opened lids to reveal a blue human eye. Blite recognized this as an acknowledgement of his presence.

"Leave my crew alone," he repeated.

"Overspill," said Penny Royal. "Eight must be controlled."

"I've no idea what you're talking about."

"Previous difficulty," said Penny Royal, then, "Fixed."

The eye-stalk abruptly retracted and Blite just knew that was all the response he would get. After a while longer he stood and left the hold, just in time to hear Martina's shout of, "Oh no! No!" As he walked back towards the bridge she rushed past him, his bed sheet wrapped around her body; she paused to give him a horrified look, then ran on. He halted, turned and walked back down the corridor to Medical. Greer glanced over at him, still seeming hazy, but also apparently puzzled at her surroundings.

"Still want to be beautiful?" he asked.

It took her a moment to understand him, then her expression turned indignant.

"I am beautiful," she said.

He released the reinforced straps holding her and went to find Brondohohan on the bridge. The man looked over at him with a pursed mouth and annoyed expression.

"I see Ikbal has stopped scratching," said Brond. "And suddenly I can distinguish between reality and hallucination."

"It's like sharing a ship with a tornado," said Blite, seating himself in one of the chairs. "I don't think there's any intent to hurt us, this time, but it might just inadvertently rip us apart."

"A mental maelstrom," said Brond.

"Quite."

Haber moved back in with Chont after another day, and only a little while after that did Blite learn what their problem had been. They had always been close—a closeness some had described as practically tele-pathic. After their visit to the engine room they'd found themselves *really* sensing each other's emotions, along with the babble behind coherent thought. It had been just too intense, even frightening. Martina refused to speak to him for quite some time afterwards but, when he forced a meet-ing with her, she reluctantly accepted that all he had done was knock her out.

Finally, the U-space drive shut down, for they had arrived at their destination. Blite was on the bridge with Martina and Greer, and all three looked at each other and failed to react. They had planned to abandon ship at this point yet, during the journey, something had changed. Faced now with the actual moment, they did nothing.

"We're just out from an E6 green-belt planet," Leven announced. "Penny Royal is presently focusing ship's scanners on all orbital objects."

"It's looking for something," said Martina.

"No shit," Greer replied.

"Can you give us a view?" asked Blite.

He then immediately felt the push and shove of thrusters as the ship's aspect changed, swinging a milky yellow orb into view.

"You can control thrusters?" Blite asked.

"It seems I can do anything I like," replied Leven, "until I do something Penny Royal doesn't like." Then, after a pause, "It's found something."

"Show me," said Blite.

A frame appeared superimposed on one side of the planet, which then expanded, but there was nothing in it. Blite was about to ask about that when Leven said, "I'm not even sure what it's found. There's some kind of odd low-level U-space signature there. Penny Royal just sent a heavily coded pulse to that area." Another pause. "Ah, chameleonware."

As Blite watched, the designated area of space shimmered and something folded out of it. The thing looked like a spinning top a hundred feet across, its spindle a weird semi-organic tangle. After a moment, he saw that the rim of the thing was an old-style Tokomak fusion torus—much like those the Polity had used to power orbital weapons.

"Some kind of particle cannon?" Martina suggested.

It didn't look much like a cannon to Blite.

"It's powering up now and that U-signature is strengthening." The focus on the object drew back, and Leven then highlighted something in red—a tube spearing down towards the planet from one end of the object's spindle.

"Some bizarre kind of ionizing scoop-field to feed the Tokomak from the atmosphere," said Leven. Then, "The resultant energy is being U-transmitted away."

"Where to?" asked Blite.

"I can't tell—it's just going into U-space."

The focus closed in again to show the object speckled with lights like spider eyes, a haze of energy all around it. Next, just a moment later, it folded out of existence again.

"Chameleonware re-engaged," said Leven needlessly.

Blite stared at the empty frame, the machine they had just seen sitting leaden in his mind. Penny Royal had activated the thing or, rather, reactivated it, and it was now putting out a great deal of power. He had no idea what this was all about, but didn't like it at all. Even when the frame closed, he still seemed to feel the Tokomak out there, grazing on and fusing atmosphere and feeding the resulting power into *something*.

Leven now said, "Penny Royal just began scanning the surface."

Was there a link between that machine and an object down on the surface? Blite felt certain there wasn't, that the machine had been activated and now the black AI was focusing on other concerns.

The fusion drive fired then—the orb of the world rapidly expanding. Blite felt a relaxing of tension as the rest of the crew joined them, still none of them showing any inclination to make a rush for the shuttle. Haber asked what was going on and Martina explained, replaying a vid of the machine they had just seen. They discussed the thing and speculated, but could come to no conclusions. Haber and Chont eventually wandered off while Brond and Ikbal installed themselves in the other two chairs.

Over the ensuing hour, Penny Royal adjusted their course and Blite realized its intention was to scan the entire surface.

"Any ideas what it's looking for now?" he asked generally.

"The initial scan was for orbital objects," Leven replied. "This scan is mainly focused on recent surface impacts."

"So something was in orbit here and Penny Royal is now checking to see if it crashed into the surface?" Blite suggested.

"So it would seem."

"Another of those machines?" he asked.

"Maybe."

The waiting became interminable and over the ensuing hours crew left the bridge and returned. Blite himself went off for a sleep for a few hours, returned to check on progress, then went to get something to eat. He was just finishing his food when Brond announced over the intercom, "Planetary scan's done—it's now scanning out into the rest of the system."

Blite returned his tray to the refectory synthesizer and sauntered to the bridge. He was the last to arrive—everyone else was there.

"A ship has been detected," said Leven. "It's on an out-system course, operating on fusion with hardfield scoops deployed. Best guess is that it is collecting as much fuel as possible for a long journey without U-space drive."

"Could be an alien vessel," Chont suggested.

"Hardly," Leven replied. "It's Isobel Satomi's *Moray Firth*."

ISOBEL

Trent had disabled most of the cameras in the bridge, but he hadn't known about all of them and hadn't come close to finding the concealed ones. Still he was trying to take the ship's systems out of her control and probably believed he was succeeding. He was only making progress because she allowed him to, and she could take it all away with a thought. Now, having assured herself that he wasn't doing anything unexpected, she returned her attention to her present task.

The glue where her human shoulders had been had set firm. Its nano-fibre bond into her carapace was so deep that neither the pulse-rifle now affixed to her right shoulder, nor the proton cannon joined to her left could come away—unless the carapace concerned was torn off. She'd angled the weapons upwards, accepting her hooder mode of movement and engineering for that, where her head tilted slightly upwards. Generally, from what she knew about hooder anatomy, the rows of eyes running down either side of her face were supposed to be employed for the meticulous dissection of prey. And now she'd noticed that a hard ridge vertically divided what had been her face. However, she'd discovered that these new eyes could focus better than human eyes at long range. This might have been a puzzle, had she not known more. Also, infrared sensors had appeared on the back of her cowl, and essentially these would be on top when she was down and scuttling along the ground. She might have supposed that these were for the sensing of distant prey, but the creature she was becoming sported more sensors than feasible in something that had evolved naturally. And of course that was right.

Knowing just what sort of transformation she was undergoing, she had loaded as much about hooders as she could find out. Recent studies claimed, with a great deal of backup evidence, that hooders were the devolved descendants of biomech war machines. These, it turned out, had been built by one of the three supposedly extinct alien races.

With the weapons now bonded in place, Isobel linked into their targeting and brought up cross hairs in her upper pair of eyes. As she turned her cowl, and thus the weapons, they tracked around the storeroom. She had done the best she could with the resources at her disposal. But still the weapons would need to be sighted in to ensure accuracy, preferably in a large open space. Next she linked into one of the storeroom cams, rose up to face it, and gazed at herself.

Her human arms and legs were gone, what remained having been rapidly absorbed into her growing body and displaced by hard carapace. The limbs themselves she had eaten, just as she had eaten Gabriel. The only difference being that she had eaten her own bones, whereas Gabriel's sat in a well-chewed stack over to one side. Their laminations and other reinforcements rendered them indigestible, even to a hooder. She had also consumed two boxes full of carbon-fibre fabric, for the growth spurt she had experienced had made her incredibly hungry. Now, from the tip of her tail to the top of her cowl she measured ten feet. Her body segments had more definition, but had yet to acquire the outgrowths which had led some to equate a hooder's body to a terran vertebrate's spine. Nothing remained of her human face.

Within her cowl, she had two rows of eyes—six pairs—while at either end of the ridge down the centre of her "face," jointed limbs were folded. These terminated in curved spatulas with small spikes extending from their bases along their inner faces. She knew these were incredibly sensitive and with them she could even feel faults in flat metal that human hands could not detect. On either side of the face ridge, inside the two rows of eyes, glassy tubes had begun sprouting. She had just started being able to move these, waving them ineffectually from side to side. But she knew they would later grow telescopic sections and toothed ends that could bore through flesh. These, she understood, were for feeding on "white fats" and body fluids, with the nightmare now circular mouth at the bottom of the ridge used for larger items.

Rows of jointed limbs terminated in glassy scythes, which had grown early on from the sides of her face. They always remained scalpel sharp, perpetually shedding their inner faces to expose new lethal edges, much in the way a cat sheds its claws. Beyond these lay tangled organics that had recently bubbled out to fill the gap between her face and her cowl. They had the appearance of offal, but were now hardening where they connected to her cowl. The latest additions, on top of all of this, were black tentacles. These were seemingly sprouting at random and one of these had now grown pincers. She knew that later on some would sprout delicate manipulators, similar to those found on an autodoc.

In all, she possessed more appendages to manipulate her environment than any human being. She could control her own ship and she could use all the human-formatted controls easily enough. She could also take things apart in ways no human could manage without supplemental tools. She'd first-hand experience of this, after adapting the weapons now bonded at the base of her cowl, or rather her *hood.* Only one or two problems remained. She knew she'd have to open out various parts of this ship as time progressed, because she was going to grow a lot bigger. And, in her dealings, she would definitely need human agents. This was why she'd decided that synthesized proteins would have to do for a while, and that she would not be killing and eating Trent. Time now, she felt, to venture back out into her ship.

Isobel turned to the door, switching off the lock with her mind—also disabling Trent's recently added security feature that sent a signal to the bridge. She then opened the door with an insectile limb, the uppermost in the long arrays running down either side of her body. As she moved into the corridor, she ensured that the cams Trent presumed he controlled didn't alert him. They continued to display an empty corridor in his screens. Then she paused. The heavy dragging noise she had made in exiting had been considerable, despite her care. Trent would hear her coming long before she reached the bridge door, so she initiated her grav-harness. The thing strained to lift her increased weight up off the grav-plated floor, and she progressed with light touches of her limbs to propel her forwards.

Even though she took as much care as possible, she still managed to make a loud clattering just before reaching the bridge door, as she tried to kill her momentum. However, a glance through the cams showed that Trent had not noticed. He was utterly absorbed by the ship's exterior sensor data, and she could now see an image displayed in the laminate of the chain-glass front screen. Isobel was about to enter, when what he was looking at suddenly hit home: there was a ship out there!

Through her haiman augmentations, she keyed into the data and began scanning through it. This ship had just dropped out of U-space over the nearby planet. It was of a design familiar in the Graveyard but wasn't one she particularly recognized. It had spent some time there, probably scanning the area, before briefly submerging itself in U-space to come out here. Her first momentary delight upon seeing this vessel was instantly banished. Rather than some random traveller she could ask for help, this appeared to be a ship that had come specifically to this area in search of something, and that something might be her. This could be an enemy. She now needed to be in full control of this situation.

Isobel surged through the door without bothering to open it. Trent looked round and came up out of his seat, his face pale with horror, and groped for his gun. But she was on him in a moment, using one of her forward limbs to slap the weapon from his hand with such force that she felt his wrist break. She slammed him back and down, switching off her harness at the same time so she pinned him to the console with her full weight. He struggled underneath her, terrified, shouting, and she froze. She now struggled herself, fighting the urge to begin feeding which was almost agonizing in its intensity. She needed to tell him she wasn't going to kill him, to reassure him, but all that came out of her main mouth was a grinding hiss. This was one aspect of her plan she had neglected.

While he continued to struggle, only exciting that part of her that wanted to tear into him further, her more rational self keyed through to the ship's intercom. She then heaved her weight off him and backed up to the door. He threw himself from the console and glanced once at his gun, which lay on the floor right beside her, then backed up to the other side of the bridge as far away from her as he could get. Trent was looking all around for something he could use as a weapon, seeing nothing and finally, hopelessly, settled into a fighting stance.

Isobel rapidly found numerous recordings of her own voice, from when she had been human, and fed them into a speech program. She struggled to try and connect that to her thought processes, then, realizing it would take at least a few minutes, just selected five words. She strung them together.

"I . . . will . . . not . . . harm . . . you," she said through the intercom.

"Like you didn't harm Gabriel," he spat back.

She kept working the program even as she selected more words.

"One time," she managed. "No . . . deceleration."

She did not have the required vocabulary in her own recorded speech. Not once, in all of it, had she used the words "self" and "control" together. However, as the program began to make the required connections, she did find the second of them and added, "No me control."

"Is there anything of Isobel left in there?" he asked. "You can't even speak."

Still he had not relaxed his fighting stance and he was edging back towards her. She knew precisely how he thought. He supposed his only chance against her would be to get hold of his gun again. Obviously, he had not studied the data aboard this ship on hooders, or he would know that nothing less than a proton cannon could harm her. She felt a surge of irritation with him, facing her like this. Not only was she turning into a hooder, but she could turn him into a smoking smear with just the weapons now attached to her carapace. While continuing to struggle with the language program, she reached down with one of her lower limbs and almost dismissively sent his gun skittering back towards him.

"Kill . . . me . . . then."

The fool didn't hesitate. He threw himself forwards into a roll, snatched up the pulse-gun in his left hand and came back up onto his feet. She resisted the urge to fall on him, and turned her face away. She might be practically invulnerable but really didn't want to lose any of her eyes or fine manipulators since, as she understood it, they could take days to grow back.

Pulse-gun shots stitched their way up her body and then concentrated on the back of her hood. She felt slight impacts followed by warmth that rapidly dissipated. The back of her hood warmed up even more, became noticeably hot, and that heat spread out and down. It was quite pleasurable, in fact. A beep sounded; his gun telling him he had only a few shots left. Isobel let them hit and turned just as he tried a fast reload, but fumbled it because of his broken wrist, dropping both empty and full combined compressed nitrogen and power cartridges to the floor. He was panting, but he didn't try to retrieve the full cartridge. Isobel stared, frozen again, his vulnerability so *tempting*. He broke the spell by reaching up with the barrel of his gun to tap it against that damned earring of his, and now she felt anger, swiftly ramped up by analysis of its cause. Of course, his earring annoyed her now because it was a reminder. The purple sapphire was precisely the same colour as her human eyes, or rather, as they had been.

"Are you done now?" Isobel finally enquired, now her voice synthesizer program was completely connected. "Or would you like to try a few of those neat kicks you learned?"

He just stood there, staring at her, and while he did so she distracted herself by considering how she might glue a portable voice synthesizer to her carapace.

"I'm done," he said, struggling to holster his weapon, then cradling his broken wrist.

"Then go down to medical and get yourself fixed up," she replied. "Spear at least left us an autodoc you can use."

She moved aside from the door and held herself as rigid as she could, though she couldn't stop her facial manipulators reaching yearningly towards him. After a hesitation he moved forwards, stooping to sweep up his gun cartridges before exiting through the door. She read the wariness in his expression but at least there was no disgust there. Gabriel, she surmised, would not have been the same. He had been showing signs of the same xenophobic reaction to her as he had in the past towards prador and shell people. Perhaps this was why she hadn't held back with him, she reasoned. But she also recognized that Gabriel's reaction to her might have been the more sensible one.

She decided the acceleration chair by the console would be a hindrance, dipped her hood low and swept it sideways. The chair tore from its mountings and crashed into the wall of the bridge. Next she rose up over the console to inspect the other ship's image in the laminate screen. Almost as an afterthought, Isobel closed the armoured shutters across the front screen—it might be a ten-inch thick slab of chain-glass, but an energy weapon's flash-through could damage even her. Now she noted the other ship's thrusters were firing, bringing it in closer, so she directed a com-laser at it.

"Hello," she sent, "I'm glad someone's turned up—we were going to have a long journey otherwise." She decided it best not to allow her present image to transmit too.

There was no response, but Isobel was aware of how her ship was being constantly scanned. She targeted the other ship through her sensors, but didn't power up her single railgun. In reality there was no need, since the gun could power up, aim and fire all within milliseconds. Anyway, of all the enemies who might have sought her out here, she couldn't think of one who wouldn't take time to gloat before opening fire. Most likely, such an enemy would want to board and make things personal. Which, as she now was, she would much prefer. It was just rather odd that whoever was aboard that other ship, whether an enemy or otherwise, wasn't talking.

Trent . . .

She hadn't been paying attention. The man had just opened the airlock into the small escape shuttle. Doubtless he hoped to get to that other ship, where he rated his chances of survival as being better. She watched him lug his bag of belongings into the airlock and close the door behind him, then she locked both doors.

"Trent," she said, "I let you shoot at me once to demonstrate the futility of trying to kill me. Now I've allowed you to try and escape to demonstrate the futility of that." This was of course a lie. If he had thought to disable the airlock sensor he would've been gone before she noticed. "Any further foolishness like this and I will terminate our agreement. I leave you to consider the nature of that termination."

She contemplated how delicious that might be.

He started to say something but she cut off the microphone. She would deal with him later. Returning her attention to the bridge screen's viewing laminate, she blinked her rows of eyes, sure some shadow had flickered during her brief distraction. She replayed the last few seconds in her mind. A shadow had briefly coagulated around an external door in the other ship, before shooting across towards the *Moray Firth*. Then it left her field of view.

She checked sensor data but could find nothing, which was odd. Her sensors should have picked up that moving darkness, just as the cam had. That meant her sensors had been compromised, which meant either her ship's system had somehow been penetrated, or someone or something out there was using sophisticated chameleonware. She immediately focused on all doors opening to space, while powering up anti-personnel lasers. Next she ran a scouring program through the lasers, so they ran a firing pattern all around her hull which should hit anything man-sized or above.

"Ouch," said a voice in her mind, and all the lasers shut down.

It was just a silly word, but suddenly Isobel was terrified. She could not even begin to trace where it had come from, or how the lasers had been shut down. She had to be utterly compromised—something had completely penetrated both her ship's computer system and her haiman enhancements.

"Thorvald Spear," said the voice contemplatively.

The *Moray Firth* jerked and shuddered, as if a giant had grabbed it and was shaking it to see what might rattle inside. Next a sound penetrated the hull like the scrabbling of a thousand clawed feet. And following that, clear as could be, she saw a warning icon signalling that the engine section's maintenance door was now standing open.

Isobel swept round, then hesitated. The voice had been bland, but it was one she recognized. Fighting her terror, she headed back out of the bridge. But as she moved down the central corridor, the movement impelled her other part into greater prominence. Terror fled, supplanted by rage and an odd twisted excitement, the emotions of the hunt. She finally reached the airlock into the engine compartment, which was now closed. Again she hesitated. Could she even cram herself into the human-sized airlock? Of course she could—the airlock was made to take two or even three people at a push. What about air? If the maintenance door was open, there would be none in the engine section now. But hooders came from an environment where air was scarce and, though they could die from its lack, they could survive for a long time without it. What could she do? It was Penny Royal . . .

Cursing to herself, she opened the outer airlock door and squeezed inside. The lock then refused to cycle out its air—because, although it could recognize something was inside, it wasn't getting any working space suit readings. She overrode it and, as the air drained, she felt sphincters closing all over her body and something glazing her eyes. She opened the inner door and entered, compressed both physically and mentally like a spring.

This rear section was cylindrical, with all the fuel tanks and other equipment related to the fusion drive to the back. Pipes webbed the inner hull, leading to steering thrusters all around the ship. A fusion reactor squatted nearby, like a huge iron hockey puck caught in a spider's web of pipes and ducts. Above was the sphere containing her second-child ship mind, and in the middle lay the U-space drive. This resembled a huge wine bottle fashioned of polished aluminium, with matt-black radiator fins extending to the walls and electromagnetic projectors jutting to four quarters. It was partially concealed by the black and silver mass shape, stooping over it.

"Hello Isobel," it said, in her mind.

Isobel immediately wanted to launch a physical attack, but managed to suppress the urge as she surged forwards, her human self knowing how suicidal that would be. She drew cross hairs over this figure, but she couldn't fire. Sure, the proton cannon *might* damage the black AI, but it certainly *would* damage the U-space drive, which could well be suicide too. It might be dormant since Spear had knocked out the tuning of its Calabi-Yau frames. However, it still contained torsioned spacial knots which, if they unravelled, might tear apart everything in here, including Isobel.

"What do you want?" she managed.

"A resolution, and a change of course," it replied, suddenly sweeping away from the drive and in the process turning into a shoal of black, sharp-edged fishes. This mass crossed the engine section in a blink, to poise, wavering, directly before Isobel. All instinctive and logical responses froze inside her. She felt herself being inspected, so deeply that nothing could be hidden. Was this how the religious felt, she wondered?

"How does it feel to tear them apart?" Penny Royal asked.

"Damn you," she said and, no longer caring, triggered both her weapons.

The guns did not fire but the very action tripped other relays inside her. All her rage at Spear, at Penny Royal and at any who had crossed her waxed strong and hot. All her sense of loss at no longer being human howled at her from some deep dark well and rose. All the human horror at what had been done to her, and what she had become, yanked hard on the threads of her being. A wave travelled through her from hood to tail and she coiled and collapsed, louse-like, to the deck as if to stop herself flying apart. Then another wave, black and full of knives, fell upon her.

Again? She asked in some part of her being.

I know the original form now, Penny Royal replied.

Visions of alien destruction pursued her into darkness, watched over by something white, pure and utterly lethal.

When she finally recovered her senses it was to the sound, transmitted through the ship, of Trent pleading to be let out, for he had been trapped in the airlock for six hours. She shouldn't have been able to hear him, she thought. Then she realized the maintenance door to the engine section was closed and it had recharged with air. In silence she released him, while in her mind she checked and rechecked a diagnostic test of the U-space engine. It was now fully functional once more. Maybe Penny Royal had come into this system to find its own destroyer or perhaps it sought something aboard that vessel. Why it had then stopped on its way out to repair her U-space engine, she just could not fathom. She had no idea what it had done to her either, to leave spreading patches of grey on her carapace and to turn her red eyes orange. She could only understand the deep and violent grief the AI had left with her, for that was precisely in keeping with all its gifts.

SPEAR

The Golem provided nothing—was a bust as far as obtaining data about Penny Royal. I therefore returned to studying the pyrite storage inside the ammonite fossil, which I had brought aboard. Meanwhile, Flute kept slinging us away from the sun to cool down, before returning to manufacture more railgun missiles. I watched this process sometimes, but mostly ignored it. I only stopped my work for a length of time to observe how Flute mined pitchblende from a belt of dust which ran around the supergiant sun in an orbit as wide as that of Uranus around Sol. When I finally couldn't figure out what was going on and felt an exciting lack of familiarity with the process, I decided to ask.

"I am drawing dust into the ship through a Buzzard hardfield intake," Flute replied.

"And then?" I prompted.

"I sieve the dust of major impurities and then the rest is mixed with water then enzyme refined. Next, uranium-238 is para-magnetically extracted."

"Enzymes—how did you make them?"

"This ship has a stock of them for just this purpose."

Of course: this ship was made to be capable of restocking its armoury, so ensuring a supply of such an enzyme wasn't improbable. This meant that other equipment used in this process would also be aboard.

"What do you do with it next?" I asked.

"I melt the uranium and form it into shaped ingots, these being used to line a separation grid in the neutron fast-saturation chamber, the one adjacent to the fusion reactor. Here it is transmuted into fissile plutonium-239," Flute replied. "Meanwhile, I'm building the bomb mechanism in the ship's weapons assembly chamber. It will contain pressure-metalized hydrogen, a hardfield tetragonal box and a single fifteen-kiloton CTD. The expected blast yield is two hundred and thirty megatons."

I didn't know the mass of Penny Royal's planetoid, but if I could slam this device down through one of the tunnel entrances, I felt sure that—if the planetoid itself didn't fly apart—Penny Royal would be leaving the other entrances as vapour.

"Carry on with the good work," I said, heading back to my own tasks.

When the pyrite crystals in the ammonite were scanned aboard the *Moray Firth*, a few things had been flagged for my attention. However, I just hadn't felt inclined to examine them then. Now, with nothing I could do to hasten my arrival time at Penny Royal's planetoid, I did have time and the inclination. What had been discovered astounded me: the ammonite contained a human mind.

Further examination revealed that it was a stripped-out version of what it *might* have been, when inside someone's skull. Whether it was from a real person, a copy from a real person or an AI-created facsimile was debatable. I then found it became active when I applied some power. It was thinking and in some manner *doing*—then, after a period of time, it switched to an entirely different quantum circuit. After a further period of time—about six hours at the speed it was running and one hour for me—it switched back to its original circuit. I was baffled. I just couldn't see the purpose of this because, upon further observation, when it switched circuits it retained no awareness of what had taken place before. It was thinking and doing but trapped in the same perpetual loop of thought and action.

I tried influencing that loop by injecting random data. Certainly there was an effect, but again, after the switch-over it lost all memory of the previous cycle. In doing this I began to notice how other processes, outside its mental patterns, were influenced. There were reactions to my input, which did change whatever the trapped persona was doing. I had to run Hilbert space calculations to divine this, many of which ran on aug processing exclusive to my own mind. Then the penny dropped . . . to coin a phrase . . .

What I was seeing was a stripped-down human mind, without much of the baggage we all carry but with sufficient capability to function as a human being. It was living in a virtuality loop. Here was a mind trapped in an artificial reality, forever performing the same tasks. Also, from my outside perspective, it seemed one quantum circuit was activated after the other. However, further analysis revealed that to the mind inside they were acting in concert—this apparently related to some weird time crystallization effect. It was one mind interacting with itself. It was time, I felt, to find out what it was actually doing. I wanted to take a look.

Auging through to these circuits was no easy task. I couldn't connect in fully and understand what I was seeing, because I needed to at least identify something recognizable there so I could translate the rest of the programming. I started off by trying to interpret everything that lay outside the mind, or minds—the rules, the dimensions and material. Eventually, after hours of work, I felt I had something and routed data through the hologram projector. A shape appeared, flickering and changing rapidly and sometimes filling up the projection cylinder. This flickering slowed as the program discarded the most unlikely data, became contained in an area as wide as a football, then finally something resolved. It took me a further few seconds to realize I was looking at a pair of ancient wrought-iron pincers, and that their tips were glowing. Subsequently, translating the virtuality became just a matter of brute force computing and soon I was ready to peer inside, and so I did.

The victim hanging by his wrists from the chain was probably moaning in agony. I didn't have audio so I couldn't hear that. However, his body was clearly covered with burns and blood. At that moment the torturer was over by a brazier, heating his pincers and his poker. I took in details, noting objects scattered on the floor below the victim and identified them as toes and fingers. The whole scene was sickening, and yet prosaic—a standard setup you might find in any fantasy or historical virtual game. The torturer turned away from the brazier, raising the glowing poker. This loop was coming to an end, I realized. And, as the torturer walked round behind his victim, I could guess how it ended. I just took a moment longer to confirm that the blood and burns on the victim's face were all that distinguished it from that of the torturer. Then I shut down the feed and, as quickly as I could, shut down the power supply to that particular circle of Hell.

Here was a person constantly reliving the roles of both torturer and victim, yet remembering nothing. What was the point of it? Gazing at the ammonite, I realized that it was just another of the grotesque wrecks Penny Royal left behind. Maybe it was a toy to the AI, maybe it was a prototype.

Or maybe it was something that had been discarded, like one of the scraps virtuality designers edited from their programs. Was this just a piece lying on the cutting room floor? More than anything, it brought home to me the callous brutality of the thing I was hunting.

"Flute," I said. "Are we done here yet?"

"We have everything we need," the mind replied.

"Take us to these coordinates." I sent the shifting coordinates first taken from the ersatz fossil before me. "Get us underway immediately."

No more delays—it was time to fry a black AI.

10

SPEAR

The moment my ship exited U-space, I was at the scanner getting a long-range image of the planetoid. Also, for some very obvious reasons, I had now decided to rename my ship the *Lance*. The rock didn't look like much—just another of the multitude of dark wanderers between stars. But to me, it felt as if I now stood at the gates of Mordor, gazing upon the distant fortress of Barad-dûr. Of course I also felt sure I had been here before. However, the planetoid wasn't visible on the screen fabric all around me, which displayed just the immediate open vacuum and the distant jewelled swathes of stars, so I felt as if I had yet to make any dangerous commitment.

I had all the ship's sensors scanning every band of the EM spectrum it was possible for them to scan. In addition, I had recognition programs running, so any data went into secure storage to be checked for anything dangerous before being shunted into analysis. I'd heard some stories about this place, of ship minds driven mad by signals they'd picked up from here. There were tales of human and prador crews driven to murder each other simply by glimpsing something on screen or hearing something over a speaker. It could all be apocryphal, as was so much about Penny Royal. But, knowing that AI's capabilities, I wasn't going to discount it either.

There was nothing at first, then I began to pick up chatter. After it had gone through checks and filtering, I recognised space suit radios. The communications were coded, but not unbreakably so—in fact they just used an old wartime military code. Flute cracked it within a few minutes, and a minute after that I heard the first words.

"Pull out now! We've got company!" said some woman.

"What do we have in space near to the planetoid?" I asked Flute.

My ship mind drew a small red frame over part of the screen fabric to the left of me and expanded the planetoid to bring it into view there. He was using frames now to highlight things on the screen, but why, I wasn't sure. All I hoped was that the change from a scope-sight to frames was a sign that my ship's mind was no longer thinking quite so much like a prador. A chequered pattern flickered across this larger frame, pausing every now and then to expand images of the objects that accompanied the planetoid on its dark journey. First to appear was a prador in-system kamikaze. This was a huge fusion drive, seemingly jury-rigged to a sphere that had contained the device's mind and world-busting CTD. The sphere had a hole torn in its side to expose a void inside, rather like a mollusc shell where the meat had been stripped out by a predator. Scan readings showed the whole thing was completely dead. Next up was a Polity-designed watch satellite, looted and dead again, with no chameleonware to hide it.

"Both of these have location beacons stuck on them," Flute observed.

"Any indication of the age of the beacons?" I asked.

"None."

They could have been put there at any time, then. Though I guessed that those I was hearing down on the planetoid had placed them, which rather indicated their purpose here.

Thereafter Flute studied a series of asteroids, conglomerations of rubble, dust and technological debris. The latter was so melted and deformed it was hard to tell what it had been previously. Then we paused over an area of empty space for some minutes.

"What's up?" I asked.

"I don't know," said Flute, "there's a strange U-signature at this location but I can't see anything. I suspect something is concealed by chameleonware."

Could that be Penny Royal?

"Target the location with a particle beam," I ordered, then wasn't sure what to do next. If it was Penny Royal I should hit it immediately, without warning and hard, but there might be something or somebody else there who I had no wish to kill. I decided on a half-measure. "Try a com request first and if that doesn't work, fire a ranging laser at it—that should be enough warning. If there's still no response, then beam it."

I sensed the com request going through via my aug, but there was no response. The ranging laser stabbed out next for a full thirty seconds, again without response. Next the particle beam lanced out, a beautiful lethal blue against vacuum, and splashed against a hardfield.

"Cut it," I instructed, "but be ready."

I watched through ship's sensors. Was there something there? Briefly a sphere had appeared—a glassy shimmer around some object. The sphere then winked out and shortly after it the object did the same.

"It just U-jumped," said Flute.

"Location?"

"Unknown—perfectly concealed."

I replayed the sequence of events in my aug and slowed things down. The object had been enclosed in some kind of spherical field—and that couldn't have been a hardfield because that was impossible. I speculated on it being a chain-glass sphere that had decohered before the thing inside jumped, though why one would want to so enclose an object I had no idea. The thing inside had looked like a Tokomak-powered orbital weapon. Perhaps the Polity had placed it here, or perhaps it was one of Penny Royal's toys? I simply had no idea.

"Okay," I said, feeling really uncomfortable with my lack of knowledge. "Keep scanning."

Next up something quite weird appeared, the sight of which immediately dispelled my anxiety about the previous object. Here a large snake floated in vacuum. It resembled a large thick-bodied cobra, but four limbs were folded below the spread of its hood and it had a long thin ovipositor extending from its tail. It was grey and stony-looking because its chame-leonware was out. Staring at it, I felt something tighten up in my chest as I remembered the jungle planet Durana. It was a real memory too, this time—nothing false or doubtful about this.

"Do we have any readings on that?" I asked tightly.

"It is difficult to tell," Flute replied. "There does not seem to be any visible damage to the item so it may be on minimal power. There is a beacon, but it is some distance from the thing and producing a different signal. I can hit it with a railgun round from here."

"Do not fire," I said immediately. Of course Flute's reaction to seeing an object like this had to be somewhat visceral. Not only was he seeing something built in the shape of a lethal and apparently extinct prador parasite, he was also seeing what was quite obviously a Polity assassin drone. But what the hell was it doing here? A number of possibilities occurred to me. During my researches before entering the Graveyard I'd picked up on plenty of other data concerning the war. Many drones like this one had been disenfranchised by the end of conflict and had gone looking for action elsewhere. Perhaps this one had gone looking for trouble with Penny Royal and ended up brain-fried. Another possibility was that it had disavowed the Polity, as a certain number of its kind had. Maybe it had come here to join Penny Royal, or it could be a guardian, ready to power up and come after the unwary.

"Keep a watch on it and if it begins to move then let me know," I said. "Is that everything in near space around the planetoid?"

"Everything that might represent a danger to us," Flute replied. "I have also identified the source of those signals as a ship down on the surface." The frame about the planetoid expanded, pulling its surface into closer view. Then another frame appeared over part of the surface and expanded that in turn, bringing it into focus. Here rested a large ship, a thing like a big white beetle devoid of legs, with a large open framework behind it and behind that a fusion drive. I noted the space-suited figures moving towards the beetle nose from a nearby tunnel—one of the door-ways into Barad-dûr.

"Take us in closer," I instructed Flute, and felt the surge of the fusion engine kicking in. "Put us geostationary above that ship and maintain."

Had someone come to negotiate with the devil? If they had, then it was likely they were unpleasant types just like Isobel Satomi. As we drew closer, the last stragglers boarded the ship down on the surface—this confirmed by someone called Mona as she berated them for their tardiness. However, it didn't launch as the *Lance* drew closer. This Mona, whom I assumed was the captain, probably knew that if I intended to attack, such a move would render them vulnerable.

"Put a com-laser on them—standard Polity com-coding," I instructed.

"You can talk to them on their suit frequency," Flute noted.

"I know I can, but I don't want them to know I can listen in on that." I paused. "Filter out everything but direct communications between me and whoever I end up talking to. Is that understood?"

"Standard hostile contact communications," Flute replied, and I didn't know whether that was from a Polity or a prador war manual.

After a moment another frame opened in the screen fabric, and out of it a heavily built but attractive woman gazed at me suspiciously. "Who are you and what do you want?" I recognized Mona's flat tones at once.

"I might ask the same question of you," I replied, then to my ship mind, "Flute, give me a close-up view of the open framework body of that ship."

The screen fabric image expanded and I could now see objects inside the framework: hockey-puck fusion reactors stacked like coins, coils of s-con cable and skeins of optics. I could also see other less easily identifiable items of hardware. I felt a sudden surge of disappointment which, after a moment, settled leaden inside me.

"We are capable of protecting ourselves," said Mona, and at that moment hardfields flickered on above her ship.

Bravado—by now she had to know that a Polity destroyer was sitting in space above her and, even though it was an old destroyer, she must be aware it outgunned her by an order of magnitude.

"That's a dangerous place to be, down there," I tried.

"Well, it wasn't," she replied.

"Flute, give me a close-up on that nearby tunnel entrance."

The frame swung aside and focused in to show me a couple of grav-sleds beside that dark maw, both loaded down with looted hardware.

It was highly unlikely that if Penny Royal was in residence it would allow salvagers here to tear out the infrastructure. Obviously they'd beacon-marked that space debris for later collection—the kamikaze and observation satellite. But they must have beacon-marked the assassin drone as something to avoid.

"We work for John Hobbs," said Mona.

I had no idea who this was but, by her tone, I assumed he was some sort of big noise in the Graveyard. What should I do now? I had a large fusion bomb specially made for this place and now no one was home.

"I was looking for Penny Royal," I said.

"Then why don't you piss off back to the Polity?" she replied.

"Pretend," I said, "that I am a very stupid person controlling enough armament to turn you and your ship into a hot smear on the rock down there, and tell me Penny Royal's location."

During a pause she spoke over suit radio to some other member of her crew down there.

"What do you reckon?" she asked.

"Some Polity dipshit looking to get screwed by Penny Royal," a man replied.

"A dipshit in a Polity destroyer, mind."

"Yeah, there is that."

"I don't have to pretend you're stupid," she now replied to me. "You haven't done much checking of information sources outside of the Polity, have you?"

"What relevance has that?"

"AIs tell lies," she said.

This wasn't really news to me, since that was something I had learned during the war. Certainly suppression of information about Penny Royal had been frequent. But why now, why lies a hundred years after the fact?

"If you could explain further?" I suggested.

"What should I tell him?" she asked her comrade.

"The truth—I don't suppose he's here after the salvage."

After a long pause she said to me, "Okay, some decades ago Penny Royal got on the wrong side of some alien technology and got smeared. When we heard the news, we came here to see what we could find, but there was still too much signal traffic down here and too much life in automated defence systems. Later, a drone called Amistad came here, put Penny Royal back together and took it off to the planet Masada. There the drone was put in charge and Penny Royal now acts as its enforcer."

I just sat there gaping at her. All my efforts, all the knowledge I had acquired and all the risks I had taken to get this far and . . . nothing. Penny Royal wasn't here. I felt stupid and incredibly frustrated and wanted to scream. I also wanted to reject what she'd just told me, but it was evident the AI wasn't here and why should she lie? The moment passed, then, and I began thinking clearly again.

Now I understood why these events had been suppressed; why I was only learning about them now. Penny Royal was a mass-murderer who, under Polity law, should face obliteration for its crimes. Polity AIs were very firm in their contention that death was the punishment for murder, with no exceptions. They wouldn't want it known that Penny Royal had, apparently, been let off the hook. This confirmed what Sylac had said when he spoke to me in that virtuality before my resurrection—how Polity AIs didn't stick to their own rules about the punishment of murderers. I also realized why it had been so easy for me to get the coordinates of this place from Isobel and why, at the time, I'd felt she was concealing something. She had known Penny Royal wouldn't be here and, understandably, had felt no reason to stop me heading off on a fruitless quest.

"Flute," I said tightly, "take us back out."

As the fusion drive kicked back in I gazed at Mona. "Thank you for your candour."

She looked abruptly relieved as she saw on her instruments that I was pulling out, and now she was curious. "Why did you want to find Penny Royal? For most sane people that AI is one to avoid, and you don't strike me as crazy."

"Vengeance," I replied. "I want to destroy Penny Royal."

"It killed someone you knew?"

"It killed many people I knew," I replied. "I was on Panarchia when it bombed my division out of existence."

"But there were no survivors on Panarchia," she said, puzzled.

I stared at her in annoyance. I hoped that, by the time I returned to the Polity, that historical inaccuracy would have been noticed and corrected, bearing in mind my own resurrection.

"I'll leave you to your salvaging now," I said. "I take it you're avoiding the assassin drone up here?"

"We are—power up something like that and you could find yourself and your crew dead, and your ship in pieces, before it realizes the war is over."

"Very well," I replied, then, "Flute, cut com."

As we slowly pulled away I sat in moody contemplation. With Penny Royal back in the Polity fold, my chances of destroying it had just dropped down a well. Masada was a place I had already researched while gathering data on hooders. When it turned out its gabbleduck species was the devolved descendant of the Atheter, the Polity had become very interested in that world, as the Atheter was one of the supposedly dead ancient races. Its warden, Amistad, had been raised to the status of planetary AI, then for some reason downgraded to a planetary warden. Nevertheless, he was still a war drone. Since his arrival there one of those gabbleducks, by technological means, had un-devolved into a high state of intelligence. I'd also picked up rumours of dangerous Jain technology and, as always when that stuff was around, dracomen were present too. This was not good because the place would be under heavy Polity scrutiny and I had no doubt that some serious military hardware was in the vicinity. It was a bad place to get heavy-handed, and I therefore had a lot of thinking and planning to do, which was why it was madness to say what I said next.

"Flute, that assassin drone out there," I said. "I want you to head over to it and take it in through the rearming hatch."

"Assassin drones are dangerous," Flute observed.

"Hunting black AIs is dangerous too, yet you've made no comment on that." I felt the steering thrusters kicking in to alter our course and, when Flute did not reply, I continued. "The war is over, Flute, you're programmed for loyalty to me, and you're really in no danger from an assassin drone made in the shape of a prador parasite."

Even as I spoke, I wondered why I was doing this. I knew that presuming the drone might contain information relevant to Penny Royal, even if inactive, was a rationalization. My impulse to pick up the drone came from somewhere deeper. The thing looked exactly like the assassin drone that had accompanied Jebel Krong's commando unit on the planet Durana. It might even be the same one. I realized this impulse was some twisted attempt to reclaim my past.

After a long pause Flute replied, "It is an atavistic fear in two respects."

"Two respects?"

"Yes."

I shrugged and left it at that. At least it meant my ship mind was managing to consign the war to history. I now turned my attention to a screen frame, bringing the assassin drone into focus.

The sight of the thing sent a shiver down my spine, and I was no prador. My reaction had more to do with a growing dislike of how every-thing around me felt familiar, which translated into an extreme dislike of coincidences. The thing drew rapidly closer and I could tell by the sounds permeating the ship that the armaments loading hatch had opened. The drone fell out of sight for a moment. Then Flute kindly provided me with an alternative view as it manoeuvred the open hatch towards the drone, brought it in, then the hatch closed. I understood perfectly that this was a dangerous thing to do, but I felt compelled to rescue this comrade—even if it turned out to be just a lifeless metal snake.

A few minutes later it proved it wasn't lifeless at all, as an alarm klaxon sounded throughout the ship. Flute said, "The drone has the fusion bomb."

TRENT

Trent looked along the stilt-houses gathered on the shore, then inland towards the Carapace. It was a suitable name for a place mostly built by shell people, but also occupied by Graveyard faecal scum. They called the place "Carapace City"—a case of optimism over reality, since it was ques-tionable whether the place could even be called a town.

"Well, you're up to your neck in it now, aren't you?" he said to himself.

His boss was in the process of finishing her transformation into a monster. She'd killed and eaten Gabriel. Trent still felt sick about that, and still felt as if he'd dropped into some alternative reality. He'd checked that storeroom and found the remains. There was dried blood on the floor, a few items of internal hardware, some scraps of indigestible clothing and a neat stack of thoroughly chewed bones. He guessed even a hooder couldn't eat bones reinforced with ceramal laminations.

"Fuck it," he said, and kicked something at his feet. The thing rolled away like the stone he'd thought it to be, then sprouted legs and scurried off towards the murky sea and disappeared. "Bollocks," he added.

He'd thought he'd beaten her, that while she was ensconced in that storeroom he'd managed to break her control over the *Moray Firth*. She'd soon shown him otherwise. However, she needed him as a human interface with the world, as a gopher—someone to fetch and carry the things she needed from outside the ship. When he learned this, he decided that on the first opportunity he would run, drop every association with her and ship out. But she had to come here to this shit hole. Still, it would have been manageable, he'd enough funds to buy passage out on another ship down here. But no, she'd thought of that. He reached up and touched the sore point behind his ear.

She'd been quick and firm, grabbing him with her many limbs and closing her hood over him as he went down on the floor. He'd thought that was it; that it was his turn to join Gabriel. But the scalpel manipulator travelled coldly up the side of his face and behind his ear to slice with neat precision. It was like losing one of his main senses when his aug dropped away. Since he'd opened his account with a cortical print, and his bank didn't maintain any more than netlink exchange and a cash machine on this stinking world, he couldn't access it. There was no branch here where, without the aug, he could get the required cortical scan to prove his identity.

Of course, he perfectly understood her actions in relieving him of his aug. And, as his finger travelled to where his purple sapphire had hung, he understood the source of most of his anger. Losing his aug and all that entailed was bad, but why had she taken the jewel too? Did she know what it meant to him and did she know about Genève? By taking that jewel from him, she'd ensured that he wouldn't run, as she held hostage the only thing he really valued. He lowered his hand, remembering his sister and his last days on Coloron, hunting down her killers and making them all pay. He took that jewel from the last of them—the jewel they'd killed her for because it had been a real, documented one. It was valuable and had belonged to their mother, being originally from a mine on Titan. He didn't even know why they'd intended to sell it. Maybe for drugs or augmentation, maybe for passage off that world. That hadn't really mattered.

Trent swore again, then decided this was the last time he'd express his anger or frustration, as he ascended stairs leading up from the shore. He really didn't want to be here or go to Carapace City, but what were his choices? This place was a dead end for many, which accounted for the largest portion of those occupying that city. Last time they'd come here, with Spear, the requests they'd received for passage off-world had numbered in the thousands. He just didn't have the cash to get away, so for now he'd just do Satomi's bidding. Right now, this involved ordering much-needed supplies which, of course, Isobel would pay for when they reached the *Moray Firth*.

Fuel for the fusion reactor, which in turn powered the U-space drive, wasn't a problem. The reactor was an old thing but at least it could run on deuterium, which they refined out of seawater here and sold cheaply. The problem was fuel for the fusion engine and the ship's thrusters. The first was really old and used tritium-encased micro-beads of frozen deuterium. The thrusters, which were positively antique, used nitrogen tetroxide, which would have to be either made by or bought from a retailer in the city.

Reaching the top of the stepped pathway, he could view the city. At the centre sat the Carapace, a dome of beige composite which resembled the carapace of a terran crab more than any prador. Underneath it resided the market, along with more established concerns. It was his ultimate destination but before he reached it, he would have to make his way through the surrounding shanty town, then the inner streets. It was a place where many visitors had disappeared—generally ending up in the market as stock body parts just an hour or so later. He needed transport through there. Pausing, he glanced to his left towards the spaceport. Behind it lay a car park and taxi rank. He could have hired a lift but the charges were astronomical and the chances of being kidnapped or forced into some other money-making scam were high. There was a better option.

Trent turned to the right, following a winding path that led downwards, bracketed on either side by primitive plants like stringy cacti and various ground-hugging bryophytes. At one point, something the size of a man's torso scuttled across the path in front of him and he drew his gun to track its progress. He realized, just as it disappeared into a rocky crevice, that he had just seen a crustacean from the prador home world—a creature bearing some similarity to prador but sitting lower down on the food chain.

Within a few minutes the canal came into sight and he was actually happy to see shell people, a couple of barges and a jetty to which a number of water scooters had been moored. He holstered his weapon as he drew closer, then took a moment to lift his breather mask and check the air, because the bad air here mainly clung around the coast. It still smelled rank but seemed breathable, which he soon confirmed with one of his watch functions—one he hadn't used in all the years since he had auged up. A shellman, not as fully transformed as the one Spear had met, stepped out of a booth as Trent reached the foot of the jetty. This one just looked like a ragged soldier with an organic flak helmet welded to his head. Thorny organic armour had turned his hands into lethal weapons.

"I want to hire a scooter," said Trent snappily.

The shellman eyed him from head to foot, then turned to peer at the canal.

"We've got a reaverfish in," he stated.

Shellmen were easy enough to deal with, just so long as you ignored their alterations and made no stupid references to their worshipful attitude towards the prador. Trent had been about to comment on reaverfish being a prador food item, so surely no problem to those who aped the prador, but clamped down on that. Reaverfish grew larger than the Earth's great white shark, possessed an excess of sharp fins and had tongues that protruded like a sawfish's nose. They were also far nastier than the great white shark. Moreover, if one of these things attacked you, it wasn't making a mistake.

"I've got a gun," he replied, now trying to keep his voice level. "And reaverfish can die just like anything else." He was thoroughly aware that he wasn't in a good mood and that when he was like this he often became provocative. Really, he didn't need any more trouble than he was already in.

The shellman turned to study him again. "One zil of diamond slate then—and you get ninety-eight muzil back if you return the scooter before this time tomorrow."

It was expensive but nowhere near as much as a taxi driver would have charged. It also meant he'd be completely in control of his own transport and the canal would take him right through into the dome.

"Two muzil a day," he stated.

The shellman shook his head. "Escalating scale of one muzil extra a day, unless you want to contract for a longer period."

"I'll pay you eight muzil for five days," said Trent, and smiled through gritted teeth. "Non-refundable if I return before then."

The shellman pretended to consider that carefully. But it was noticeable that he had six scooters available, and that there weren't any empty places at the short jetty.

"Very well." He returned to his booth. As he did so, Trent turned away to open the screamer pouch at his belt, extracting four small, flat, hexagonal crystals of diamond slate. The man returned with the scooter's ID key and held it up until Trent handed over the crystal. As Trent closed his finger and thumb on the key's tab, it read his fingerprints and DNA—no one else would be using this key for the next five days. The keys could be reprogrammed and the scooter could be stolen, but this little bit of security would deter the casual thief. Also the scum here tended to avoid stealing from the shell people. Their community was tight knit and they came down hard on outsiders who stepped out of line.

"Here." The shellman led him over to one of the water scooters, but then paused to point back down the canal towards the sea. "And there's the reaverfish."

Something big was swimming towards them, its main body was submerged but an arc of fins jagged up out of the water like the wings of diving gannets, with a double-finned tail carving from side to side about ten feet behind.

"What weapon?" asked the shellman, indicating the fish.

Trent pulled aside his coat to expose his pulse-gun. The shellman appeared doubtful about this, so Trent pulled his coat round further to expose a series of cylinders on his belt, and the man dipped his head respectfully. This was all a bit overcautious, since the damned fish was unlikely to be able to catch a water scooter.

Keeping an eye on the approaching predator, Trent stepped out onto the scooter and mounted it, inserted the key and fired it up. He felt the water-tractor begin humming underneath his seat, and cruised out into the centre of the canal to head towards the city. Glancing back, he saw the reaverfish was a lot closer than expected, its double-finned tail whipping back and forth to create more of a wake than the scooter itself. He accelerated and realized that he wasn't getting ahead of the thing, so wound the throttle right back to its stop.

"Persistent fucker, aren't you," he said, drawing his pulse-gun.

He aimed carefully and fired, but the jolting of the scooter sent his shot into the water to the left of the fish, kicking up a cloud of steam. He swore, studied the controls on the body of the gun and turned on gyro laser sighting. Now he put a blue spot on a point just back from the fish's bow wave, clicked on the gyro and the gun came alive in his hand as it tried to keep itself aimed at that point. He fired twice and the fish thrashed, briefly raising its head out of the water and shaking like a dog smacked on the nose. He grinned, but lost it when the scooter hit the edge of the canal and bounced away, nearly flinging him from his seat. Finally managing to wrestle the vehicle to the centre of the canal, he looked back at a raised shark-like head. The reaverfish opened its mouth to expose plenty of black pointy teeth, then its lower jaw split along a vertical slit to expose even more. It protruded its chainsaw tongue from this particular opening.

"Will you fuck off!" Trent shouted, accelerating again.

The fish surged forwards, its tongue scoring the back of the scooter and clipping his leg, its mouth trying to get a grip on the scooter's tail section and coming away with a chunk of cowling. It fell behind, obviously baffled by this, shook its head to expel a twisted sheet of bubble-metal, then came on again. Trent stared with disbelief at his leg. It had torn his trousers and now blood was welling. Turning angrily, he fired again, but the gyro nearly tugged the gun from his hand, it now having acquired a target somewhere up in the sky. He holstered it and concentrated on his driving, going as fast as he could through a series of bends in the canal, then opening the scooter up as it straightened out. Now there were dilapidated buildings on either side of the canal and shellmen and other disreputable characters were looking on.

Trent concentrated on his navigation, going as fast as he could while avoiding barges and protruding rigs. The light changed and his concentration was so intense that he only realized he'd entered the Carapace as the waterway opened out ahead. The terran hue was from sun-plates set in a ceiling high above. He was now entering a small lake with vessels drawn up all around its perimeter. Behind these was a chaotic panoply of tall buildings, multi-level streets and market stalls, all swarming with humanity. Now on open water he accelerated once more, pulling away from the fish which he'd either hurt or had tired in the chase. Near the end of the lake, he turned his scooter, bringing it to a halt to face the approaching reaverfish. He could have headed for the edge, dismounted and been away with no problem. However, he needed this—he wanted to feel effectual again.

"Right, you fucker," he said, and accelerated towards it.

ISOBEL

The idiot, thought Isobel, as she viewed the scene. Trent's antics showed up in the laminate above her chain-glass screen, projected by the numerous pin cams she'd attached to his clothing when she removed his aug, and the silly keepsake of his sister. What had she told him? Just make a few low-key enquiries to see if traders there had what she required.

Don't draw attention to yourself—because if you do people like Stolman in the local mafia will start taking an interest. However, she recognized Trent's impulse and understood it to the core of her being. He had probably been driven a bit stir crazy, trapped aboard the *Moray Firth* for so long, and had felt the need for some action. She too felt the need for it, though this didn't stem from boredom, but the perpetual nag of what she was becoming. In fact, if he did get into trouble she knew she'd be glad of it. She could then accede to her own impulses and have an excuse to leave her ship, to hunt and to kill. Meanwhile, however, she had to suppress her urges and attend to other business.

While the U-space drive was out she'd been unable to use her U-space communicator, their tech being integrated. And even when the drive was operating again, it had still been impossible to use it. The communicator was old design and, unlike newer models, couldn't operate from within that continuum. Now, time to get things organized.

Isobel put out a call and waited. U-space communication was supposed to be instantaneous but that was a lie. In reality the connection time was constrained by the amount of power you wanted to use, by U-space oddities between points A and B in a continuum where distance was supposed to be meaningless and, of course, by how long it took whoever she was calling to answer. After eight tedious minutes, a tone sounded and an icon blinked up in the laminate. She mentally opened it to see who she was speaking to but, for the moment, did not allow her own image to transmit.

"Morgan," she said to the beefy, bald and heavily scarred individual who appeared.

"Isobel," he replied, dipping his head in acknowledgement.

She studied him for a moment. He could easily have corrected the deep scar that ran from his forehead across his right eye, transecting his nose to end in a lump on his top lip. His mismatched eyes—one blue and the other brown—could've been corrected too. As could all the other dents and hollows on his face and the mottled pink and grey of his skin. He could, should he so wish, look like an Adonis. However, he was a man who enjoyed the shock of his brutal ugliness just as he enjoyed the brutality of his trade. He was her chief of coring and thralling. He was someone who enjoyed inflicting pain and horror and so was perfectly suited to his role. He would also be the one, she felt, who could more easily accept her current appearance.

"Morgan," she continued. "I am now going to let you see me since you, and others you select, will need to know what I now look like." She considered delivering some sort of warning, but instead allowed her image through.

Morgan jerked back from his screen, his mouth dropping open, then shook himself and leaned forwards again.

"Gruesome," he said admiringly, then grinned horribly. "You're going all the way?"

Isobel considered that for a second. Her transformation into a hooder had been continuing apace, but now, since Penny Royal's recent intervention, that change itself had taken a different path. The grey patches were now regularly distributed—at her joints, at the tips of her limbs and at the rooted sides of her plates of carapace. They were spreading too, like the effect of heat discoloration in metal, leaving ivory white behind them. Studying this effect at a nanoscopic level, Isobel had found deep changes involving s-con threads and laminations of fullerene and other materials. Her carapace was growing even stronger than its already extreme hooder invulnerability. As for her eyes, which were turning lemon yellow, the changes there were due to genetic changes in a photo-luminescent bacteria living inside; she could not fathom their purpose. Of course Morgan saw none of that—he just saw the monster.

"Not out of choice—that's out of my hands," she said, briefly contemplating how that second phrase no longer applied to her. "However, don't ever be fooled into thinking I am in any way crippled by this form or that my mental faculties have been damaged. I am in fact so much more capable than I was before."

Truth there and lies. She was very capable now, but perpetually having to fight for rationality.

"Okay, Isobel." He nodded. "What do you want?"

"What is the status of our latest cargoes?" she asked.

"The *Glory* is on its way but the *Nasturtium* is still in orbit here. I'm aboard and we're still waiting on the next load from the warehouse."

"What about the *Caligula*?"

"In space dock and ready to blow out a few cobwebs."

"Very well, I'm sending you some coordinates. I want you to head straight there once you've prepared, even if the rest of your cargo hasn't arrived."

"No delivery?"

"No, our clients in the Kingdom will have to wait a while—I have more pressing business. I want the *Caligula* fully armed, with a full complement of our troops aboard. I also want you to bring the planetary cache of CTDs . . . in fact, look upon this as a war footing and bring everything you think necessary."

"Wow," he said. "Something nasty?"

"You're damned right. Don't let me down." It had taken another internal battle to come here, rather than head straight for the planetoid. The hooder in her wanted to go directly after Spear, but the more logical human part of her mind had to accept certain realities. Firstly she was low on fuel and secondly, because he now controlled a Polity destroyer, Spear was a dangerous prey indeed.

"As you say, Isobel," said Morgan.

She cut the transmission and returned her attention to Trent.

FATHER-CAPTAIN SVERL

Father-Captain Sverl grated his prosthetic ceramal mandibles together, raised his great soft bulbous body up on his prosthetic ceramal legs and made a groaning sound beyond the vocal apparatus of any other prador. His first-child Bsorol backed away, still expecting a blow that hadn't come in many decades. Bsorol was ancient now too, his carapace knotted with strange whorls and outgrowths and his leg segments bent through a hundred years of artificially maintained adolescence.

"Leave now," Sverl clattered.

The first-child turned and headed for the sanctum door, which ground open to reveal Bsorol's two assistants—prador that had once been second-children. Like the other twenty-two aboard this submerged dreadnought, they were now just a spit away from being first-children, but for their own distortions and prosthetic replacements for body parts that would not grow back—the growth retardant effecting them all differently.

As the diagonally split sanctum doors closed, Sverl considered his options. Bsorol, who had been analysing Polity data traffic for the best part of a century, had informed him that Penny Royal was back in the Graveyard. The rogue AI had somehow come to terms with the Polity AIs. Did this mean that Sverl could drag himself from his hideaway under the sea, leaving the Rock Pool to exact vengeance? Was vengeance still what he wanted?

Sverl's war had been a hard one. He had lost two of his capital ships to the Polity, he had come close to dying when his own ship had been hit and he'd spent years recovering from radiation burns that had left him infertile. On his subsequent return to the war, during a simple mission while he accustomed himself to controlling a dreadnought, a Polity assassin drone had boarded his ship. It infected him with parasitic worms that nearly killed him again. He had to exterminate his own children to root out the infection on board—Bsorol and his other children were the last of his family, retrieved from the prador home world later in the war. Then he lost half his body mass to long and agonizing surgical procedures to remove the parasites. After that he received demotions when temporary insanity drove him to attack and destroy two rivals, thus undermining the war effort. The final insult came when he was made an outcast, this upon refusing a summons to return to the Kingdom when the new king decided to terminate the war.

Sverl bubbled anxiety and annoyance as he went over to his array of hexagonal screens and inserted one claw into a pit control.

He just hadn't been able to return. He had invested and lost too much, suffered too much to obey the one who had called a halt to the war. He had never been able to accept that the war was over for him, as his hatred of the human race and its machines went too deep. Or that's what he had thought then—so he'd remained in this borderland, this Graveyard.

The screens all came on, showing various views of the Rock Pool's human community. Many of the humans had such a dislike of their own original form that they were distorting and changing it, and how Sverl envied them their choice. He then switched to two particular views he had put in place for his study of human crime, but his heart wasn't in it, his mind still ranging into memory.

Years passed before he heard rumours of the black AI, the rogue creation of the Polity. It gave him some satisfaction to know that there was something out there that terrified even the Polity's most lethal AIs, and he took an interest, gathered data. He soon learned that this Penny Royal was adept in technologies unavailable even in the Polity. It could transform beings, grant wishes and might be able to provide Sverl himself the means to realize his greatest wish. He needed to understand why weak fleshy beings and atrocious constructed intelligences had held against prador might. How had it been possible for them to turn the tide of the war, before the new king simply gave up? However, Graveyard gossip had it that Penny Royal's gifts were poisonous and the technologies and transformations it provided could turn round to bite the recipient.

Sverl hadn't believed that for a moment, not then.

Investigating the claims, he had found more rumour than truth and recognized this as Polity propaganda. Of course Polity AIs wouldn't want it known that a being more powerful than them existed and was willing to provide for their enemies. Almost certainly those same AIs had started the rumour mills. They had built up a mythos around this Penny Royal, causing those who might have sought it out to avoid it. They had created a legend, something like that of the prador Golgoloth—frightening tales to scare children. And Sverl had considered himself no child.

Sverl withdrew his claw and the screens automatically shut down. He turned to gaze at the masses of equipment, terrariums and tanks occupying his sanctum, still undecided about what to do next. In retrospect, he realized his hate of the Polity had distorted his reasoning all those years ago. That his mind had been damaged throughout the war exacerbated this. He'd been selective about which Penny Royal stories he'd chosen to believe, listening to tales of those who had gained precisely what they wanted. He'd also been supremely arrogant, as all father-captains were, sure that if there were any catches in a transaction he'd be sure to see them. Thus he had chased down rumour and then firm data. He found the location of Penny Royal's wanderer planetoid, and went there.

Sverl shuddered to remember his state of mind back then. He'd resolved to demand the means to understand the success of humanity and its AIs. He would take that knowledge to the Kingdom and contact those dissatisfied with the new regime. He'd next gather forces around him and usurp the new king, then lead the prador to slaughter humanity, as was their right and their destiny. And so he'd gone to confront Penny Royal in its burrows, while a fortune in diamond slate was unloaded from his shuttle above. He'd deluded himself that the flower of black knives he found was only a *being*, conveniently forgetting that it was also a hated Polity artificial intelligence.

In a maelstrom of pain, madness and expanding mental horizons, Penny Royal transformed Sverl. Afterwards, the father-captain climbed to the surface on new prosthetic limbs rather than grav-engines and hardfield repulsion. He definitely felt much more intelligent and potent. And certainly he was more personally dangerous, as Penny Royal had also provided him with a lethal Golem which Sverl now controlled with a thrall unit. He also quickly began to understand more about the war and why it had gone the way it had. He became aware of the aggressive prador society's drawbacks, which included its avoidance of employing artificial intelligence. But still, though he understood specific details, a general understanding of the Polity lay beyond him. He felt, at that time, that some deep contemplation would be required, for he had yet to grow fully into his greatly expanded mental horizons.

Before even the shell people came, Sverl landed his dreadnought deep in the ocean of the world they subsequently named the Rock Pool. Other dispossessed prador joined him there and began building their underwater city. Trade was established with still other prador enclaves throughout the Graveyard. When the shell people arrived and began their strange physical worship of Sverl's kind, the immediate instinct of his fellow renegades was to exterminate them. However, that basic paradigm-changing understanding of the Polity still eluded Sverl, and he persuaded them to leave the humans alone. For perhaps they might help him towards the greater understanding he sought. He allowed them to establish and he studied them.

Throughout this time, Sverl also studied himself. Firstly, he noted the extra organic growths and crystal extensions from his major ganglion and recognized them as the source of his extended intelligence. But he did not then understand precisely what they meant. Over time he noted his body's gradual physical changes and, running intermittent tests of his genome, he discovered that it too was changing. Investigating further, he found picoscopic processes driving the change, but could not discern what was driving *them*. Only in recent years, with equipment purchased from the Polity, had he discovered underlying femtoscopic processes. He had understood less than one per cent of these. In the end, only his gross physical changes had revealed the truth.

As his visual turret sank into his main body it also spread, drawing his two eye-palps further apart while they shortened. Eventually they disappeared altogether, those eyes then residing in two pits to the fore of his carapace. The vision in his other turret eyes also started to fade. His mandibles, being fashioned of hard metal, remained unchanged. But these sank lower on his carapace while his mouth widened, a split developing from each side and working its way backwards. Doubtless, if he had still possessed manipulatory limbs beneath him, they would either have shrunk or dropped away. To his rear, he sprouted a fleshy tail which, under examination, he found to contain developing vertebrae. All this remained a mystery to Sverl, until a sickening revelation occurred to him when he was studying the shell people above.

While the shell people were humans trying to transform themselves into prador, he was a prador unwillingly being transformed into a joke of a human being. His whole carapace was taking on the shape of a human skull and it was softening, while that horrible and baffling tail was the rest of that disgusting soft creature. He surgically removed it but, over agonizing months, it grew back again. Meanwhile, small delicate white teeth sprouted inside his mouth and his eyes acquired pink fleshy lids that sprouted lashes. At the same time, when he wanted to listen closely to something, he found himself raising his front two pairs of forelegs off the ground—because they were developing nerve connections to his auditory system.

The method of transformation was darkly and grotesquely humorous, in a way Sverl would never have understood as a prador. But there was more, much more. On one level, he seemed to be developing into the organic or human aspect of the enemy, while in his major ganglion he grew nubs of human brain tissue. Understanding this made him realize something he had missed in the decades since his initial transformation. The crystal extensions of his organic brain were, in themselves, *artificial intelligence*. Penny Royal had given him the ability to understand the enemy, by turning him into *both* its aspects. He was an amalgam of prador, human and AI. And in the years to come, he felt sure that the first of those would eventually disappear.

As his AI and human components steadily grew, his anger and hatred faded, while large questions expanded in his mind. His need to understand an enemy changed, slowly transforming into a need simply to understand.

PENNY ROYAL'S PLANETOID

Mona drew her scooter to a halt in a long straight tunnel which speared into darkness for five miles in either direction. It was three metres across and perfectly circular through its length. She dismounted and walked over to its curved wall, and reached out to touch the smooth, almost polished stone with one hand. Her glove sensors detected the complete lack of faults beneath her fingertips. Still no answer to the puzzle that had been bothering her ever since they came here for salvage: where were the machines or the machine that did this? Part of the puzzle had been solved—they now knew why there was no rocky debris, the by-products of a boring machine. The stone around these tunnels was denser than elsewhere in the crust—any debris had been shoved aside and melded into the surrounding stone. Appalling amounts of energy must have been involved, yet there was no sign of the incredible machine that had created the tunnels. However, there were thousands of miles of caves worming through the crust of the planetoid and Mona knew she stood no chance of exploring them all.

Dropping her hand, she returned to the scooter, turned it round and began heading back. It might be that there just wasn't a machine or, rather, that the machine concerned was Penny Royal itself. If that was the case then the implications were frightening. The black AI was terrifying enough, but if it could manipulate matter on this scale itself . . . Mona shook her head. No, that couldn't be right. There had to be machines somewhere, or the figures just didn't add up. Penny Royal couldn't have done this alone over the sixty or so years it had occupied this place. The task would have required a hundred Penny Royals, or some vast iteration of the black AI no one had ever seen. The thought sent a shiver down her spine.

"Mona," Gareth interrupted her thoughts over com, "we've got another visitor."

"Another visitor?" she asked, accelerating.

"Yeah, I recognize this ship—it's *The Rose*."

"What the hell is Blite doing here?" she wondered. "Last I heard he was smuggling tech artefacts in the Polity." She paused as she turned into a side tunnel leading to the place they'd dubbed the "Atrium." This was a large spherical chamber with a flat gridded floor only a few hundred metres back from the entrance they were using and just beyond that lay their ship. "Don't answer that—if he's here then it's probably for the same reason as us."

"He's welcome," said Gareth. "We're all but done with this place."

True, they were done with it now, because they had a full load to haul back. This was heading to Montmartre for John Hobbs' salvage organization to process. But in reality they hadn't delved very deeply into this place at all. She was sure there was a lot more to discover here, technological treasures to be revealed. Unfortunately she would not be the only one thinking that—other salvagers would arrive as the news spread that Penny Royal was no longer in residence. Blite was probably just the first of many. But at least he wasn't the kind who'd resort to piracy and leave them trying to breathe vacuum. Mona had no doubt that Isobel Satomi, with her special problem, would be taking an interest. It was also quite possible that her ultimate boss, with his similar special problem, would take an interest too. Mona felt slightly sick at the thought of ever encountering Mr Pace.

She drove into the Atrium, the scooter's fibre-rod wheels absorbing any juddering from the floor grate. Ahead she could see some of her crew loading their last two grav-sleds. One now held white oblate spheres, packed with technology they hadn't been able to identify. The other one contained five skeletal Golem. The Golem would have been almost valueless, were it not for the fact that Hobbs had found a buyer in the Polity. Apparently, a forensic AI wanted to examine them and would pay in diamond slate.

Mona dismounted and headed towards the exit tunnel.

"What's *The Rose*'s position right now?" she asked over com.

"Same as that destroyer—sitting right above us."

"Any communication?"

"Blite wants to talk to you. Shall I patch him through?"

"Yeah, go ahead."

A screen image opened in the lower right-hand quadrant of her space suit visor to show the familiar face of Captain Blite. She thought he looked tired, a bit worried and thinner than he had been the last time she saw him.

"Hello, Mona," he said. "Long time no see."

"So it is," she replied, "and before you waste your time: no, I'm not going to negotiate search territories, nor am I going to provide you with any data. If you want data on this place you'd better make a deal with John Hobbs. We're done here—for now, anyway—and we're on our way out."

He dipped his head in acknowledgement then said, "I'm not here for the salvage."

Mona immediately auged open a private channel and, blocking transmission to Blite, spoke to Gareth in her ship. "You heard that?"

"I did," Gareth replied, "I've put up hardfields and the cannon is online."

"So what are you here for?" she asked Blite. "I do hope you haven't branched out."

It wasn't uncommon for some salvagers to go rogue and resort to piracy, though Blite had never seemed that sort.

"It's not a case of what I'm here for," he replied. "I have a passenger who, as far as I can gather, wants information on any recent visitors here. I did tell it I would ask, but it's on its way down to you anyway."

It's on its way down to you?

"Mona," said Gareth privately, "the hardfields just went down and the cannon went offline."

Mona spoke to the four crew still working in the Atrium. "Get these sleds to the cargo cage—now!"

"Oh shit," said Tanner.

"What is it?" She headed over to where he and Iona were standing. They were staring at the sled where they'd stacked the Golem—and his comment made perfect sense when she took a look herself. The five skeletal Golem had been loaded like logs and were piled to the rear of the sled. They were now slowly extricating themselves—the one on top of the pile lowering a foot to the sled as it began to climb off. Five polished ceramal skulls were now raised, curiously scanning their surroundings with darkly glowing blue eyes.

"Who's your passenger, Blite?" Mona asked.

"There's something in the cargo cage," Gareth interrupted, overriding Blite's reply.

"What?" she asked.

"I don't know—the cams just went out and some objects there were briefly activated."

Over suit com Mona said, "Everyone, back to the ship now! Fast as you can!"

The four crew didn't need to hear the order again and immediately ran for the exit in painfully slow low-grav motion. Mona ran for her scooter, mounted and started it up, turning it towards the exit. She saw the four head out of sight, then heard Iona scream and Tanner's cursing, terror in his voice. Mona stopped her scooter and considered heading back into the tunnel system and thence to one of the other exits. The nearest was twenty-eight miles away. But in the end she'd have to return to her ship . . . She paused and now auged in Blite's reply to her question.

"I'd like to tell you that there's nothing to fear. But even though me and my crew haven't really been harmed, I don't know how long that will last," he'd said, looking somewhat guilty. "I'd like to help you get away from here in one piece, but there's no advice I can give. We are all powerless."

A darkness filled the exit tunnel—a darkness full of knives. The Golem had all climbed from the grav-sled and were now standing in a neat row like troops ready for review. A shoal of sharp obsidian fish flowed into the Atrium, seemingly all connected to a spread of silver threads. These threads then drew the shoal together and the whole mass coagulated into one black irregular lump. This began growing spines, the well-known form of Penny Royal expanding and rising from the floor on a silver trunk.

Mona watched her visor screen dissolve into static and weird code begin running on the heads-up display. Something then engaged with her aug with an almost audible clunk. Events began a perfect replay in her mind, accurately recalled in a way that was alien to human memory. She felt every detail of her brief exchange with Thorvald Spear inspected thoroughly.

So this is how I die, she thought.

Something vicious arose to respond, and something else, cold and immense, inspected that briefly, before closing it down.

11

TRENT

As he headed straight towards the reaverfish, Trent drew his pulse-gun. He suddenly felt foolish doing this, especially when he heard shouts and cat-calls from the surrounding jetties and docks. But he decided to carry it through and, as he drew closer, the fish raised its head out of the water. Trent took this as a challenge and responded by accelerating even more. The thing withdrew its tongue and slammed closed its tri-section mouth, lowered its protruding fins, and dived.

Damn.

Trent wound the throttle forwards and swerved round, kicking up a huge explosion of spray. He then accelerated away from where the monster had gone under, spotting a dark shadow coming up beside him. He swerved again as the thing exploded from the water, and snapped off half his clip into its massive green-grey body. It came down with a huge splash, the wash throwing his scooter over at an angle, and turned towards him—mouth gaping and tongue shooting in and out. Two things impinged at once: a big blood-red eye gazing right at him, and the edge of a floating jetty coming up fast. He fired the rest of his clip into that eye then slammed the scooter back over, wrenching the handlebars round.

In the next moment, he found himself travelling upside down through the air for a second before hitting the water.

White water swamped him for a moment, then he surfaced, immediately loading another clip and quite proud that he'd managed to hang onto it. He kicked water and scanned around for the fish, but saw only the scooter bob to the surface and right itself with its gyros. He turned towards the nearby jetty, and saw the fish there. It was half up out of the water, its weight tilting the jetty, jerking occasionally and flapping its fins. A great green chunk was missing from the bloody prow of its skull.

Gotcha, he thought—glad to have been dunked like this since he'd pissed his pants.

From the foot of the jetty, a mixed group of shellmen and regular humans were making their way out, the lead figure carrying a coil of rope and a grappling hook. As Trent kicked water, he thought these might be for him. But when the crowd reached the reaverfish, a shellman jammed the grapnel in behind its head, then the whole group hauled it fully out of the water. More people were flooding onto the jetty too, carrying various edged implements, baskets and bags. Of course, such a creature was a huge source of food and starvation wasn't uncommon here. He snorted to himself, holstered his weapon and stroked out to his scooter, whose engine was still ticking over. Mounting, he brought it in on the other side of the jetty, which was practically half-sunk now, shut it down and unwound the mooring cable. Someone took the loop from him and dropped it over a bollard, then reached over to help him across. Only when he was off the scooter did he recognize the person standing before him and realize his danger. Instead of him seeking out traders, the mafia had come to him.

"Impressive," said a tall white-faced individual, the rapidly growing space in the crowd revealing a skeletal Golem behind him.

Trent gaped at the thing. Its polished bones were enamelled with colourful geometric patterns, so it looked like an artefact from some Mayan tomb. The thing was bigger than normal, possessing heavy joint motors and unfamiliar reinforcing along its limbs. Other almost organic-looking technologies further bulked it out. This gave it the appearance of a giant of a man who'd been skinned, rather than a silvered Golem skeleton.

Trent began reaching for his weapon but the Golem moved so fast the air snapped around it. Beside him in a moment, it clamped a skeletal hand about his wrist. In his ear it whispered, "Tush."

"I don't think so," said the man, briefly giving the Golem a worried look.

Trent heaved against the grip but he might as well have fought a docking clamp. He found the situation puzzling. Why was a Golem accompanying a local mafia lord? The androids were generally moral creatures, adhering to the spirit if not the letter of Polity law even when they were outside the Polity, so how come one of them was here with Stolman? He was definitely up to his neck in just about every crime in the book. In fact, the only reason Trent and Isobel knew about him was because he'd supplied captives for coring. He'd even purchased some back to sell to the prador here. The only Golem that would willingly work for someone like him was a broken Golem, but they were a rarity and notoriously unstable—often as dangerous to their master as to their master's enemies. But then, skin crawling, Trent remembered another kind of Golem inhabited the Graveyard. Those belonging to Penny Royal.

They could be found scattered about the Graveyard in concealed bunkers, in private collections, or just dumped somewhere awaiting discovery. Trent even knew of one sitting in a drinking den as a bar ornament, aboard the space station Montmartre. They had little value beyond that of scrap, because they couldn't be activated. Generally people kept well away from them because, on the rare occasions they did activate, it meant Penny Royal was near and bloodshed would ensue. Either Stolman had found a way around the activation problem or the black AI was here. Neither option boded well.

Trent glanced at the surrounding crowd. Most of the people here were intent on dismembering the reaverfish—great dripping green chunks already filling baskets and bags. Its fins had been severed and stabbed like kebabs on a long glass spear. Those that were watching the interplay between him and Stolman were obviously interested but wary and showed no signs of intervening. It wasn't a good idea to get on the bad side of someone like Stolman. Should Trent shout for help?

Should he ask for favours since he had landed their supper for them? No. The Golem could easily depopulate this jetty in just minutes. Also, did he want to escape?

"Come with us," said Stolman, gesturing peremptorily.

The Golem pulled Trent further onto the jetty, then propelled him towards its rear, releasing him in the process. His gun hand now free, Trent hesitated until a skeletal hand rested on his shoulder. He turned and gazed into gleaming dark blue eyes devoid of pupils, and shuddered.

"Try anything," said Stolman, "and it'll rip the skin off your back."

Trent tapped the butt of his weapon regretfully and continued.

"Over there," said Stolman, pointing to clusters of tables and chairs scattered before one of the waterfront bars. "We'll take a drink and have a little chat."

Trent shrugged. Were Stolman and his Golem any more of a danger to him than Isobel? In fact, if he played this right, Stolman might even be his way out of here. He headed over, pulled out a chair and sat down, folding his arms. Stolman sat opposite him. Trent's back felt itchy with the Golem standing so close behind. He stabbed a thumb back at him.

"Penny Royal's?" he asked.

"It was," said Stolman, "but now it's mine." He smiled cadaverously. "We finally managed to activate it a few months ago."

Trent dipped his head in acknowledgement, but wondered if that was quite true. Isobel had told him about her visitor, and the repairs to the U-space drive confirmed its identity. This Golem might just have activated due to Penny Royal's presence in this sector of space—Trent had no idea how close the AI needed to be to set them in motion.

"So," said Stolman, "tell me what Isobel Satomi is doing here."

"Why would you want to know?" asked Trent. "You should understand that taking too much of an interest in her affairs might be dangerous."

"Not quite so dangerous now." Stolman indicated with a nod to the Golem behind Trent. "But I'm only asking if there's some way I might be of help."

Trent closed his eyes for a second and took a slow breath. So, Stolman had inadvertently activated a Penny Royal Golem and now he thought he had the power to play in Satomi's toy room. But there might be even more to this. Did Stolman think he could take her on? The question then was if he was right. If Stolman had gone up against her in one of her strong-holds, she would have annihilated him, but right now she was isolated. Was Trent's best option to throw in with Stolman? He couldn't decide. The Golem here might be obeying the man, but there was no telling how long that would last. Nevertheless, Stolman undoubtedly had other resources too and with the Golem might be able to take the *Moray Firth*. If it was just Isobel as she had once been aboard the ship, before her further transformation, Trent reckoned Stolman's chances would've been high. But just how lethal was Isobel's new form? Could she, in that form and armed with a proton cannon, take a Golem down? And how long would it be before her reinforcements arrived? Isobel would surely now be talking to others in her organization, summoning resources to pursue her new goal of vengeance against Spear.

"I imagine that if she'd wanted your help she would've asked," Trent replied, now scanning his surroundings. He noted various mean-looking individuals casually placed about the area—more of Stolman's people, no doubt. "Y'know," Trent continued, "Isobel hasn't expanded her operation for a while because of what Penny Royal did to her—she's been looking for a solution. However, the last contender for her crown ended up in a prador meat farm."

Stolman shrugged. "So what? I'm just interested in how I can help."

"No," said Trent. "Like just about everyone trapped on this damned hole you're interested in the *Moray Firth*. What are you planning, Stolman?"

"I understand," the man replied smoothly, "that she has been making enquiries about various kinds of fuels. It occurs to me that she's stuck here until she can get hold of them."

By now the bar owner had realized people were actually sitting at one of his tables and had come shuffling over. In keeping with the retro feel of the place, he wore a stained apron over clothing that must have been copied from some historical catalogue. He even held a paper pad and pencil in his hand. He also looked frightened—shooting glances at the Golem as he walked over to stand obsequiously beside Stolman, pencil poised.

"What you got?" Stolman asked.

"Reaverfish on the menu today, Mr Stolman, sir."

"I'm not hungry. Got any beer?"

"Snapper and Amstel, sir."

It struck Trent that if he walked into a bar in the Prador Kingdom, he'd probably find Amstel there.

"Snapper's a local brew," Stolman informed Trent. "The shellmen make it and it's surprisingly good."

"Really?" said Trent, sure now that the man was glad of the interruption, and deliberately delaying getting to the point.

"We'll try that." Stolman tilted his head to one side, still gazing at Trent. "That okay with you?"

"That's fine," Trent replied.

"Two beers, then."

The barkeeper scribbled something on his pad, just for form, then headed back into the building.

Two men were now approaching, lugging some bulky hardware. One had a backpack and one was carrying something that looked like a gun, but with a power lead running to the pack. Trent began to turn to study them more closely, but the Golem suddenly clamped its hands on either side of his head, forcing him to continue looking forwards. Someone out of sight relieved him of his pulse-gun. A droning sound cut the air and Trent felt suddenly hot, sweat breaking out on his forehead. Wisps of smoke rose from glowing dots on his clothing. Stolman watched him as he tried to brush these away, nodded an acknowledgement to his men, then returned his attention to Trent.

"That's better," he said. "Now we can really talk."

The Golem released him and Trent looked down at himself. Of course, he'd been stupid, but reviewing everything, he couldn't remember saying anything particularly damning. Now he realized Stolman had been speaking largely for Isobel's benefit. She must have loaded him with spy gear when she cut off his aug.

"I don't see what we have to talk about," he said, glancing at the two with the hardware. He now recognized their machine as an antediluvian inductance weapon, used to burn out pin cams and microscopic microphones.

"The *Moray Firth*," said Stolman, "its defences, who else is aboard, its access codes . . . I suspect you have a perfectly good idea of what I want."

"Isobel is a haiman," said Trent. "I don't have access codes and I don't have any way of getting you through the *Firth*'s defences."

Stolman ignored him, instead watching the approaching barman. He continued, "I think we'll enjoy this beer, then take this conversation somewhere more private."

Trent decided that this Snapper beer had better be good, because it might be his last.

SPEAR

"What do you mean, 'the drone has the fusion bomb'?" I asked.

"The drone activated the moment I brought it into the munitions loading bay, it then subverted the inner bay door and came aboard," replied Flute. "It immediately headed for the weapons section and is now wrapped around the fusion device."

Oh, great.

"Has it communicated with you?" I asked, casting around. My gaze eventually fell upon a laser carbine, leaning against the horseshoe console at my feet. I studied it for a second, then wondered what the hell I'd been contemplating. I got lucky with the severely damaged Golem Daleen. But I would not be getting lucky with a functional assassin drone, no matter what weapon I might have to hand.

"It has not, but it is perpetually trying to seize control of ship's systems. While it's using only electromagnetic means, I am at present managing to stop it."

"So you won't be able to stop it if it gets physical?" I suggested.

"This ship does not contain the requisite internal defences," Flute replied.

Of course, this destroyer had been built to fight the prador, whose drones were too big even to enter. And the likelihood of something like a small second-child getting in, without the ship having been thoroughly incapacitated first, was remote. Destroyers like this simply weren't built to deal with anything other than the prador enemy.

"I want to speak to it," I said, standing up.

"It is blocking all com to itself, but I am pressurizing the armoury so you can address it through the ship's intercom."

"How long?"

"You can speak now."

For a while I just didn't know what to say. I didn't know how long the thing in the armoury had been somnolent, if it had been so at all. Alternatively, whether it was still loyal to the Polity or had been subverted by Penny Royal. It might not even be sane.

"Can you give me an image of it?"

"No, it disabled the cams."

"Very well—I'll speak now." I paused, cleared my throat. "I once saw a drone just like you on Durana, during an attack on a prador Ucapium mine. We didn't get introduced. It was just there, carrying the eggs of a particularly nasty prador parasite. I wonder how that went?"

No reply.

"That is, if you are the same assassin drone?"

Again no reply.

"I think I was hit." I grimaced. "Well, let me be a little more exact there. I know I was hit by Gatling fire and lost consciousness. That was when we ambushed a prador patrol. I've no idea what happened afterwards."

Still no reply.

"I imagine the mission was accomplished, since when I checked I found that Krong survived the war. Anyway, he didn't have a very high failure rate." I paused for a second. "So, tell me, what is your name?"

"Riss." The word hissed from the armoury sounded more like an exclamation of annoyance.

"Your name is Riss?"

"My name is Riss," the drone replied in a breathy whisper.

"Kind of appropriate really."

"I am female designation," the drone hissed acidly.

"Right . . ." Why the drone had felt the need to tell me that I'd no idea.

"You have a prador second-child mind aboard *this* Polity destroyer," said Riss.

I headed for the door, noting the emphasis. "Yes, when I salvaged this particular boat the previous occupant wasn't aboard. Incidentally, you do know the war has been over for a century?"

"My kind does not have human problems with time."

"Yeah, of course—some sort of atomic clock inside you, accurate down to the millisecond. But then relativity can screw around with things like that. I often think that the good old organic conception of time can be more practical. I mean, would I really want to feel, deep inside myself, how much time has passed since Panarchia? Feeling the weight of the years I spent as quantum processes, inside a chunk of ruby, might drive me mad."

"My kind does not have human problems with madness."

I paused then, because the repetition didn't sound too good. I might be dealing with something damaged.

"You have got to be kidding me!" I exclaimed. "Or do you exclude from 'your kind' the mind that previously occupied this very destroyer? The one who in later years took up residence inside that very planetoid out there?"

"Where is Penny Royal?" asked Riss.

Now that sounded better, and I started walking again.

"Apparently on the planet Masada, acting as the heavy for an AI warden called Amistad. It seems there must be a statute of limitations on AI murderers. I never knew that."

Riss emitted a perfectly in keeping reptilian hiss.

I finally reached an airlock into the nose section, opened it and stepped inside, not having to wait for pressures to equalize before going through the second door. Beyond it, catwalks wound here and there between the main nose-section components and masses of solid foam filling. I could just see the bulk of the railgun and the loading carousels through skeins of optics and s-con cables, tube-feeds, conveyors and structural beams. There being no grav-plates here, I turned on my boots' gecko function, tramped down one catwalk and stepped out onto a curving mass of hard foam. I walked up the curve along a path towards the central cylinder of the main armoury. Of course this wasn't where most of the munitions were kept, since they were distributed against being destroyed by one hit. But it was where most of the assembly or refinement took place.

"So I take it you're not pleased about that?" I asked.

"Penny Royal should die."

"Oh I agree, and that is an end I intend to accomplish."

"What is your name, human?"

"Thorvald Spear, bio-espionage, late of Berners' division on Panarchia before Penny Royal fried it. I'm a one-time captive of the prador and one-time comrade of Jebel U-cap Krong, in whose service I met a drone just like you. I was recently resurrected after having been dead for over a hundred years."

Riss didn't respond to that, not then.

The path led me to an opening through which ran a missile conveyor assembly, which I had to squeeze past to get inside. To my right I noted neat racks of the missiles Flute had manufactured, and at the end of another conveyor, I saw the edge of a loading carousel packed with the same. The spherical mass of the bomb was clamped at its poles and equator, positioned about halfway along the armoury. On either side of it, ship's robots lay neatly folded and inert. Maybe Flute had tried to use them and Riss had disabled them. Or Flute hadn't even bothered trying to activate them, knowing they were no match for the thing now wrapped around our bomb.

I moved further into the armoury while studying the drone. Just as *she* had appeared in vacuum, she resembled a huge cobra with its hood spread. I could see four manipulators extending down below and an ovipositor extending from her tail. However, she now looked very alive as she probed some mechanism on the bomb's surface with her manipulators, her body in constant motion. She looked as if she were trying to get a good grip on the weapon so as to squeeze the life out it. Her body was metallic, like mercury, nacreous and slightly translucent, so I could see the shadowy movement of its internal workings. In her way, she was quite beautiful. But then you can admire a tiger's grace before it eats you or, more appositely, you can admire the patterns on a snake's skin before it strikes.

"Nobody survived Panarchia," she said as I drew closer.

"History often has to be revised as new facts arise," I replied, annoyed by this constant response from anyone who knew anything about that world.

"All were accounted for," Riss insisted.

"Well," I drew to a halt, "I'll be the first to admit that my memory isn't that brilliant. But I distinctly remember, shortly after the bombardment, seeing the prador try a full thrall on Captain Gideon before trying out the spider version on me."

"Standard humans cannot survive thralling," Riss observed.

"I was dying before U-cap rescued me."

"You are incorrect," said Riss, apparently about to say something more but then falling silent. However, by then my annoyance had taken a firmer hold.

"You seem mightily inclined to preach about what's possible and what isn't. I thought that kind of thing was more typical of us stupid, limited human beings!"

"Fascinating." Riss now released her manipulators from the bomb mechanism, raised her head and swung it round to inspect me. Her eyes were a blank bright blue and positioned just like a cobras. However, she briefly blinked open a third jet-black eye, positioned in a small turret jutting from the top of her flat skull.

"What's fascinating?" I asked, still irritated.

"I do remember you from the attack on the Durana mining complex. I was that drone," Riss replied. "They managed to place you in a stasis pod and you were evacuated for medical treatment."

"So?" *Surely I had died there . . . surely that was the place?*

"My kind does not have human problems with time."

Again that sentence.

"Are you damaged?" I asked.

"I lost system function during my encounter with Penny Royal fifty-eight years ago, but function is now restored," Riss replied.

Ah, I would have to be very careful with this snake.

Riss continued, "I will allow one textual communication from your aug giving a precis of your story until now. If I am satisfied, I will relinquish control of this fusion device."

I felt like telling her to fuck off, but that wasn't a great idea. Assassin drones were deliberately manufactured to be paranoid and aggressive and they were made quickly, which tended to generate a lot in the way of copying errors. I couldn't rule out that this one might also be suicidal.

I paused, staring at her while I checked out available resources in my aug. I then collated fact and memory. This started with the background I had passed to Isobel and I added my memories of Panarchia. Then I loaded my recollections of the world where Jebel had rescued me from the prador. Lastly came Durana, where I had died. Then I detailed how these memories were reacquired during my resurrection and listed everything that had happened since. I ran all this through a text conversion program, then through an intelligent precis program. I ended up with ten thousand words of text, just as my aug signalled that a new com channel had opened. When I transmitted all this to Riss she froze for a second, blinked her black eye, then steadily unwound herself from the bomb.

"Are we good?" I asked.

"Fascinating," said Riss again. "It seems we are of similar purpose and, though you are suffering some confusion, you seem very capable indeed."

"Flute," I said, "put us on course for Masada. We need to go and have a talk with the warden there—this Amistad."

Riss snaked towards me, propelled by some sort of grav, maglev or hardfield interaction, odd distortions appearing in the air all about her.

"I am not in the least bit confused," I stated.

"You are if you think Penny Royal bombed Panarchia *before* our attack on Durana, when we targeted that Ucapium mine," Riss replied.

"Oh yeah?" I said, wondering if the drone had anything to gain by lying—if it even could. I then groped for independent facts with which to refute its information. Finding none, I continued weakly with, "Well, what happened to you?"

THE WAR: RISS

It was always like coming home, because this was the place she was made for: the odour of decay on a seashore, the clattering and bubbling of prador speech and the constant background rumble of their hard armoured feet traversing the corridors. The spatters of green blood on stone signified the casual violence of the hierarchy and, as constant background, she could hear the hiss and rumble of heavy hydraulics and the sounds of other positively antediluvian machines. These were all the sights, smells and sounds of a prador dreadnought. Coiled in an alcove, she was loaded with limeworm eggs and concealed by chameleonware. She'd located one of those hiding places second-children used if they wanted to avoid a cracked shell from any passing first-child. Here Riss, assassin drone, Special Series Seven, awaited the arrival of her first victim.

It had been surprisingly easy to get aboard. Something major had happened in the Prador Kingdom, which was causing disarray out here on the front. Three prador capital ships had abruptly retreated from Polity forces that they could've easily overcome. They'd now gathered to orbit this system's single ice giant, as something about said major event had called for a mandible-to-mandible meeting between the three father-captains. Their security had been almost non-existent, contemptuous, even. It had therefore taken little effort for Riss to attach herself to a shuttle, slipping inside the ship where the meeting was taking place. Riss had some interest in the events that had led to this meeting, but her main focus was on her mission. Her awareness was taken up with the tight *gravid* feeling of her meta-material body, and the urge to relieve herself of that feeling by depositing her millions of parasite eggs amidst as many prador as possible. Until that moment, she kept them warm, alive and cosy in a special container inside her, in her womb, her children . . .

Such was the frantic activity aboard this ship that it wasn't long before a second-child—a nicely healthy specimen with just a few healing cracks in its shell—felt the need to dodge into the alcove to avoid two first-children facing off in the corridor. Riss uncoiled as the second-child backed towards her, raised her cobra head and darted forwards. She brought the underside of her spread hood down onto the young prador's shell. It was done gently, almost caressingly, but the sticky lower surface adhered to the carapace. She then squeezed just a few hundred of the microscopic eggs into a pressure chamber at the base of her collimated diamond ovipositor, hooped her body up into a loop, and drove in the long thin spike. She precisely targeted a juncture between one back limb and the main body. With a minor convulsion, she injected the eggs, then immediately flipped herself away into the back of the alcove, ensuring her chameleonware was still optimal even while she revelled in a feeling that was almost . . . orgasmic.

The second-child whirled round, its claws up and snapping at the air. Riss recognized the creature's instinctive response to a parasite attack. Had Riss actually been a limeworm parasite, and had she not withdrawn as quickly as she had, the second-child might well have snipped her in half. This example of the kind now lowered its claws, vibrating its mandibles together in obvious prador confusion. It knew that something had hurt it and that it had reacted in a way it didn't understand. But now the pain was fading even as the eggs spread through its body to encyst in its soft tissues.

Turning back towards the corridor, it watched the two first-children move out of sight, then darted out and away, the incident here already forgotten. Later, the encysted eggs inside it would hatch out into juvenile worms. These would eat it from the inside, growing and dividing, penetrating its gut and then exiting via its rectum. They would feed on ship lice as they grew to adult form and mated, moving on to infect other prador. It was a particularly nasty biological weapon, but one Riss had no compunction in using, for she was made precisely for this task. Riss, effectively, was the weapon. And now, the urge to expel just a few more of those eggs drove her out into the corridor.

Second-children were fine but, being constrained on where they could go, they weren't the best of vectors. Riss closed in on the rear of the nearest first-child. Here was a confrontation between the first-children of two separate father-captains. At present, because they were both about the same size as and thus evenly matched, they were still threatening each other and manoeuvring. Chameleonware still operating, Riss attached herself to the rear of the nearest one and punched in her ovipositor, this time injecting a larger load of eggs. The first-child began the instinctive turn but, because of the threat before it, did not go all the way. Its opponent, however, saw this as an opportunity. It slammed into the first prador with a shuddering crash and tried to close a claw on one of its legs.

As they grappled, Riss slid underneath the first to target the second, driving her ovipositor into it the base of a manipulator limb. That done, she slithered away, noting the two first-children now backing away from each other. They were reassessing their position as some pragmatic sense suppressed instinct. Then they went their separate ways, both now biological time-bombs and as good as dead.

Now the prize.

Riss began closing in on the inner sanctum, negotiating architecture familiar because it had been programmed into the root of her being. Outer corridors swarmed with armed and nervy prador, and the signs of conflict quivered and bubbled here and there on the floors. However, Riss resisted the urge to inject more eggs, for the three attacks had taken away the edge, relieved some of the urge. Aboard this ship were three father-captains. Admittedly, father-captains did not travel as widely as their first-children, but certain other circumstances made them much better infective vectors. Their sheer body mass enabled them to produce millions of limeworms before the internal damage killed them. Every single member of their brood would visit them at some point and become parasitized. They tended not to admit to themselves that they had a problem and one result of this was a steadily growing madness. Since the father-captains controlled such formidable weapons, this could become a huge hindrance to the prador war effort, which was what, after all, Riss was here to undermine.

Despite the high concentration of prador in the corridors, Riss reached the diagonally divided door to the inner sanctum without discovery. Certainly, she'd had to evade all manner of detection devices, but again the prador here were being slack with their security. The drone had seen this before and had put it down to the prador's almost psychotic denial of the reality of assassin drones. Here their certainty of the current battle, despite what had caused these three ships to withdraw, had exacerbated their natural arrogance. This was going to be a pleasure—

"Assassin drone Riss," said an internal voice.

"I hear you, *Primeval*," Riss replied through her internal U-space communicator to the distant Polity dreadnought.

"You are to desist and withdraw," the dreadnought AI continued. "No further action."

Riss emitted an involuntary hiss. This caused a nearby first-child, who was armed to the mandibles, to swing round in suspicion—inspecting the apparently empty floor before the doors.

"Why?" Riss eventually asked.

"The facts of the matter are not entirely clear," said *Primeval*, "but it seems that the prador king has been usurped, and that the usurper has called for a ceasefire. It may be that the war is about to end."

"I hardly think that likely. This is probably just some ploy to wrong-foot us—to gain some advantage."

"If that is the case, then we are failing to see it," *Primeval* continued. "Our analysis shows a ceasefire gives us the advantage, since our industrial output of weapons now exceeds that of the prador."

"It seems foolish for me to withdraw now," Riss argued. "I still have a full load of limeworm eggs. And three father-captains are on the other side of one last door."

"Orders are orders," replied *Primeval*.

"But who's to say they won't start fighting again?" said Riss, sure of her own utter reasonableness. "The prador here owe loyalty to the previous king and might decide on a schism from the new one."

"They have already signalled their intent to withdraw and are calling in all their troops, drones, kamikazes and attack boats."

"Perhaps I should just stay—"

"The order is direct from Earth Central."

"We're stopping? We should finish this—they'll only attack again when the new king is established."

"It's a direct order from the top, Riss: withdraw now."

"But—"

The signal came directly through the same communications channel—a code Riss hardly recognized until it self-assembled and did its work. It inserted itself in Riss's version of an autonomic nervous system like a mental laxative. Riss hooped, squeezed and opened, spraying a jet of white carrier fluid filled with her entire load of eggs. The prador, seeing the stream apparently appearing out of nowhere, scribing a dripping line across the sanctum doors, centred one Gatling cannon and fired. It tore a trench across the floor where Riss had been discharging herself just a second previously.

Now attached to the ceiling, Riss felt a sense of emptiness beyond the physical. She squirmed to safety, heading out towards the dreadnought's open hatches. A stream of recalled drones and armoured prador were flowing through, but the chamelonware still held. She would eject herself out into space, beyond the reach of the ship's U-fields and wait to be picked up. Beyond that, she just had no idea what to do next, for she faced the end of her entire reason for existence.

ISOBEL

Crouched inside the *Moray Firth*, now down in the Rock Pool's small space port, Isobel damned herself for her stupidity as she watched her cameras on Trent fail. She had embarked on this venture with Thorvald Spear—an activity she wouldn't have contemplated a few years back. She wouldn't even have met him back then, and so been enticed by his promise of a cure. One of her lieutenants would have negotiated with him and taken him to the destroyer. Though a more likely scenario would have been Spear being dragged off to be tortured, then cut-auged of everything of value in his skull before being dispatched to the prador.

Trent had been right about her ceasing to expand her organization while she searched for a cure. But she wondered if he'd known about the pin cams and been diplomatic about her other failings. She acknowledged that her disgust at the changes she'd been undergoing, complemented by an over-reliance on her haiman augmentations, had led her to isolate herself from the plain muscle and firepower available to her. Now she found herself here, trapped alone in her spaceship and in danger of falling foul of a two-bit shell-world gangster—of the kind she'd once have squashed without a thought. It was humiliating, and it could not be tolerated.

However, now she could act; now she could *hunt*.

She had briefly considered contacting Morgan again and having him bring reinforcements here. Then she thought about putting *Moray Firth* back in orbit while Morgan dropped a bomb on Carapace City. But no, that might piss off the mysterious father-captain here. Though prador had no particular love for humans of any kind, they definitely wouldn't appreciate humans bombarding one of their worlds. And, like all father-captains, Sverl was sure to be sitting inside a warship. A better idea would have been to bring down forces to raid the city, wiping out Stolman's petty organization to deliver a powerful message to similar wannabes like him.

But better still, she'd decided, to deal with him herself. Wasn't she capable?

One part of her wasn't sure, the other part was utterly certain.

Stolman had a large and lethal-looking Golem at his disposal. According to the conversation she had overheard, it was also a Penny Royal Golem.Whether that made it more or less dangerous she wasn't sure, but she was fairly sure Stolman was controlling it through his own aug. It was therefore highly likely that she'd be able to subvert his control over the thing with her own haiman abilities. And, that aside, she was now much harder to kill than a human being, and Golem, though incredibly tough, were still susceptible to proton cannon fire.

With a mechanical clattering, Isobel swept out of the bridge and headed back through the *Moray Firth*, excitement rising. She stopped to attach her speech synthesizer and then pulled a hover trunk out of storage and activated it. Into this went explosives ranging from those that could bring down a building, to anti-personnel grenades like the ones Trent had carried. She put in a rocket bundle: six armour-piercing missiles she could fire remotely from the trunk and mentally guide to their targets. Then, just for good measure, she added extra power supplies and reloads for her shoulder-mounted proton cannon and pulse-rifle. Anything else? Yes, there was something else and, just like the proton cannon, she found it still gleaming and unused. The mosquito autogun shrugged out of its packaging once she accessed and instructed it. Then, taking delicate steps, it walked over to the hover trunk and folded itself inside. That would have to do—there was no room for anything more.

Isobel felt the trunk would help for appearance's sake, but she also put her grav-harness back on and took a shoulder bag filled with some of her portable wealth. The more such items she took with her, the more she would look like an intelligent technical being rather than an escapee from a zoo. This would lessen the chances of someone deciding to open fire on her. Just to complete her ensemble of harmlessness, she folded down both her weapons on their mountings and put shrink coverings over them— two discs of polymer composite that closed up into black casings. These wouldn't prevent her using the weapons, but would make them look less lethal. It was the difference between someone walking into a space port with a holstered gun, rather than one in hand.

She exited her ship through the usual airlock, broadcasting to the watchers that she was leaving, adding, "I am highly adapted, so I don't want any panic or unfortunate mistakes."

"We observe here," someone replied.

"I'm not a shellman," she explained. "I'm something you may not have seen before."

"Bsorol makes us aware of your biological history, Isobel Satomi," the voice assured her.

Bsorol?

Isobel dipped her hood to inspect the steady bleaching of her cara-pace. For a second she'd thought she was talking to one of the shell people here. But now, hearing that name, she analysed word order and emphasis, and realized she'd been talking to a prador through translation software.

Once out of her ship, she scanned what passed for a space port here. Hers was one of three ships. The other two, though large, were still just shuttles. She noted a saucer-shaped one that looked to have come from one of John Hobbs' salvage ships. There was also a brick-like object, the main detachable cargo section from an old Polity in-system hauler. The drive section, still up in orbit, would doubtless have been adapted to U-space travel. Scattered about the field were a couple of shellman guards and some standard humans unloading cargo from the hauler's shuttle. All of them were looking at her, which probably meant they'd received a warn-ing from the watching prador. As she gazed back, she suddenly found herself fighting a strong urge to chase after them. Instead, she dropped down onto all her legs and scuttled across to the terminal building. She was briefly irritated by the feel of hard stone and wished for something she could grip more readily, her hover trunk rushing to keep up.

First, she went through a security arch where an automated voice issued her with a warning: "Deployment of any weapon in the terminal building will be terminal for you." This statement was odd because, though a recording, it sounded as if it had issued from a prador translator. But surely prador did not possess a sense of humour? A short tunnel led her to a pressure door that hesitated before opening to admit her to the building. A few people were scattered inside, but not so many as when she'd come here with Spear. Some showed no reaction to her at all, some stared, while one woman let out a gasp and turned and ran at full pelt for an exit. This probably meant she had some knowledge of the hooders of Masada. Again the urge to give chase arose in her, and again she beat it down. Meanwhile, across and to her left, two prador stood watching.

Both were clad in bulky armour. This was a blue-green she recognized as a Polity alloy, made some time after the war, based on metallurgy learned from the prador. She suspected it was one of these that she'd spoken to earlier. Choosing an exit to the car parks and taxi ranks, she began moving. One of the prador immediately centred a Gatling cannon on her and tracked her as she crossed the area. In response she kept her hood turned so she could draw cross hairs over the prador—the delay between thought and firing just microseconds. Was this a pointless gesture? What were her chances of survival if it were to open fire on her? Though she did have the body of a hooder, it was still weak compared to the adult form. Moreover, could even the latter survive a fusillade of prador alloy slugs, which were harder than diamond and heavier than plutonium? As she reached the pressure door exit and went through, her tension drained. She pondered on how if something had kicked off, nobody else in the vicinity—or indeed the building itself—would have survived.

Ahead lay a small car park for hydrocars, with just a few vehicles present. A foam-stone road cut across nearby and here waited three taxis, their drivers sitting around a nearby table, positioned on a mound coated with blue-green mosses and sprouting fan fungus. They were playing a game involving dice and occasionally sipping from drinks through straws, which they inserted via holes in their breather masks. They all turned to look at her, then leapt out of their seats as she began to approach.

"There is no cause for alarm," she called. "I simply require a ride into Carapace City."

By the time she reached the table, two of the drivers were back in their cabs. This time she found it easier to resist the urge to give chase, because the other driver hadn't fled. He was a squat fat amphidapt who looked like a by-blow of a man and a cane toad, clad in black trousers and shirt with a slick rubbery look, which was probably the only sort of material that could survive his damp warty skin.

"What the hell are you?" he asked.

"I am Isobel Satomi," she replied.

He tilted his head, considered that for a moment while a long purple tongue protruded to lick over his right eyeball. Then he nodded. "You're the gal who got screwed over by Penny Royal."

Isobel repressed the urge to grab him and remove his tongue. It was not the observation about her being screwed over that annoyed her, but being referred to as a "gal."

"How much to take me into the city?" she asked instead.

"Ten muzil," he said, casting an eye over her trunk as it settled beside her.

She reached out with one thin black tentacle—the one with the pincers—and snipped the polymer coating over her pulse-gun. The coating shrivelled and dropped off. She raised it and aimed it at his face.

"Try again," she suggested.

12

SVERL

Sverl gazed with distaste at the image of the single prador, expanded to fill ten segment screens, standing in the audience chamber adjoining his sanctum. Sfolk, who was one of Vlern's brood of young adult males, was quivering with fear. Adults generally didn't put themselves at the complete mercy of any other adult. However, Sverl had made sure that if any of Vlern's brood wanted to present a request, they had to come here. It was a way of keeping them subjugated, which was necessary to prevent them running amok. They had done so when Vlern died, and would do again, given the opportunity.

Vlern had joined Sverl shortly after he sank his dreadnought in the sea, seemingly of fellow feeling about the war's end. Like other Graveyard prador, he had been intent on acquiring allies to avoid being picked off by the King's Guard. Contingents of the Guard were still in the vicinity, hunting down such rebels. However, though Vlern had seemed perfectly sane and coherent in initial communications, the reality was rather different. He had been a very old prador, sans legs and mandibles. Dying nerve tissue meant he couldn't take any more prosthetics either, and he was as mad as a tankful of reaverfish. He'd spent the ensuing decades here under the sea muttering to himself, being fed flesh paste and tank-grown child's blood. Frequent interventions on Sverl's part were required to keep him from sending his children against his neighbours—and to ensure he kept those same children in a state of arrested development. Some decades ago, Vlern stopped being able to eat properly and ended up choking on flesh paste. The first Sverl learned of his death was when one of Vlern's five first-children, then making the transformation into a young adult, tried to take control of Vlern's old destroyer to kill off his siblings.

Sverl's initial instinct had been to leave the first-child to it. But his second instinct, surely a result of his ongoing transformation, had been to stop any killing before it started. It was just so wasteful to allow the few prador here to start tearing each other apart. Using his single Golem and his children he intervened and took control of Vlern's ship systems. The drive and weapons were then unavailable to the five, who were all transforming into adults. He divided living space on the destroyer for them, then divided up Vlern's second-children, drones and other resources amongst them. All first-children and young adults had necessarily been required to fight their instincts during the war—so they were to behave or pay the penalty.

Over the ensuing years, there had always been trouble from these five. The trade in human blanks they'd conducted was a case in point, blanks being humans cored of their brains and subsequently controlled by prador thrall technology. This trade might not have been so dangerous here where the Polity supposedly couldn't reach, but it had brought some very unsavoury characters to this world. Their constant infighting and attempts to murder one another had often seemed about to get out of control. And one attempt to assassinate Sverl had resulted in the loss of one of his own children, which could never be replaced. Now there was more trouble on the horizon.

"So tell me what you want," he clattered, his on-screen image one of himself from over fifty years ago. It would not do to let any of the prador here see his true appearance, for they thought his behaviour alone dubious enough.

Sfolk shifted his feet about and snipped at the air with one claw. He was frightened of Sverl's reaction, but for the moment Sverl wasn't angry at all. He was still slightly amazed that the five had come to an agreement and chosen one to present their request.

"Our population only grows smaller," said Sfolk.

"Very true," Sverl replied. "And as I recollect you and your brothers have played no small part in that."

Again the snipping. "You are *wrong*."

Sfolk wasn't denying the truth of Sverl's words, just expressing what many prador here now felt. Sverl just didn't speak or behave as he should. Sverl was all *wrong*. It was also a protest from the young adult, because Sfolk clearly didn't know how to approach the matter in hand with someone who didn't *feel* like a prador.

"Just get to the point," said Sverl. "I promise I won't crack your shell for anything you say now, but I will crack it if you continue wasting my time." Of course Sverl hadn't delivered a cracked shell for decades. If he felt the need to do so, he would send in his drone with the big manipulator arms, currently sitting in an adjunct to the audience room.

"We want to go," said Sfolk, now cringing.

"Go where?" Sverl asked distractedly, glancing at those screens not occupied by Sfolk. Some interesting stuff was going on in the human realm and the petty politics down here were annoying him.

"To the Kingdom."

Now Sfolk had Sverl's complete attention.

"You want to return to where you'll be stripped of your limbs, attached to a grav-plate, then injected with hydrofluoric acid, before being skimmed out over the sea?" he enquired.

The old king died like that, so rumour had it, and it was now the favoured punishment for renegade prador.

"We are not our father," Sfolk asserted.

"True enough . . ." said Sverl.

"Our children are not our children," Sfolk added.

Ah.

So that's what all this was about. The second-children Sfolk and his brothers controlled were in fact their brothers. They had no offspring of their own. Sverl emitted a very unpradorlike sigh and settled lower on his limbs, resting the tips of his claws against the floor. Perhaps it really was time for the likes of Sfolk and his sibling to go. Certainly, living here under Sverl's regime, they were losing touch with the realities of the outer universe. If they truly thought they could go back to the Kingdom with protestations of innocence they were being very, very naive. Their father had been the rebel and they had been under the control of his pheromones when he rebelled, but in prador terms, thinking those excuses would work just made them a little bit crazy.

Admittedly, it was possible that the new king, who had made some decidedly odd decisions himself, might give them amnesty. But that the five's mindset even allowed them to think it was a possibility showed they weren't fit to join prador society. That they supposed there might be justice or mercy there at all had to be Sverl's fault. They had found it here and so expected it was normal, little realizing how human softness had infiltrated their world. But, of course they weren't thinking straight. Sfolk's last comment implied that they were thinking about what was completely lacking here: females.

"Return to your ship," said Sverl. "Tell your brothers that I am thinking about it and will give them a decision within five days."

Sfolk's shock was comical. He had come here expecting to leave at least with a cracked shell if he managed to leave at all. In a way that was a good thing—it showed that Sverl's rule over them had not completely killed their survival instincts.

The audience chamber doors opened and Sfolk whirled round and departed, two second-children waiting to conduct him from the ship. Sverl waited until the doors had closed before switching the ten screens back to more interesting views, and began contemplating possible futures.

Not counting Sverl, this enclave under the sea included seven adult males in total, plus their children in various forms. But there were no females and as such it was a dead end. Sure, there seemed to be evidence that Cvorn—one of the other prador—had growth tanks. However, that just made the dead end an inbred genetic one. With the five new adults now wanting to leave, there was definitely going to be trouble. Why should Sverl fight it? He had himself been contemplating leaving to go in search of Penny Royal. For he was at last coming to appreciate that his feelings about that AI were far stronger than his attitude towards the Polity or the prador king—or even the war itself.

In deep introspection, and with a degree of depression, Sverl continued gazing at his screens. Then he began to perk up as members of the local human mafia beat up another human. This was not uncommon and usually only evinced a passing interest from Sverl. But in this case the victim was a servant of Isobel Satomi who, in a way, Sverl felt might be a kindred spirit.

Sverl had never quite been able to nail down when Satomi had visited Penny Royal—whether it was before or after Sverl himself—but similar results had ensued. She had asked for haiman abilities and Penny Royal had granted its own interpretation of her request. Penny Royal's dubious activities were fairly well known to the prador nowadays and so it was generally avoided. Yet humans didn't seem as cautious, even thought what it did was firmly embedded in their history and mythologies. A large proportion of the human race had once believed in supernatural beings—a belief that generally did not survive interstellar travel. Some had believed in entities who granted wishes—for which the price was always too much. One of these scenarios involved paying with your soul, a mythical form of consciousness that could survive the death of the body. Hence a human phrase, "Selling your soul to the devil." But the whole idea of getting more than you bargained for was entrenched in their psyche with other cautious phrases like, "Be careful what you wish for." This perhaps explained why the many stories about Penny Royal didn't quite match up to the reality as Sverl had found it.

If all Penny Royal's deals were the equivalent of that curious human term "a poisoned chalice" for the other party, Penny Royal wouldn't have been able to do business in the Graveyard. Yet the AI had acquired wealth and power and resources. Certainly some did end up regretting their bargains. Sverl's searches had turned up a few cases where some had been driven to take their own lives or had returned to the Polity for help. Nevertheless, there were nowhere near as many as rumour would have it. Sverl had located four, possibly five twisted agreements, if the rumours about Mr Pace were true. But right now, in the Graveyard, there was only one example other than Sverl, and that was Isobel Satomi. Now she was here again.

On her last visit, Sverl had discovered that someone connected to her wanted to buy one of his second-child minds. Sverl had immediately decided one of the *specials* should be provided. Now she was back again. And, judging by this Trent's replies to Stolman's questions, the deal had gone drastically wrong.

As he reviewed recorded footage transmitted via his Golem, which he had allowed Stolman's people to find and apparently activate, Sverl's fascination increased. This Thorvald Spear was seeking Penny Royal and had apparently recommissioned the AI's old destroyer using Sverl's *special* second-child mind. He had also left on this destroyer, having reneged on his deal with Satomi and sabotaged her ship. Satomi now wanted to hunt him down. She knew he'd gone to Penny Royal's planetoid—presumably mistakenly as the AI was now aboard a small salvage vessel called *The Rose*. It also seemed, from some of Trent's garbled comments, that Satomi had encountered *The Rose* and quite possibly the black AI. This apparently explained how Isobel's drive was functional again, following Spear's sabotage.

Sverl settled down on his legs, resting the bottom of his bloated body on the floor. He felt tense, excited, and confused. He could perfectly understand that Satomi was out for revenge on Spear. He could also see why Spear was out for revenge against Penny Royal, judging by the potted biography he'd checked. But he couldn't fathom Penny Royal's motivations. Certainly they had changed—else the Polity wouldn't have accepted the AI back into the fold. And now Sverl was questioning his own way forward. His earlier feeling that his long sojourn under this ocean was coming to an end was growing stronger. In fact, he was starting to feel puzzled as to what had motivated his own century-long procrastination on this world.

BLITE

Penny Royal had become decidedly chatty. Well, in its terms, Blite felt. As the *The Rose* approached the AI's nameless planetoid—a place Blite had sworn never to visit—the AI had made an announcement: "I am here to obtain information about a human called Thorvald Spear, who it is likely has visited this place." Terse replies then ensued to Blite's further questions. He learned that this Spear was now travelling the Graveyard aboard Penny Royal's former destroyer. Perhaps the AI had given Blite and his crew information to reassure them in some way. It wasn't really working.

"So what's it doing down there?" Brond wondered, when Penny Royal had left the ship.

"Obtaining information," Blite replied, to which Ikbal issued a snort.

When Blite had seen Mona and her salvage crew down on the planet, he had felt a sudden altruistic impulse. He would talk to her and try to obtain the information Penny Royal required, whatever it was. That way the crew might be more likely to survive the experience. They might not have to go through the terror he and his crew had faced and, to a limited extent, learned to live with. However, he just wasn't quick enough.

"Shit," said someone called Tanner, on the surface. "Oh shit."

Mona hadn't been using particularly complex coding for their suit transmissions, so it hadn't been difficult to listen in. They'd heard Mona tell those inside the cave system to get out just as Penny Royal was going in. Had Tanner just run into the AI? Would he survive the experience?

Blite fixed his gaze on the screen, which showed a close-up of Mona's ship and the entrance the crew had been using to access the cave system. He watched as four space-suited figures stumbled out.

"Shit—I'm alive," Tanner added.

"Let's hope it lasts," replied one of the others.

"Get back now," instructed the one called Gareth, who was monitoring from their ship. The instruction was hardly necessary, because the four were already running towards it. "Where's Mona?" Gareth asked.

"She was behind us," Tanner replied.

After a long pause Gareth just repeated, "Get back to the ship."

"I wonder what it's doing with her?" asked Brond.

Greer, who had just entered the bridge with Martina, said, "Do we want to know?"

"We do want to know," said Martina as she inserted herself into one of the seats. "Penny Royal seems to have changed. It seems to be showing none of its previous nasty inclinations. Even what it did to us, it quickly corrected. But let's see how it behaves with other people. Let's see if the change is real."

"Golem," said Brond.

Blite swung back to the screen to see five skeletal Golem marching out of the cave entrance, just as the four crewmen entered Mona's ship. Two grav-sleds, with just a few chunks of salvage on each, trailed after them. They walked in lock-step over to the cargo cage, and waited as the two sleds slid into the cage, whereupon they followed them inside. Blite worked his controls, trying to focus in closer on their activity. They unloaded the meagre salvage from the sleds, then loaded one with other items already within the cage. Then all five seated themselves in the cage, while the reloaded sled floated back out and headed over to the cave entrance.

"Uh?" said Brond.

"Beats me," Blite replied.

"I'm okay," said a space-suited figure, now walking out of the entrance. Mona's voice was shaky and she'd spoken as if she disbelieved her own words.

"What happened in there?" Gareth asked.

"Yeah," said Blite, inserting himself into their space suit com, "what happened?"

"It's rude to butt in like that, Blite," said Mona, now walking towards the spaceship. "And what the hell are you doing ferrying that particular passenger about?"

"I didn't have much choice in the matter—I don't really control my own ship anymore."

"I'm sorry to hear that," she said, the implication there that she couldn't do anything about that. "Anyway, Penny Royal just read me like a book and now has all the information it requires. It informs me that we can take everything we have in the cargo cage right now and that we can return if we wish, but we won't find anything of value."

"What about the Golem?" Gareth asked.

"They apparently have 'holding personalities' and will obey us after a limited fashion until we deliver them to the destination we've been given."

Mona now reached the airlock to her ship. "Get everything fired up, Gareth, we're getting the hell out of here." She entered the airlock.

It wouldn't surprise Blite if they dumped the Golem at some point during their journey back to Montmartre space station. Then again, maybe not. It didn't seem likely that Mona could persuade her crew to enter the cargo cage to eject them.

Blowing out a ring-shaped cloud of dust, her ship began to lift on chemical thrusters. Then, just a few hundred feet from the ground, it peeled upwards and ignited its fusion drive, the back-blast causing another dust storm on the surface below. Igniting the fusion torch that close to a planet of any kind generally wasn't done, but Blite supposed they were anxious to leave. Within a few minutes, the ship was spearing past Blite's just a few miles away.

"Best of luck, Blite," Mona sent. "I don't envy you."

Her ship dropped into U-space before it was properly clear of the planetoid and the effect caused another backwash. *The Rose* shuddered and twisted in some indefinable way, while weird lighting effects, like travelling lines of nacre, sped over the surfaces of surrounding equipment.

"She's in a hurry," Brond observed.

"Understandable," Blite replied.

"Perhaps we should have asked her for a lift?" suggested Martina, just to air the thought, just to put it out there.

"Perhaps," said Blite, but he knew that none of his crew felt so inclined. They really had no idea about Penny Royal's aims, but were all now in it for the duration, until the end. Precisely why they all felt this way, Blite couldn't say. Perhaps Penny Royal had reprogrammed them.

"Here it comes," said Ikbal. "Our passenger returns."

Glittering darkness exited the cave mouth, stretched up from the ground towards them and snapped out into space. Forming into a disc, it crossed the intervening distance improbably fast. In fact, when Penny Royal made this kind of crossing, Blite had measured an intermittent U-space effect. The ship clattered with the AI's arrival, and Blite noted the hold door open and close. However, he didn't need these indicators to know Penny Royal was back. It was as if he could feel the thing breathing on the back of his neck, though it breathed not at all.

The Rose began to move, steering thrusters diverting it and the fusion drive firing up. They watched while the ship swung round the planetoid.

"It's looking for something again," commented Leven. "And it seems a little agitated."

Blite was daring to aug into his ship's system more than before, and observed it was performing a deep scan of the surrounding space.

"*It's using the same codes as before,*" said Leven, speaking direct to Blite through his aug.

"*Before?*"

"*When it located that power plant.*"

"*Ah.*"

After one full orbit of the planetoid Penny Royal drew the ship into a stationary orbit. Then through the system, Blite observed a powerful U-space signal being transmitted with that same coding.

"Something just arrived," Leven announced a moment later, opening up a frame on blank space.

"I think we've been here before," said Blite, his words confirmed a moment later when one of those spinning-top power plants shed its chameleonware.

Unlike the one before, this was already fully active. In addition, as far as Blite could surmise, it had been elsewhere. The things obviously hid themselves, so it wasn't a stretch to understand they could run and hide somewhere else upon discovery. As the thing concealed itself once more, *The Rose* began to move, orientating back towards the planetoid.

"Something's happening down there," said Leven, throwing up a view of the surface. Blite fixed his attention on the screen. A ball of fire blew out of a cave mouth and the ground behind it lifted and collapsed, issuing a dust cloud. Leven immediately pulled back the view, to show similar explosions all around the planetoid, numerous collapses etching out the underlying labyrinth of tunnels.

"Why?" he asked.

"Eliminating dangerous toys," Penny Royal breathed.

The Rose now accelerated, the fusion drive ramping to full power. Blite could sense that they were done here now.

"Where now?" he asked.

His answer was, inevitably, a memory.

He sat on this bridge, two of his old crew with him, studying a report on a particular world. They were discussing whether it might be worth doing business there. They decided against it because, really, there wasn't much to trade but there were plenty of chances to die.

Blite came out of the memory feeling sick again.

"Why the hell—" Blite began then stopped himself. Penny Royal might answer his questions, but it did so in a manner which wasn't at all comfortable. Now, gazing at the puzzled expressions around him he said, "We're going to the Rock Pool."

"And why are we going there?" Martina asked. "There's nothing there but shell people, prador and Graveyard scum."

"Maybe I'll ask about that later," Blite replied.

ISOBEL

As the cab sped towards Carapace City, travelling faster than was probably usual for this driver, she looked ahead. She had already penetrated one aug network and, using search engines, had drawn plans of the place in her mind. Coming closer, she found another smaller aug network and recognized it as one arising from those odd Dracocorp augs. These were organic augmentations, apparently made by a company set up by Dragon, the self-named trans-stellar alien entity. She decided to avoid that one. She'd encountered these before, worn by Separatists out of the Polity, and recognized them as a trap. One person could use the network to assume dominance over others who were linked in. She penetrated other computing systems, too—cam systems and simple communicators—but avoided the dangerous stuff such as free drones and Golem. Perhaps fortuitously, there didn't seem to be anything big here; anything which might cause her serious problems. Interlinking all she'd gathered so far, she began dispatching further search engines.

Her first glimpse of Trent, after his pin cam removal, sat in the recorded memory of an ancient security camera. She realized Stolman and his heavies were the ones wearing the Dracocorp augs. Perhaps the computing particular to those augs, coupled with Stolman's supremacy in the network, had enabled him to activate the Golem. Perhaps that was the answer, given that Penny Royal wasn't in the vicinity to activate the tech.

Using further cams, she managed to track Trent to a boat, which headed off along a narrow canal that extended from the central pond. But she could find no further cams nearby and there was no computing in the boat or it would have left a trace. The option of using satellite imagery was out too, what with the dome over the central part of the city. Checking ahead, she tried penetrating some tight security systems in the canal-side houses to track him further.

"Looking for someone?" a voice asked.

Isobel immediately felt the predator in her arise, with the urge to attack. She upped her security as she sought the source of that voice. She tried to trace it but found all her attempts slewing away to random computing all over the city.

"I'm here," said the voice.

A channel opened to one of the security systems she'd been attempting to penetrate, and thence to a specific camera. Though viscerally wanting to attack, she instead assessed the dangers and intellectually was tempted to just pull out and shut down. However, she reasoned that the one she could now see had picked up on her very quickly, and it would remain a danger even if she did pull out.

Just in front of the wall-mounted camera hovered a plain grey drone, rather like a small surfboard with sensors around its rim. It had two topaz eyes to its fore and what looked like limbs of some kind folded up underneath its forward section. She studied it for a moment longer but could divine little from its appearance. When attempting to study it in the virtual world, she just found a glossy surface from which her mind slid away. This was why she'd been intent on avoiding both Golem and drones. They were AI and they could be tricky. The thing she was looking at might be a few centuries old and might even be a planetary AI, slumming it in a beat-up drone body.

"I'm looking for Trent Sobel," she replied. "Anyone you're looking for?"

"Nah, I'm not looking for anyone in particular," the drone replied. "I just like to keep my finger on the pulse."

The cab had now slowed to pass through the rather less affluent outer suburbs of the city. Here the driver had to negotiate around decaying cars, piles of rubbish and some rather esoteric street planning. At one point, it slowed to a crawl behind a wide electric cart loaded down with what looked like dried-out cacti. Indigents in the area took this opportunity to rush up and bang on the cab to draw attention to their distinctly crappy wares. When they saw Isobel half-coiled across the back seats they rushed away just as quickly.

"And Trent Sobel?" Isobel enquired.

"He's not having a particularly good day, and it's going to get worse unless you get to him soon."

"So you've been taking an interest?"

"I always take an interest in Stolman," said the drone. "He's an interesting sort of guy—what with him sitting at the head of the local Mafia and a pre-enslaving Dracocorp network. And now he's supposedly controlling a Penny Royal Golem."

Supposedly?

"So you're a voyeur?"

"Call me a student of human fallibility."

"Can you give me Trent's location?"

"Sure." The drone sent a data package, which Isobel immediately blocked.

"Just tell me, please."

"Well, you are a suspicious type," said the drone, "but then in your trade I guess you have to be. And I'm guessing your recent transformation might have distorted your perspective somewhat." A noise that could only be described as a titter ensued, then the drone continued, "Tell your driver to take you to the Reaverson Warehouse, Eastish Fourteen."

"Eastish?"

"Compasses don't work here. Oh, and here's a cam you might find useful."

The package was smaller this time and Isobel routed it into secure storage and made a cursory external examination of it. Then, with as much caution as possible, she opened it. It was simply a code-breaking program to a specific cam in what was supposed to be a secure network. Isobel used it, and immediately opened a view into the Reaverson Warehouse. Ascertaining at a glance that Trent was still alive, she now decided to satisfy her curiosity.

"You're a Polity drone," she said. "Yet you're watching crimes being committed and doing nothing. Why is that?"

"This ain't the Polity and not every AI is trying to attain sainthood," the drone replied. "And really, what can you do with that mess called humanity, until it feels inclined to raise itself out of the mire it so enjoys? I mean, look at you, Isobel. You've got wealth, power, haiman abilities and yet still you persist in your sordid little pursuits—even when the possibilities open to you are practically infinite."

Isobel fought to suppress a sudden surge of almost insane rage that had her writhing on the back seats of the cab. Finally getting it under control, she managed, "I have a particular problem, as you may well have gathered, caused by Penny Royal. And I'm trying to deal with it."

"Sure, yet still you're the head of a human organization that cores and thralls other human beings to sell to the prador."

"Fuck you."

"Not this side of eternity, my little centipede." The drone paused for a second, then added, "Oh, you should check out Taiken Fuels, just a few hundred yards up from Reaverson's. You should find everything you need for your ship. See you around, Isobel, or maybe not."

The drone cut all connections, while Isobel fumed. Fucking supercilious Polity minds. They could be so super intelligent, but they had no real idea about her. About the alliances, responsibilities, commitments and the sheer difficulty involved in relinquishing something she'd fought so hard to build, and it had no appreciation of just how vulnerable she'd be if she let it go. They never went through anything like this—just adjusted themselves either physically or mentally to suit current circumstances.

"Fuck it," she said out loud, then to the driver, "Take me to Taiken Fuels, Eastish Fourteen." Better to disembark some distance from the Reaverson Warehouse so she could reconnoitre.

"Okay," the driver replied.

At that moment, Isobel noted a horrible damp smell in the cab and the beads of moisture that had appeared on the back of the driver's neck. She didn't suppose her writhing about in the back here and clattering together her mouthparts had done much for his nerves.

The warehouse district looked much the same as such places had centuries ago. Wide streets for big carriers ran between the two- and three-storey blocks. The place was dilapidated, with rubbish overflowing from large rusting skips and strewn about the streets. Empty packing crates and chemical barrels littered any available free space. Isobel flowed out of the cab and paid the driver after he unloaded her hover trunk. As the vehicle pulled away with a crump of over-stressed fibre-wheels, she glanced into the glass-fronted showroom of Taiken Fuels. A shellman, squatting on some sort of platform, stared at her with his mandibles drooping and human mouth hanging open. Ignoring him, she moved back towards Reaverson's, pausing behind a broken-down auto-handler dray to plan her next moves. She also needed to fight the urge to just go careering in.

After receiving a beating and initial questioning, Trent had been dragged back towards a wall of plasmesh crates. For a moment she thought the three heavies were just holding him there. But when they stepped away, she realized they must have smeared him with adhesive because now he was stuck spread-eagled in place. Stolman had pulled over a chair to watch, while his staff brought out various items to place on a table beside him. Isobel focused the camera, noting some fairly standard torture items as well as a cut aug. Really, the aug would have been enough. The vibrational paint peeler, heat-gun, small atomic shear and abrasion plate had to be for Stolman's enjoyment only. She understood the inclination because she had taken part in such scenes herself on many occasions but now, oddly, she felt a contemptuous disgust.

So how should she approach? There were eighteen armed thugs in and about the warehouse, plus the Golem and Stolman himself. There were two autoguns positioned within the warehouse too. The exterior cams probably connected directly into the Dracocorp aug network, and there were sub-AI security drones covering every entrance. If her aim was to rescue Trent, which she must or she couldn't really justify being here, she'd have to move quickly and the Golem would be a problem. Even with the weapons she possessed it would take time to shut it down—time in which one of Stolman's thugs could take a shot at Trent. As she opened her trunk, she decided that she'd try accessing the Dracocorp aug network after all, followed by an attempt to access the mind of that Golem. If Stolman had managed to activate it, then surely it shouldn't be so difficult to take control away from him.

Isobel made tentative connections to the network and carefully began weaning out data and recognition codes. She quickly understood that she could make no true penetration of the network without being included within it, and so needed a Dracocorp aug of her own. She began to model one in her mind, taking up more and more data threads to process through it. In a moment she'd almost reached the point where she could communicate—and actually become part of the network. She then found that the moment she did so, Stolman would know someone else had joined. At that point, her modelled aug would become partially subservient to his. Moments after that, he'd know who she was and could shut her out again.

However, there was something she could do. She calculated that for at least a few minutes, she could scramble his connection to the Golem. But whether this was a good thing, she couldn't tell. The Golem might just shut down completely and do nothing. It might become fully conscious and, with it being first enslaved to Penny Royal, become even more dangerous than it was now.

Isobel made her decision and instructed the autogun, which delicately stepped out of the crate and then scuttled up and along one wall. She loaded up with grenades and other armaments, also stripping the covering from her proton cannon. She then selected targets down the street for the missile bundle, took a calming breath as she checked the whole intricate network of her attack plan, then stepped out from behind the auto-handler dray. Streaks of fire flared behind her as the missiles fired, and she felt an ecstatic joy rising up inside her as she surged forwards.

THE WAR: RISS

"You are a drone," so the station AI had said. "Your physical appearance and function can be changed and I can reformat your mind."

Riss remembered the crowded final construction bay aboard Factory Station Gdansk 12. This was where she'd been posted to learn her fate at the end of the war. There had been thousands of drones there: war drones built to resemble just about every creature imaginable, terran or alien. Giant scorpions, spiders and ants had been there in abundance, although snakelike forms such as her own were not so prevalent, since many drones liked to have plenty of limbs with which to manipulate their environment. Distinguishing assassin drones from plain war drones had more to do with mental signature than shape—the former tending to be much more taciturn and moody. While there, Riss was reminded of the chaotic departure from her original factory station. She and a few other drones had fled Factory Station Room 101 shortly after it surfaced from U-space. The station had been hugely damaged, its AI was insane, and its secrets were thereafter buried by lies about it being destroyed.

Near to Riss, on Gdansk 12, there had been a pair of drones fashioned like sharks. There was also a particularly irascible drone—somewhat like a giant chromed lobster with particle cannons in its mouth. From these drones, Riss had gained useful intelligence. She learned that many drones, attack ships, destroyers and even some dreadnoughts had gone AWOL since confirmation of the war's end—just like Room 101 had done earlier in the war. Apparently, these were now heading out of the Polity, unable to accept the end of their function. They were contemptuous of slow humanity and intent on starting something new. Riss had been tempted to head for one of the broadcast rendezvous points, but not tempted enough.

"Are you going to?" she had asked.

"Going to what?" asked the Gdansk AI.

"Change your appearance and function and reformat your mind?" said Riss. "You are, after all, obsolete now."

"I am going to go somnolent and wait," replied Gdansk.

"Mothballed."

"Not a description I like and, even so, I don't think it will be for long."

"Me neither," Riss had replied, heading for the exit.

In the months and then years following the war, a buffer zone was formed between the two realms, by agreement between the new prador king and the Polity. Even as Riss travelled out towards this, hopping from ship to ship, this borderland had acquired the name the Graveyard. It was appropriate, since the Polity worlds here had received the brunt of the prador attack when they weren't conserving resources for the long haul. The nearby prador worlds too had been subject to a space runcible attack, whose source had been the perimeter of a black hole. The munitions were world-frying x-rays and planetary rubble, travelling at a significant portion of the speed of light.

Riss found ruination, but also occupation. Prador and humans were still there, while salvage hunters and the lone scum of both races were arriving, and a strange outlaw culture began to form. Sometimes hitching rides on ships, sometimes just hanging in orbit over worlds scattered with the titanic remains of industrialized warfare, Riss waited. She did so with the long patience of a machine for the renewal of conflict, for her purpose to be reinstated. There were moments of excitement—border infringements by prador foolish enough to disobey their king, or human rebels hoping to restart conflict. But generally sanity, of a kind, prevailed.

Riss was resting above yet another war-shattered world, thirty-two years after the war, when things changed for her. She'd noticed salvagers below were busily taking apart a crashed Polity attack ship. Then they were running back to their ship, shooting at something in the ruination behind them. Their grav-sleds, loaded down with valuables, had been abandoned. Maybe a somnolent prador drone had been unearthed, though that seemed unlikely near the wreck of a Polity attack ship. Maybe one of Riss's own kind had activated and driven them off. Any of a hundred other dangers could have been the cause of their panic.

Eventually they reached their ship and from high in orbit Riss could only detect some odd movements and twisting of shadow behind them. They boarded and launched at once, the ground around their ship seeming to lens as if seen through some intense gravity field. Thereafter everything was fine until the ship reached orbit, then it just died—with no power output at all. Riss continued watching, not feeling any need to intervene—at least not yet. An airlock opened, expelling a human, sans space suit, out into vacuum. And now Riss felt it was time to take a look.

Riss grav-planed over to the ship and tried to scan deep inside it. None of the salvage crew was in evidence, though there was a dark area within that she couldn't penetrate. On the way in she caught hold of the dead human, for there still might be something there that could be saved. Then she dragged the body into the ship's open airlock and closed the door behind. The airlock was receiving no power so refused to pressurize but, when Riss opened it manually while it was still evacuated, that lack of power also prevented safety latches clicking in. Leaving the corpse behind, Riss headed directly to the area she'd been unable to scan— towards the sounds that seemed to be issuing from some hell—and came upon the edge of it in a dropshaft leading to the engine room. Ahead lay darkness with something seemingly suspended within it, glittering like flakes of mica, and Riss froze. The screams of pain and terror just went on and on, beyond the point where any human could have the energy to sustain them, but still Riss did not go on.

The drone recognized this darkness, and fled.

Riss headed for the airlock, happy to be ignored. Only now the corpse awaited, standing upright, seemingly woven together with silver tendrils, its eyes like flat pieces of obsidian.

"You . . . not know meaning . . . of no purpose," it said.

Riss tried to get past, but hands closed on her snakish body with inhuman strength. Something penetrated, straight in through the route *Primeval* had used to make her expel her last parasite eggs. The thing inside inspected every part of Riss's mind, focused for a long moment on events surrounding her inception. It was apparently curious about the secret Riss had been forced to keep concerning Factory Station Room 101 and its disappearance. Then it abruptly grew and devoured the foundations of Riss's mind, leaving emptiness behind, overlaid with a thin veil of consciousness and memory. Released at last, Riss reached the airlock and managed to expel herself out into vacuum, writhing there as the ship came alive again and accelerated away under fusion drive, eventually dropping into U-space.

SPEAR

"Penny Royal was right," said Riss. "I had not known the true meaning of being without purpose."

"Time to scrap yourself, then," Flute interjected before I could reply.

"But something else must have happened," I said. "How else could I have found you where I did?"

"I cannot say what impelled me. I spent ten years on the edge of oblivion with only one thread keeping me from it: the need to find Penny Royal again. I did, but whether to demand back what it took from me, try for some portion of vengeance or to just achieve that oblivion I don't know."

"So what happened?"

"Penny Royal just slapped me aside after it had finished with me. I had no consciousness at all until you brought me aboard this ship—the *Puling Child.*"

"Consciousness?" wondered Flute, then drawled, "Sure."

"Flute, unless you've got something positive to contribute," I said, "shut up."

Riss had swung her head like a compass needle towards where Flute was located and opened her black eye fully. I really didn't need my ship mind pissing off this drone. Thus far, it had been quite open and cooperative, but there was nothing to stop it deciding to give Flute a terminal injection through his case.

"I'm calling this ship the *Lance* now," I said.

"Why?"

"Because my name is Spear so it amused me. Also, because the piece of Penny Royal I have remaining aboard has similarities . . . there are other reasons too. It's complicated."

"Too complicated for a—" Flute started muttering, then must have decided that wasn't a positive contribution.

We were under drive, heading towards Masada, where I hoped the drone Amistad could supply missing answers, but we were weeks away from there yet. I'd searched the available data and it did seem that the events on the mining planet of Durana happened before Penny Royal bombarded Panarchia. And now my memories just didn't make sense.

"I know about that piece," said Riss. "Have you looked inside?"

"Looked inside?"

"The spine."

Riss said nothing further and, though it's pretty difficult to read a machine, I felt sure it was frightened. I studied said machine, and it, *she*, blinked her black eye at me.

"I've got other concerns," I said, "like why my memories just don't line up with reality. The chronology I had was the Panarchia bombing, followed by the prador capturing and thralling me, Jebel rescuing me, then me serving with Jebel prior to being killed."

"Sometimes the human mind, in an effort to repair itself, knits things together in the wrong places," Riss suggested.

"Yes, I'm sure that's a problem your kind never suffer from," I snapped, but the jibe had no strength to it, as I considered the . . . possibilities.

The jungle world where Jebel rescued me from the prador wasn't all that clear in my memory. I had put it down to having had a spider thrall dug into the back of my neck at the time. However, it didn't really seem all that different to Durana. I had memories of Panarchia, Durana and the world where Jebel found me, plus the hospital ship and some other events. Yet, the time when I was lying on the ground, after Krong attacked my prador captors, could just as easily have been stitched on.

It could've been a memory of what happened after the second-child shot me during the ambush on Durana. So what did that mean? Was it that I had served with Jebel Krong, was badly injured and hospitalized, went back into service and ended up serving on Panarchia during the bombing and so ... died there?

No, how could that be right? I distinctly remembered seeing the results of Penny Royal's depredations after Panarchia, and gathering data on that too. The absolute physical proof of that was the ship I was sitting in right at that moment. I had extracted information from a prador mind on its location, supposedly after Panarchia.

Nobody survived Panarchia ...

Everybody who knew anything about that world insisted on that fact and I—with my faulty stitched-together recollections—denied it.

My recollection ...

I stood up from the horseshoe console, glancing over at Riss, who then watched me silently as I headed for the door. In a moment I found myself in my laboratory, standing beside the glass cylinder containing Penny Royal's spine. How much coincidence can a story stand without seeming fake? The one survivor of Penny Royal's main atrocity, before the AI went AWOL, has discovered the location of Penny Royal's original ship. That one survivor chooses to use one of Penny Royal's victims to get him to that ship. Upon seeking out Penny Royal in its hideaway, that survivor picks up another of the AI's victims, who suddenly awakes after half a century of slumber. I had no idea what it all meant, but I felt damned sure I was being manipulated.

I opened the lid of the cylinder, reached inside and closed my hand around the spine. Again, I felt that weird and uncomfortable connection with the thing as I lifted it out and carried it over to the central table.

"Okay," I said, "let's see what we can find out."

With the assistance of Riss, I spent the weeks-long journey to Masada studying the spine. Riss possessed some highly sophisticated scanning gear within her body which I didn't have in the equipment available to me. The first thing we discovered was that the thing was active. It contained time crystals—cyclic quantum processes that required no input energy at all. It also used other processes to suck power from its surrounding environment, including the zero-point field. There were still other reactions which were hard to define, involving matter transmutation and the braking of the spin state of atoms.

"There's a U-space transceiver in there," Riss observed at one point.

It was difficult to map out because, like many of its systems, it was distributed. Like a lot of them, it ventured into the realms of picotech and perhaps even femtotech. We managed to ascertain that it was receiving more data than it was transmitting, which it was laying down in quantum storage throughout its entire mass. A rough estimate gave us a storage density ranging into terabytes per microgram—which meant this spine was capable, for example, of storing the minds of many thousands of human beings. It could even hold maybe as many as ten planetary AIs.

"It is also quantum entangled," Riss later added, even as we fell into orbit around the planet Masada.

"Probably with Penny Royal," I suggested.

"I am suspicious by nature," Riss told me. "And measuring the spin states of atoms is no easy task because it requires some intricate work with U-fields. However, I have managed to do some of that work using adaptations of my own U-space transceiver, and I am now considering whether or not I should kill you."

I turned towards the drone which, as usual, was coiled at the end of the table. Her head was raised to gaze at the arrays of scanning devices we had built around the spine.

"What?"

"I can't say for sure what the Golem Daleen saw that drove it to attack you, because its mind was obviously damaged and reformed by Penny Royal. But I'm guessing it saw you as an instrument of the AI that all but destroyed it."

"If you could elaborate," I said, taking just a small pace back.

"The spine is quantum entangled with a ruby memplant—the one that resides inside your skull."

13

TRENT

Trent had been here before. He'd lost count of the number of beatings he'd received as he worked his way up through the Separatist movement on Coloron. And if it came to counting which of his bones he'd had broken, it would have been easier to count the unbroken ones. Still, it hurt like hell and Stolman's men had been especially vicious. He reckoned that came down to the desperation they felt at being trapped here in the Rock Pool, and the need to take it out on someone.

The pain from his testicles still made him feel sick and the ribs down one side of his chest were all busted. So was his right forearm, many of the fingers on his left hand and the bones in the arch of his left foot. His insides felt a mess too and he knew that if he didn't get to an autodoc soon he would be pissing blood, if not dying. As for his jaw—definitely broken, over on that patch of floor where most of his teeth lay. How the hell Stolman expected him to reveal everything about the *Moray Firth*'s security now he didn't know. He could hardly speak.

"I do hope Satomi realizes what a loyal soul she has in you," said Stolman.

Trent just grunted. Even with everything he could tell Stolman about the *Moray Firth*, the man stood no chance. After any attempted attack, Isobel would just head for orbit and call in reinforcements. Stolman would end up as meat paste and quite likely, if he was still alive, Isobel would come after Trent because she wasn't the forgiving sort. As it was, he knew his only chance of survival now was to keep quiet for as long as he could. He could hope Stolman would tire of torture and resort to the cut aug on the table beside him—and that afterwards he would allow Trent to live. Then, when Isobel came to crush Stolman, there was at least a chance she would forgive Trent. He could rightly claim he had fought not to reveal anything that could be a danger to her, until unable to conceal everything in his mind.

"Cut off his clothing." Stolman sat back and waved a hand airily. "Let's see how much more cooperative he gets when we start grinding off his skin. Oh, just out of interest, Trent, the longest anyone has lasted is to the knees."

Wonderful.

Trent strained against the glue sticking him to the crates. A lot of it had been smeared on his clothing, so if they started cutting that away then maybe he could pull himself free. Almost certainly he would lose the skin off the backs of his hands and part of his scalp, but that would be better than what was coming.

"What?" Stolman abruptly stood up, his chair crashing over behind him. Further behind him Penny Royal's former Golem, which had been standing against the back wall, abruptly stepped forwards. "Cover! Weapons!" Stolman bellowed, just as explosions detonated outside.

Hi, Isobel, thought Trent tiredly.

Another detonation blew smoke and debris into the room via an access corridor. Stolman's men quickly pulled out a wide selection of lethal hardware in response and took cover. Glancing at Trent, Stolman reached for a hand laser at his belt, but the instinct for survival had taken over and he was already running before he could pull it. All sorts of weaponry ended up directed towards the corridor's entrance, including the two autoguns, just as a second explosion sent a disc-shaped security drone bouncing inside. Next, a mosquito autogun came through the smoke, spitting pulse-fire. This picked up one man and flung him back, shredding him at the same time. Trent thought, *And that's for my balls, you fucker.* A protruding arm caught two shots next, the owner shrieking, but the gun moved on to a more immediate target, its shots splashing and ricocheting from ceramal bones.

Another explosion sent crates tumbling from a stack even as Stolman's autoguns concentrated on the mosquito. The thing moved across the floor at high speed and took out one of the other guns, but then ran into the blur that was the Golem. It just picked the gun up and smashed it against the floor before discarding it. Yet another explosion brought sheets of chain-glass raining down. Incendiaries began filling the area with boiling smoke. Pulse-fire stabbed down five times, each time finding a target—then the red slash of laser carbines and one proton beam speared upwards towards a hole in the roof. Trent eyed the source of that proton beam, which had to be the greatest danger. Its operator was crouching behind a loading robot, but the next explosion tipped the robot over to crush the marksman.

A little messy, thought Trent, *but acceptable.*

Just then, some force tried to suck him away from the wall of crates, then slammed him back into it. With his eyes watering, Trent watched an I-beam clang end-on against the floor, then topple. When he looked up it was at sky, since most of the roof was now gone. Something dropped through the hole, a proton beam stabbing down from it repeatedly, like a cutting torch slicing through confetti. A man tumbled through the air, trailing fire, then two more men just burst like ignited hydrogen balloons. How many? Trent had lost count.

Isobel descended like some Aztec goddess, spewing fire all around her and writhing in returned fire almost as if relishing the feel of it. After the initial fusillade, her firing grew intermittent then finally stuttered to a halt as she drew to a stop in mid-air. Then she abruptly slid sideways to crash through a simple glass window into an internal office. She came out clutching a figure, Stolman, and descended to the floor.

"And thus," declaimed a voice, right beside Trent, "do the scales drop from my eyes."

He looked into two luminous dark blue eyes. The Golem held Stolman's atomic shear up in one hand. Trent just stared at it, and waited for the end. Suddenly it swung round in front of him, vibrating under numerous autogun impacts, light flashing all around it and a hot metal stink filling the air. Trent looked up as Isobel's proton beam stabbed out again and took out this remaining autogun, which had obviously been damaged but had managed to restart itself. Why hadn't it shot at Isobel? Obvious: Stolman must have realized she was all but invulnerable to its shots and so directed it against Trent. Petty vengeance. But why had the Golem stood in the way of those shots? Because it was moral now? Stolman's Golem? Or *Penny Royal*'s Golem?

"It's not listening to you any more, Stolman," said Isobel.

The Golem moved closer and used the atomic shear to cut behind Trent with infinite precision.

"Snickety snick," it said, "doubly quick."

So accurately did it cut, that when his left hand dropped away from the crate only a thin layer of glue and plasmesh coated the back of it. Eventually he fell away, landing on his knees and supported by his one good hand, biting down on a yell. After a moment he again looked across at Isobel. She was hanging over Stolman, who she must have knocked out, like a snake about to strike.

"So what do you think we should do with him?" she asked.

Something involving a lot of pain, Trent felt, but right then he was more concerned about the damage to his own body. He wanted nerve blockers and an autodoc, pronto. When he didn't reply, she turned slightly to gaze to one side at the Golem, who now stood motionless, the light gone from its eyes. It shifted slightly as if in response to some unheard signal, but this movement took away its balance and it fell to the floor like a sack of scrap.

"Damn," said Isobel. "It's inert again." She dipped her hood to inspect Stolman, "But maybe that won't last."

Rearing up again, she next moved her variety of limbs in a smooth rippling twist—the end result was her grav-harness coming off and skidding across the floor towards Trent. He reached out and took it up, standing mostly balanced on one foot, and slowly and methodically donned it and tightened up all the straps. Isobel watched him, alien, unknowable. It was going to hurt like hell when it took his weight off the floor.

"Go back to the ship," she said. "Get yourself fixed up." Then she dipped her head downwards to look at Stolman, who had just emitted a low groan and was recovering consciousness. "I have some fuel to buy," she added.

Trent studied the harness controls, then tapped in instructions with his good hand. The harness slowly took his weight, his broken ribs grinding.

"What . . . 'bout . . . ' im?" he managed through his shattered mouth.

"I'm hungry," Isobel replied.

Trent was up through the roof and sending himself towards the space port when he heard the first muffled scream.

SVERL

Sverl just couldn't keep still. The fight at Stolman's place had triggered some remaining prador instinct in him, and he'd just wanted to be in on the action. And Isobel Satomi? He was utterly fascinated by the changes she had undergone. After Trent exited through the warehouse roof, Sverl increased his control of his Golem. Very carefully, because Isobel was haiman and might notice, he deliberately blocked the affectation of glowing eyes and made it turn its head for a better view.

Isobel fed like the hooder she'd become; stripping away skin and flesh while Stolman shrieked in agony. She'd sliced away his face, the muscles around his neck and had peeled away the clothing on his upper body. She started in on his chest before he fainted. Then, obviously bored with this game and with better things to do, she drove tubular feeding mouths into exposed but undamaged arteries in his neck and spent the next ten minutes draining him dry and finally killing him. As she did this, Sverl felt her tentatively reach out to his Golem via some virtual Dracocorp aug, but then withdraw to concentrate on her feeding.

She ate faster now, picking Stolman up off the floor and simultaneously turning him and stripping him. Bigger chunks of muscle, fat and sometimes bone went into her larger mouth. Sverl recognized her ravenous appetite. What prador wouldn't? Obviously this had distracted her from her intent to try and seize control of the Golem, and now Sverl realized he had a decision to make. If he wanted to now become active and go in pursuit of Penny Royal—though to what end he wasn't sure—here was a golden opportunity. Satomi was intent on going after Thorvald Spear who was intent on going after Penny Royal. Following either of these would lead Sverl to the AI. He should allow Isobel to take control of the Golem and use it to maintain his link with her. Eventually, when she caught up with Spear, Sverl could establish contact with his second-child mind. After all, it wasn't as loyal as a buyer might suppose . . .

After consuming all his soft tissues, Isobel left Stolman's harder parts scattered over the floor—his larger bones and skull. Sverl felt a moment of panic, not sure if he was ready to relinquish control of the Golem. But she didn't try, for Stolman had obviously not satisfied her appetite. Picking up a stray human leg on her way, she went over to drag a partially intact corpse from the rubble. After finishing the leg, she began devouring that. As he watched her, Sverl sent an instruction to Bsorol, his nearest attendant first-child. He immediately set off and, by the time Isobel was discarding the remnants of the second corpse, had returned with the carcass of a small reaverfish. Sverl didn't hesitate. He chopped the fish in half with one of his claws and, retaining the tail end, he held it up to his mandibles like an ice-cream cone. Sverl munched away happily as he watched the show.

A third corpse now—was Isobel going to eat them all? This one was badly burned and after a moment she discarded it, moving on to one that had merely been decapitated, which was obviously preferable. Along with her human form, had Isobel lost that strange human inclination to enjoy cooked meat? Sverl was thankful it wasn't one he'd acquired along with his other human characteristics. The prador here in the ocean looked askance at his odd behaviour anyway, so would definitely see such a change in tastes as dangerously aberrant.

Isobel finished with the third corpse and that, at last, seemed to be enough. Though it was difficult to understand the behaviour of alien creatures, Isobel was certainly easier to read in this form than her previous human one. She was obviously dazed, now coming out of a feeding frenzy. Quite probably her insides ached and certainly she had expanded—gaps showing here and there between the plates of her chitin carapace. Isobel straightened up abruptly, then turned and faced the Golem. It was decision time for Sverl and suddenly it was no decision at all. Of course he would allow her control of it.

She reached for it through her virtual aug, opening up the bandwidth and reading how to control it while incorporating the correct degree of autonomy. Sverl allowed it its own responses because, in the end, it wasn't just a telefactored machine. It was a distinct being in and of itself, though strange and quirky even in prador terms. Its eyes glowing, it stood up.

"Snackety snack," it said, swinging its head from side to side as it surveyed the carnage, then, "I love you, Isobel."

Sverl was baffled by this, until he realized that some of his own feelings must have been leaking through—and he had, just in the last hour, acquired a deep feeling of kinship and affection for her. Isobel also seemed puzzled by this statement, for she hesitated for a long drawn-out moment before issuing verbal instructions.

"Follow me," she said through her voice synthesizer, "I have fuel to buy."

Outside the warehouse an armoured car had arrived, along with a fire robot, which wouldn't now be required since the flames had failed to take hold. Armed shell people enforcers had disembarked from the car, but hesitated to do anything more. In Carapace City they enforced a limited degree of public order because chaos was bad for business. As Sverl finished the first half of the reaverfish and picked up the next, he tuned into their communications. They knew this was Stolman's warehouse and were aware that he had made some sort of play against Isobel Satomi. They also knew what she now looked like and, as she exited, with Stolman's Golem behind her, they made the sensible decision to stand aside.

The shell people had little love for Stolman—he'd been getting far too powerful and arrogant.

"Is Stolman dead?" asked one brave soul as she passed through them.

"He is," she replied simply, and moved on.

Sverl now noted another watcher in the area. The battered-looking Polity drone was hovering up by a nearby warehouse's second-storey loading hatch. Through the eyes of his Golem, Sverl observed it for a short while, but decided there was nothing to be done. The thing presented the persona of a reckless erstwhile war drone, taking a tour of the backwaters and rough houses of the Polity line. But it had been here too long and its subtle interventions betrayed it. The thing was almost certainly a watcher placed here by Earth Central Security. Sverl had considered sending one of his own prador drones to destroy it, but success was not a foregone conclusion. Moreover, even if it worked, ECS would only send something more difficult to spot.

Isobel moved on to Taiken Fuels. Taiken himself would doubtless suffer one of his problematic bowel movements, brought on by his own radical physical changes, before he realized there was money to be made. Sverl was about to turn his attention to other things when something intruded on his connection with his Golem.

"You really need to keep your eye on the ball, Sverl," said a voice.

Sverl immediately traced the communication to the ECS watcher, then ramped up his com security at once.

"What are you talking about, drone?" he enquired.

"Well, while you've been having a grand old time watching Isobel smear Stolman and having a lunch break, you haven't been paying attention to your other feeds."

"If you could elaborate," suggested Sverl, frantically checking his screens and alerts.

"Your Beta satellite," the drone explained. "You really should check out the view."

Sverl inserted his free claw into a pit control even as the alert made itself known. He dropped the remaining reaverfish and came close to experiencing a problematic bowel movement of his own.

This changed everything.

BLITE

Great, the Rock Pool, thought Blite. It was another place he'd decided he never wanted to visit. Any place occupied by a large group of people turning themselves into prador had to be a bad place to go to. The prador the shell people worshipped were here too. To be frank, the entire Graveyard had also dropped off his "desired destination" list a number of years ago.

Blite grimaced. Sure, there were fortunes to be made here. Some collectors paid premium prices for wartime artefacts, and salvaged technology always had a price, despite being antediluvian in Polity terms. There was even money still to be made in rescuing people or memplants. However, the dangers were greater too. Betrayals were frequent, non-payment and other underhand practices could occur and transactions could get bloody. The Graveyard was full of nasty people like Isobel Satomi and legendary villains like the indestructible Mr Pace. This was why Blite had stuck to the Polity in recent years. Yes, he had tended to push the borders of legality, but not in ways that might get him dead.

"No strange U-signatures detected, and Penny Royal isn't searching," commented Leven. "I don't think there's one of those hidden power plants here."

"You're still with us, Leven," said Greer. "You've been a bit quiet lately."

Leven had no reply to this.

"So why are we here?" wondered Brond.

Blite felt a flash of irritation, since this was a question one or another of his crew had been asking ever since they entered the Graveyard. It put pressure on him to ask similar questions of Penny Royal, and he'd already learned he didn't like the way the AI often answered.

"I'm not acquainted with metaphysics, so why don't you go ask our passenger?" he snapped.

"Okay," said Brond. He sat back, loosened up his shoulders as if he was preparing for a fight, and gazed up at the ceiling. "Penny Royal, why are we here?"

There was no verbal reply, but Brond suddenly didn't look very well. His mouth dropped open and his hands balled into fists. Blite wondered where he'd been taken in his own mind—or if he'd been reliving one of his own memories.

"We don't have no choice in the matter," Brond whispered, then swallowed noisily.

"But why is Penny Royal here?" interjected Martina. She had sense enough to direct her question to the rest of them, rather than to the AI itself.

Dead silence met this. Brond had no answer and Blite knew he certainly didn't.

"Clear as mud," grumped Ikbal.

Blite returned his attention to the world below on his screens, then eyed the indicators that would show if the hold door had opened again. He abruptly came to a decision, though whether his orders would be allowed he had no idea.

"Perhaps you should ask?" Brond suggested to Blite.

"He does seem to have a better connection," Martina agreed.

"We really shouldn't just ride along with this," said Greer. "We must do something."

"Mebbe," said Ikbal, watching Blite warily.

Blite felt another flash of anger. Before they left Masada there had been at least some degree of respect for his position as captain and owner of *The Rose*. Now his crew felt that any of them could come to the bridge, even when it wasn't their shift, interrupt him, have discussions about what they should do, and generally act as if they were part of a committee rather than part of his crew.

"All right," he said, "that's enough. You, Ikbal, and you, Martina, aren't on duty right now so you can fuck off back to your cabins or the rec room. And you, Brond, can shut the fuck up. When I want anyone's input I'll ask for it. Is that understood?"

By now, Ikbal and Martina were out of their seats.

"Oh, and if you're feeling at a bit of a loose end then maybe it's about time you checked the maintenance roster," he added. "I've noticed how it's getting just a bit ratty in the living quarters and I haven't seen any clean-bots out of their niches for a while." He paused, realized he was panting and at the point of going into a rant. He deliberately forced himself to calm down. "That would be your area, wouldn't it Ikbal?"

"It would, sir," replied Ikbal, understanding his captain's mood at once and quickly leaving the bridge.

"And what's that look for?" Blite asked Martina, who seemed affronted. "Do you think that because you offered to fuck me I'm going to give you some slack? I want you to check the manifest of our stores right now—we have to be getting short of something."

Martina turned away and stormed out huffily, but Blite knew she would do as she was told. He now turned to Brond. "We've got contacts here, I'm sure. Check our files and see what you can find."

"Yessir," said Brond, and immediately began applying himself to his console and screen.

"And you, Greer, check coms down on the planet and see if anything odd is happening down there."

Greer likewise applied herself.

"Now, where was I? Oh yeah, Leven . . . why've you been so quiet lately?"

"You all may be forming the opinion that Penny Royal is a changed character," replied Leven. "I, on the other hand, being closer to that black AI on the mental plane, am not entirely of that opinion."

"Which still doesn't explain your reticence," said Blite, not bothering to dispute that "changed character" claim.

"The tiger might not want to eat you today, but it's still a tiger. Always best to keep one's head down and try not to annoy said tiger."

"Interesting metaphor," said Blite, "but now you might be prodding it with a stick, because I want you to contact whoever runs that space port below and get us permission to land. Then I want you to land us."

"Thank you so much," said Leven. "You'll be glad to know that no permissions are required. The space port was built by shell people for the sum purpose of luring business to this world. The only ships that might have a problem here are ECS vessels, what with the renegade prador under the sea nearby . . ."

Blite said, "Take us down, then."

As thrusters fired and they began to draw closer to the Rock Pool, Blite speculated. Penny Royal had spent a lot of time in the Graveyard and it was known to have dealings with the prador. Could it be that the AI's presence here involved these contacts in some way? If it did, then their feelings towards Penny Royal might be due for a rapid change, just when they were slightly more comfortable with its presence aboard. If the prador were involved with the AI, danger could materialize at any time.

SPEAR

The moment the *Lance* surfaced in the Masadan system, we found a Polity attack ship sitting in our path. The thing was a long narrow wedge of midnight and looked precisely what it was: deadly. A microsecond later, it splintered off missiles from its own substance. These disappeared in micro U-jumps, which would have been impossible during the war, since the technology didn't exist then, and reappeared just a couple of miles either side of us.

"What's it saying?" I asked.

"It wants to know what we're doing here above this particular piece of Polity property," Flute replied. "Also why we happen to have restocked a railgun magazine which, according to historical record, should have been practically empty. Why we have a multi-megaton fusion device aboard, how I was obtained, what we've been doing in the Graveyard, who other than myself is aboard, what our business is here and, incidentally, why it shouldn't vaporize us right away."

"You've provided details?" I enquired.

"I have," Flute continued. "Now it wants to put Golem aboard, it wants full access to me and is currently in a U-space conference with a forensic AI in preparation for a full investigation of us and this ship."

"Touchy, isn't it?" said Riss.

I glanced at the drone, coiled over by the wall with her head down. She had decided not to kill me just yet, since that wouldn't resolve the puzzle of my connection with Penny Royal's spine. Of course I was grateful for that, but I had my own problems with that connection.

"This place has a bit of history, that's why it's jumpy," I said. "I want to talk to that ship."

"Go ahead," Flute replied.

"Polity attack ship, what's your name?" I asked.

"Oh, human communications, is it?" the attack ship rejoined with affected boredom. "My name is *Micheletto's Garrotte.*"

"Huh," said Riss, "someone fancies itself as a Borgia assassin."

"Well," added the *Garrotte* AI. "At least I'm only named after an assassin, and am not an anachronism incapable of being anything else."

"Screw you," said Riss.

"Surely not—you only screw prador."

"I think we're getting away from the point here," I tried.

"Hardly," said the *Garrotte.* "An interesting trio you have there. A Room 101 hash-up of a drone, a prador kamikaze that didn't quite make it to the front and a recently resurrected, deluded and vengeful bio-espionage agent. Now, are you really the types I want orbiting a protectorate world, occupied by a similarly recently resurrected member of the Atheter race? In a Polity destroyer which was once occupied by Penny Royal, and now contains a continent buster?"

"Bringing us back to the point," I said. "This was a Polity destroyer but under rights of salvage it now belongs to me. This also means you've no right to put Golem aboard, or a forensic AI."

"No right?" the attack ship asked disbelievingly. "You are seriously deluded if you think you have rights extending . . . hold on a minute."

After a brief silence, Flute said, "It just recalled its missiles."

"Ah, Amistad is talking and has just intervened," said Riss, her head abruptly jerking up and her black eye opening.

"It's moving away," Flute added.

I could see that. The attack ship abruptly peeled away from us, with no steering thrusters or any other visible drive propelling it. Then it just disappeared back under the chameleonware that must have originally concealed it.

I had no doubt that watch stations along the edge of the Graveyard had spotted us on the way out and that this thing had been forewarned. U-space tracking had obviously become more sophisticated since the war.

"What's going on?" I asked.

"I have been denied access to our weapons," said Flute.

"What?"

"Wartime programming," Flute explained. "I have been disconnected from weapons control and the only way to reconnect is by physical intervention. Further programming has also been added. Should I attempt to reconnect to our weapons, while in the vicinity of Masada, the fusion bomb will detonate."

"Best you don't do that, then," I said. Having been reminded that Flute originated from a prador kamikaze was giving me worrying thoughts. "Riss?"

"We are now good to approach Masada," the drone explained. "Under protectorate law, only warships controlled by Polity AIs are allowed to approach this world. Those under private ownership must be boarded, assessed and thereafter controlled by Polity AIs. In this case Amistad, the warden of Masada, has allowed the rules to be relaxed. I have been designated the Polity AI boarding contingent."

"What about that forensic AI and my ownership of this vessel?"

"Your salvage claim has been approved and no further investigation is required."

"Take us in, Flute," I instructed, then sat back to ponder the oddity of this situation. Were I a Polity AI, I would want to strip this ship down to its individual components and study each of them at the sub-molecular level. I would also be very wary of allowing Penny Royal's former craft near a world where the AI had apparently been given amnesty. Especially while it was controlled by someone who wanted to hunt that AI down, which they must have surely worked out by now. Something did not add up here. A lot of things didn't add up.

"I want to talk to Amistad," I said, even as the fusion drive kicked in to take us on the last leg of our journey to Masada itself.

"Amistad will speak to you, face-to-face, down on the planet," said Riss. "Further communications with him have been blocked."

Now, to give us some scenery, Flute had called up a truncated view in-system onto the screen wall. I could see the sun, but with its glare toned down. The gas giant Calypse was off to one side—like an onyx marble amidst the complexity of the Braemar moon system. And Masada lay ahead, enlarged in a subframe, aubergine in hue with its moons highlighted in their courses around it. Notable too were the other items around that world. Here were a veritable swarm of satellites and various space stations, including a massive one still under construction.

Before coming here, Flute had updated astrogation data files so had known we couldn't surface from U-space closer than two parsecs from Masada. I had no doubt that around that world lay the means of preventing anyone venturing too close: USERs, underspace interference emitters, dipping their singularities in and out of U-space to cause local disruption fields. And doubtless there were big weapons too, in case a hostile ship managed to penetrate too close. Perhaps this last explained Amistad's lack of paranoia about us now approaching the world, but it certainly didn't explain that "no further investigation required."

Too many things didn't add up, including the attitude behind that phrase. Then there was the mysterious connection I had with Penny Royal's discarded spine, plus my apparently erroneous memories. I was beginning to entertain the suspicion that I was a piece being moved around a chessboard, but with no idea who was playing me.

14

SVERL

In response to the new arrival the Polity drone had pointed out, Sverl immediately issued a recall to all his children, some of whom were out hunting reaverfish. Then he issued recalls to various pieces of equipment scattered about the world—including drones, survey robots and some of the closer perambulating mining robots and refineries under the sea. Others that were more distant might have to be abandoned. If he wanted to retrieve any satellites, he could pick them up when he was in orbit, if that was where he was going . . .

It was time for him to act, surely?

But how? Penny Royal was finally here, the supposed target of his vengeance. Could he simply wait for *The Rose* to draw closer, surface his dreadnought and deploy its weapons to destroy the ship? Penny Royal might be dangerous, but it was aboard a simple salvage ship and surely couldn't survive the blast of a crust-breaking prador kamikaze.

However, such destruction would be too impersonal. And if Sverl was completely honest with himself, plain vengeance wasn't all he wanted, if he wanted it at all. He wanted a confrontation, resolution, explanation and answers to questions he could feel but just didn't know how to ask . . . maybe he was even hoping for absolution?

So again: what should he do? Sverl could think of no possible reason why Penny Royal might come here, beyond himself. Perhaps the Polity's acceptance of the black AI was justified, perhaps it had changed and was now coming to right wrongs and give explanations. Or quite possibly it was coming to correct past mistakes and its methods hadn't changed at all. Perhaps it had come to erase those mistakes . . .

Sverl champed his mandibles, utterly conflicted. What if Penny Royal was coming to cure him, to set his transformation in reverse? Did he, like Isobel Satomi, want a cure for his ills? Did *she* any longer want such a cure? She appeared quite comfortable in her new form, while Sverl himself was ambivalent about his own transformation. He froze for long minutes, his thought processes locked until the need for a response drove him to action. He turned back to his screens and inserted both his claws into pit controls. He could at least get some of his other local problems out of the way.

"Sfolk," he said to the young adult prador peering from one screen. "I am now relinquishing control of your ship's system. You must decide amongst yourselves what you do next."

Sfolk made a sound that had its human equivalent in, "Uh?"

"I will not stop you returning to the Kingdom," Sverl continued, "but must warn you not to expect justice or fair treatment there. In the Kingdom only might is right." He paused before sending the signal that would remove his lock from their vessel's engine and weapons. Was it such a good idea to give them control of their weapons now? Perhaps he should delay . . . No, he decided not. The Five would probably be squabbling for the next ten years about who controlled what, and most likely would return to their fratricidal pursuits.

"That is all," Sverl added, and closed down the connection.

He now turned his attention to two more screens, from which two wholly adult prador gazed at him. "Cvorn and Skute, I give you fair warning that I am relinquishing my rule of our enclave."

Only as he said the words did he realize they were true. Penny Royal was here and Sverl felt certain some resolution of his vague aims was in the offing, although whether that would be confrontation with or destruction of the AI he didn't know. Thereafter . . . he knew he couldn't stay here.

"Why?" asked Cvorn, while Skute just bubbled—Sverl felt sure the latter had been sliding into senility for some time.

"The time has come for me to take care of some matters that have remained unresolved for . . . some while," Sverl replied.

"You wish to kill the rogue AI, Penny Royal," Cvorn stated.

No, yes, maybe, thought Sverl. How could he possibly explain the complexities of the situation to one of his former kind? Cvorn was intelligent for a prador, but would still become first confused, then angry. This would translate into suspicion verging on paranoia towards Sverl's activities. He sometimes wondered how he'd managed not to end up in an all-out battle with his neighbours during their time here. Then, abruptly, it hit him. He'd never revealed to any prador his encounter with Penny Royal, yet somehow Cvorn had learned of it. What else might the old prador have learned? What might he know about Sverl's transformation?

"Yes, I am going to kill the rogue AI," he said carefully.

"So you know its present location?" asked Cvorn.

"Yes," Sverl replied, his own suspicions increasing, "I know its location."

"And you're leaving?"

"Yes, I'm leaving," said Sverl, deciding it better to pretend he'd be searching for the AI, rather than revealing Penny Royal was aboard the descending ship. If he did, Cvorn might open fire on *The Rose.* He continued, "I have also relinquished control of the Five's ship and have left them to decide their own command structure. They want to return to the Kingdom . . . for females."

"Yes, apparently so," said Cvorn.

Now suspicion transformed into paranoia and Sverl began to pay a lot more attention to his data feeds. Most of his children and drones had returned, the two from the space port were just entering the sea and would be back in just minutes. Only three of the distant reaverfish hunters would take some time to arrive. Two of the big mining robots were trundling inside, with a big refinery—one that weaned useful pure metals out of seawater—coming in close behind. But there was a lot of other movement out there too—as children, drones and robots similarly returned to the three destroyers. These belonged to Cvorn, Skute and the Five respectively.

"Is there something you want to say to me, Cvorn?" he asked.

"Just that you've made a serious mistake, Sverl," said Cvorn, "I put that down to what you're turning into."

In this situation, a human military commander would never have replied in such a fashion. Sverl was also now thoroughly aware of his mistake. Any other prador would have had to ask, thus giving Cvorn a chance to brag and threaten. But Sverl just cut communications and considered the situation as it now stood. Cvorn and Skute had long since refused to return to the Kingdom because, like Sverl, they felt that ending the war was a big mistake. Their rabid hate of humanity had not waned and it had taken all Sverl's powers of persuasion to stop them ripping apart the first shell people to arrive here. And, in later years, he'd barely prevented them from eradicating Carapace City. He'd told them it was better to learn from the humans, so they could gauge how best to exterminate them in vast numbers, rather than just wipe out a few—the kind of argument prador liked.

But apparently Cvorn, possibly Skute and quite likely the Five, had been well aware of Sverl's encounter with Penny Royal and the changes he had undergone. Typical of prador, they no longer considered him one of them. It was likely they were now preparing to act against him and he must be ready for that.

Why they had not moved against him before now could be down to an established principle of prador military tactics—that two destroyers had a destructive power equal to one dreadnought. In preventing the Five from controlling their ship, he'd maintained a balance of power here. And by relinquishing that control, he'd shifted that balance. Sverl immediately tried to link through to the Five's destroyer, and was completely unsurprised to find his access to its systems now blocked.

While previously he'd considered laying a trap of some kind for the AI here in the ocean, for surely it was here for him, the situation had now changed. If he stayed down here, his ship stood a good chance of being destroyed. But he faced yet another mental conflict. The humans in Carapace City and elsewhere were now in danger. In fact, "in danger" wasn't really strong enough. Even if Cvorn and the others didn't act against him, they would certainly exterminate the humans here as soon as his protection was removed. Sverl was very much against that and wondered if his long fascination with them could now be styled affection.

What could he do?

One of the human traits he'd acquired, and could really do without, was a tendency to be indecisive and procrastinate. However, he was part AI, so could also think with utter logic and come to the most rational conclusions. He coldly considered options as he watched *The Rose* descend towards the space port. He couldn't fully protect the shell people and himself. The three prador destroyers possessed CTDs, atomic and even chemical weapons. Just one of these could annihilate Carapace City, and he simply didn't have the hardfields and anti-munitions to stop one getting through. Especially if he was using them to protect himself.

Sverl began to prepare. He first sent an alert to all his children to bring them to battle readiness and applied a higher level of security protocol. He didn't want the others sneaking some weapon either close to or aboard his ship. Next, he began ramping up power accumulation from his fusion reactors and running diagnostics on his weapons systems. It then occurred to him that now might be a good time to get a little sneaky too. His ship rested on the seabed, but was adjacent to a drilling and mining installation he'd been using to obtain hydrocarbons. That installation had now shut down—its equipment being withdrawn— but a convenient mineshaft still lay available. He selected one of the midrange CTDs from his weapons cache, set up automated systems to transfer it to his drone cache, then ordered two drones to transfer it down the mineshaft.

This one device would be enough to cause plenty of damage to Skute's ship and minimal damage to the other two. He could've chosen something more destructive, but the resultant tsunami would have swept away Carapace City, while this lesser device should result in a wave only a few metres high. Next, he selected other devices from his armoury, some of them of Polity manufacture, and set them loading to his railgun carousels. He paused then, with everything in motion around him and the volume of noise in his ship increasing. He had done all he could here for now.

Time to make a call.

The call he made was through Carapace City's communication network. He used only a static image of how he'd once looked—as he'd appeared when he last used this channel, four decades ago. He also ensured it remained completely and deliberately unsecured, though he kept tracing software running.

"Yes," snapped a shellman, his gaze off to one side, probably watching his strange recent customer departing.

"Taiken," said Sverl, waiting for the man to look at the screen. Taiken, of Taiken Fuels, the most powerful trader here and de facto ruler of the shell people, swung his attention back to the screen. His eyes widened in shock and his mandibles dropped to expose his human mouth.

"Father-Captain Sverl!" he exclaimed, then made a gobbling noise only vaguely reminiscent of that made by an obsequious first-child. The cam on his system tracked him as he made some half-human attempt to grovel.

"You must order the population of Carapace City evacuated inland, immediately," said Sverl. "You are all in extreme danger."

Taiken just crouched there for a moment with his human mouth trying to frame words and failing. Eventually he pulled himself back upright and managed, "Why?"

"You are a shellman so understand that you are all here on sufferance. Only my intervention with my fellows has prevented them from eradicating you. I am now no longer in command here and soon my fellows will begin cleaning house. Their first action is likely to involve them firing a CTD at your city."

"They wouldn't," Taiken said, showing that thoroughly irritating human tendency for self-deception.

"They would," Sverl affirmed. "And then they would take great pleasure in hunting down any survivors. The best chance your people have of surviving is to head inland and disperse in the mountains—the mountains because there may be actions out here in the sea that will result in tsunamis. My fellows have not appreciated my protection of you and your people, so my departure from this ocean may not be a quiet one."

"But we're shell people," Taiken managed.

By now, at least five other individuals were overhearing this exchange. Sverl traced four of them. Two were shell people and Taiken's competitors, another was a standard human competitor who had arrived from off-world a decade ago, while the fourth was Cvorn. Usually Stolman or one of his employees would be listening in too, but not anymore . . .

"And you are deluded," Sverl replied, "if you think that changing yourselves has raised you in prador estimation. While we may hate the humans of the Polity, they do have our respect, whereas for you people we only hold contempt."

"But I thought—"

Sverl interrupted. "You have been warned—and I calculate you have less than a day and a night to get out. That is all." Sverl cut the communication to Taiken but, leaving the com open, he now began to apply some security. Cvorn and the humans were easy to block out, but the remaining listener was still there.

"Drone," Sverl said. "I know you're listening."

"You're surprisingly smart for a prador," it replied.

"I know you're ECS," said Sverl.

"No shit, Sherlock," said the drone. "And I know what you are too."

It took Sverl a moment to translate the first phrase, then a further moment to digest the second one. How many didn't know what had once been his most intimate secret? He continued, "As you heard, the people of the city are in danger. Taiken, if he can bring himself to accept my warning, will only pass it on to his own people."

"Hence your lack of security on that call," said the drone.

"And hence my speaking to you now. My fellow prador here will certainly act against the human population there, even if they don't act against me."

"I would say that 'fellow prador' might be stretching things a tad, especially since you're showing such concern for the disgusting humans here. So I take it you're leaving us, Sverl?"

"I may be," said Sverl, irritated. "But I'm speaking to you as I'm sure you have ways of spreading my warning, convincingly, amidst the entire human population there. And of course, being an ECS drone, I'm sure you are sufficiently *moral* to want to."

"Already doing it," said the drone. "Your little chat with Taiken is now playing on every piece of computing in Carapace City. I'm setting up embarkation points, have seized control of all robot transportation and am having it converge on these. Even now, grav-coaches and other large vehicles are taking on passengers to ferry them inland. They'll be deposited in the mountains." The drone paused for a second. "Already over six hundred people have boarded in the initial panic . . . I've also made contact with the captains of the two ships whose shuttles are in the space port and am organizing Galaxy Bank payment for them to take on passengers. One trip up only, unfortunately, since both captains want to get away from here just as fast as they can. But still, between them those shuttles could get over a thousand away from here."

Sverl took a moment to absorb that, then began to run some checks. The drone wasn't lying: it really had set all that in motion in just a few minutes. Recordings of his exchange with Taiken were running on four of his screen feeds from the city and a list of embarkation points was up on other screens along with instructions. He also noted that all fire klaxons, reaverfish alert sirens and other warning devices were either sounding or flashing. The drone had just demonstrated how powerful it was and how deeply it had infiltrated here.

"Shame the other two ships at the space port are . . . unavailable," he commented.

"Yes, a shame," said the drone, "but, as we know, people on Satomi's ship would end up either eaten or sent for coring. While their fate aboard the other ship could be even worse. Incidentally, Blite's ship just changed course." The drone paused for a second, then continued, "So, Sverl, with Penny Royal arriving here you decided to act. And in acting, you shifted the balance of power down there. Your 'fellow prador,' who incidentally learned of your transformation over twenty years ago, now see an opportunity to attack something they find more detestable than shell people. Bit of a pickle you're in there."

"You're remarkably well informed."

"I certainly am. Anyway, this has been on the cards for a while. Even without Penny Royal, you may have agreed to release the Five's ship with the same result. By the way, they do intend to head back to the Kingdom, after they've fulfilled what they see as their side of their bargain with Cvorn. Silly of them—they'll end up sizzling in some prador sea."

"Thank you for filling in the detail for me," said Sverl drily.

"Maybe you can give me some more detail in return. You said 'less than a day and a night' but a more accurate timeframe might be useful."

"I can be no more accurate than that," Sverl replied. "I will delay for as long as possible, but the onset of conflict is down to Cvorn and the rest." Meanwhile Sverl checked up on *The Rose* and felt a moment of bafflement.

"Okay." Sverl imagined the drone shrugging. "I'll do what I can for them, but there's almost certainly going to be a lot of deaths."

"Goodbye, drone," said Sverl and cut the communication.

He gazed at his screens, still baffled and, in a strange way, disappointed. It seemed Penny Royal was not coming directly to him. *The Rose* had just fired up its steering thrusters and was now grav-planing away from the space port, heading directly towards Carapace City.

TRENT

The autodoc worked over his torso first, slicing him open to expose shattered ribs. It repositioned some pieces, discarding others, then bone welded them—in some cases fitting dissolving clamps. Before sealing up his flesh, fat and skin, it inserted tentacles to make repairs to the internal damage. It turned out this wouldn't have killed him but would have, as he had supposed, had him pissing blood.

Trent lay there, naked and conscious, trying not to look at the thing working but morbid curiosity occasionally drew his gaze back. The doc had offered him complete unconsciousness but he had demurred, going for nerve blockers instead. He had relayed the feeds from cameras positioned on the hull of the *Moray Firth* and was also checking news feeds from Carapace City. There had been one small item about the battle at the Reaverson Warehouse. This was surprisingly detailed, and was also correct in its suppositions about what Stolman had been after and how Isobel had responded. It even showed footage of him winging away in the grav-harness, then had a later clip of Isobel departing the place with Stolman's Golem in tow. Now there was only one repeating broadcast, this being a communication between the prador father-captain under the sea and a shellman called Taiken. Isobel needed to get back here, and fast.

The doc finished its work inside him and closed him up neatly. The scar lines of the new skin welds precisely overlay those left previously— the last time it repaired his ribs. It then moved onto his hand and began to take it apart like a Meccano model. Holding a remote control in his other hand Trent flicked back to the four cam views outside, and saw that Isobel had arrived.

Gazing at the stretch of space port lying between the *Moray Firth* and the terminal building, Trent watched Isobel writhe towards the ship. Surprisingly, despite the news, she had succeeded in her aims. Behind her walked the Golem and behind it came a large grav-sled loaded with barrels. A primitive wheeled hydrovane fuel tanker was also trundling its way. Isobel came in through the airlock while the Golem led the grav-sled to the hold door, which was already opening. By the time Trent heard her clattering down the corridor towards him, the fuel tanker had parked and was attaching itself to a fuel port. Then the door into Medical opened and she entered.

"How are you?" she asked.

Trent stared at her, thinking how prosaic that sounded, coming from her as she was now. He also realized how such a visit and apparent show of concern from her wasn't really normal—it wasn't really the Isobel he knew. Remembering Stolman's screams, he glanced down at the mess of his injured hand as it was being steadily reassembled.

"Being repaired," he said, his clamped and bone-welded jaw aching and still not feeling right. He was also conscious that his tooth implants were too white. "Just another ten or twenty bones to go. You've seen that communication?"

"I've seen it," she replied, raising her hood so her rows of eyes were directed towards his face rather than his hand. He noted that she was bigger now, fatter and longer with gaps in her carapace exposing skin that was a lovely shade of cyanosis blue.

"We need to get out of here," he said.

"Yes," Isobel agreed, but she didn't sound sure.

"Problem?" he asked.

"Another ship arrived," she explained. "It was aiming to land at the space port but then diverted to Carapace City. It's Blite's *The Rose*."

"And?"

"Penny Royal was aboard *The Rose*—I told you how our U-drive was fixed."

"How does that change anything?" he asked. "Surely your main target is Spear?"

"It is," Isobel agreed, dipping her hood in acknowledgement, "but I have my contacts and have just received a further notification. Spear's ship just arrived in the Masadan system. He's still looking in the wrong places for Penny Royal."

"We can't go there." It was stating the obvious, really. Neither of them wanted to put themselves within reach of Polity justice.

"No." There seemed some doubt there, and some confusion, though she was rather difficult to read.

"What's bothering you, Isobel?" Trent asked, surprised he felt able to ask her such a question and amazed that they were having a conversation at all. Isobel generally gave orders and expected them to be obeyed. She didn't often show doubt, very infrequently discussed such matters and never sought advice.

"Why is Penny Royal here?" she asked.

Trent shrugged, then wished he hadn't as he felt broken bones grating together. "Why did it fix our drive? Why was it accepted back into the Polity and why did it leave? I find it difficult enough working out the other people's motivations, let alone something even Polity AIs puzzle over."

"Penny Royal could reverse the changes I'm undergoing," she said flatly, almost testingly. "It has answers. It can bring matters to a . . . resolution."

Trent abruptly felt very worried about her. Sure, Penny Royal could reverse the changes she was undergoing, but was it likely to do so? Even if the Polity had accepted it, that didn't mean it'd become any less nasty. If it was acceding to the will of Polity AIs, it might well carry out her death sentence . . . though of course that didn't tie up with it repairing their drive. However, it wasn't her statement about changes that worried him, it was her comments on "answers" and "resolutions." These were very vague, which wasn't like Isobel at all.

"Your best option," he said, "is to stay well away from that AI and just go after Spear if he ever comes back out of the Polity. Or, even better, forget both of them and just get back to business."

"Business," she said. "Why?"

"Money, power, leverage," said Trent. "We had a chance to take that dreadnought from Spear and that would have resulted in plenty of the first. Now he's inside it and in full control, so going after him and killing him isn't going to benefit us in any way. We would probably have to destroy the ship to kill him, even if we could. Better to go back to business, Isobel, then try to hire in some Polity expertise to deal with your . . . problem."

Isobel turned away, the door opening automatically ahead of her.

"I don't know that it is a problem anymore," she said as she departed, then clattered her way towards the bridge.

Trent looked at the autodoc as it closed up his hand and considered shutting it down. He still might have time to get to an airlock and out. Even if things were about to blow up with the prador, his chances of survival out there still might rate higher than they were in here aboard the *Firth* . . . with a captain who might even enjoy being a hooder. He was still procrastinating as the ship engaged grav and began to ascend.

BLITE

"Well, we wanted to go to Carapace City," commented Brond.

Blite glared at him then said, "Leven, do you have any idea of our precise destination?"

"No," the Golem mind replied, "but unless Penny Royal wants to destroy a few buildings when it puts us down, there's a clear area right beside the Carapace itself." The mind paused for a second then continued, "That's presupposing our ultimate destination is Carapace City and not somewhere beyond it."

Blite tried to weigh all the options, but just couldn't see his way clear. Penny Royal had demonstrated how it could descend from this ship to a planetoid and Blite had no doubt it could travel in the same way down to a planet. In fact, since it had showed itself capable of manipulating U-space, he wondered if it needed his ship at all. So why, upon allowing him to descend to the Rock Pool, had it now diverted his ship? Surely it could have abandoned it at any point to head wherever it wanted to go?

He braced himself angrily for whatever might ensue, sorted and rejected questions to ask and settled on, "Penny Royal, what the fuck are you doing?"

There was no reply, verbal or otherwise.

"Greer," said Blite, "any ideas?"

Greer, who had been monitoring general coms as they descended, just in case there was any unfortunate response to their presence, turned to look at him. Blite thought she looked ill.

"There's a com exchange being broadcast throughout the city, between the father-captain under the sea and Taiken Asmolus," she said.

Blite groped for a moment to remember. "Oh yeah, the shellman boss here. What's it all about?"

"I'll transfer it to your screen," she said woodenly.

Blite swung his attention back to his screen, as it divided to show Taiken on one side and a prador father-captain on the other. Blite took it in and by the time the list of nominated embarkation points had appeared, he felt precisely how Greer looked. So, some sort of power shift under the sea. Father-Captain Sverl was either stepping down from his position of power, something prador only did on the way to a disposal pit, or was being usurped. And apparently the new guys weren't anywhere near as tolerant of humans as Sverl, in whatever form.

Beginning to feel sweat beading on his brow, Blite reviewed what he knew about the situation under the sea. Sverl occupied a prador dreadnought, while other prador occupied three destroyers, but little was known of them other than that. All four vessels were likely undamaged and carrying something close to the full complement of armaments, for surely they'd have been repaired and restocked over the many years since the war. That stock would include continent-busting kamikazes, a wide variety of other CTDs and atomics, particle cannons and near-c railguns. There was enough firepower sitting under the sea to take out not only Carapace City, but this entire world. He had thought earlier that if Penny Royal clashed with the prador, the result could be a real danger to him and his ship. Now he just felt the overpowering urge to giggle hysterically. The AI hadn't really needed to do anything more than bring them here.

"Is Penny Royal somehow involved in this?" wondered Greer.

The question abruptly sobered Blite. The AI hadn't departed this ship, but that didn't mean it hadn't been interfering down there in some way. Maybe it had been talking to the prador? Maybe it had taken sides and helped set one side against the other? It was rather a strange coincidence that all this had blown up on the AI's arrival here. Perhaps events here were all perfectly in keeping with Penny Royal's plans, whatever they were.

"I've no idea," he hedged.

"Damn," said Brond.

"What is it now?" Blite asked tiredly, as they rapidly drew closer to Carapace City.

"A ship just took off from the space port," Brond replied.

"I'd hardly think that surprising in the situation," said Blite, but then grudgingly added, "It's probably evacuating people—we know some of those transports were taking people to the port for that purpose."

"No, they were to take people to the two shuttles there, but there was also a spaceship down," said Brond. "I didn't think to run an ID check on it until I spotted it launching just now. It's Isobel Satomi's *Moray Firth*."

Blite just stared at him.

"Strange it being here," Brond added.

"Her wanting to come here isn't strange at all, since this was her next most likely port of call after we visited her," said Blite. "But her U-drive was trashed before Penny Royal popped across for a visit."

He shrugged. It seemed Isobel Satomi was part of the black AI's plans too, but since he had no idea what those plans were, he had no clue what part she might have to play.

SPEAR

As Riss and I descended to Masada in the *Lance*'s shuttle, specific instructions arrived about what I must do with my ship's erstwhile crew. I was also able to aug into the local AI net, though Amistad himself still wasn't talking to us. My aug immediately began updating its science files and, even though I was impatient to get to other data, I allowed it to do so since it wasn't as if I was wasting any time. Astoundingly, the update lasted a full twenty minutes as it loaded new advances in my areas of interest—in adaptogenics, micro- and nanotech and biotech. Then, as we descended to land at the space port, which sat on a foam-stone raft on a plain of flute grass, I linked through to their main war history database. Here, I checked to see what changes might have been made concerning Panarchia. Updates had been made to the space battle's casualty rates for this planetary system, since some supposedly destroyed drones had been discovered. They were found in the list of those who'd joined the AI diaspora after the war. However, the number of casualties reported on Panarchia itself remained exactly the same at 8,078. Apparently, there were still no survivors reported. Did the AIs doubt my memories as much as I now did?

Next I checked my own military file, which was something I hadn't really done in any detail before. Why should I? I remembered it all. There I found my service record and discovered that I had indeed served with Jebel U-cap Krong before Panarchia. I'd been severely wounded and transferred in a stasis pod to a hospital ship. After my recovery, I served with Berners' division and died with it on Panarchia. If all this was true then, plainly, my memories of being thralled by the prador were false. The horror of what ensued was false and even the psychosomatic itch I sometimes experienced at the back of my neck was false. In fact, it seemed that everything that had driven me this far was based on a lie.

As the shuttle landed—without any intervention from me since this was controlled by some small portion of Amistad's mind—I took a look at news updates concerning Penny Royal. There was a whole new file available concerning my salvage claim on the *Puling Child*, its confirmation and name change, along with a surprising amount of detail about its prior location and condition. Absorbing this, I felt my mouth go dry. I had been led to that ship by false memories, because apparently I had never interrogated a first-child to find its location . . . I shook my head, not wanting to pursue that, then returned to the data. I could see that my dealings with Isobel Satomi, the purchase of Flute and my subsequent visit to Penny Royal's planetoid were detailed too. I was about to call back to the ship and ask Flute just how much he'd told that attack ship AI. Then further information was flagged for my attention and, absorbing it, I started to get angry. Penny Royal wasn't even here anymore.

"It's not fucking here," I said out loud.

"I can see that now," Riss immediately replied. "Seems it left here at just about the same time you were taking control of the *Lance*. Did you also note the subsequent location traces?"

I had noted them, and I was quite frustrated about that. Penny Royal had seized control of *The Rose*, and a sighting of that ship had been reported by a member of the very same salvage crew I saw. They'd also been visiting the AI's wanderer planetoid in the Graveyard. If I had waited around there for just a while longer, the AI would have come to me. Thereafter, no further reports—Penny Royal had disappeared again. I turned my attention then to local news and data. I wanted to gather whatever I could find about a small salvage and smuggler ship called *The Rose* and its crew, and all available detail on Penny Royal's sojourn on this planet.

"We may well be wasting our time here," I suggested, as we reached the airlock.

"We need data," opined Riss.

I was still angry, but I did agree.

I donned a breather mask and we disembarked, then I stood watching as an auto-handler trundled over to a small cargo door in the side of the shuttle. It was there to take away the ship's dead crew finally, along with their non-human fellow. I felt a momentary reluctance, because there might have been something yet to learn from the Golem Daleen—then I auged an instruction to open that door. The handler inserted big spade-like hands and, one by one, took out three cylindrical cold-store coffins and loaded them onto its cage trailer. Next it took out the smaller container—about the size of a pressure cooker—in which resided Daleen's AI crystal.

"Daleen will be encountering a forensic AI soon enough," said Riss.

"Yeah," I said. "Did you pick up anything on the others?"

"Forensic AIs in their future too," Riss replied. "The remaining relatives, if having any interest at all, have agreed to an attempt at brain reconstruction."

I wasn't surprised—Polity AIs would want to extract every scrap of information available about the events aboard my ship a hundred years ago. And still I was surprised at the hands-off attitude towards me and that ship itself. I turned away and, with Riss in tow, headed over to the edge of the space port platform. I rented a gravcar, then headed out to the coordinates Amistad had provided, which took two hours.

The observation tower raised its platform high above the lethal wildlife here, while a tough ceramic conveyor engine deep in the muddy ground drove it along. As we approached in the rental gravcar—the only way of getting out here safely, what with recent hooder activity—I stared at the platform, puzzled by how wrong it appeared. A brief aug search showed me how it had been much expanded from its original form, which did look right to me. Again some hint of someone else's memories. Something else, which looked like another tower in the making, was being constructed nearby. Perhaps the aim was to raise a number of similar towers to support a mobile city.

A simple locator frame flicked into being on our car's screen, outlining a small gravcar platform. This came into view to one side, just before the intelligence down there took control. I released the joystick and sat back, taking in the view: the gas giant Calypse was poised on the horizon in the aubergine sky and the chequerboard of squirm ponds gleamed distantly. They were now worked by robots rather than slaves of the Theocracy. I could also see a long tubular building to one side, made of woven flute grass. This contained the corpse of a giant albino hooder that had apparently been called the Technician. Beyond that lay a convoluted structure of similarly woven grass, which was the home of the newly sentient gabbleduck.

"I suppose my own particular concerns aren't considered important, in the light of what's happened here," I said grudgingly.

Masada was a world used to being at the centre of major events. Until just a few decades ago there had been a ruling theocracy here, with the majority of the population enslaved to constant labour on the planet's surface. Then had come rebellion involving alien technology, followed by Polity intervention and quarantine. After the quarantine, an alien attack ensued, shortly followed by the resurrection to sentience of one of the creatures here—a gabbleduck. This was apparently descended from one of the great extinct civilizations: the Atheter. Since then the world had been reclassified as a protectorate, with a Polity warden in charge to prevent more chaos. I'd studied this history with interest, but over the last few hours my focus had been mainly on very recent events. Because the present warden of this world, Amistad, had of course brought Penny Royal here.

"You shouldn't assume your concerns don't count," Riss replied from where she was coiled on the seat beside me, her head up and nose pressed against the screen. "Penny Royal is taken very seriously indeed."

"More seriously than million-year-old biomechs, resurrected aliens, Jain technology and Dragon?" I wondered.

Riss turned to peer at me, her black eye open and sparkles appearing in its depths. This was a second outward sign of the huge amounts of data the drone had been processing ever since we boarded the shuttle.

The other sign had been an increase in her body temperature—such that I knew it would be dangerous to touch her nacreous skin.

"Penny Royal is in the same category," the drone said.

"That being?"

"A potential gigadeath weapon and paradigm-changing intelligence."

I didn't pursue that, since it made my quest for vengeance seem like a rather petty and irrelevant detail.

Our car descended slowly, as if the one controlling it wanted to give us plenty of time to take in the rather intimidating view. As it settled, a map appeared on a small console screen courteously informing me of my destination. This gave me the option to upload it to an aug, gridlink or portable hardware. I just memorized it and stepped out of the car, sniffing at the damp air before pulling on my breather mask. However, I had no need of the map as Riss shot out after me and writhed on ahead, leading the way. A door at the rear of the parking platform swung open as we approached, to reveal a couple of people clad in flute grass camouflage combats. However, they abruptly stepped aside when they saw Riss. We moved on inside as they headed out towards an armoured troop transporter, one of them commenting, "One of his wartime buddies, I bet."

Riss headed up some stairs and I followed, feeling the waft of an air differential but seeing no sign that the interior air was breathable. By way of a long tubular corridor and another set of stairs, we came to a doorway. This gleamed with the glassy lemon scale of a hardfield, which blinked out as we approached. A further two steps brought us up onto the original observation platform. Amistad turned to face us, his polished chrome legs clattering noisily on the scarred metal.

"You don't need the mask," he said.

Amistad was bigger than the gravcar I'd arrived in, a perfect rendition of a scorpion in gleaming metal. That outer shiny coat was doubtless nano-chain chrome vanadium alloy, which was resistant to just about any weapon that didn't need mounting on a tank or some larger vehicle. I removed my mask and hung it at my belt, annoyed at yet another false memory—that upon first meeting Amistad, I felt I was back in the presence of some long-time comrade in arms. The feeling diminished as I walked out to stand before him, as I found myself checking either side of the platform for a spiny shadow.

"By now you know that Penny Royal is no longer here," Amistad observed.

"So I understand," I said. "It was last sighted in the Graveyard."

"And is quite likely to still be there."

"But what I fail to understand," I continued doggedly, "is why that creature ended up here in the first place and why it wasn't recycled through a scrap-metal plant ages ago."

"You know the story by now, Thorvald," said the warden of Masada. "The data is available and I know you have been accessing it."

"I do and I have," I said. "You resurrected Penny Royal after its encounter with the same Atheter technology that caused problems here. But you reawakened it without the supposedly bad part of its eight states of consciousness. Upon discovering that eighth state, Penny Royal destroyed it and now all is forgiven—all the thousands tortured, maimed and killed. Seems to me that, just like in any human society before the Quiet War, the law doesn't apply to the rulers."

"You know the story," said Amistad, "so you must know why amnesty was granted."

"I know the reasoning," I said. I crossed my arms, suddenly feeling cold. "You classified Penny Royal as eight separate intelligences and considered the destruction of the eighth state execution of sentence. But of course that kind of ruling doesn't apply to a human with some multiple personality disorder, does it?"

Amistad snipped a claw in the air, and his eyes gleamed red for a moment. I realized this wasn't a threat, just annoyance.

"And, of course," said Riss, rising up beside me, "in the case of Penny Royal you screwed up."

"That is as yet to be determined," the scorpion stated.

"Face up to it, Amistad, Penny Royal played you," said Riss.

I turned to peer at the drone, not sure what she was implying. Was she talking about Penny Royal escaping on Blite's ship? The AI had made its move while Amistad had been dealing with some difficult compromises on Masada—arising from this human-occupied world now containing a sentient alien autochthon. This autochthon would have been quite within its rights, under Polity law, in ejecting the whole human population. But, going back to Penny Royal, whether the AI had committed some crime in boarding *The Rose* hadn't been proven. For me there was no doubt: the crew of that ship had probably been killed by the AI or transformed into something terrible. I considered what was running inside the fossil I now carried in my pocket.

"Not so. Penny Royal was free to depart at any time it chose."

"You know that's not what I'm talking about," said Riss. "The data, as you said, is available. This includes all the files pertaining to your encounter with Penny Royal on the edge of the caldera."

While the assassin drone and erstwhile war drone settled to glaring at each other, though perhaps there was more going on than I could see, I again accessed that same data and quickly ran through it. Penny Royal had learned the location of its missing "eighth state of consciousness" at the bottom of the sea here, seized it and brought it back inland. Amistad had tracked it down to the edge of a caldera where, in a dramatic diorama, Penny Royal had destroyed the container that housed its eighth state. I was still none the wiser.

"You're a one-trick pony, Riss," Amistad eventually replied. "And you can't kill an AI with an injection of parasite eggs, even if you had any."

"Admit it," said Riss, "you fucked up."

I'd had enough of this.

"What the hell are you two on about!" I snapped. "Riss?"

"Tell him," the assassin drone said, her gaze still locked with Amistad's but her head flicking briefly towards me.

Amistad again clicked a claw at the air as if trying to sever some thread—perhaps the one of his own involvement. As this world's warden, he was effectively stuck here for now, though he could never cut the ties of responsibility.

"Okay," he said, "I fucked up."

"I'm still as clueless as before," I stated.

Amistad swung towards me, breaking the staring contest with Riss, who now deflated a little.

"There is evidence to indicate that Penny Royal did not in fact destroy its eighth state of consciousness, but had uploaded it from its container before I arrived at the caldera."

"Which means," said Riss, stretching up again, "that it's still subject to a death sentence."

"It means that portion of Penny Royal is still subject to such a sentence," Amistad shot back.

"Look, fuck all that!" I interjected, "Penny Royal, whether it's divided into eight fucking states or suffering a psychotic break, is guilty of exterminating Berners' division on Panarchia!" I paused to pull up some other figures. "Since Panarchia, it is directly guilty of having killed three thousand five hundred and twenty-three human beings and forty-seven AIs." I groped in my pocket and held up the ammonite fossil. "This is what Penny Royal does—it's a sadistic torture-loving machine! This is what that fucking thing is!"

Amistad, who until that moment had been in constant, if minimal motion, now froze.

"What is that?" he said.

"This," I waved the fossil at the warden of Masada. "This is quantum storage giving the location of Penny Royal's planetoid, but it has room in there for something else. A torture virtuality. You have no idea—"

Amistad moved, fast, the sound of its feet like a series of firecrackers going off, and was looming over me in a second. His massive claw came down and with a delicate precision, which seemed impossible for something so large and heavy, it plucked the fossil from my hand. I took a step back, half expecting an attack, but the big scorpion just retreated. Then, as if sampling some delicacy, it inserted it into its preoral cavity, turned it with mobile setae, then swallowed it.

I turned to glance at Riss, who was now facing me.

"I never saw that," said the assassin drone. Saw what? I wondered.

"It's always recording," said Amistad, as if agreeing with Riss. "So are the dead actually dead?"

I turned back to Amistad who froze again. Noting my attention, he snipped the air again then said, "It's a self-referencing time crystal.

The human mind within is a recording, running in a simplified state. I will transmit it to the Soulbank."

"So now you see the kind of thing Penny Royal does," I said, feeling I had somehow lost impetus.

"As you should know too, personally."

"What?"

"Since learning of your pursuit of Penny Royal, I have taken an interest in you, Thorvald Spear," said Amistad. "Have you yet admitted to yourself that your memories have been added to and tampered with?"

"I don't know for sure . . ." I didn't want to tell the warden that, though I agreed all the evidence pointed that way, I just couldn't *feel* it to be true.

"You have memories of being captured by the prador, with a companion," Amistad stated. "The prador tried out a full thrall on your companion, who died during the process and whose body died shortly afterwards. They then tried out a spider thrall on you. You survived for a while, in a great deal of pain, and were dying when those same prador were ambushed."

"By Jebel U-cap Krong," I replied.

"No, just by a squad of ECS commandos led by someone who'd never met Jebel U-cap Krong. The man with the spider thrall was called Jasper Frettle, not Thorvald Spear. While his companion, who was killed by full thralling, was a woman called Yonella Frettle—his wife. They weren't soldiers, but citizens on a Polity world. The planet was just being settled when we first encountered the prador and the two were captured when the prador later conquered their world. They were only some of those on which the prador attempted to use thrall devices before they finally admitted that normal humans were too weak. They realized that their limited supply of humans from Spatterjay were the only subjects robust enough to take thrall technology."

"What?" I said stupidly.

"Jasper Frettle couldn't live with those memories, so when the process became available he had them edited out of his mind," Amistad continued relentlessly. "Some may consider that weak, but others consider it a necessary requirement given a potentially unlimited span of life.

Just like all such edited memories, his were stored. They still exist in what might be called the miscellaneous files of Soulbank. Those previously inhabiting your memplant, and now also in the soft matter of your brain, are an edited and distorted copy. I have to wonder when Penny Royal managed to get hold of them—and how long that AI has been making its plans . . ."

"What!"

"They never actually told you where your memplant was found, did they?"

"It was in a shop . . . jewellery . . ."

"Yes, Markham's Exotica lies about two hundred miles from here, in the coastal town called Chattering. Though I do believe she's opened a branch in the space port's shopping complex which you recently left."

I just gaped at Amistad, aware that Riss was studying me very closely. Maybe the assassin drone was again wondering whether she should kill me. Maybe, in her position, I would be wondering the same.

"Of course," Amistad continued, "there's no actual proof that Penny Royal visited Markham's. However, Penny Royal was sighted by one of the clear-up teams on Panarchia after the war—in fact most of that team did not survive the encounter."

"Returning to the scene of its greatest crime," I spat, at a loss for anything else to say.

"Doubtless," Amistad agreed. "After the war, it was discovered that one bio-espionage expert in Berners' division possessed an early Sylac memplant. Instructions were transmitted to the clear-up teams there to scan for that memplant's beacon, but it wasn't found. It was assumed that it must have been destroyed in the CTD conflagration. The old ruby memplants are rugged, but did get destroyed."

I knew it would take me a long time to agonize over all this and incorporate it. Penny Royal had found my memplant, jiggered with my memories, then placed it in a jeweller's?

"This changes nothing," I said. "Penny Royal still has to pay."

"Of course," said Amistad. "But first you have to find it or, perhaps, wait until it finds you."

"I am going to kill Penny Royal," I affirmed, feeling the hate in the pit of my stomach. But, even as I turned away, I felt that hate briefly transform into a miserable emptiness. If some of my memories weren't my own, would I discover the same about my emotions?

15

ISOBEL

As the *Moray Firth* reached orbit, Isobel fervently rejected Trent's advice. It was true that to kill Spear she'd probably have to destroy his ship and so gain no revenue from acquiring it. And it was also the case that killing him that way would be impersonal and without satisfaction. However, there was one factor which Trent had neglected, which was very important to her business in the Graveyard—reputation. When the changes to her body were noticed by her competitors and the words "she was fucked over by Penny Royal" were finally spoken, her enemies had immediately grown bolder and had needed slapping down. The reaction to her being duped by a mere mortal would be so much worse. She might even draw the attention of Mr Pace, and she couldn't allow that. At least, that is how Isobel justified her intentions to herself, to bring Spear down and rip him apart.

But now she had to cease questioning that goal and decide how it might be achieved. Gazing at a screen showing the Rock Pool below, she believed her decision to leave the surface was the right one. If things were blowing up between the prador it would get mighty unhealthy down there. In that respect, it was also likely to be dangerous up here too.

However, she had her reasons for not leaving the system. She had instructed Morgan to take the *Caligula* and the *Nasturtium* to the coordinates of Penny Royal's planetoid, because that had been Spear's next known location. From there she had hoped to find a way of tracking him down. She had known that salvagers had been working there and they might have information about Spear they could pass on. That was irrelevant now, what with her learning that he'd gone to Masada, where it would be suicidal to pursue him. However, Penny Royal was Spear's target, so if she stayed with the AI, currently onboard *The Rose*, then certainly Spear would come to her sooner or later.

It all seemed perfectly logical, so why did she feel a deep core of frustration on leaving the Rock Pool? It stemmed from the predatory part of her—a part of her that was getting increasingly aggressive. Spear was her target, but he had only taken advantage of her condition—which was caused by Penny Royal. Actually, the black AI had always been a target for her vengeance, but an unattainable one. Her realistic side had always known that she stood no chance against the AI. Only that logical side of her was not so strong now. Not only did she see Spear as prey—as someone to hunt and tear apart—she saw Penny Royal in that way too. Moreover, now she was putting distance between her and that prey.

Isobel bit down on her frustration, mentally opened up a U-space com to the *Nasturtium* and waited, only to receive no response. Next she tried the *Caligula*, but no luck there either. Morgan must be on his way to the planetoid, meaning she wouldn't be able to contact him until he next came out of U-space.

She left the com channel open, so the man would know she wanted to talk to him at the first opportunity. And with another mental instruction, she increased the magnification through her sensors to give her a close-up of Carapace City. She then tracked down Blite's ship's current position. *The Rose* rested in a clear area just at the edge of the Carapace itself. She had no idea why the black AI had chosen that location, nor what its involvement in the coming storm might be, though it was surely involved.

"So," said Trent, walking into the bridge, "what's the plan?"

She whipped round towards him, stopping herself from falling on him at the last second. He jerked away from her, his expression frightened as his hand dropped to the butt of his gun. He took his hand away while allowing himself a steadying breath and stepped on into the bridge, pausing for just a second to eye the Golem standing back against the rear wall.

"Snickety snick," it said, but even with her close connection to the thing, Isobel couldn't fathom where that had come from.

She returned her full attention to Trent. He was moving with care, looked exhausted and had lost a deal of body mass. He seated himself carefully in a chair, then sipped from the cup he was carrying. To distract herself from the attractiveness of his vulnerability, she assessed the damage done to her bridge door. When she entered the ship most recently, it had been a squeeze to get through the airlock. The internal corridors had also felt claustrophobic. The dents and scratches around the door were inadvertent, but a sure sign it was time to start remodelling the internal spaces of her ship.

"Was it such a great idea bringing that thing aboard?" he asked.

"I control it completely," she said, "and it may provide some . . . connection to Penny Royal."

"You're sure?"

"I'm sure."

He grunted doubtfully, then said, "I'm guessing you think that staying on Penny Royal is a sure route to Spear?"

"I sent Morgan and the bulk of our muscle, along with the *Caligula* and the *Nasturtium*, to Penny Royal's planetoid. The moment I am able to contact Morgan again I'll summon him here—if we're still here then."

"So we're staying," he said.

She dipped her hood in response, already remodelling the blueprint of her ship in her head as she turned back to study the screen. She had to suppress thoughts about how enjoyable it would be to peel the flesh from Trent's bones and how *good* he would taste. Internal walls would have to go, she decided, leaving structural members in place. She would leave Medical and some other human areas in place, but the rest would have to be opened out. She wouldn't use the human airlocks any more, but the hold doors. Perhaps she should turn one of the holds into an airlock itself? Trent's cabin would stay—even if he didn't survive to occupy it, then someone else could use it . . .

Now for a new design of space suit . . .

"Maybe hanging in orbit right here isn't such a great idea either," Trent suggested.

Isobel focused on him distractedly without turning, using only her outer cowl sensors, which mainly functioned in the infrared. Even as she did this, she was loading instructions to the cache of mothballed large-maintenance robots she had aboard. They would begin with the partition walls and the conversion of one hold into an airlock. The suit, she decided, would have to be infinitely expandable—made to take new sections and extensions, for she was a growing girl. She would make that herself out of monomer fabric she had aboard. Then, even as she began playing with some tentative designs in her skull, she realized that both the suit and the remodelling were signs of acceptance of what she was becoming.

She now turned to the skeletal android, loading instructions to it, and dispatched it to assist in the remodelling. Trent watched it go, still obviously in disagreement with her decision to keep the thing.

"Agreed, we should change course," she said abruptly, present circumstances beyond the ship coming back into focus.

In her mind she mapped the local system. The Rock Pool possessed two small moons but, if prador heavy weapons were about to be deployed here they would offer little in the way of safety. The next planet out was presently on the far side of the sun. But further in than the Rock Pool, about a quarter of an orbit round the sun from it, lay a smaller world. This was burning and molten on its sunward side but scattered with giant crevasses on the other. These could easily hide a ship. Perfect.

Isobel paused, noted that during her introspection Trent had headed off to his cabin. She fired up the fusion drive and began heading away, scattering grapefruit-sized com satellites as she went. She would conceal herself, watch and wait. And then, when Spear eventually put in an appearance, she would strike. Though whether she would strike Spear or Penny Royal first she wasn't sure.

SVERL

The patterns of movement out there had changed. Analysing them closely, Sverl realized that the recalled children belonging to Cvorn, Skute and the Five were heading rapidly for whatever cover they could find—if they hadn't already made it home. Robots and other assets in the ocean were still converging on the three ships, but this was probably in an attempt to cover that other movement.

The other prador were about to head for the surface; action was imminent.

His attention now focused on one of Cvorn's perambulating factories. It had ceased moving and was now driving its rock anchors into the bottom. This could be seen as an attempt to save it from damage, since it was so close, but Sverl was suspicious. He withdrew a claw from one pit control and inserted it in another, then connected via his thrall control units to his weapons. He took control of two particle cannons, targeting coming up on two of his array of hexagonal screens. All the other weapons had children at the controls, but they would only react to threat as trained or follow orders, which meant a delay. If anything came from that factory, he would need to act fast.

"Get to cover," Sverl instructed his remaining three second-children out there. They had a chance of survival, since the main action of any battle would certainly take place out of the ocean. Above water, weapons could be deployed faster and more effectively. He would return for them one day, if he could. It was not as if he had many kin left to spare. Everything else, including his remaining perambulating factory and various robots, he would have to leave too. Time now to move—he didn't want to be the last to leave the ocean.

"Prepare for battle," he instructed those aboard, and set water tractor drives running to give his dreadnought clearance. "Respond as you have been trained."

Immediately the water out there clouded as the tractor drives stirred tons of silt from the bottom. Sverl switched to sonar and ultrasound imaging, noting that billows of silt were now blowing out from under the other three ships as they too set themselves in motion. As he studied the images, they blinked; a shimmering diamond pattern fleeing across both screens. He reacted immediately, firing one particle cannon at Cvorn's factory, which had to be the source, meanwhile considering the workings of fate. If he had not just switched to ultra- and infrasound imaging, he wouldn't have seen the recognizable interference caused by cavitating torpedoes.

He also felt a moment of regret. Right up until now there had been a chance, however remote, that the others weren't going to turn hostile. But even as he regretted their predictably prador-like behaviour, he calmly assessed his initial plans and planned responses. Then he felt his own prador excitement growing at the prospect of, as the humans would put it, taking off his gloves.

His particle beam stabbed out slowly through the seawater. It created a growing glassy tube where seawater turned to superheated steam, then ionized hydrogen, oxygen and ozone and smashed other elements to radioactive isotopes. The tube held for a few seconds before turning into a boiling explosion that simply wiped out the view in that direction. Meanwhile Sverl used every source of scanning to track down the torpedoes. The beam finally reached the factory, the red-orange glare of vaporizing steel and carbon lighting up the ocean just as he located the torpedoes. There were two of them, curving round a few miles out. They would approach from the opposite side of his ship to the factory—the side that was out of reach of his particle cannons.

"Quadrant Six, rail, five kilotons, two miles," he instructed the relevant gunner.

The missile shot out at low speed—at full railgun speed it would simply have smashed against the seawater as if facing an exotic armoured wall. The resultant explosion would blow back, taking out railgun and gunner. A few hundred feet from the ship, it fired up its own drive and accelerated, a burning magnesium glare behind it and great bubbles of superheated steam rising to the surface.

Sverl now saw that his ship had enough clearance from the bottom. Taking his claw from the weapons pit control, he reinserted it in one of the drive controls and fired up his vessel's multiple fusion engines. If the fired missile didn't disrupt the two torpedoes' cavitation drives, or destroy the things, surely his fusion drive would? Then again, surely Cvorn would have known that?

His great ship bore the shape of a prador carapace—a great chunk of exotic metal six miles across, sprouting weapons turrets and sensor arrays like high-tech barnacles. Now, it began to rise rapidly, seemingly poised on top of a newly ignited sun. Sverl touched the ocean tractor drives to set it turning, bringing the two particle cannon ports round to the side. Then a massive detonation either destroyed the two torpedoes, or destroyed any view of them, but he suspected they'd just changed course.

"Quadrant Two, be aware of possible incoming as we breach." He withdrew one claw from the drive and again reinserted it into weapons, meanwhile asking himself how *he* would have done it. The torpedoes would have their own momentum, so it was a simple calculation to judge where they might exit the ocean's surface. Another few touches with the tractor drive had his ship turning further.

"Seven and Eight, loose forty of those Polity grav mines directly after we breach," he instructed. "Use a swarm two dispersion, close at one mile."

"Father, they will pose a danger," replied the second-child at the rail-gun and subsidiary weapons arrays in Quadrant Seven. Aboard any other prador ship, posing such a question would have resulted in summary execution. Well, at least after any battle. But Sverl's children had learned that he expected their input and would, to misapply a human metaphor, provide carrots rather than always wielding the big stick.

"Further dispersion will be by CTD blast from below," Sverl replied, opening up a control unit link to the big CTD in the mineshaft, which now lay a mile below his ship. "The grav mines will be driven out by the blast front and may well intercept the rising destroyers."

They were a neat and simple Polity toy, those mines. The grav-engines could be easily shielded because they had just one setting—neutral buoyancy—and they carried proximity-detonated CTDs. They would be a second unpleasant surprise for Cvorn and the rest; the first being what was about to happen below.

BLITE

First had come a rumble and *The Rose* shook underfoot, but Blite had thought nothing of it because he had been on many seismically active worlds. However, the crowd moving down the adjacent road paused as one, as if they had all heard the first footfall of some approaching giant, then picked up their pace. A sense of panic infected the sulphide-laden air. Apparently earthquakes weren't a common occurrence here.

Standing on the hull of his ship, Blite swung round to peer out to sea through his monocular. He could just see a purplish glare penetrating to the surface of the ocean at the far horizon. It could have been a visual effect characteristic of this world, but when that light changed to a deep red-orange flash, Blite thought otherwise.

"So everyone's fucking off but us," said Ikbal.

The Rose had landed and powered down—with nothing now available to the drive systems. A clattering had started up, followed by an ear-piercing tinnitus whine. Other sounds had followed, until the inside of the ship was filled with a cacophony worthy of an automated factory gathering pace. It became unbearable, hence Blite relocating outside and allowing his crew to follow him.

"Some are getting ready to fuck off," he replied to Ikbal, "but they all should have left long before now to be far enough away." He glanced across at the nearby houses in this more salubrious portion of town. The evacuation seemed well organized, fast and pretty calm, but there had been damage to the city and it was still ongoing. He counted four fires, one blazing merrily in the upper floor of a nearby three-storey building. Its flames were now flicking through a peaked roof tiled with some sort of stone—the tiles cracked with sounds like gunshots and slewed to the ground in pieces. He turned his attention to Brond and Martina, who had set up a remote console, linked to the ship's sensors, there at least being sufficient power to operate those. "Any idea what that was?" he asked.

"Particle beam fired a couple of miles down," replied Martina grimly. "Looks like it hit something—steel and carbon spectra."

"Shit." Blite raised his monocular to his eyes in time to see the ocean boiling out there, and a bright glare below. "Shit, shit," he added.

First up came four towers, spearing out of the ocean like giant brass asparagus shoots. Below them rose the turret they were attached to, then the rest of the enormous ship was gradually revealed. Blite swallowed drily. He had heard that there was a prador dreadnought down there, but the reality had failed to impinge until now. The behemoth continued to rise, like an island being pushed up by some seismic event. Weapons turrets and pits decorated its surface and, from one of the latter, objects began spewing out. Blite increased magnification to pick out one of these and set his monocular's chameleon-eye lenses to track it. The thing looked like a thick silver coin, until it engaged chameleonware and disappeared.

"Now those," said Brond, "are Polity grav mines."

"Unusual," Blite replied, trying to keep his tone calm and analytical. "Prador tend to dislike using Polity tech—they see it as an admission that it might be superior."

As the dreadnought cleared the ocean, particle beams stabbed out and down from two turrets and two bright flashes ignited above the ocean. They were two yellow suns, expanding and flattening as a blast front rolled out across the ocean.

"What was that?" asked Greer, sitting on the edge of the hull with her feet on one of the nacelle struts.

"Secure yourselves now!" Blite shouted, dropping his monocular to swing on its neck strap and reaching to unreel the safety line from his space suit belt. He squatted to clip its hook over one of the hull-mounted rings. "Close up your suits too!" he added, sweeping his suit visor across.

While the others secured themselves like Blite, Chont and Haber were still running back to the ship. They'd been investigating the edge of the Carapace, where it was attached to the ground. Arriving, they quickly scrambled up a ladder on the side of the ship, then fixed their safety lines to that.

"Any detail on that explosion?" Blite asked Martina and Brond over suit radio.

"All of it," replied Brond. "Two cavitating-drive torpedoes exited the ocean a couple of miles from that ship and fired up rocket motors. The father-captain must have been wise to them because he nailed them straight away."

"Blast power?"

"About a megaton each—directed. Some sort of armour-piercer."

By now the blast front had reached the shore and Blite didn't need a monocular to see it. An explosion of white water marked out the edge of the sea from horizon to horizon, then disappeared in a boiling line of dust. As it drew closer he saw chunks of vegetable matter being hurled up into the air, but felt a momentary relief. If he'd seen rocks being picked up, he'd have known that a safety line wasn't enough. Hitting the less salubrious suburbs of Carapace City, the blast front picked up even more rubbish as it flattened flimsy shanty dwellings. Blite dipped his head and waited.

It reached them a moment later and their surroundings disappeared in dust and debris. The wind tried to wrench Blite from the hull of his ship, but just didn't have the strength. However, a square bubble-metal sheet ten feet across came out of this chaos, slamming sideways just beside him and tumbling onward. He licked his lips and took a steadying breath, then raised his monocular to his visor and clicked it onto the attachment points on his suit's helmet. Linking into his suit's system, the device's imaging was now visible inside his visor. He adjusted it through its spectrum to try and get a view through the dust. Infrared just gave him a sun glare now a few miles above the sea, with something else visible down to one side, probably still below the ocean. Ultraviolet was no better. He was about to give up on it, since the dust was already clearing, when another bright light ignited under the sea. This grew, and grew until it blotted everything else out. He detached the monocular—the glare now perfectly visible without them.

"And that?" he wondered out loud.

A moment later his perspective abruptly changed. And though he still stood on the hull of his ship it seemed he was floating out above the sea, peering down and down, into the depths. A massive blast there had ignited the surrounding ocean and he could feel the force of it rising up. Then he was back again, trying not to throw up.

"Penny Royal?" he managed.

"Captain," said Greer.

He glanced over to her and saw her pointing over the side of the ship, towards the hold door. Blite now identified the vibration he'd been feeling through his hand, as he squatted with it resting against the deck. The hold door had opened. He stood up, just in time to see one of the globular objects, which he'd last seen when he sat on one in the hold, rise into sight. The hole open into its internal complexity gleamed like a shattered red eye.

"Screw this," he said and detached his line, walking over to the edge of his ship. He now had a clear view of Penny Royal exiting the hold, in sea-urchin form but with a much more open formation than usual. It had an intricate tangle of silver and black at its core. Five more of those globular objects circled it like huge white soap bubbles. And, more prosaically, one of them was spooling out a heavy s-con cable attached somewhere inside the ship.

After a brief pause Blite asked, "What are you doing?"

The next moment Penny Royal delivered its reply, though whether this was a memory or some kind of manufactured experience, Blite couldn't tell.

He was lying on sand holding up a shield, fending off the blows from a big studded mace wielded by someone dressed for some serious SM. He knew, absolutely knew, that if he relaxed his grip on that shield he would be beaten to death.

Then he was back to reality, stumbling away from the edge of his ship, no longer nauseous but just plain scared. He swore quietly. He was going to be a lot more parsimonious with the questions henceforth.

The AI began to rise, the object towing the cable remaining behind it, while the others abruptly shot away. Blite tracked their flight out towards the ocean, then lost them in the remaining dust. He tried again with his monocular and picked up one of them, hovering out towards the edge of the city about fifty feet above the ground. Then he realized he was seeing something else beyond.

The ocean heaved, a low dome of water tens of miles wide rising. Then the surface exploded upwards in spume and steam, as doubtless massive bubbles of superheated steam breached. The whole mass collapsed again with slow grace, but from its edges a disturbance fled. Blite tracked it inwards and watched a wave mounding up as it drew closer to the shore. He lowered his monocular, then searched around for somewhere nearby to reattach his safety line. The mounded wave hit the shore and just kept coming—the ocean simply seeming to eat up the land lying between him and it. He considered swearing, but decided he'd done enough of that.

"Just lost all power," commented Brond.

Blite looked around. Why had it suddenly grown darker and colder? He raised his monocular again, but it was dead. He reattached it to his helmet to run a diagnostic, but his suit just flashed a power failure warning in his visor, which worryingly simply faded. Again he surveyed his surroundings. On the nearby road, powered vehicles had failed too. After a moment, he realized that he could no longer see the fires over in that direction. He turned towards the three-storey building that had been burning nearby and gazed dumbfounded as the flames died. Then the glow of embers inside the peaked roof just faded.

"What the hell?" he wondered, forgetting his earlier decision about profanity.

Penny Royal was now about a hundred feet up, which was perhaps the full extension of that s-con cable. Beyond it, high in the sky, the prador dreadnought was now little more than a glowing speck.

"Disruptive entropic effects inevitable," whispered Penny Royal. "Your ship's reactor does not provide enough power."

The AI was sucking power out of everything around them, Blite realized, but how and what for? He was damned if he was going to ask and end up flat on his back in another Roman arena virtuality.

"Now Cvorn and the Five make their move," the AI added. "Skute's ship is damaged, but on its way up nevertheless."

Blite switched his attention to the ocean and found his view of it distorted, as if he was seeing it through a slice of amber. The tsunami, which was now little more than a mobile pile of slurry and plant matter, had nearly reached the city. It was about six feet high, but Blite knew such a mass of water would annihilate the rest of the shanty town, probably bring down some of the stronger buildings around him, and could easily turn over his ship.

Beyond the wave, the captain now saw two prador destroyers rise from the ocean on fusion drive. They resembled the dreadnought, but were sleeker, more horizontally stretched-out versions. They were also much smaller—each being about two miles long.

"The wave," said someone, Blite wasn't sure who.

It hit an invisible wall and just stopped. Blite raised his gaze and saw something he hadn't realized until now. That amber tint in the air stopped about fifty feet up, where those globular objects hung in the sky. Penny Royal had created a massive curved hardfield around the ocean-facing edge of the city.

A shield, he thought, *of course.*

Was this, Blite wondered, a demonstration of some previously unseen altruism on the part of the AI?

More explosions ensued above the ocean and one of the destroyers tilted, some of its outer protrusions had been torn away and a glowing dent was visible in its hull.

"The mines!" Martina's shout was just audible in Blite's closed-up suit, and over the constant roaring that surrounded them. He glanced over at her and saw she had manually opened her visor, and did the same.

The undamaged destroyer abruptly dropped, green lasers stabbing out all around it and lighting up the steam and spume out there. The damaged destroyer also began firing, even as a third began to emerge from the waves. Further detonations ensued, multiple blast waves carrying across the ocean towards the land, and the city. Now, as the tsunami began to ebb, the hardfield began to rise and reconfigure as those spherical objects repositioned themselves in the sky. The airborne field began to form an oval stretched out across the sky facing the ocean, its lower edge now fifty or so feet above the ground. Its upper edge was now maybe two or three hundred feet up.

Blite watched the dying tsunami flowing in. Though its force had been blunted by the hardfield, it was still strong and high enough to wipe out the more distant parts of the shanty town. A blast front followed it, picking up spume and debris on its way in, but it wasn't as powerful as those first two waves—seemingly dying even as it reached them. He slapped his gloved hands together and huffed out vapour in air turned decidedly chill, stood up and nearly fell over. He was more careful with his footing as he realized that ice was forming on his ship's hull.

"They've got the dreadnought's mines nailed," said Brond.

"Well," said Martina, "the prador did work out how to see through simple chameleonware during the war."

The laser strikes continued out there, the subsequent detonations progressively further from the three ships, which now hung above the ocean at the same level.

"What I don't understand," said Blite, "is why they aren't going after the dreadnought."

The world abruptly turned a blinding actinic white, as something detonated against the oval hardfield. The ground and his ship shifted and he went down on his backside. Penny Royal was a black star against that light with streaks of pink lightning issuing from the tips of its spines. And Blite felt the twist passing through his body that he often felt when *The Rose*'s space drive engaged. Steam and smoke rose all around and Blite spotted the fire in that three-storey building briefly flare back into life. Seen through the force-field the glare died, fading to a red macula. As Blite steadied himself and rose up into a squat, he realized he could now no longer see the edges of the shielding. He glanced behind, seeing that amber hue there, and it was now above, too.

"Unfinished business, I reckon," said Ikbal, now close beside him. He nodded to the surrounding buildings. "The people here were kidding themselves if they thought the prador considered them anything more than vermin."

Two more blasts ensued, one above, and one behind. These faded too, snapping out like oxygen-starved acetylene flames. A particle beam played across the shield, leaving a diminishing shadow in its path, then winked out. Penny Royal had once terrified Blite, but at length he had grown accustomed to it. He was suspicious of it and sometimes it annoyed him. It left him often baffled, certainly respectful and never less than afraid of what it might do. Now he felt a growing awe.

"Return inside now," the AI's voice whispered out of the air. "Danger increasing."

"Increasing?" said Ikbal disbelievingly.

Blite just detached his line and headed for the ladder.

SVERL

In the sanctum inside his dreadnought, Sverl gazed at his screens in disbelief. He was now sitting in a low geostationary position directly above Carapace City. The unexpected shielding had been of an odd design. It was curved, but all the science he knew had it that the energy losses in distorting such an interface in this way outweighed its effectiveness. It also had no anchored projectors which would take on the kinetic load. Neither could he see any heat sinks or energy convertors for the transformation of such a load to be shunted away. It had initially been powered by *The Rose*'s fusion reactor, but that alone couldn't have provided enough power to stop dead the tsunami—let alone the ensuing CTD blasts or particle beams. But of course this was Penny Royal, and the technological know-how down there lay beyond the prador's scientific prowess. And, unless they were keeping things under wraps, it was beyond the Polity AIs too.

Again checking data, Sverl tried to work out what had been done, and how. Penny Royal had somehow anchored the shield to realspace and used some entropic effect to draw power from that. The temperature down there had dropped rapidly, both behind and ahead of the shield for nearly twenty miles. It dipped below the freezing point of water within the first few miles, rising in a simple curve to the limit of that distance. The energy from the first CTD fired from Cvorn's ship had routed back, raising the temperature again. But then some U-space effect had kicked in, diverting the bulk of that energy into underspace. Then Penny Royal somehow steadily drew on this again to expand and strengthen the shield. It now completely enwrapped Carapace City, the visible part of it being a dome. But the whole thing formed a perfect sphere, for it also lay underground.

Stunning, and terrifying. How could Sverl ever have contemplated petty vengeance against something capable of doing *that*? However, more than ever he now wanted a confrontation of a different kind, resolution, absolution, something . . . He could no more contemplate avoiding the black AI than he could now consider attacking it. There was mystery here; the AI was the source, the centre, the point where Sverl *had* to be. There was a further puzzle too. Why had Penny Royal defended the city? Sverl took just a moment to come up with the answer, and then wondered if some remnant of his prador arrogance might be kicking in.

Because of me.

Without him, the prador enclave would not have existed on this world. Without him and the changes Penny Royal had wrought in him, Carapace City wouldn't have been able to exist either, containing as it did the shell people and other humans. No normal prador would have allowed that—only one tempered, or perhaps twisted, by his change into an amalgam of prador, human and AI. This place was a disaster waiting to happen. Even without Penny Royal's arrival, and Sverl's response to that, the others would have turned against him at some point. In the ensuing battle, the humans here would have been annihilated. Penny Royal had apparently taken responsibility and come here to prevent that—and in essence to clear up a mess of its own making. But what next? Was Sverl next on the black AI's agenda?

Procrastinating . . .

Sverl abruptly realized he had been studying the data and thinking about what it might mean for far too long. Now his prador kin were pig-headedly trying to penetrate a shield that only became stronger after each attack. They were consistently failing to adapt quickly to the new and the different—so now was the time to act. Now, while that shield protected the city, Cvorn and the others had allowed their hatred of humanity to override common sense. So, while they were so distracted, Sverl could get heavy-handed. It was time for some payback for both the attack on him and the deaths caused down there. Cvorn and the others might have failed to destroy the main human population, but they had, by Sverl's estimation, managed to vaporize hundreds. Those living outside the city were simply gone. The few hundred who hadn't waited for automated transport out and fled on foot had been killed by their own instinct for self-preservation.

"All gunners," he announced, again taking control of two of the particle cannons himself, "fire at will—hit those destroyers."

Targeting images abruptly proliferated across his screens and his children responded with everything from the standard dour, "We obey," to a few clattering cries of prador delight. He felt some parental pride as firing commenced just a second later, the thrumming of railguns permeating the ship as they hurled down missiles, these travelling nearly as fast as the particle beams that stabbed down with them.

Skute's ship took the first blow. Three railgun missiles hit it in succession, the first two vaporizing against exotic metal armour. But the force of their blasts did knock the ship down to just above the ocean, compacting it horizontally too so that nothing inside could have survived. However, the third missile penetrated right through, blowing a molten plume down into the waves. Even as Skute's ship slid sideways on failing engines, the next missiles impacted above the other two destroyers. But these exploded on projected hardfields because the other two had seen the danger at the last moment. Both ships dropped after successive hardfield impacts. They were forced back down into the ocean, glaring like stars and seemingly unravelling as they fired out s-con sink cables. The sea boiled around them as energy convertors aboard turned the energy from those impacts into massive pulses of heat and dispersed light.

So you did prepare, Sverl thought, *though it seems Skute was as senile as I supposed.*

The burning remains of Skute's destroyer ploughed into the sea beside the coast, hit the edge of the landmass and bounced up. Then, just as the debris came down again in a cataclysmic crash, a hundred miles south of Carapace City, Sverl's screens and control unit links alerted him to danger.

The moon?

How had they positioned those?

Three railgun missiles hit his ship before he managed to get his hard-fields up. The impact sent him staggering, his claws coming out of the pit controls. A series of screen segments went out, then automatically switched to other views. He saw a glowing hardfield generator hurled inward from his hull to then tear through the ship's infrastructure. Other areas filled with fire, while he glimpsed one of his children falling out through a hole in the hull into vacuum.

Arrogance always has its cost.

Glancing round his sanctum, he saw that nothing was damaged or had come loose in here, then forced himself back to his controls. He was aware that at least two of his remaining precious children were gone. However, the others had reacted perfectly as per their training, and quickly focused on the new danger. A layer of rocky camouflage had slewed away from that irregular lump that could only just be defined as a moon. Underneath this, two near-c railguns were spewing a perpetual fusillade of iron-based missiles that must have been manufactured from the moon's own substance. All of the dreadnought's energy was being sucked up by its shields, convertors labouring to turn the impact shocks into heat. This was now being spewed from the ship's dark side, as jets of stored water turned to HO plasma—a store that could not last for much longer. If only Sverl had the kind of technology Penny Royal had used—that way of shunting the energy into U-space then drawing it back to power his shields . . .

Meanwhile, on the planet below, the two remaining destroyers were exiting the ocean under fusion and anti-grav drive, the massive accelera-tion probably killing any of the unprepared aboard. For just a second Sverl considered the formula, supposing that two destroyers were no match for one dreadnought. With Skute's ship down, the advantage should be his, but he now knew that wasn't true. By positioning those railguns on the moon, Cvorn and the others had managed to take the advantage. He was nailed; he couldn't even fire up his drive to run because the energy drain would weaken his shields. He had, at best, the time it would take for the two destroyers to clear atmosphere, then a second fusillade from them would tear him apart.

SPEAR

As I headed to the space port and my shuttle, I found myself sinking into a black depression. Even the magnificent sight of a massive hooder, hurtling through the flute grasses below like an enraged monorail train, failed to lift it, especially when the sight felt so *familiar* to me. Riss was also without much to say, and I wondered if AIs could be as subject to the foibles of mood as us creatures of flesh and blood. Of course they could— they could do everything we could do and more—and they could also cease to be subject to them any time they chose. Thinking this, I remembered how I wasn't so different, really. Running a feedback program through my aug's nano-connections in my skull to restore the neurochemical balance in my brain, I felt the mood fade and a "natural" optimism return.

"Let's land," I said.

Riss turned towards me with her black eye closed, but opened a mouth I hadn't seen open until that moment. It was pink inside with white fangs, and the long sharp tongue was red, mottled with purple.

"It's dangerous down there," she replied, mouth movements now matching speech and imparting an appropriate hiss. I wondered if some internal conflict was making her neglect her outward appearance. Yet, this physical accompaniment to speech might have implied the opposite. It could be that *previously* she had been neglecting her outward appearance.

"I just linked in to the hooder beacon network so I know all their locations and none of them will be close to where we set down," I replied. "We need to talk."

My depression was certainly absent now, but the initial reasons for it remained. Instead of perpetually chewing these over in my mind I wanted someone to bounce them off, and I wanted to do it here. I'd spent too long aboard the *Lance* and wanted to extend my break from it. I set the car to descend, aiming for a large flat rock, on a mound where a channel of muddy water divided into a Y.

"Surely we must hurry back to the Graveyard?" said Riss. "We might miss Penny Royal if we don't go now."

"The Graveyard is a big place, and Penny Royal will still exist even if we don't manage to find it there," I replied. I took my hand away from the controls as the car abruptly took over. Instead of coming down on the rock, it slewed sideways and landed on the sloping ground beside it, on a bed of short flute grass shoots.

"Penny oysters," said Riss. "Somehow appropriate."

Getting no further explanation for the manoeuvre, I queried the car's computer and received an automatic message from some submind of Amistad's. Apparently landing on the rocks here was frowned upon. Such a landing would crush the many penny oysters that occupied them and these creatures were protected. Further enquiries rendered the reason for the protection order: penny oysters contained a great deal of the genetically encoded knowledge of the Atheter. They essentially belonged to the single sentient Atheter living on this world, an entity that had named itself the Weaver. The Polity did not want to annoy it by the inadvertent destruction of parts of its databank.

I pulled on my breather mask and stepped out of the car, hard shoots crunching under my boots as I walked over to the rock, hearing the swishing of Riss's progress behind me. I stood there gazing down at a scattering of translucent domes each about an inch across, stuck to the surface of the stone like limpets. Inside these, I could just about identify the slimy movements of the molluscs they protected.

"I don't know what I am," I said.

Rising beside me Riss replied, "Neither do I."

I glanced at the snake-like drone. "You don't know what you are, or you don't know what I am?"

"Both."

The sun was setting. Some odd illusion suggested that the now-greenish orb was sinking into the clouds, and was about to settle on the land over there. Riss's reply didn't particularly baffle me. Recollecting the drone's story, I imagined that not knowing what she was must be a constant affliction for her. She had been made for one purpose only and was now obsolete. Then Penny Royal had screwed with her mind, leaving a void that had eventually filled with vengeance against that AI.

"Penny Royal tampered with my memories, added to them and maybe subtracted from them too," I said. "But memory is merely one aspect of a mind's structure. I have to wonder if its software has been tampered with too, as well as the information in storage."

"Yes," was the full extent of Riss's assistance with that matter.

"I no longer know what is and isn't true, or whether I can trust myself," I said. "Do I really hate Penny Royal? Yes, I was killed at Panarchia by that AI and lost a lot of friends there. But I never really saw the things it did after that event and I had absolutely zero time to nurture my supposed need for vengeance."

"All you do know," said Riss, now turning towards me and opening that black eye again, "is what *isn't* true about yourself."

I nodded. It was growing darker now, stars appearing in the aubergine sky and the vast nebula displayed across it etching itself into existence. It was a beautiful sight, one which I of course somehow already knew. But, at that moment, it didn't seem to matter. I could appreciate it, even against a background of unwarranted familiarity. "I was never captured by the prador and I never suffered under one of their spider thralls. I never saw the atrocities committed by Penny Royal after Panarchia and I never grew to consider myself the ultimate tool of retribution against that AI." I paused to watch one of this world's fast-moving moons come tumbling up over the horizon. It threw shadows all about us, one of them quite odd.

"Y'know," I continued, "if someone wanted to fashion a tool—a hunter intent on going after Penny Royal no matter what—that would be me. Yet it would appear that Penny Royal itself forged me."

"Perhaps it wants to be punished," said Riss, now turning to look behind us.

"So I am its form of suicide, or something?"

The drone's lack of reply made me think she had no more answers than I did. As I stood there contemplating my situation, I raised my gaze to further stars now blinking into existence. Straight away, I saw something up there, cruising across. For a second I thought it was one of the orbital objects, until it drew to a halt. I was looking at an old-style ship's crab drone: a two-foot-wide pill of metal, with two glinting topaz eyes close together on its rim and claws folded in on either side of them.

"We're being watched," I said.

"Oh, really," Riss drawled.

Riss was still looking behind us, so, with the skin on my back creeping, I casually turned around. It had squatted down where the watercourse divided; a great bulk nearly the size of an African elephant. In this light and in its present pose, it did look something like that animal too. It was drinking—I could now hear the slurping sounds—but then it finished, reared back and sat on its haunches. Its body sagged into a pyramid of flesh, its tiara of green eyes gleaming below the shiny dome of its head. It snapped its big duck's bill open and closed as if it was relishing the drink, exposing white spiky teeth inside.

"No beacons on these," I suggested quietly, thinking of the hooder alerts.

"And especially not on this one," Riss replied.

This one?

I now saw that it held a tricone in one of its black claws—three laterally connected cones of shell with something glistening in the ends of each. While we watched, it inserted a long talon into one cone and levered out part of the mollusc's triple body. It inspected the morsel for a moment, then inserted it into its bill and champed it down. It then levered out the other two parts and ate them, studying the empty shell before discarding it. Then, in one rippling movement, it was across the stream and heading up the slope towards us. I felt a momentary frisson, for I knew that no part of me had ever seen a gabbleduck feeding.

"Be aware," grated a voice nearby, "that if you attempt any violence I will be forced to either stun or eliminate you—that includes you, snake drone."

"Really?" said Riss.

I glanced around to see that the crab drone was now hovering just a couple of yards behind us.

"Really," it replied. "I might not have the Watts myself but I've got narrow beam masers pointed at both of you from orbit."

Now I understood what Riss meant by "this one"—the drone was its protection. And here, rapidly approaching us like an eager two-ton puppy, came this planet's autochthon. The Weaver, as it was known, was the resurrected and only living example of an Atheter. Descendant of a race that had, arguably, exterminated itself. Thankfully the creature slowed as it drew closer. But still it loomed over us as it stooped down and inspected us both in turn, as if short-sighted. Seemingly satisfied, it settled back on its haunches again. I stared at the thing, and it stared back. I now saw that it carried various bits of technology, hanging from a wide girdle made of intricately woven flute grasses. And affixed to the side of its head was what looked suspiciously like a G-Chrome aug. Reaching down to its girdle, it bifurcated one of its forelimbs so each section displayed three claws, and plucked off an object with one set.

"Why?" it said, quite distinctly.

"Why what?" I asked, the frisson failing to depart, because all of this felt so new for a change. But I also wondered what the chances were of me setting down just there—on the one place on this planet where this creature had stopped for its evening meal. I knew there was such a thing as coincidence, but my recent experiences made me feel it wasn't as common as one would suppose.

"Is existence more important than veracity?" the Weaver enquired. The object it held wasn't anything I recognized. The nearest approximation was that it resembled the internal auditory workings of a human ear, fashioned out of blue metal and glass. It had to be some newly recreated piece of Atheter technology. "Penny Royal," it added with something like a sigh.

"What about Penny Royal?" I asked, frisson turning to excitement.

Of course, in the years since this creature had been resurrected it was quite likely to have had its encounters with the black AI.

"Do you like your iteration?" it asked.

It was definitely pinpointing something about me—how I wasn't the genuine article—but how it knew that and why it was here talking about it I had no idea. I was reminded of the Dragon Dialogues, and of Delphic oracles. Perhaps some of the nonsense it had spouted as a regular devolved gabbleduck had stuck, before its ancestor's mind had been uploaded into its skull. Perhaps it just couldn't speak straight. I thought very hard about my reply.

"I dislike my false memories and I dislike doubting my motivations, but I like being me, and existing."

A crackling ensued behind us and I whirled, half expecting the crab drone to be launching an attack. However, the air was shimmering over the rock and penny oysters were splitting off it and rising. They swirled in a circle there, then danced in a neat line overhead—I realized my mouth was hanging open, and closed it. The molluscs came to float above the gabbleduck, which raised its free claw. The things dropped and circled that claw, shifting as they did so in kaleidoscope patterns.

"Follow the pattern," said the creature before us, whereupon it caught one of the oysters with its other claw, levered out its soft part and tossed it into its bill. "Knowledge is in the pattern. Eat the world."

I turned to Riss. "Have you any idea what it's talking about?" Familiarity had returned because some part of me, or whatever I was connected to, had heard the gibberish spouted by gabbleducks.

"One current theory is that the more of this world's genetically-modified life forms it eats, the more knowledge of its kin it acquires. It follows that to acquire all the knowledge of its former kind, it must eat everything living on this planet." Riss gave a snakish shrug. "It is not a theory the AIs subscribe to."

"Let's get the hell out of here," I said, turning away and walking back to our gravcar. Riss followed, saying nothing. I felt a terrible disappointment. From such an unusual, rare and coincidental encounter I'd felt excitement. I'd expected, I don't know, some sort of revelation? And yet, all I'd found was a creature as wrapped up in its own concerns as any of us, when not trying to maintain a facade of gnomic mystery.

I had to resolve my problems myself; find my own answers. Nothing had really changed for all the solutions still lay with Penny Royal—which I might or might not kill in the process of obtaining them, if it didn't kill me. Yet, when I reached the gravcar and sat down inside I felt empty. The route back to the space port lay clear in my aug and, intellectually,

I planned to head from this world straight back to the Graveyard. There I would search for my nemesis, the black AI. However, as Riss entered and coiled up on the seat beside me I keyed into the maps of this world and ran a search. In less than a second I located the coastal town called Chattering and, as I took the car up into the sky, I studied the town's map to find Markham's Exotica.

16

SVERL

"The city will be undefended," something close by whispered.

Sverl pulled his claws from the pit controls and whirled, bringing them up to rend anything that had entered his sanctum. A black diamond hung in the air, seemingly extruded from elsewhere—the visible portion of a shadow filled with hard sharp edges.

"Defend the city, Sverl, as they run."

Sverl gazed at this thing, which had to be either some projection from Penny Royal or some extension of the AI through underspace. A thousand questions clamoured in his mind, but each negated the next, to leave him dumb. The diamond, or whatever it was, folded in on itself and disappeared—winking out with a crack at the last.

Defend the city?

Sverl turned back to his controls. "Prepare for rapid descent," he ordered. "All gunners prepare to open fire on the destroyers and intercept anything from them fired towards the city. I will control our shields." In the extended AI component of his mind, he system-linked his ship's remaining hardfields to its weapons. They would now cover gaps, shift out of the way of firing from his gunners and move to intercept anything from the destroyers his gunners couldn't hit. Then he waited, not quite sure what to expect, but guessing it would be spectacular.

The city's hardfield began to change shape. His instruments showed him that the underground section had disappeared and now the skirt of the remaining dome was rising, some odd spherical objects seemingly clinging to it. Within a minute, the field straightened into a ten-mile-wide disc above the city. The field was also darker now, with hardly any visible light getting through. It began to shrink rapidly, growing darker still— then a star ignited at its centre. A moment later, the whole thing snapped into a single tight disc half a mile across, ringed by those objects. From this issued a flash that temporarily blinded Sverl's sensors. When they came back on, a microsecond later, he saw a coherent beam of white light issuing from it—a white laser half a mile thick.

In the smoke-filled air above the city, the beam was visible in both human and prador spectrums. Beyond the Rock Pool's atmosphere it faded out, but remained visible to other sensors. It struck the moon, which turned to a glaring silver bauble as the beam cut right through it. Plasma and molten rock exploded out of its other side in a two-hundred-mile plume. A few seconds later the moon exploded—three great chunks of rock and rubble flying apart with laceworks of glowing magma. Then all this matter expanded violently in a spherical plasma cloud.

Sverl reacted immediately, diverting power from his shields to fire his fusion engines again. These were now hurling him back down towards the planet and the city, grav-engines set to negative to hurry the process. His dreadnought entered atmosphere in a moment, its hull rapidly heating and leaving a vapour trail. Meanwhile his gunners again opened fire on the two destroyers, which were now eighty miles up from the ocean. The railgun missiles cut red streaks through the air—travelling so fast they were ablating on the way in, their impact power reduced but still considerable as they hit protective hardfields. Returned fire was almost immediate, and Sverl ran his own interceptions as his ship descended to fifty miles, spinning on steering thrusters as it did so. It now had its main drives pointed downwards, decelerating hard. Internal grav took much of the sting out of that deceleration, but Sverl still slammed belly-down against the deck hard enough to wind himself, which wouldn't have happened if he'd still possessed a carapace.

Nothing more had been fired at the city, because Cvorn and the Five had expected Sverl to go straight after them. They weren't therefore wasting any energy on that target—yet. The two destroyers continued accelerating upwards, their fire concentrated on Sverl's ship, while he centred his fire on them. Within just a few minutes the dictum concerning the relative power of dreadnoughts and destroyers began to yield results. All three ships were managing to intercept anything thrown their way but, while Sverl's shield-energy convertors were managing the load, the two destroyers were beginning to glow. Their armour was turning red-hot as excess heat distributed around its s-con layer, even while they ejected their maximum in the way of HO plasma cooling.

"Time to warm them up a little more," Sverl clattered contentedly, just before opening up with all seven of his available particle cannons.

By now the destroyers were up out of atmosphere. It must have been obvious to Cvorn that Sverl had placed his ship between them and the city, and was keeping it so positioned. Risking his own destruction, Cvorn diverted a portion of his firing elsewhere—ejecting ten low-speed railgun missiles to travel concentrically round the world away from the main battleground. It had been done subtly, as if the accidental result of a hard-field generator imploding near the railgun concerned. However, Sverl recognized it for what it was, even as his particle beams struck the hard-fields of those other ships: spite.

The two destroyers glowed like stars, but still managed to keep enough power flowing to their engines to continue accelerating away. Their next manoeuvre was risky indeed, but not as dangerous as staying where they were. Distorted copies of the two stars now became visible, strung out in a long line behind their course. These reflections were blurred, as if seen through the edge of polished diamond slate. And, with hardfields still projecting and while under particle cannon attack, they submerged into U-space and disappeared.

All firing from Sverl's dreadnought abruptly ceased.

"Stay alert," Sverl instructed.

"Those ten missiles?" said the astute gunner in Quadrant Six.

"Precisely," Sverl replied.

An hour later the missiles came over the horizon, travelling at twenty thousand miles per hour just a hundred feet above the ground. Sverl opened fire with particle cannons and, upon counting eight targets vaporized, realized Cvorn had been even more tricky. In a flash of insight, he abruptly brought his ship down in a hard descent, landing in a blast of fusion flame. He settled the ship half on the rubble of the space port and half in the ocean. His sensors now penetrating the depths, and working with ultra- and infrasound, he waited. Five hours later diamond patterns fled across his screens once more. Two hours after that, when the cavitating torpedoes left the ocean, he nailed them just twenty feet above the waves. He took them down before they could even fire up their rocket motors to take them in towards Carapace City.

Now, with the danger apparently over, Sverl decided it was time to face his own personal demon. He would, he decided, leave his ship in his personal ground transporter. He would head to Carapace City and confront Penny Royal. However, when he finally almost reluctantly directed his sensors there, to locate the precise position of *The Rose*, that ship was gone.

TRENT

The creaks and groans in the surrounding canyon could be heard in the ship, but Trent could only just detect them over the other sounds inside. He'd woken from a semi-drugged post-operative slumber, to the sound of atomic shears slicing through internal partitions of carbon foam. He next recognized the crackle of laser cutters, the clattering of robots and the stink of everbond glues. When he finally managed to get himself moving, showered, with some coffee down him, he opened his cabin door to find things much changed.

Steps now led down to a grav-plated walkway traversing the length of the ship. The walls and other cabins were missing, their partitions and various other components stacked towards the rear ahead of the engine section. His own cabin was a slightly distorted cube, sitting at the intersection of internal cross-members. Medical still existed in a similar form, though one side of it opened to a wide floor, across which some of its instruments had been affixed. Storerooms and laboratories were now just open floors—their racking, storage and instruments still in place, but more widely spaced. He could see all the way to the bridge, whose rear section had been opened out. Isobel was at the centre of the floor, now occupying the area where her laboratory-cum-workshop had been. Assisted by the Golem, she was doing something with a tube of monomer fabric, and looked like some monstrous insect cocooning its prey.

Trent stepped down onto the walkway, paused for a second, then went back to his cabin. Inside he stripped off his first choice of clothing, then donned an undersuit and space suit and clipped the helmet at his belt. Isobel was obviously redesigning the inside of her ship to suit her new form, which he now knew to be more resistant to vacuum than his own. Removing internal partitions and bulkheads might not have weakened the ship much, but it certainly wouldn't be healthy for him if there was a hull breach. Newly clad, he headed for the platform Isobel now occupied.

She turned her cowl towards him, slowly, almost distractedly. He surmised he hadn't come upon her unawares this time, so she'd managed to suppress her first instincts. He knew for sure now that she was fighting not to kill him; that she was trying to retain enough humanity so she wouldn't instantly regard him as prey. She was, he felt, even more dangerous now than she had been when she attacked Gabriel. She also seemed a lot less balanced and logical. Trent was sure that if she didn't kill him herself, then she would probably drag him into some situation in which they would both end up dead.

"I considered doing away with grav-plates completely," she said as she returned her attention to her work, "but even my new self retains its attraction to up and down. Also its health is better under gravity stresses. Surprising, really, considering that it is a form that was modified by the Atheter into a war biomech, so it must have been used in vacuum combat."

Trent now had some inkling of what she was doing. The tube of material ended in an open spoon shape with shimmershield projectors around its rim. In addition, it had a console inside the rim's base, with multi-jointed, intricate robot arms extending from that to the outside. There were strengthening ribs throughout, maybe some sort of heating system, along with various power supplies, oxygen packs, weapon ports and other items attached. Running down the length of the thing were rows of holes rimmed with electrical molecular bond seals. Those were where her legs would protrude—demonstration if any of her tolerance of raw vacuum. Isobel was making a space suit to fit her new form.

"Enough now," she said, abruptly pulling away from her work and relinquishing the suit to the Golem. "We have to get moving."

"Moving?" he queried.

"It may think it's managing to sneak away, but that's not going to happen."

"Sneak away?" Trent asked, feeling stupid.

Isobel clattered across the floor to him and he repressed the urge to leap aside, just stepping out of her way with apparent calm. She went on past him, an odd spicy smell accompanying her. Perhaps this had something to do with her latest surge of growth, after her heavy meal down in the Rock Pool. She was now over twelve feet long and all those gaps in her carapace had closed up. Her hood was now a yard across and she had sprouted more black tentacles amidst the other steadily growing manipulators there. He hesitated to go after her, but followed after one look at the Golem, who of course always appeared to be grinning.

"You've been asleep," she said, "and you haven't updated yourself."

"If you recollect, I did have some problems to overcome," he replied as he tailed her up the walkway towards the bridge. "And of course I no longer have an aug."

"The blow-up between the prador has occurred," she explained perfunctorily. "Three destroyers attacked the dreadnought and one was destroyed. Meanwhile, Penny Royal erected a hardfield barrier around Carapace City. When the dreadnought subsequently ran afoul of a rail-gun emplacement on one of the moons, Penny Royal used the energy from the hardfield to destroy the emplacement. The dreadnought then defended the city from the remaining destroyers until they fled, while Penny Royal sneaked off."

By now Trent was on the bridge floor, gazing through the screen at the canyon in which the *Moray Firth* currently sat. Black crumbly rock rose to either side, with yellow-gold runnels of molten sulphur flowing down the sides and a stream of the same churning below. Disc-shaped objects like mushroom caps clung here and there to the stone. He didn't know whether they were living or just some sort of mineral formation. He repressed his immediate urge to utter a brainless "what" and just took the time to absorb what she'd told him.

"That's an appalling amount of energy," he said, sitting down in the single seat remaining on the bridge floor.

"Stolen energy," said Isobel, as a view opened in one corner of the screen's laminate. It showed a truncated view of the solar system, with a white dot rising from the Rock Pool. "Penny Royal generated a small hardfield anchored to realspace and used an entropic effect to take energy from the real. It absorbed energy from attacks on the field and routed that into U-space, tapping it to expand the hardfield all round the city."

"All *round* the city?"

Isobel dipped her hood in acknowledgement. "A spherical field completely enclosing it, even underground. Energy from subsequent attacks was also routed into underspace." The *Moray Firth* was on the move now; Trent could feel its engines in his bones. Isobel continued, "When the emplacement on the moon began firing on the dreadnought, Penny Royal drew all the underspace energy back into the real, routing it through a lasing and collapsing hardfield. The white laser shot, as far as I can calculate, possessed ninety-eight per cent of the total energy thrown against the hardfield. So we're talking about a laser blast effectively powered by a gigaton-range CTD."

"The moon?" Trent asked quietly.

"Mostly vaporized."

Neither of the moons here were very big, as Trent recollected, and certainly a dreadnought possessed the firepower to take out objects like them. But still, Penny Royal wasn't a dreadnought. This was why Isobel had never gone after the AI, despite her hatred of what it had done to her. She'd always possessed sufficient survival instincts to avoid confronting something that could smear her like a bug. Now, as the *Moray Firth* rose out of the canyon on this inner planet, broken black mountains and sulphur fumaroles slipping past all round, she appeared intent on following the AI.

"I still think you should drop this, Isobel," he suggested.

As if in reply, armoured shutters drew across the chain-glass screen, shutting out the view. For a second the screen just showed the inner face of the heat-treated ceramal, then the laminate fired up to display the view on screen. Ahead lay the blackness of space, and stars—this system's sun now lying behind them. It was only evident through a glare reflecting from a sensor spine projecting to the right.

"You might not even be able to follow," he said, trying not to sound too hopeful.

Isobel turned her hood towards him, and he wondered how he'd ever get used to the horror that was now her face.

"*The Rose* is heading out from the Rock Pool's gravity well," she replied, a little distractedly. "It's an old cargo ship so its drive parameters are unshielded. When it goes into U-space, I can weigh its energy balance and determine its coordinates."

"It might have been unshielded before . . ."

"If Penny Royal is shielding, then we'll find another way."

She turned back towards the view, obviously deep in sensor data. A moment later, graphics appeared along the bottom of the screen and Trent recognized them instantly. She was accessing the ship's weapons and they were all powered up and ready to fire.

Trent just sat there, feeling a sense of doom. His mood was probably due to the psychological damage he'd sustained along with his injuries. But if she was accessing those weapons, they might well be a part of those "other ways" she was considering. It seemed her earlier idea about getting answers, or some resolution from the AI, had slipped her mind. The main image on the screen now changed to show Blite's *The Rose*.

It was under fusion drive against a backdrop of stars, the *Moray Firth*'s targeting frames now blossoming all over it.

"Isobel . . . don't," he managed.

She was tighter now; coiled like a spring. Emitting a hiss, she turned towards him, scalpel knives clacking together in her hood. They shed slivers of a material like glass, sharpening themselves.

"It would be better if Penny Royal doesn't leave at all," she said. "Spear will come here to the AI's last known location."

"You saw what it did down on the Rock Pool," he argued. "Do you think for one second you'll be able to—"

Oh Hell. She was firing the weapons.

He could feel thrumming throughout the ship as the railgun fired, then he saw the impacts flashing on *The Rose*'s hardfield on screen. A surge of acceleration tried to throw him out of his seat and he hurriedly latched the safety harness in place. Isobel skidded across the floor, her hard feet tearing up metal. Something flashed out there, the screen blanked and the *Moray Firth* jerked as if slapped by a giant hand. Trent felt his gut tightening and experienced an almost painful awareness of his recent injuries. Just as he'd thought only moments before, she was going to get them both killed.

"Chameleonware?" said Isobel in disbelief. "They don't use chameleonware."

The *Moray Firth* abruptly changed direction and the screen came back on, an image flashed up of *The Rose*, so it couldn't be using chameleonware itself. The next moment, the ship's sensors seemed to be trying to fix on something indefinable. He glimpsed a massive object looming out there, now sliding to one side of the screen. The laminate then went completely white, before another image surged forwards to occupy it. Now another image stared back at them, which clattered prosthetic mandibles and bubbled, noises which were instantly translated into speech he could recognize.

"Isobel," said the prador Father-Captain Sverl, "we need to talk."

Great, a prador dreadnought on our ass.

"Isobel," Sverl repeated.

"No," she stated. "Never."

The weapons were firing again, striking flat hardfields and lighting the massive dreadnought looming beyond.

She was attacking?

"Isobel," said Sverl once again, managing to impart his huge disappointment through that one translated word.

Another lurch ensued, followed by an emergency dive into U-space that set Trent's ears ringing and made his bones feel as if they'd turned to fracturing glass. The screen went grey, shot through with swirls and flickering lights that sucked on the eyeballs, before turning white. At last, Isobel had found some remnant of sanity.

"It can't follow us," she said, rage evident even through her speech synthesizer. "I can shield my drive parameters."

The U-jump abruptly terminated, space returning to the screen laminate. The stars were dim and widely scattered here.

"It cannot follow," Isobel repeated. "It was told to guard the fucking Rock Pool."

Trent didn't question that. Obviously her communication with the father-captain had been much more extensive than the portion he'd heard. He waited long minutes, and finally Isobel relaxed, as much as her new form allowed.

"*The Rose* went into U-space," she stated, her cowl turned towards Trent. "And I have its coordinates."

Great. Wonderful.

"Wouldn't it be better to wait at the Rock Pool?" he asked. "That's surely where Spear will be heading next."

"No . . . not there," she hissed. "Spear's not coming here. He won't be leaving Masada because Penny Royal is going to him." She paused . . . to consider? "I need to arrange a new rendezvous with Morgan. We're going to need some serious firepower for the endgame."

"And where will that be?"

"Masada."

Trent felt himself relax into weary acceptance. There was something liberating about being certain of the time and location of your own death.

SVERL

Sverl felt very disappointed and just a little bit hurt. Didn't Isobel Satomi understand how close he and she were? Didn't she understand their fellow feeling?

He squatted in his sanctum and contemplated her reaction to him. Their verbal communication had been brief and pointless, but communication on other levels had held whole encyclopaedias of meaning. He had sent her his life story and his questions in one informational missile, and it punched through all her defences to then unravel. He knew she could handle the data with her haiman augmentations, and he thought she would understand. The bounce-back had been interesting, since his programs had rooted out much detail on her life and sent it back to him. Then all was overwhelmed by a surge of emotion: an insane rage undershot with human terror.

Now, mentally riffling through portions of Isobel's life story, Sverl understood part of her reaction. Her early years, in human terms, had been traumatic. She had been powerless when she saw her family slaughtered, then powerless in drug-dependent sexual slavery and only climbed to power as a mafia whore. By penetrating her defences so easily, Sverl had made her powerless again, hence her human reaction of fear. However, her rage was something else, human on its surface but driven by what she was becoming. Next reaching the more recent parts of her life, Sverl divined her intentions. She intended to hunt *both* Spear and Penny Royal—her hooder element overriding the rational human in her.

Sverl clattered his mandibles in frustration. He wanted to pursue her to see if she had some insight, or some answers he needed. He could, in an instant, because she had failed to adequately shield her drive. He also wanted to go after the source of all his . . . confusion: Penny Royal. However, he could do neither. Penny Royal had saved his life, but in repayment he knew he must protect Carapace City. He had no doubt that Cvorn and the Five had left watchers in that system and if he left they would return here to finish it off. He was stuck here for now.

Even as he considered his dilemma, it got a little less complex when it became evident where Isobel was headed. He couldn't go there. No matter what his need for resolution with Penny Royal and regardless of his intense curiosity about Isobel. The Polity AIs on Masada would not respond well to a prador dreadnought approaching their territory, especially near a world occupied by a resurrected Atheter. There were probably assets in place around that world capable of defending it against an entire war fleet. He would be vapour before he even had a chance to explain.

A visit there would also be suicide for Isobel but now, knowing more about her and what she had become, Sverl doubted that would stop her. He emitted a pradorish sigh, accepting that his curiosity about her was unlikely to be satisfied. He then sent a repeating U-space communication—a general instruction that his Golem would receive the next time Isobel's ship entered the real. It was a survivor, that one, so it would know what to do.

It was also unlikely that Penny Royal would stay on Masada. The AI was on the move, set on some unfathomable course that Sverl doubted would limit it to one world. It must eventually go where Sverl could intercept it without running into Polity firepower. What to do?

His tentative communication to a Rock Pool target was met with an immediate response. "Well that could have gone better, and it could have gone a lot worse," said the Polity drone down there.

"I will need to leave," said Sverl, "but if I go, then Cvorn might come back."

"True enough," said the drone. "When members of your erstwhile kind are on the losing side they love the opportunity to resort to spite. I'd bet the farm that Cvorn is checking feeds from watch satellites and sensors scattered all over this system even now."

"This world needs to be protected," said Sverl. "Can't the Polity do something?"

"As you well know, Polity or prador intervention in the Graveyard is frowned upon," said the drone. "If Polity forces were to turn up here, then your king would have to respond, by which time the turd trajectory would be fanwards."

It took Sverl a moment to sort out *that* strange colloquialism, his thoughts straying to the strange human obsession with certain bodily functions.

"But prador forces are here already," he said in annoyance.

"Renegade prador," said the drone, "who are private individuals with no allegiance to the Kingdom. Just like the private individual humans down here, with their lack of allegiance to the Polity."

Sverl contemplated giving up on them as he had, effectively, before. He couldn't. Penny Royal had protected Carapace City and if Sverl left it, to go after some vague resolution from the black AI, its response might not be so good. Sverl glanced at one of his screens, now showing a cloud of debris spreading equilaterally around the planet. It was visible from below as periodic meteor flashes—all that remained of that moon.

"But don't you fret," said the drone. "I'm sure your strange need to get close to something even I might get nightmares about will be satisfied."

How did the drone know about that?

"What do you mean?"

"Consider the situation," said the drone. "Penny Royal came here to resolve the problematic situation caused by transforming you. I now suspect it's in the process of resolving another problematic situation, one caused by the changes it made to Isobel Satomi."

"You are being obscure."

"I don't have all the data—my updates from the Polity and elsewhere are limited as I might be captured out here. However, I do know that Thorvald Spear is himself a Penny Royal creation. He hired Isobel Satomi to take him to the AI's destroyer, betrayed her and wrecked her drive— actions certain to put her hard on his tail. Penny Royal then went and repaired her drive. Later, after the events here, it went into an unshielded jump to Masada, where Spear is located."

"You're still being obscure."

"I can't really be clearer. Penny Royal will know, down to the nth degree, the extent of Isobel's changes and how she will react. It's leading her to the kind of resolution you yourself seek."

"And still seek," said Sverl, still not sure he understood what the drone was suggesting. "You said my need will surely be satisfied?"

"It will, but meanwhile you must stay here to deal with Cvorn, who will undoubtedly hatch some plot to extract vengeance from you—by annihilating the people down here."

"And I must also deal with the Five," Sverl added.

"No, not the Five—you do them an injustice," said the drone. "You also haven't been checking your data."

Sverl was dumbfounded for a moment, then did some verifying. In just a moment he discovered what the drone was implying. The two prador destroyers had emergency U-jumped out of this system in different directions. Cvorn's jump had taken him in towards the Polity, while the Five's had taken them towards the Kingdom.

"You have further data?" Sverl asked.

"I have. The emergency U-jumps took both ships six light years away. The Five jumped again—heading straight into the Kingdom and almost certainly looking for females."

"So that really is their aim?"

"It is."

"Very well, Cvorn only. But let us return to the matter of my satisfaction. You seem very sure but haven't explained yourself."

"Simple enough, really. Penny Royal seems to be in the process of sorting out the messes it made in the past and tying up unfinished business. It also seems to be laying the groundwork for something else—but for what I have no idea. Anyway, you, Sverl, are unfinished business. My guess is that even if you don't go in search of Penny Royal it will, at some point, come for you."

Sverl wasn't sure if he liked that idea, but it would have to be enough. He would stay here and wait to intercept whatever Cvorn threw this way. He had no choice.

"Isobel is going to die," he stated.

"Not necessarily, but going where she's going, she's certainly biting off more than she can chew."

That particular metaphor translated directly into the prador language and was much used even now. Sverl guessed that all sentient races with mouths and stomachs would have metaphors that were much the same.

"I don't see how there could be any other outcome but her death."

"You don't? Is death the resolution *you* seek?"

"No."

"Neither is it the one Isobel seeks. Always remember that Penny Royal gives its victims what they want—often providing more of what they want than they in fact wanted."

"I don't understand."

"Few people do," the drone replied, and broke the communication.

SPEAR

The edge of the rocky shelf on the seaward side of the town was just visible from the hotel's enclosed balcony. Beyond it lay the mud pan, then a flute-grass peninsula separating it from the sea. And on the mud pan were scattered the shells of dead tricones. The coastal town of Chattering sat on a long flat rock, saved from the grinding mouthparts of those molluscs through being surrounded by that briny mud. Had it been further inland, the rock would have been ground down to nothing in a couple of centuries.

"They have a whole craft industry here devoted to making objects from the shells," said Riss.

"What kind of objects?" I asked, grateful that the drone was now speaking to me.

After I told her we wouldn't be heading back to the ship and the Graveyard yet she had snapped at me. She wondered if I'd lost my enthusiasm for hunting down a mass murderer, and generally made acerbic comments about my lack of devotion to duty. It had been a rather hollow tirade, I felt, as if her heart wasn't in it.

"Fancy boxes, vases and cups—all the usual tat." The drone turned from gazing out across the town to study me. "So now we're going to visit a jewellery shop."

"Yes, we are."

"I doubt you will learn anything new there," she replied. "It's not as if anyone there will know Penny Royal's location."

"I'm feeling my way," I said. "I think that leaving here now would be too hasty. There are things to learn here." I turned and stepped from the balcony back into the apartment, which I can only describe as the Masadan version of rustic. It possessed furniture made of woven flute grass bonded under a thin layer of transparent resin. A kitchen area consisted of a vending machine providing a few strange drinks and snacks—the intention doubtless being for me to spend my money in the restaurant on the floor below. In addition, the bathroom was a single sanitary booth of the kind designed for small spaceships. I walked over to the bed, picked up my rucksack and shouldered it.

"Are you coming?"

I headed for the door, Riss emitting an irritated hiss as she followed me down into the foyer. A fat jovial catadapt man sat behind the counter. He stood up and grinned.

"Don't forget your mask," he said.

I reached into my rucksack to take it out and he nodded, his grin freezing in place as he transferred his gaze to Riss. The revolving pressure door took us out onto a narrow street formed from the town's base stone. This had footpaths worn into it alongside the buildings, while its centre had been tiled level with slabs of hard white ceramic to carry the few groundcars here. I breathed the muggy swamp air for a moment, started to feel out of breath, then donned the mask. Checking the map in my aug, I turned right and headed along the path, that weird feeling of déjà vu hitting me strongly. I'd never been to this world before, yet I felt that I could find Markham's without a map. I picked up my pace, trying to shake off the feeling. But, unlike previous occasions, it just grew stronger the closer I came to my destination.

At the centre of the town was a small square, overlooked on four sides by little baroque churches that could have been transported here directly from some ancient Italian town on Earth. One of them was still in use—religion being a difficult affliction to cure even in people who'd suffered under the vicious Theocracy here. The other three had been converted into an administrative centre and shopping malls. At the centre of the square an object was concealed behind scaffolding draped with silvery monomer. There was still, apparently, much debate about what to do with the Cage. Some felt it should be retained as part of their history and as a curiosity for tourists. Others still remembered friends and relatives dying in it and wanted it torn down and replaced with a fountain.

I headed through the archway, sans doors, into one of the shopping malls, or converted church. The shoppers stopped to stare at my companion, but moved on as if embarrassed by their gauche parochialism. Here were various concerns packed with Polity products: augs, shimmershield breather masks, atomic shears, suitcase-manufactories—the whole works. And behind another window, I saw mannequins in the forms of various human adaptations and guessed what was being sold there. Ahead lay Markham's, which possessed a complete chain-glass front with a shimmershield glinting across the single rectangular entrance. Behind the glass, jewellery glittered in various standard displays. Then every now and again, hardfields picked up items and set them dancing through the air, intermittently flashing holograms to give the prices.

I halted and stared at the place, finding myself horrified by its unexpected crassness. I turned and gazed at the other shops within the converted church with a weird feeling of offence rising in me and ended up looking through the arched entrance towards the Cage. Around me the noise and bustle faded, as did the shops, and I saw the previous interior of the church, stark and spartan.

Rows of people were down on their knees on the stone, their clothing ragged and bulging at the fore as if each and every one of them was pregnant, the men included. But the cloth in fact concealed their scoles—large aphid-like creatures that fed them oxygen in exchange for blood. They prayed loudly, ever casting a wary eye over the black-uniformed proctors, the Theocracy's religious police. These patrolled the building, swinging shock batons. I felt my eyes filling with tears as I looked towards the open wooden doors and the Cage.

The five inside it were naked, starving and hollow-eyed. They knew the ten days they had been given to make their peace with God were coming to an end, because the oxygen bottles had been wheeled out and the crowds were gathering. In the compartment below the Cage, bound faggots of dry flute grass had been stacked—but these wouldn't burn on this airless world, hence the oxygen to feed the flames. This was a spectacle theocrats came to see from afar, even from the cylinder worlds of Faith, Hope and Charity. I couldn't save them, neither could our revolutionary cell. But the thermite block I'd inserted amidst the fuel would bring about a quick end and might even take out a few of the viewing theocrats. I wouldn't stay to watch. I'd had enough, at last, of pointless rebellion, and now the wealth I had slowly and secretly accumulated would buy me passage with smugglers off-world. I felt bad about this, but knew it was time to look after myself.

"You can come with us," the smuggler captain had said. "Or we can drop you off at outlink station Miranda."

"Where are you going?" I had asked.

When he told me about the Graveyard and the pickings to be had there I was undecided, but now I was certain. I would go with them. I wasn't sure that years spent killing Theocracy vicars and proctors would make me a good fit for that strange utopia that was the Polity. I headed out of the church, my proctor's uniform tight and uncomfortable across my breasts. It had been made to fit a man now decaying under the flute grass rhizome mat. The burning was nigh—because those in the church were standing to follow the Vicar of Chattering out into the milky sunlight—

"Spear!"

The shops returned and the Cage was again shrouded in monomer. I blinked and focused on Riss, who had risen up with her flat cobra head only inches from my face, the single black eye wide open. I realized I was down on my knees and that, all around, people were watching me with suspicion. I quickly stood up, not wanting them to mistake my prone position as a sudden impulse to pray.

Hallucination? No, I had just experienced someone's memories with a clarity normally only open to AIs. It frightened me and I had no idea what it meant, though I guessed there was some connection to my previous experiences of déjà vu and odd memories. This was, I now felt sure, something Penny Royal had done to me—and coming here had unlocked this memory.

"What's the matter with you?" Riss asked, now looking up at me from waist level. Her ovipositor was noticeably raised, as threatening as a scorpion's sting.

"I'm fine," I said, not wanting to explain, not knowing how to explain. I met the gazes of a few of the people standing around. "I'm okay—dizzy spell. I had the O2 of my breather set too high."

They began moving away. Whether they believed me or not I couldn't say, but they didn't seem to want to get involved. I began walking towards Markham's again.

"What did it do to you?" Riss asked next, confusing me utterly, ovipositor still poised.

"What?"

"The spine."

"I don't understand."

"I told you that you and it are entangled," Riss explained. "There was a data transference, though whether from you to it or it to you I don't know."

I could see no reason to lie, so said, "Memories." I tried to gather my thoughts and continued, "Ever since I was resurrected, I've been experiencing odd moments of déjà vu and occasionally remembering things that I'm pretty certain never happened to me. I put it down to faults in the reconstruction work on my implant. Just then I had a big one." I gestured back towards the Cage. "I remembered being present here before an execution and deciding to leave this world, to buy passage on a smuggler's ship out to the Graveyard. I was a young woman—one of the rebels here."

"One of Penny Royal's victims," Riss stated.

Yes, that was certainly possible. I stared at a series of jewelled rings, spinning in a circle before me within Markham's display. Then I dropped my gaze to a strangely unnerving glass sculpture—some kind of arthropod with lights glowing in its depths—and considered that nightmare diorama trapped in an ammonite fossil. Penny Royal might well have killed many of its victims, but there was no guarantee it had completely erased them. Some it had certainly recorded. Could it have recorded more than just a few? So was I getting an accidental bleed-over from recorded memories contained within the spine, or from Penny Royal via the spine? Or was the introduction of those memories into my mind a deliberate act on the part of the AI? It being deliberate seemed more likely. What were the chances of one of the AI's victims having been here—right in the very church where Markham's opened for business and subsequently put my memplant ruby up for sale? I stepped over to the shimmershield and entered.

She was waiting in the middle of the shop. She appeared anxious, wary and she gazed at me as if she knew me.

"I've been expecting you," said Gloria Markham.

17

This system lay on the edge of the borderland. Here the Graveyard ended and the Polity began, and a red giant sun was steadily boiling the oceans from what had once, long ago, been a living world. Isobel transferred her gaze from the glowing sphere before her to a frame which she mentally opened up in the laminate. This expanded to fill a quadrant of the screen, showing a large asteroid—but that wasn't what held her attention.

Just out from this asteroid were three ships, growing rapidly larger as the *Moray Firth* drew closer. These were the *Nasturtium*, the *Glory* and the much larger and more lethal-looking *Caligula*—a ship the colour of old oak, with atmosphere wings folded halfway back into its hull. A big teardrop-shaped weapons nacelle extended forward from below its shark-ish nose. Isobel opened another frame.

"So you brought the *Glory*," she said.

Morgan, who had recently transferred from the *Nasturtium* to the *Caligula*, squinted at her then replied, "Seems they received a cancellation on their stopover. Our clients all of a sudden decided they didn't want to do business with us anymore."

This gave Isobel momentary pause. Had her clients in the Kingdom been monitoring her activities and decided she was no longer a safe option to supply their particular kink? Had the king cracked down on them or, and now she might be being paranoid, had some other influence been at work, maybe even Penny Royal? She shook herself, dismissing that line of thought.

Her clients cancelling meant she had an extra ship, but it also probably meant the *Glory* still had its human cargo aboard. Perhaps it would be better to abandon that cargo here for later collection, since carrying the evidence of their crimes to Masada would make her men rather edgy. Not that she intended to let any Polity monitors or military anywhere near them. It would be a quick in and out operation beneath the Polity's notice—a fast conclusion to the hunt—the kill.

She paused, closing all her eyes and trying to suppress the predator inside. She needed to think a lot more clearly about this. Despite her anxiousness to be on her way, she knew that Morgan and the others would rebel against following her to Masada. This would be the case whether or not they were carrying evidence of their crimes, and she needed to do something about that.

"It will be useful," she said, referring to the *Glory*.

"So where are we heading now?" Morgan asked. "I'm not too happy about sitting this close to the Polity—I'd bet we're being watched even now."

Confirmation—she could not allow Morgan or the rest any choices. She blinked her numerous eyes, another subframe opening in the laminate. This showed an object like an extended dumb-bell, crusted all over with sensors. The structure glinted with lights from thousands of portals, coilgun barrels the size of sequoias sprouting from each end. This was the nearest Polity watch station. The obvious weapons weren't all it possessed, apparently. There would be USERs in there or intelligent U-space missiles, plus runcible gates linked to installations inside suns or placed on the event horizons of black holes. These would be capable of routing appalling amounts of power. However, such stations were here to watch for some major push by the prador, so a few human ships like hers were surely beneath their notice.

"Don't let that concern you," she said. "This border is as leaky as a prador door seal—we've had our agents and Separatist agents crossing it for years."

"We're crossing it?" said Morgan, alarmed.

"Don't be silly," she lied. "Our business remains in the Graveyard. I'll be coming over to the *Caligula* shortly to go into more detail about that—I'll want full control of its weapons for what's to come." The rest wasn't much of a lie. She had already penetrated the *Caligula*'s systems, as she had penetrated the other two ships, but they weren't her main concern. While she controlled those systems remotely there was always a chance, once Morgan and the rest knew where they were going, that they would try and maybe succeed in mutinying. She needed to be within physical reach of the people, not the computers. She understood now that she had relied on computer omniscience for too long.

"I'll be with you shortly," she said. "Inform the captain of the *Glory* that my agent will be arriving on his ship shortly too."

"Your agent?" Morgan enquired.

Almost without conscious thought, Isobel looked through cams inside the *Moray Firth* to where the Golem was working—making refinements to her space suit.

"Yes, my agent," she said, and cut the communications link.

Fear was the key. Her presence aboard the *Caligula* would enforce the obedience of all aboard and the presence of a skeletal Penny Royal Golem aboard the *Glory* would do the same there. That was as far as she could extend her physical control. The *Nasturtium*, if its captain managed to rebel, would be an acceptable loss.

"You will take charge of this ship," she said abruptly, turning to Trent.

He looked hopeful, but only for a moment, perhaps realizing that "taking charge" didn't mean he would be able to flee in the *Moray Firth*.

"What are you going to do?"

Isobel turned away from the screen and her consoles. "I'm going to ensure absolute obedience," she replied and set off back through her ship.

Soon, with Trent hurrying to catch up, she arrived at her laboratory platform, where the Golem held her bulky space suit stretched out over its arms. She quickly began donning it, with the Golem's attentive assistance.

Trent watched all this seemingly with tired acceptance. She knew he thought that taking the hunt to Masada was suicide, and knew he had given up trying to persuade her otherwise. He was a fool—there was a reason she was in charge with him subordinate. As the seals closed on her limbs and around the fixings to her weapons, she considered how all the work she'd done aboard the *Moray Firth* could have been wasted. Surely it would be better for her to remain aboard the *Caligula* now? It was the larger ship and so would have more room for her. It had more firepower and more resources aboard. Why had she retained her silly sentimental attachment to her old ship for so long, while keeping the *Caligula* moth-balled? She just had no idea, though she saw a connection to her earlier attachment to her human body.

"Return to the bridge," she said to Trent. "You can monitor from there."

It didn't really matter where he located himself aboard, since he wouldn't be operating any of its systems. And whatever he did, or didn't do, made no difference whatsoever. But right then, she just wanted him away from her. Closing her suit had felt like abnegation—she was denying herself prey by putting the suit between them—and that made her feel even more like attacking him. As he walked away, she swept off the platform and down to the hold she'd designated as her airlock, the Golem stomping after her. She entered through the back cargo door and felt the monomer fabric of her suit stiffen slightly as the door closed and the air evacuated.

As the outer cargo doors opened on hard vacuum, she felt a surge of excitement—in complete contrast to her previous worries and her rage. It felt a little like going after Stolman, but now something martial was raising its head inside her. Moving to the lip of the hold, she gazed at her three other ships as the *Moray Firth* drew closer and began to decelerate. They were still some miles away and not very clear visually in the dim red light of the local sun. She was about to clean up the imagery using her haiman augmentations when the ships abruptly snapped into sharp and exact focus.

What?

Next gridlines and targeting frames appeared across her vision, just momentarily, but as they faded she *knew* precise distances, power levels and weapons complements. Attack plans blossomed in her mind in intricate detail.

My eyes . . .

It was something to do with them, and something to do with other changes inside her. Trying to understand what had happened as best she could, she realized all this had stemmed from some unconscious part of her—it included her augmentations, but was more sophisticated. Inside her, mind and machine had just taken a step closer than even haiman integration could manage.

I am a hooder.

Apparently hooders were biomech weapons, but she'd never thought very deeply about what that might mean. They were capable of withstanding powerful weapons, but where was the rest? Where was the tactical mind and where were the thought processes, the actual armaments and everything else implied by the words "biomech weapon"? It struck her that the hooders of Masada were as devolved, mentally, as the gabbleducks—the descendants of the Atheter. So what was this? What was happening to her?

Penny Royal.

What had the AI said during their last encounter, when it had initiated these further changes?

I know the original form now.

Isobel's excitement increased as she finally understood the full potential of her change. Previously she had been transforming into one of Masada's hooders. These were animals, mindless shadows of the biomechs they had once been. Penny Royal's further intervention meant she was now changing into the original hooder form. The Polity had been sitting on data, so new insights into Masada's hooders were under wraps. But major events had occurred on Masada. An alien machine had all but destroyed Penny Royal there, before Amistad resurrected the AI. That machine was destroyed in turn, mainly down to a hooder—an almost legendary albino hooder rumoured to be millions of years old. It was named the Technician.

I will be even more powerful now.

Isobel twitched her cowl, sending instructions to the Golem poised beside her. It immediately launched itself into vacuum; a skeletal missile perfectly on target for the *Glory*. She too then launched herself, her trajectory precisely and instinctively calculated. As she travelled, she felt the need to move her limbs but thought that ridiculous until she tried. Pale pink fire flickered around them and she felt them digging into the soft rhizome-coated loam of vacuum, gripping the quantum foam of the universe to accelerate her towards her *target*.

"Isobel! Isobel!"

It was Morgan, trying to talk to her. She was a missile, unreadable energies washing around her, and the *Caligula's* automated defences had immediately come online. She felt a moment of chagrin, knowing she would have to reach out to shut down those defences, but before she could use her usual methods some other part of her reached out first. The defences went offline. A potential firing pattern blossomed within her and it had nothing to do with the Polity weapons she carried. She saw the induction wave would cause a surge through the *Caligula's* reactor. The ensuing sub-space fold, as carefully shaped as an origami model, would force the U-space drive to initiate while being completely out of balance. Then, feeding on the power surge, the *Caligula* would be crushed in its own warp . . .

Noo!

Isobel forced away that *other*, lost her grip on space and found herself tumbling, everything that occurred before now a momentary fantasy. Her mind could now label all the energies she'd used and actions she'd made and intended to make. But just a moment ago these weren't thoughts but feelings—and the resulting actions were as easy and as unconscious as walking, running, breathing . . . the beating of her heart. And now they were gone again. She slammed into the hull of the *Caligula* and bounced away, leaving a definite dent, horror rippling through her. This was almost worse than her urge to kill and rend and feed. She had almost, without real conscious thought of her own, annihilated one of her own spaceships.

Isobel writhed in vacuum, unable to grip anything that would lead her back to the ship, but finally had to admit defeat and use the impellers on her suit. Slowly re-establishing control, she used prosaic haiman functions to penetrate the warship's systems and get it to open a hold door. She collapsed inside on functioning grav-plates, noticing crates of weapons stacked all around her as the hold charged with air. She noted too that her space suit had split open and, unlike the last time she had found herself in vacuum, she felt no ill-effects at all. She abruptly, angrily, stripped away the suit and discarded it. Perhaps she was being foolish, but she felt sure that her future held no need for such basic protection.

"Isobel!"

Morgan was first through the bulkhead door, followed by four armed heavies, two of whom she vaguely recognized. She swung towards them and noted the heavies instinctively reaching for their weapons.

"You've changed," Morgan added.

What was he talking about? He'd seen her transformation already. She reached out with her augmentations to gaze through the cams here in this hold, and looked upon the new Isobel. That had been no fantasy out there—something had definitely happened, some deep change had occurred. She could see, without calculating, that her length had increased to fifteen feet, with a consequent reduction in her girth. Her carapace, all of it, was now a perfect ivory colour and her eyes glowed a bright almost jewel-like lemon yellow.

I'm beautiful, she thought.

She was also, she realized, incredibly hungry. Those here must have realized this on some instinctive level even as she did, for they all began backing away, even Morgan.

No . . . control.

Her Golem had arrived at the *Glory* and entered, and was now positioned on the bridge, while the *Nasturtium* remained under her mental control. She wanted to get going, and now, but the hunger wouldn't leave her and she found herself edging towards Morgan and the others.

No . . . stop.

She checked the cargo manifest of the *Glory*, confirming that it still included eighty-six mindless human beings, with prador thralls installed inside their empty skulls. She sent her instructions. When the captain of that ship questioned the order to shift part of that cargo across to the *Caligula*, the Golem beside him rested a hand on his shoulder and said, "Snickety, snick."

It was enough, and he obeyed.

BLITE

Blite had never felt anything like it. *The Rose* shuddered, and he sensed a sickening *twist* travelling down its length. It seemed to try and turn him inside out as it passed through him too. He rolled out of his bed, realizing he was floating up above the floor just a microsecond before the grav-plates came back on and dropped him on it.

"Bollocks," he said, almost resigned.

Who was on watch? Brondohohan and Ikbal, though the others would be on the bridge soon enough after that, whatever it was. He struggled to his feet, swaying, still feeling an odd wavering effect from the plates underneath his feet. He then staggered over to his cabin door and out. Chont and Haber were ahead of him, Martina and Greer trotting up the corridor behind.

"What the hell was that?" asked Greer.

"I don't know," Blite replied.

"We're out of U-space," said Martina.

He nodded and turned to head after Chont and Haber, only now realizing the truth of her words. The buzz was gone; the perpetual hum and tension of the U-space engine had ceased.

"There's something big, black and nasty out there," said Brond the moment Blite reached the bridge and dropped into his chair. "It's called the *Micheletto's Garrotte* and it's some sort of modern Polity attack ship."

"How did it knock us into the real?" Blite eyed the deadly looking black spike of a vessel shown on the screen.

"It didn't," said Ikbal. "That was something else, sited in a suspiciously regularly shaped asteroid out there. Seems we ran into a USER, because the U-space entry barrier was recently extended to here." Ikbal looked round from his instruments. "Now we're surrounded by modern splinter missiles that could U-jump right in here at any moment. They're all capable of even tracking us through U-space too—that is, if we stood any chance of getting through the USER effect."

"So what now?" Blite asked, bracing himself.

They all knew he wasn't asking the question of them.

"The *Garrotte* AI is being particularly stubborn and aggressive," Penny Royal whispered. "It seems I am not trusted."

Blite sighed with relief that he wasn't to be reintroduced to his memories, or anyone else's for that matter, then said, "Oh, really." He shot a look at the others, just to ensure that they would keep their own comments to themselves.

"It will be necessary for me to take some action," the AI added.

Shit.

Already, *The Rose* was filled with a huge tension. Blite reached out towards the console, stop-motion images of his hand tracing the movement. He called up a tactical display to reveal the *Garrotte* just fifty miles away, while the five splinter missiles surrounded them at a distance of just a mile. His instruments also showed him a U-space storm too fierce for *The Rose*'s U-space engine to drive through. It would not wane for some time, even if the USER, located on an asteroid just over one light minute away, was shut down.

"You're talking to the *Garrotte*," he said, phrasing it so it wasn't quite a question and hoping in some way to prevent or delay Penny Royal from taking "some action."

"Yes," the AI replied, but added no more.

Blite opened a general Polity com channel, though he imagined the ship out there was listening on every channel he knew about and some more besides.

"Polity attack ship," he said. "This is Captain Blite of *The Rose*." He paused, trying to find the words. "I have a crew of five people, all of whom are innocent of any capital crime. We are, essentially, hostages of the other resident aboard." Again the pause. "Who, I have to add, has been innocent of any capital crimes since being aboard and even saved the lives of thousands of people in Carapace City on the Rock Pool." Yet another pause. "Penny Royal has also returned to me memcordings of crew I lost in a previous encounter with it. I suggest you think very carefully about any actions you might be inclined to take."

"Oh goody," replied the *Garrotte* AI, "the slow drag of human speech yet again."

"Yet again?" Blite enquired, anxious to keep some dialogue going, even though the light inside *The Rose* now seemed as solid as amber and something was certainly going to happen.

"Oh yes, I had the pleasure of a chat with one Thorvald Spear. He happens to be inside the ship your supposed kidnapper used to occupy. Do you think Penny Royal has come to claim it back? I would have to be very harsh if that was the case."

The *Garrotte* was babbling—probably this human conversation had been assigned to some insignificant part of its intellect, while the active part concentrated on its main concern.

"What does Penny Royal say?"

"Oh lots and very little," said the *Garrotte*. "But I cannot allow you or it to approach Masada and this time I'm getting no interference from Amistad. In fact, much to my delight, Penny Royal is considered such a danger that I have been authorized to use my full complement of weapons—if necessary."

"And what about us?"

The tension changed and Blite felt something like a USER surge travel through his body. On his tactical display, one of the surrounding missiles blinked out of existence.

"The fuck?" said the *Garrotte*.

Penny Royal now replayed something, undoubtedly for the benefit of Blite and his crew, since AI-to-AI communication with the *Garrotte* would have taken a microsecond. It was the voice of a woman, whom Blite just knew was military, and was lecturing to an audience.

"Legally, we are on dodgy ground," she said. "In Polity law, we are here in this system under sufferance. We have been given no carte blanche to take any military action out here. By deploying a USER here we are actually infringing on the law concerning 'deliberate isolation of autochthons'—even though the Weaver is the only sentient alien here."

"I think you know better than that," said the *Garrotte*. "And where's my fucking missile?"

"I do," hissed Penny Royal.

The lecturer now continued, "Polity AIs make it up as they go along; choosing the laws to best suit their own needs or purposes. However, until the laws are changed, we are still in infringement."

It occurred to Blite that Penny Royal was buying time by using recorded human speech, but surely this must have occurred to the attack ship AI? Probably, but it was equally as likely to be waiting for Penny Royal to act, before responding itself. The captain gazed at the time display at the bottom of his screen, and counted down the seconds since the missile disappeared.

"The Weaver hasn't actually complained," said the *Garrotte*, "nor has it instructed us *not* to take any military action. As for this 'isolation of autochthons,' you seem to have dragged that out of the mists of time . . . what exactly are we isolating the Weaver from? Do you think it might want to cosy up to the prador?"

"You won't know until such a time as you cease isolating it," replied Penny Royal, obviously not finding a suitable recording to use. "It could be that it has its own communication routes and that some of those you stop are here by invitation."

"Like you?"

A short pause ensued, then came a flash from a massive explosion just over one light minute away. This was followed by a further outpouring of x-rays as a singularity began to eat its surrounding asteroid.

"I thought so," said the *Garrotte*. "Time to take the gloves off."

Blite grabbed his safety harness and pulled it across as the tension within his ship ramped up to an unbearable level. *The Rose* shuddered, the sound of its U-space engine labouring reached them, and they submerged into that continuum. The ship now crashed and appeared to twist all around them, error codes began filling the surrounding screens and a breach klaxon began to sound. He heard Haber scream and bit down on a scream himself as he found himself gazing into something impossible for his mind to accept. Then, with another shuddering crash, they were out of it again. Through the main screen Blite now saw the planet Masada. A microsecond later his tactical display showed U-signatures all around them, one of them oscillating weirdly and spearing towards them. A massive flare ignited outside—the main screen blanking to black safety.

The Rose jerked as if going over a subspace pot-hole. Haber and Chont shot backwards across the bridge and crashed into the rear wall. Greer was clinging with heavy-worlder strength to the base of Brond's chair with one arm, her other arm wrapped tightly around Martina.

Another explosion ensued, massive, megaton range like the last. Blite's tactical display showed this spreading as it hit their curved hard-field, the impact shock driving *The Rose* a hundred miles from its previous position. Without the stabilizing effect of internal grav, and another force employed by Penny Royal causing the very air to resemble amber, they would all have been dripping smears on the ship's bulkheads. Blite smelled smoke then heard the worst sound a space man could hear: the roar of air escaping into vacuum. A particle beam stabbed and probed out there, blue shot through with criss-crossing spirals of black. Tracing it back to its source, he could now make out the *Micheletto's Garrotte*. This beam ground across the ship's hardfield like a drill skittering on hard metal and now *The Rose* began shuddering.

"I think we've had it!" someone shouted over the roar. Blite wasn't sure who had spoken, but had to agree. Penny Royal had taken on something advanced and lethal here and might well suffer a defeat. Maybe the AI could survive that, but Blite suspected he and his crew would not.

Then it all stopped.

The beam winked out and there were no more explosions. The amber loosened and flowed, allowing the smoke to dissipate into vent fans running at full speed, while the sound of air escaping ceased at once.

"Are we dead?" asked Ikbal, and now Blite realized it was him who had spoken before.

"Not yet," Brond replied.

Those two words, Blite felt, covered their entire situation since last leaving Masada—which was now uncomfortably close. They waited, wondering what the hell was going on. Finally a voice issued from the speaker.

"You have got to be fucking kidding me," said the *Garrotte* AI.

"Like I said," Penny Royal replied. "Some are here by invitation."

SPEAR

Gloria Markham was an attractive woman of indeterminate age. If she'd had no Polity anti-ageing treatments or cosmetic work, and just been subject to the medical tech of this world before Polity intervention, I would have put her age at about thirty, solstan. However, I knew that many had availed themselves of Polity medical tech since intervention and, judging by another aspect of her, she had too. She wore a tight clinging skirt and an undercut top—a particular fashion affectation found only here. The blue fabric clung to her upper arms and shoulders and the tight ring collar was high on her throat. The material below that clung to her breasts, but didn't reach down to cover them completely. Below them a triangular hole had been cut, revealing their underside, while the point of the triangle terminated at her belly-button. The centre of this cut-away section revealed a circular scar a couple of inches across, ridged around its circumference with mauve and black scar tissue. The top was designed to reveal the scar left by a scole—an aphid-like creature. This bio-engineered parasite had enabled humans to survive on this oxygen-depleted world. Really, if she hadn't used Polity medical technology to negate the effects of the scole on the human body, even after it was removed, she would have looked about eighty now, or been dead.

"This is about my mother," she said, after greeting me with that, "I've been expecting you."

"It is?" I said.

"It is," she replied, giving me a head-to-foot inspection that made me feel quite uncomfortable, before glancing at Riss and frowning. Then she stepped past us to lock the shop door.

"My mother was a rebel," she explained, as she led us through an arch into her cramped quarters to the rear. "She fought the Theocracy for thirty years and that battle changed her. She started to enjoy the killing a little too much as she grew tired of the cause but powerful within it. She ended up becoming dictatorial and accumulated wealth for her own ends. By the time she abandoned the cause she was as hated and feared by those within it as those we were fighting, but I loved her."

She gestured me to an uncomfortable-looking stool, gazed at Riss again, now as if she disapproved, then headed over to a sideboard crowded with bottles.

"So you were a rebel too," I suggested, deciding just to go with this as I sat down.

"I was, though if you talk to any Masadan now they'll tell you they were freedom fighters too. The number of supposed rebels here has increased a hundredfold, while the number of ex-pond workers has diminished almost to zero." Her smile was twisted and sad as she turned round, then she banished it and held up a bottle and two glasses. "Wine?" she enquired, a little too brightly.

"Certainly," I replied, if it would put her at her ease, going on. "So she bought passage off-world on a smuggler's ship," I said. "To the Graveyard."

"How can you know that?" She sat in the chair on the other side of a low polished obsidian table, clinked down the glasses and poured.

"Call it an educated guess."

She frowned, shook her head in puzzlement, then continued, "She stayed with the smugglers for eight solstan years, but eventually they ousted her when she tried to strangle the smuggler captain. She then applied her skills to more lucrative work, more suited to her skills. I don't know how many contracts she carried out, but they numbered into the hundreds."

"Contracts?" Riss enquired from a thick hand-woven rug where she'd coiled herself.

"She was a killer—I told you. She hunted and killed people. Her past turned her into what she was. The Theocracy made her, just like it made many who are in the Tidy Squad even now."

"Let me guess," I said. "She was eventually hired for a hit that killed her?"

"Yes." Gloria nodded an affirmative. "I researched all this many years ago—compiled all the data . . . She was hired by a big salvage operator in the Graveyard, one John Hobbs. He provided her with weaponry and expertise, promising a fortune in diamond slate if she killed something that had destroyed one of his ships and slaughtered its crew."

"Penny Royal," said Riss.

During an uncomfortable pause I tried the wine. It was a deep blood-red and very good. Only as I sipped it did I remember that they grew grape trees here and guessed this must be a local product.

Gloria gave a tight nod. "My mother hunted the rogue AI for decades and irritated it enough for it to send one of its Golem after her, which she managed to destroy. Eventually she found the location of its planetoid and went there in a converted prador kamikaze with a crust-breaker rocket." She sat back and crossed her legs, took a large gulp from her glass and fixed her gaze on me. I was aware that she was looking for something from me, but I wasn't sure what it was. I was too busy remembering the derelict kamikaze I'd seen out by that planetoid and remembering my own plan to bomb Penny Royal. Obviously that initial attempt had failed and I wondered how likely it was that my efforts would have succeeded.

"What happened then?" I asked, returning to the moment.

"I don't know," Gloria smiled tightly, "but one day I intend to ask her."

"So Penny Royal returned her," said Riss, just a step ahead of me.

Gloria nodded and stood up. Facing me she unnecessarily straightened out her clothing, then paused to give me a lingering look before turning abruptly. She walked to a wall crammed with old still pictures and framed pieces of screen fabric running old scenes. She pushed one of these aside—one cycling a moving image of a woman similar in appearance to Gloria herself, presumably her mother. This revealed an inset hand-safe, which she opened. Inside rested a small box made of polished tricone shell. She took this out and returned to her seat, opening the box on the table.

"My mother, Renata Markham," she explained, looking up and meeting my gaze very directly. I started to get some intimation of the undercurrents here and glanced down at my nascuff. I realized that shutting down one's libido also shuts down sensitivity to a particular kind of body language.

The ruby cylinder resting in its wool packing was smaller than the one Sylac had made for me, being of the standard kind that could be purchased now. So it was of Polity manufacture? No, of course not—Penny Royal had just made it easily accessible by standard methods. I imagined that Renata Markham had resided in some other esoteric storage before the AI loaded her to this jewel and brought it here.

"So tell me about the visit you received," I said.

"I don't remember the words," she said. "It came in the night . . . I heard a sound in the shop and went out to investigate. The front windows were black and there was Penny Royal hovering just below the ceiling—a ball of black spines. I recognized it at once since it's been on many news reports . . ."

"Then?" Riss prompted.

"I don't remember the words, as I said. But it talked to me somehow. A ruby memplant rested on my counter, larger than this one. I was to put it in a brooch setting and display it, but I couldn't allow anyone to buy it. Eventually someone would recognize it for what it was and some representative of the Polity would be along to claim it. I asked why I should do this for the creature that killed my mother—whereupon I felt something in my hand, opened it, and found this." She stabbed a finger at the memplant. "I had this one checked and my mother's mind was identified inside, so I did as I was told." She now fell silent, staring at the object on the tabletop.

"There's more—you said you were expecting me."

She looked up then, as if remembering herself, straightened her back as she fingered the scar on her stomach and chewed on her top lip. The undercurrent couldn't be any clearer now. I considered how I should react, then made an aug link to my nascuff and fiddled with its controls. Slowly it changed from blue to red.

"When the Polity Golem came here and took your memplant away," she said, "I asked to be kept informed, and I was. I've known your location, with a few limitations, ever since you were resurrected." She paused, staring at me intently. "I knew when you arrived here at Masada and I knew when you came here to Chattering. I was sure you were tracing your past . . . have always been sure you would come here."

I thought I understood the undercurrent then. Had she become a little obsessive about me? I now considered reversing what I'd done with my cuff, but by then other feelings were kicking in and my inner lecher was thinking: *Why not?* I shook my head, half-expecting to be annoyed but feeling amused instead. Then I concentrated on the story she'd told me.

It all seemed so random. She had to do as Penny Royal asked, then someone had to recognize my implant, then the Polity had to collect it and resurrect me. I needed to eventually find out about this place and come here, and then remember someone else's memories. Finally, Gloria had to be here to tell me her story . . . But no, nothing about Penny Royal was random. Penny Royal had probably known precisely how Gloria would react, might even have programmed it into her mind. The AI had probably calculated to the second when the implant would be spotted and then collected. It might have calculated to the second when I would be sitting here hearing this.

"Tell me, Gloria," I said. "Did your mother leave this world shortly after some of her comrades were executed in the Cage?"

Gloria nodded. "My mother placed a thermal device in the ritual fire to make sure they didn't suffer. I think that act was what finally drove her to give up on the cause."

Well, no, Gloria, I thought. She'd already made that decision beforehand.

Gloria's story had been a confirmation of what I'd already felt, but perhaps a necessary one. The sensations of déjà vu, the fragments of memories and the larger recollection I had experienced here were all true memories. She had proved that with her version of events. Undoubtedly, through the spine, I was connected to other lives—lives that had been taken by Penny Royal. Why the AI needed this to be completely confirmed for me I had no idea. However, I suspected the answers were coming my way with the inevitability of the death of suns. I picked up my wine, finished the glass and put it down. Gloria leaned forwards, picked up the bottle and looked at me enquiringly. There was more to her enquiry than the wine. I glanced over at Riss.

The snake drone uncoiled and headed for the arch.

"*Riss?*" I asked by aug.

"Nearly choking on the hormones," she replied out loud. "I'll see you back at the hotel." She disappeared through the arch.

Gloria followed, probably to open the shop door for Riss, but she paused at the arch and I heard the door open and close beyond her.

"Well, how did it do that?" she asked, turning back towards me.

"Riss is a war drone of many talents," I explained. "She used to sneak into prador dreadnoughts, so obviously a shop door is no problem for her."

"Her?"

"Female-designated drone—simply because of certain physical traits."

Gloria walked back and stood close beside me. "And apparently able to sense human hormones."

I reached out and traced a finger round the scole scar on her stomach. She reached down and placed a hand over mine, holding it in place.

"I won't be staying," I said.

"That doesn't matter."

"Why?" I asked.

"Just telling the story doesn't feel like enough."

It made a kind of sense. I shrugged, so she pushed my hand down to a stick-seam at her hip. I inserted a finger and slid it down to open it. She reached down to help and was soon kicking the skirt off her feet. She was obviously proud of her body, standing there in that revealing top and a pair of all but transparent lacy knickers. She then pressed a point on her top just above one breast and the garment retreated like a living stain into a nodule there, which she detached and discarded. I was reminded of Sheil Glasser and her similarly easy-to-discard clothing. When she did nothing more than stroke her scar, I reached out, grabbed a handful of lacy material and pulled her towards me. After stumbling a little, she moved closer, stepped astride me, then reached down.

Even as she was screwing me I wondered how much of this had been preplanned: the way she had dismissed Riss, the way she had directed me to this stool rather than the armchair, the wine, how she had been dressed. Hands clamped to her waist, I sucked and chewed on her nipples and she rubbed her breasts in my face. However, when I tried to pull her head down to kiss her she pulled it away, began grunting and shoving hard against me before coming with a series of surprised exclamations. I tried to keep her moving but she leaned back, resting her hands on the table, studying me with a puzzled frown. I leaned forwards, pushed her onto her back on the table and stood over her. She just lay there watching me, expectant. I then grabbed the wine bottle, putting it to one side with the glasses. It would have been more dramatic to sweep them aside, but it was good wine. After quickly shedding all my clothing, I lifted up her legs and pulled off her knickers, since they'd been making the side of my cock sore anyway, then fucked her on the table. She started to get back into it again and was responding vigorously by the time I started to come, but my orgasm was killed a bit when, at that point, the table collapsed.

She started giggling and, after a moment, that set me off. We untangled ourselves from the wreckage, grabbed the wine and glasses and she led me into her bedroom. She dissolved a stim strip in her mouth while I just made some further adjustments to my nascuff. Over the ensuing hours we drank another two bottles of wine, took our time, then it just reached an ending that at first baffled me.

"It was nice to meet you, Thorvald Spear," she said, suddenly distant.

Climbing off the bed and pulling on a robe, she moved over to the bedroom door and opened it. I was dismissed. Still puzzled, I dressed—I would shower in my hotel. When she led the way out of the bedroom I followed, trying to think of something else to say, then gestured to the tricone shell box lying beside the collapsed table.

"Why didn't you get her to Soulbank?" I asked, nodding down at the thing. "I doubt she's wanted for whatever she did in the Graveyard, and I would bet that the AIs would resurrect her for her services to the cause here."

Gloria looked up. "Because I love her."

Of course, Gloria seemed to love a research project and an ideal, but the reality might turn out to be harder to love. Similar rules applied to hate. As I headed for the shop door she said, "You knew things you shouldn't have been able to know and I was curious about you."

"I guess," I replied.

"But now I will take her to Soulbank," she said, almost indifferently.

What had changed? I began to think that nothing had changed, but that something had been completed. For me, anyway. Once out of Markham's I strode out of the converted church into lavender sunshine. I noted that one side of the Cage's monomer covering had been lifted, and some workmen were using ancient acetylene cutting equipment on the metal posts securing it to the ground. I guess the council or committee here had come to their decision.

Heading for my hotel, I pondered how lacking in curiosity Gloria had actually been. She told me her story but asked very few questions of me. Perhaps Penny Royal had simply programmed her, with the ease of winding up a clockwork toy, to deliver her story. Her own concerns, curiosity, questions . . . being irrelevant. I really hoped that everything that came after hadn't been part of the AI's plan. But I couldn't help feeling that the AI was a completist and that it had programmed her obsession with me. The sexual act had been the full point at the end of her plot thread in my story and now she could move on, resurrect her mother—continue with her life.

18

ISOBEL

Her hunger was intense now and she knew it was going to be difficult to keep it under control—aboard a ship with a human crew of ten and a troop complement of fifty. Linking through to the *Glory*, she saw the first four cold coffins being loaded to a pulpit handler; they would then exit through a hold lock. She estimated that they would arrive here on the *Caligula* within half an hour, so all she needed to do was maintain self-control until then.

"So where are we going?" Morgan asked, as he walked behind her towards the *Caligula*'s bridge—there not being enough room in the corridor for him to walk beside her.

I must open out this ship too, she thought, trying to distract herself from Morgan and the four behind him. He was accompanied by two boosted men, a male heavy-worlder, and a woman with cybernetic augmentations. And all of these, to her present way of thinking, were just prey.

"In good time—I have some arrangements to make first."

Just then, ahead of her, a man and a woman in combat fatigues stepped out of a cabin. She halted, it was almost too much. They stared at her in shock, with curiosity, and she stared back, seeing every bead of sweat on their faces.

Control.

"Crew and the troops are to remain at their stations or in their quarters," she announced, that same announcement echoing from the ship's PA a moment later. The two ahead paused for a second, then backed into the cabin. There would have been more of them, Isobel knew. More of the crew and troop complement would want to get a look at her, at how she'd changed. She didn't know, should they all start milling around her, if she could restrain herself.

Five people were seated on the bridge, two controlling the ship's weapons and one permanently checking on the ship's second-child mind. Another two were ready at damage control and ship's maintenance stations. They all turned, with one of them, a woman, abruptly standing up and looking terrified. Isobel rapidly inspected files. This woman had once worked aboard a smuggler ship that traded with Masada, so knew all about hooders. Isobel fought to maintain calm as she moved to the middle of the bridge floor.

"All of you," she said, "return to your quarters, now."

After a hesitation, they all stood, some of them looking to Morgan questioningly. He nodded once and she suppressed the urge to let herself go here. She was in charge and yet they needed confirmation from him? No matter. They were redundant, as now she was in charge of everything they'd controlled.

"What's going on, Isobel?" Morgan asked, now sounding wary. "There's no need for this—we've always carried out your orders without deviation."

Really, did she need any of them? If Spear and Penny Royal were in orbit she could completely control the attack. If they were down on the surface of the planet, she should be able to hit them from orbit.Why had she bothered pulling together all these troops?

No . . . stupid.

Her plans would depend on the situation at Masada. She might need to divide her forces, or send troops to secure some location, or she might require them as a distraction. She mustn't return to her old way of thinking that she could absolutely control everything with her mind. She wasn't thinking straight.

The pulpit handler was halfway to the ship, the hold she had entered through standing open to receive it. She should have waited there and satisfied her need before coming here. She turned, slowly, fighting for self-control. The moment the five crew fell into the complete compass of her senses, target frames blossomed all over them and attack plans reeled out in her mind. It was an odd feeling, as if she was some three-fold being. The predator wanted to rend and tear, yet something analytical and cold was growing in her, something that mapped a route to the immediate destruction of a threat. Her human self also remained, trying to hold all three aspects together.

"We are going to Masada," she said abruptly.

Morgan looked startled while the other four glanced at each other, obviously surprised and then trying to shut down on any further reaction.

"Dangerous," he said.

"Yes, but necessary."

"Why?" he asked.

She watched him in silence for a moment, then said, "You are asking too many questions, Morgan."

"I'm sorry," he said, "but going to a Polity world, especially that one, is a hell of a risk. I don't know what the payoff could possibly be."

Isobel moved forwards and Morgan and the others abruptly got out of her way. She needed him, didn't she? Better to decide her response to such insubordination after she had fed.

"I have to return to the hold," she said. "Explanations can come after that."

They followed her as she headed back the way she had come. Through ship's cams she watched the pulpit handler enter the hold then the space doors there closed. She was eager, but knew she should not allow that to distract her now. Why the hell had she told him where they were going just then? Had some part of her wanted to instigate violence? The answer was obvious: the predator wanted to feed and was pushing her other parts. She watched Morgan and the others through the ship's internal systems and, just as she reached the bulkhead door into the hold, she saw it.

He reached up to tap three times against his cheekbone, then lowered his hand again. Her analytical part ran through all her memories of Morgan, riffled through them like a speed reader. He didn't touch his scarred face very much, and she had no recollection of him having ever made that movement before. It was a signal—a simple option when you knew all other forms of communication were being monitored. The augmented woman fell back a few paces, shaking her head and putting on a show of looking frightened. She abruptly turned into a side corridor and moved away. Isobel knew it was all an act and that she was supposed to assume xenophobia had driven this person away. While continuing to watch Morgan and the remaining three, Isobel used the ship's cam system to track the woman.

She went directly to her cabin and, of course, there were no cams operating inside. Shortly after that, a cam outside the cabin developed a fault, but Isobel was able to access it and correct it.

Too easy; a deliberate distraction.

At the bulkhead door to the hold, Isobel turned to Morgan and the other three.

"Wait here," she said, mentally opening the door behind her then scuttling backwards through it. As the door closed, she turned to eye the four cold-storage cylinders the pulpit handler had deposited on the floor. Targeting frames immediately overlaid them and she jerked back, a line of translucent pink fire travelling down the length of her body. What? Why was she reacting like this to what were practically corpses? Some sort of hidden weapon? Isobel moved to one side, putting some distance between herself and the containers, trying to order her mind. She checked recorded data on the history of these containers to check for any possible tampering. She also searched for anything unusual in the recorded footage of them being taken from the *Glory*'s hold, yet could find nothing wrong.

With more success, she simultaneously checked an old schematic of the *Caligula* against an updated one, looking for holes in security. It was well concealed and, had her mind and senses not been as ramped up as they were, she would have missed it. Hidden routes had been opened up throughout the ship from the woman's cabin. Isobel traced one of those routes down to a maintenance door in the corridor leading to this hold. The maintenance robot she required was just off that route, replacing a faulty optic cable, so she turned it and sent it creeping to a new position. Then she froze it into immobility when it detected movement, and gazed through its cam eyes.

The woman was coming and she was carrying something. Isobel focused in and identified a portable proton cannon—and the woman was screwing a giga-Watt energy canister into its underside. Morgan had made preparations to deal with what he'd thought Isobel had become, should she be a threat. But she knew these were inadequate, given what she now knew about herself. She moved back towards the door. She had to deal with this. But that new part of her abruptly wrenched her back to focus on the cold coffins. It was taking over, gathering energy . . .

A subspacial twist emanated from her, kaleidoscope refractions cutting the air of the hold. Coffins must be expelled, destroyed. Too dangerous this close. Through her haiman augmentation she sent an instruction to one of the coffins for confirmation and simultaneously ordered an emergency expulsion of the hold's air. She also directed the space door to open even while sending an order—viciously enforced—to the *Glory* for all its cargo to be expelled . . .

What?

The coffin opened and, with senses stretching into realms her previous augmentations hadn't reached, she inspected the corpse lying within. The primitive control device inside its empty skull and extending down its spine was unimportant. The blue rings of scar tissue were just organic damage and the virus that had grown from them inside the corpse was prosaic at the microscopic level. However, at sub-microscopic levels, the new part of Isobel recognized danger.

The enemy.

The wave issued from her instantly, its gravity front smashing into the four coffins and the pulpit handler—slinging them as wreckage through the space doors and far out into vacuum. In the first few seconds this wreckage travelled a hundred miles out, then the *twist*, following it out, enclosed it and collapsed. A brief star blossomed as that twist compressed the wreckage nigh to the point of fusion.

Disruption sufficient; immediate danger eliminated.

Now she was into the *Caligula*'s weapons. The *Glory* was shedding its cargo, using its fast dump mechanisms—installed against interception during potential Polity police actions. The captain had been reluctant to comply, but his second not so much so after the Golem tore out the captain's throat. Isobel fired the *Caligula*'s particle cannons, turning each in the procession of coffins into white-hot plasma. It was enough, for the enemy was in an inactive state and unlikely to recover from such a burn, though elements of it might remain in existence.

Potential threat eliminated.

Isobel swung round to the bulkhead door, as the space door closed and the hold recharged with air. As that other thing receded inside her, the predator took full control. She surged forwards, issuing subspacially generated hardfield shears and went straight through the bulkhead. The woman was stepping from the maintenance hatch even at that moment and Isobel targeted her with her own particle cannon, one shot turning her head to flaming vapour. Morgan tried to run but she came down on him like a giant iron fly swat. She rolled over him as she pursued the others, leaving just a smear of offal behind. The other three she brought down just a few yards later.

She moved on through the ship, no longer human, no longer even able to consider regaining control. And she hunted, killed and fed.

AMISTAD

Through thousands of eyes Amistad watched *The Rose* draw closer to Masada, passing a defence installation that contained one of the new gravity weapons. This device could have picked up the ship in a gravity wave and tossed it into the face of Calypse, or into the sun. But the weapon and its controlling submind remained somnolent, castrated by legalities and the protectorate status of this world. Amistad felt a frustration more related to his war drone past than his present warden status.

"Let that ship through, and allow it to land."

This communication channel had opened just a short while after *The Rose* had been knocked out of U-space by the USER and intercepted by the *Garrotte*. It was a channel that hadn't opened since Amistad's last communications with the Weaver, the newly evolved Atheter. This was some years ago now, when, under the Weaver's control, a hooder known as the Technician had destroyed a rogue Atheter killing machine. Thereafter, the Weaver had negotiated with the human ambassador of Masada, Leif Grant. Other points regarding the governing of Masada had been settled between Amistad and Weaver's Atheter AI. But after the negotiations the Weaver had lost interest, and all communications concerning the running of this world had been from its AI. However, this directive to let *The Rose* land had come direct from the Weaver, who had now disappeared.

Amistad had immediately asked why such a vessel, containing such a dangerous entity, should be let through, but there had been no reply from the Weaver. Similar questions directed towards the Weaver's Atheter AI had received nil response too. Perhaps the AI just didn't have the spare processing power to reply, since it was now busy interfering with Polity computing all around this world.

"How are you now?" Amistad asked.

The watch drone, currently stuck sideways in a mud bank a hundred kilometres from the viewing platform, emitted some hisses and squeaks before replying. The drone hadn't been a Polity employee but had turned up one day, penetrating all sorts of defences, to watch the Weaver. Unusually, the Weaver had not objected to its presence through the AI, and Amistad had quickly routed over an employment contract. The drone had watched the Weaver for over a year without problems, but now there was a problem.

"Like an induction wave tore out my grav," replied the crab-like drone.

Via its AI, the Weaver had requested much in the way of Polity manu-facturing equipment and materials. Upon receiving that equipment, it had at once taken it into its baroque flute grass home. Here all the spyware and pin-head watchers had immediately been deactivated. Polity scanning devices had also failed to penetrate its home for over a year now.

Using this equipment, the Weaver had apparently started producing various devices—though these could only be seen when it brought them out of its home. Some of these were perfectly understandable, like the atomic shear it used to cut flute grass. It had also constructed a complex hardfield generator, which it used to fold and weave both grasses and various other materials. Other devices were impenetrable, like the object it used to pull penny molluscs from their rocks, then set them floating while it fed on them. Amistad had at first thought it used hardfields to achieve this, but subsequent investigation detected interference with Van De Walls forces and subtle boson fields. It was this device the Weaver had used to bring down the watchful crab drone.

Amistad briefly replayed the incident. The Weaver had set out on one of its long perambulations, stopping to sample the odd tricone, which it seemed to relish. It occasionally snacked on penny oysters, which it always shifted through the air in precisely measured and unchanging patterns. As usual the crab drone was in tow. But today, during the Weaver's third snack on those little molluscs, it had sent them into a pattern never seen before. The drone had moved closer and that was when the complex grav pulse had hit it and, with a screeing sound, it had dropped out of the sky into the mud bank. The Weaver had continued feeding for a while before moving off, but what it did thereafter wasn't known.

The drone being knocked out of play shouldn't have mattered because watch satellites, arrayed all around Masada, were capable of closely inspecting absolutely anything on the surface. But, shortly after the Weaver polished off its last penny oyster, forty watch satellites—those covering the main continent—simply shut down. Surface surveillance had also crashed and any attempt to gather data from privately owned scanning devices was disrupted. Amistad had been trying for some time to reactivate both the satellites and the surface stuff. But it had soon become apparent that something, presumably the Atheter AI, was interfering on AI levels. Even a request for gabbleduck sightings was being interfered with, with responses to this being scrambled over communication channels and locator beacons suddenly not knowing where they were.

"The Weaver doesn't want to be watched," said the drone.

"He's up to something," interjected the *Garrotte* AI from out in space. "Something involving Penny Royal."

"When superior minds start stating the obvious," said Amistad, "I tend to start questioning the appellation 'superior'."

"He doesn't trust us," said the *Garrotte*. "After the initial negotiations about the protectorate status of this world, he began playing for time. Everything he has done and said since then has been designed to baffle and mislead."

The world had first been subsumed into the Polity after the fall of its human theocracy but, under Polity protocols, the discovery of an alien autochthon meant it could not be part of the Polity. So the Polity had decided to "protect" this alien on this alien world. Seen through other eyes, that protection translated as isolation and control.

"In the same position, would you trust us?" the crab drone asked from its mud bank.

"Probably not, but I'd tend to trust a loose cannon like Penny Royal even less," said the *Garrotte*. "I would guess this involves some weapon— some way for the Weaver to attack us."

"That's because you were formatted to think in martial terms," said Amistad.

"As were you."

"I was, but my horizons have since widened."

"So what do you reckon?" asked the crab drone.

Amistad thought about the question for a whole microsecond. "I don't think the *Garrotte* is right about the Weaver looking for a way to attack. More likely he is trying to obtain something to change his status from that of a protected sentient—to strengthen his bargaining position."

"And Penny Royal is supplying that?"

"Possibly," said Amistad, now studying the deep scan results of *The Rose* as it descended into the atmosphere of Masada. "Consider that ship's hardfield," he added.

"Seriously advanced hardfield linked into U-space tech," the *Garrotte* surmised. "So a defensive system. I guess that makes sense."

It did, Amistad felt, though the masses of singular mem-storage units aboard that ship didn't. And, really, bringing some sort of defensive system here for the Weaver just seemed too simple for Penny Royal. One also had to wonder what the black AI was getting in exchange. Atheter knowledge or technology? Should Penny Royal be allowed such?

The *Garrotte* now added, "Maybe we should relax the rules a little and inadvertently send a multi-megaton CTD imploder *The Rose*'s way?"

"It wouldn't work," interjected a distant mind, causing an immediate "oh shit" reaction amidst the three. "Events in the Graveyard are becoming clearer—the defensive technology you have spotted would stop a CTD dead."

"So how should I react?" Amistad enquired of Earth Central.

"You don't. You just watch."

Amistad's frustration increased and when Earth Central again withdrew, he did some hard thinking. After a moment he incorporated data from one of his subminds—one that had been in constant contact with a recent arrival on this world. And then he made direct contact with that arrival himself.

"How is your information-gathering exercise proceeding?" he asked.

"Well enough," Riss replied, though without much enthusiasm. "But now, since it's the great Amistad himself talking to me, rather than his submind, my suspicions have been aroused." The snake drone and Spear were in Chattering, back in their hotel after their recent visit to Markham's. Now updated by his submind, Amistad was fully aware of the events that had occurred there. And, in the light of them, he was considering his options. He could tell them Penny Royal had arrived and allow them to respond, or he could keep them locked down in Chattering as a bargaining chip. They, or at least Spear, seemed to have a part to play in the black AI's manipulations—though what that part involved wasn't entirely clear. However, even as Amistad weighed the options, the decision was taken away from him.

"I see," said Riss.

Amistad immediately checked his communications security, but there were no holes. Riss and Spear had just received a message from the *Lance*, and Spear had jumped out of a chair at the news. They now knew Penny Royal had arrived, and were being updated on its descent to Masada.

"Of course you were about to tell us all about that, weren't you?" said Riss.

"Of course," Amistad replied, giving away nothing, then re-delegated his submind to watch the two. Next, clamping down on his war drone frustration, he tried another communications channel—another one that hadn't been open for some time.

"So what are you up to?" he asked.

"Restoring balance," Penny Royal replied at once.

"You still have your eighth state of consciousness," Amistad stated.

"I do."

"It is guilty of murder."

"Yes."

"Then you are a fugitive."

"On Masada, which is not legally part of the Polity," said the AI. "Perhaps you need to talk to the Weaver about that."

Of course, the Polity couldn't go after Penny Royal without the Weaver's consent. If they'd wanted to "arrest" Penny Royal, it should have been done outside Masada's atmosphere limits—and even then they'd have been on dubious legal ground. The Weaver essentially owned Masada and had a claim on the entire Masadan system. Only the protectorate status of this world gave the Polity leeway out there. It was all, legally, very murky—just the kind of murk criminals like to hide themselves in.

"You are bringing a defensive system for the Weaver," Amistad stated.

"Yes."

Yes? The affirmative struck Amistad as far too easy. Penny Royal was up to something more complex than just bringing a defensive system. And what about Spear? Where did he fit in?

"What do you get in return?"

"Balance."

"So you've turned into an altruist?"

"What I am and what I will be is yet to be decided. And whether I will be, too."

"Now you're being deliberately obscure."

"I will enjoy a further exchange with you, Amistad, but not here, and only when your tether has been cut."

Com shut down.

Amistad chewed that over. He was bound to this world so long as it remained a protectorate; so long as it required a warden. A defensive system, no matter how advanced, was not something that could change the status of this world so definitively. Definitely something else . . .

Masada's warden reopened the channel to the *Garrotte* which had so abruptly closed previously.

"Nothing else gets in here without me knowing, do you understand?"

"Difficult now the USER's down."

"But not impossible."

"I can cause local U-space disruptions with my missiles—knock most things out as they come in-system—but if they're targeted at Masada itself, I won't have a lot of time for scanning and analysis thereafter."

"Then you'd better react at AI speeds, hadn't you?"

"Certainly," said the *Garrotte*, obviously waiting for something more.

"If you don't have time to get a response from me, in a priority situation you have carte blanche."

"At last," sighed the *Garrotte*.

BLITE

To allow for Masada's boggy surface, *The Rose* lowered landing feet that spread monomer sheets between their toes. This mimicked the webbed feet of some great bird, and would prevent them having to constantly use anti-grav to prevent the ship sinking down through the rhizome mat.

"So what is that?" Brond asked, gazing ahead through the bridge screen.

"That," said Blite, "is the Atheter AI."

The building before them looked like an ancient temple abandoned in the Masadan wilderness, with its domed roof supported by a ring of pillars. In its floor, it housed a huge disc of memcrystal, which in turn housed the only known Atheter AI in existence.

"So we just notched up from being in a dangerous situation to being in a lethal one, huh?"

"I don't know that it's ever been anything but lethal," Blite replied. "I would say that we now find ourselves seriously out of our league. This is big shit. This is a game where entry level should be planetary governor and above." He sat back, checked some of the displays before him and noted that the hold door had opened. "I'm going outside," he decided abruptly, and stood up.

"Maybe not too smart," said Ikbal.

Blite turned to glare at him, ready to bawl him out, but Ikbal pointed to another display. Apparently there were three hooders not far away. Blite deflated somewhat but insisted, "Okay, I'll visit the armoury, but I'm still going outside." He suspected the hooders wouldn't be a problem, because Penny Royal was probably outside too and that would put off even for those voracious hunters.

As he headed back out of the bridge, he noted Brond and Ikbal standing too, doubtless intending to follow. He considered saying something to put them off, then reconsidered—he wasn't their mother. The rest showed no inclination to come. Perhaps they were the sensible ones.

Opening up the armoury, he selected a portable particle cannon he'd obtained in the Graveyard, cutting it out of the claw of a much-decayed prador first-child. He also hung a couple of sonic grenades on his belt. Leaving the armoury door open, he then headed to his cabin, shucked off the soiled shipsuit he'd been wearing since the Rock Pool, and selected an enviro-suit from his wardrobe. He was about to put this on, but suddenly felt as grubby as he actually was, and decided to take a shower. It was almost as if he was preparing for some final battle on some level, some endgame event. Twenty minutes later he stepped out of *The Rose*'s airlock onto a ramp. But instead of descending, he headed to one side, climbing a ladder leading to the upper hull. Brond and Ikbal were waiting for him, trying to look cool and casual despite the company just a few yards away. Nearby, a giant flower of black blades balanced on a stem of plaited silver stood swaying in some unfelt wind.

They'd brought pulse-rifles with them and Blite wondered why—the weapons would be ineffective against hooders. But then, after a moment's consideration, he understood how they felt. The weapons were a comfort.

"I thought you were heading straight out," said Ikbal accusingly.

"Yeah, I thought so too," added Brond.

"I took a shower," said Blite, feeling far more casual than the other two were trying to appear as he unshouldered his weapon. He propped it against a sensor cone protruding from the hull.

"Anything occurred meanwhile?"

"Nothing much," said Ikbal, "except that." He stabbed a finger out into the flute grasses, where what looked like the upper part of some giant's black spinal column lay just visible. Blite swallowed drily. There was a hooder out here, close, well within striking distance of them. He then remembered just how dangerous these things were. Even being inside *The Rose* didn't necessarily mean they were safe, if such a creature decided to attack.

As he watched, the hooder abruptly rose up, curving round and away from them. He realized it was circling something out there. Then, scanning beyond it, he could see one of the other hooders—also circling something. Off to one side there was another disturbance that might be the final one of the three Ikbal had detected.

"They possess a vague memory of the servant war machines they once were," whispered Penny Royal. "And they now become confused by the new behaviour of the gabbleducks, them being the devolved descendants of those the hooders once served."

Penny Royal was very good at providing answers to questions Blite hadn't asked, but was a bit obscure when it came to the direct ones he did ask.

The closest hooder again halted, this time at a greater distance from the ship, and settled down into the grasses. The disturbance it had been circling briefly came into view. It was indeed a gabbleduck.

"Surfle peg," Blite heard distantly.

The gabbleduck disappeared into the grasses again, its course taking it directly towards the building housing the Atheter AI.

"It was carrying something," said Brond.

"They weave," said Penny Royal. "They make objects that seem to serve no purpose. And sometimes they make objects whose purpose is obvious, and they abandon both. The active mind of the Weaver speaks to them in dreams they don't understand, and those dreams are always louder near the AI."

The gabbleduck now climbed up onto a walkway leading into the AI building, still clutching the object before it. Arriving at the pillars, it hesitated, then discarded the thing like someone guiltily discarding trash. It then passed between two pillars, turned and exited between two others, dropping back down into the grasses. It muttered nonsense as it departed.

"Like votive offerings," said Blite.

"Not even that logical," Penny Royal replied.

"Why are we here?" Blite asked, and before he could curse himself for letting that question slip out, Penny Royal answered him.

"Spear will come, because he has to."

"So?"

"He and I are the lure and Isobel will respond as calculated."

Blite just waited. Penny Royal knew how much he understood and how much he was capable of understanding, and would either explain or not.

"As a human and a predator she will inevitably gather all her forces around her for an attack here—she will not be able to resist the lure," Penny Royal informed him. "Those forces will include her cargo ship. And, her trade with the prador having been terminated, one of those ships will inevitably still contain its cargo of the cored and thralled. The accelerating changes within her will starve her—and rather than feed on her own people she will attempt to feed on that cargo. The Atheter war mind growing within her will then detect the Jain element of the Spatterjay virus. Their use of Jain technology kept the Atheter locked in civil war for millennia before they sacrificed everything they were in order to be free of it—and Isobel is now close to her final war machine form. Reacting to that threat, the war mind will begin to dominate, and her changes will accelerate. They will accelerate further every time she encounters any resistance. And when she is here, she will finally be ready."

That was quite a long speech from the AI. But Blite only understood that Isobel Satomi was coming and that it was quite likely that things would soon turn nasty.

SPEAR

I quickly packed away my meagre luggage, basically just some items that weren't particularly essential. Riss eyed my rucksack and said, "I don't suppose you've got a CTD knocking around in there, have you?"

That stopped me in my tracks. When Flute informed us that *The Rose* had arrived here, I'd been shocked and knew I had to react. Subsequent events were baffling but I started getting ready to leave at once, as I would soon know Penny Royal's location down on the surface of the world. But what then?

I wasn't armed. I didn't really have the firepower of the *Lance* to back me up since it had been effectively neutered, and I certainly didn't have the option of using the fusion device. All that had been taken away from me as we approached Masada. Even if I could somehow get round that, there were weapons up there that could quickly turn the *Lance* into vapour. I allowed myself a wry smile at Riss's comment, remembering that I'd wondered what I'd use against Penny Royal when we met. Strong language it would have to be.

"I guess we're going to have to view Masada as neutral territory," I said.

"It would be nice to assume Penny Royal will do the same," Riss observed drily.

"So what do you suggest?" I said, dropping my rucksack down on the bed, then sitting down beside it.

"I don't know any more," said the drone.

That simple statement had many implications. Amistad had called Riss a "one-trick pony." The snake drone's motivations were generally absolute. First she'd been a prador killer with just one method of attack, next she sought vengeance on the one that had hollowed her out. But even that was gone now.

"I know what you're thinking," said Riss.

"You do?"

"What's my trick now?"

"Close enough."

"Answers—we have to confront Penny Royal, whether the black AI is making us do that or not." Riss paused, head pointing down towards the floor. "I am beginning to understand that I could never transcend what I was, without that self being destroyed. Vengeance filled the void and it's still there, but as an option only. I think I reflect you in that."

I nodded and stood, took up my rucksack. "Let's go."

The problems started when I tried to send the gravcar to Blite's ship's location, relayed to my aug by Flute. The car just sat there with "unable to respond" displayed in red letters on its console screen. When I started auging for an explanation, I hit chaotic disruption in the virtual world. But I did manage to discover that all gravcars had been temporarily grounded, while my destination had been put under a quarantine order.

"Amistad's blocking us," I said. "What does the submind say?"

"That it would be best if we stayed where we are, for our own safety."

"I thought so." I pointed to the console. "Can you do anything?"

"No. All gravcars are temporarily grounded, but this particular one is grounded until someone comes and repairs the grav-engine."

"Then we get another one."

"Too easy to shut down."

Riss sent something to my aug. Chattering had an all-terrain vehicle rental facility and the ATVs available needed minimal computer control. But Riss could usurp this. No outside signal could shut down a vehicle she controlled. I nodded and climbed out of the gravcar, then we took the stairs from the hotel roof back down to the street.

"It's two hundred miles," I said as we headed for the rental place.

"We can cross that in five hours—if I drive."

"But then there's the quarantine . . ."

"Something we'll have to deal with," Riss replied. "There's no actual barrier up and I'm assuming Amistad will only resort to satellite weapons to disable our vehicle, whereupon we can walk in the remaining ten miles."

"Reassuring."

His name was Steve, according to the name tab on his overalls, and he immediately refused to rent us a vehicle.

"Sorry, but I got my orders," he said.

"Who from?"

"Local cops," he replied, "but they're taking their orders direct from one of the warden's subminds."

The garage sat just by a bridge that crossed Chattering's surrounding swamp. Its doors were open and four big cargo ATVs sat inside on cage wheels. These stood taller than the vehicles themselves and contained proactive suspension in their actual structures. I turned to Riss.

"For our own safety, police are coming to conduct us back to our hotel," said the drone. "But this is low-key intervention."

I knew what Riss meant. If Amistad really seriously wanted to stop us leaving this place, he could have done a lot more than just sabotage our transport plans and instruct local cops. He could have sent Earth Central Security monitors or agents. He could have taken out that bridge using a particle cannon, or dropped hardfields in our path from orbit. It struck me that the warden was undecided about how to deal with us, so was going through the motions but without much heart. Perhaps the warden felt his responsibility lay in warning us off, but didn't extend to expending resources on actually stopping us.

"What does the submind say?" I asked.

"Everyone who is so inclined is being warned against heading towards that landing site," Riss replied. "The submind told me that we aren't unique and shouldn't consider ourselves a special case. I asked why, if we aren't a special case, we have one of Amistad's subminds completely focused on us. It's not talking to me now."

Weird.

I turned back to Steve and noted he had been watching this exchange boggle-eyed. Behind him one of his ATVs started up its hydrogen turbine engine. I auged through a decent sum to the garage's account and knew, as he froze, that he had received notification of the payment through his aug.

"We are renting one of your vehicles," I said, and headed over.

"Hold it right there!" came a shout from behind.

Not quick enough. I sighed and turned to see a man and a woman entering the building. They were both clad in pearl-grey uniforms with blue piping, wore helmets with visors down and had bulky stun guns holstered at their hips, which they had yet to draw.

"Legally," I said, "you have no right to stop us leaving."

The female replied. "True, but Steve refused to rent you an ATV and as I understand it your drone has accessed one vehicle and you were about to take it. You have been caught in the act of theft."

"I resent that," said Riss.

She turned to gaze at the drone, dropping her hand to her stun gun— then hesitated and slid it across to hook a thumb in her belt. "Resent what?"

"Being described as *his* drone," Riss replied. "Are you still so primitive here that you don't quite get independent machine intelligences?"

She grimaced then said, "Legally I can arrest you now, but I have options. Return to your hotel and stay there and I'm sure Steve will drop any charges."

I glanced round at Steve who had moved off to one side, certainly to make sure he didn't get in the way if these two cops started using their stunners.

"This is stupid," I said.

"It's no problem," said Riss. "Let's go." The snake drone swung round and continued towards the ATV. I hesitated for a second, then turned to follow.

"I said, hold it!"

Glancing back, I saw that both cops had drawn their weapons.

"This is your last warning," said the man.

Riss reached the ATV and a door folded down into a ramp, doubt-less on her mental command. Behind me I heard the crack and hiss of the stunner energy pulses and flinched. Nothing hit me and, when I looked round, I saw both cops lying twitching on the garage floor. Inside the vehicle was a large cargo area—fifteen feet across and thirty long. I followed Riss to the ATV's cockpit and took one of the seats beside her as she coiled in the driver's seat. I thought then that the vehicle was far too big, just to take us where we wanted to go, but I'd yet discover the curious workings of serendipity. Then the joystick shifted forwards without the drone actually touching it.

"Like I said, 'low key'," she explained.

Certainly Amistad must have had no real expectation of his methods stopping a determined war drone.

"So why did Amistad try to stop us?" I asked. "That all seemed a point-less waste of time."

"To slow us. To slow events down to give him time to ponder options and, most importantly, to locate the Weaver. It seems it's involved, but has apparently gone missing."

"I see," I said, not really seeing at all. "What did you use?" I asked, nodding back toward the garage, which was now receding behind us as Riss drove the ATV onto the bridge from Chattering.

"Simple hardfield just a few inches ahead of their weapons," Riss explained. "It reflected their shots straight back at them . . . Now, let's see what this thing can do."

The ATV accelerated off the bridge onto a road of flattened grasses over rhizome. It just kept on accelerating, then abruptly swerved off the road into the grasses, accelerating still. I calmly pulled across a safety harness as the vehicle exceeded seventy miles an hour, with visibility ahead apparently less than a yard. The hissing of our passage through the grasses turned into a roar.

19

AMISTAD

Amistad's frustration was increasing, because he still wasn't getting the full picture here. He paused for a moment to peer down at the metal floor below him, noting the multiple scores and scratches and one point where he had actually punctured it.

Calm down, he told himself, and subsided into stillness.

Penny Royal had claimed to be delivering a defensive system to the Weaver, which would explain why the crazy gabbleduck had gone AWOL. So Amistad was concentrating his search for the Weaver on routes leading to *The Rose*. But there were still anomalies. What was Spear's part in all this, and what was the meaning of the black AI's obscure hint that, sometime hence, Amistad might cease to be warden of the world?

So, concentrate on Spear first. He was out to exact vengeance on Penny Royal, but only because of the memories the AI had distorted and placed within his memplant. The way he had encountered the Weaver was much too coincidental and, going by their exchange, the Weaver knew about his memories. Subtle mental manipulation could explain the meeting, and secret communications between Penny Royal and the

Weaver could explain the latter's knowledge of Spear. However, he still just didn't seem to fit . . .

Amistad abruptly checked the security around Penny Royal's old ship, now renamed the *Lance*, then increased it. If Spear didn't fit, then perhaps his role was just to bring Penny Royal's ship here, which might hide a multitude of secrets. Perhaps some hidden device aboard? Amistad used local satellites to deep scan that vessel again. As the results came back, he detected nothing that hadn't been found before. The fusion device aboard was too simple to be involved. Flute was partially AI, but no more dangerous for that than the drone Riss, and the micro- and nanobot culture that was steadily being cleansed from the ship had no power to affect events down here. No, it wasn't the ship.

Perhaps then, the answer lay in the past? Penny Royal hadn't of course destroyed its eighth state of consciousness, so maybe there was something else he had missed? Amistad began reviewing recorded data again.

After the events surrounding the arrival of the Atheter device here, Penny Royal had seldom been unmonitored—either physically or virtually. Amistad listed those occasions when Amistad's perpetual security around the AI had been at its most lax. He then ran programs to sort these, based on current events and tranches of submind-generated possible scenarios.

During a visit Penny Royal made to the Atheter AI, there had been a three-second blank spot. This was partially down to a solar flare, but also connected to a server nexus being destroyed by a Tidy Squad bomb. Amistad reviewed the evidence and found that there was no evidence of any of its members being responsible, despite the close monitoring of the Squad prior to it being closed down. Could Penny Royal therefore have engineered it? Quite possibly. And during those three seconds, it could have had a whole world of communications with the Atheter AI and thence with the Weaver itself. But there was no real proof there beyond the circumstantial.

Penny Royal's visit to the Technician's corpse was another potentially connected anomaly. Amistad understood why the Weaver had retained the dead war machine's corpse. Even though it had been fried by its encounter with the Atheter device—its internal components heavily disrupted—it still contained a lot of dense tech. A Polity forensic AI had deep scanned the tech, and was now only a couple of percentage points into understanding it. It was defined as a corpse, a wreck, but even that was debatable. Penny Royal had visited it in its woven flute grass tomb, shortly after the forensic AI's visit, and Amistad had watched closely. However, nothing occurred on the virtual level and Penny Royal had only run a brief low-penetration scan of the Technician and then departed—as if reassuring itself that it would be no further problem before dismissing it. Amistad decided to review his recordings of that visit.

Immediately, it was as if he was on some invisible platform inside the Technician's mausoleum. The tubular building was fifty feet across, its lower section covered with jutting protrusions. Gabbleducks apparently used these to get about inside their structures rather than using floors. As a whole, the building consisted of woven plaits of grass that had been knitted together and bound with a resin extracted from other Masadan plants. The Technician lay stretched out in a woven grass cradle, bone white and massive, some sort of energy weapon having eaten into its carapace all down one side. Upon his first visit, Amistad had noted the lack of putrescene in the air. There was also a lack of prawn-like crustaceans, one variety of this world's natural undertakers. A corpse here would usually end up swarming with these just minutes after death—this applying even to human corpses, despite their flesh being poisonous to the creatures.

The Technician wasn't rotting and it wasn't triggering the usual ecological disposal mechanisms. Subsequent investigations revealed that the woven flute grasses that surrounded it had been combined with other plants. And when these slowly decayed together, they produced an atmospheric preservative. This was molecularly perfect in preventing this giant albino hooder's decay—almost as if they'd been designed for this purpose.

Amistad continued to watch the memory as darkness filled one of the tubelike connecting tunnels at the end of this structure, and Penny Royal flowed through. The AI was semi-dispersed, here resembling a silver tree decorated with black knife-like leaves, bent over and propelled forwards by some silent gale. Perpetually changing shape as it moved, the AI traversed the length of the Technician, rounded its hood and returned back down its wounded side, stopping halfway. Here is where it conducted its scan, before proceeding to the back of the structure and out again.

No.

Amistad was watching with a whole new intensity and ran things again, from the moment Penny Royal stopped beside the creature. He slowed things down and focused in on every detail. Beside the Technician the AI settled back into another form, with the silver tendrils forming a trunk. The knives all connected to it at their bases and extended into leaf-forms, folding out their dense crystalline structure and realigning it. And again, there it was.

As Penny Royal completed this transformation into its watching form, one of its "knives" darted across to enter the Technician through a hole in its carapace. This object returned just as the AI finished its scan and transformed back into its previous form. The knife slid back into Penny Royal's form as naturally as a stray fish rejoining its shoal.

I should not have missed that, thought Amistad. Then perfect recall revealed that he hadn't missed it—in his own original recall of this partic-ular visit, these details just hadn't been there. He immediately began checking his own systems for interference, meanwhile broadcasting warnings to local AIs and back to Earth Central. Penny Royal had been interfering, and the AI had been interfering with *Amistad.*

On looking deeper, he saw that his earlier memory of his and Penny Royal's encounter on the lip of the caldera hadn't contained its more recent detail either. He really hadn't known that Penny Royal had uploaded its eighth state from the container. Just as with this more recent memory, detail had been added later. But, unfortunately, there was no time stamp on it and no way of telling when this had happened. Nor was there any way of telling how it had been added. Or indeed why.

"You have been compromised," noted the *Garrotte*, its communication channel tight, security heavy and bandwidth limited, "by Penny Royal."

Other local AIs noted this too, and began to limit their connection with Amistad. Even one of his subminds—one with a lot more of his origi-nal war-drone self in it than others—declared independence and abruptly severed all connection.

"I have," Amistad replied. "But even so, I think I know what's coming."

"Really?" wondered the *Garrotte*, now distrusting Amistad entirely.

"Really," Amistad continued. "Penny Royal sampled the Technician—it took genetic data and probably—"

"I have four ships coming through now," said the *Garrotte*. "Sorry, work to do."

The attack ship cut the communication channel, firmly. And Amistad had a sneaking suspicion that the data had been added to trigger this very result—so he would be compromised right now.

ISOBEL

The *Caligula* smelled like an abattoir, one that had also been set on fire. The crew were all dead and the surviving seven troops had barricaded themselves in the armoury, where they had set up some heavy weapons. She'd just managed to stop herself going in after them as her frenzy started to diminish. It wasn't risk to herself that halted her, but the fact that the *Caligula* could be crippled if they started letting loose with particle cannons. She waited then, with the patience of a cat, and watched as the seven cut through a wall and rushed to get aboard a shuttle. She watched them depart, took some necessary action, then turned away from the armoury.

Even with the initial frenzy gone, the hunger remained. For now it originated utterly in the cold analytical part of her, and she continued to feed. It was no meticulous feeding, this, no instinctive hooder need to separate out poisonous black fats. She knew, on that analytical level, that such simple poisons would not affect her present form. All the way back from the armoury she ripped into the corpses, her extensible feeding members sucking at fluid. Her scalpel manipulators, some now as large as garden sickles, sliced up the rest and conveyed a constant stream to her large feeding mouth. Everything went in this time: clothing, augmentations, the laminated bones of those who had been boosted. She only realized how unselective she was being when she became aware she'd sliced up an assault rifle and eaten that.

After the fifth corpse, her body felt agonizingly tight and her temperature was now so high that the stuff she was eating had begun to smoke as she took it up. The small human part of her wanted to scream. Relief only came with a shuddering crack all down her length, as the old carapace broke open along dorsal lines. Each segment parted over new hot growths of cyanosis-blue flesh. Even as she moved on, new carapace began to extend from under the old, like the growth of fingernails under time-lapse. Her cowl, her mouth, and her manipulators were growing at the same pace too and as these got larger the pace of her feeding increased. Isobel peeled the corpse of a woman as if eating a cob of sweetcorn, chewing down flesh, bones and gristle. She fed on the spine like a stalk of asparagus then sucked in the shoulders, arms and head in one bite. Negligently, she noted her new carapace scoring the corridor walls. And, while searching for one who had crawled into his cabin to die, she had to tear out the door, its frame and part of the wall.

I am Isobel, she told herself, but was only sure of what that meant in the last human part of her mind, which now had little grip on the rest. The analytical part was now utterly dominant, the predator an adjunct to that, while the human looked on. Even so, the dominant war machine parts still vaguely retained Isobel Satomi's purpose for, powerful as it was, it was a servant or slave and still required instruction. It was going to Masada to kill both Thorvald Spear and Penny Royal. Previously, this had been nothing more than an arrogant fantasy. However, even while it was a part of and trapped inside this mentality, the human Isobel realized that success was now a real possibility. The tri-part being, this new Isobel, was quite capable of taking on the black AI. However, the war machine's vagueness of purpose stemmed from something else. Its analytical part had reacted to the Jain technology dormant in the Spatterjay virus, which it had been exposed to in the thralled corpses. And this exposure to its ancient foe had triggered a dawning awareness of its true purpose. Hooder war machines had been created to fight a particular enemy: Atheter who controlled or were controlled by Jain tech, along with the technology itself. The Jain may have disappeared as a race many millennia ago, but their tech still survived here and there, as lethal as a dormant genocidal bio-weapon.

A hooder such as Isobel wasn't designed to hunt down creatures it didn't even recognize—and the awakening part of her being was starting to sense that. Its present mission didn't come from its true masters and soon there would be a reckoning.

When Isobel reached the bridge of the *Caligula*, she realized that she couldn't enter it without wrecking it completely—and that entering it was a pointless exercise anyway. Behind the bridge she tore out walls, destroyed cabins and ripped up floors, but with a precision that left essential optics and power cables in place. She eventually coiled her now huge form in a nest of torn metal and other debris. She had fed hugely and grown hugely, but further internal growth needed to take place. She became somnolent as she concentrated the autonomous mechanisms that belonged to her analytical side on her new form's internal structures. The predator retreated, now perceiving no immediate threats and being dominated by the other. Isobel the human fought against the urge to sleep, somehow aware that this would be her last and only chance to regain some control.

First she focused on the predator. It was in fact the main mental component of the hooder she had originally been turning into. It had started to dominate her, which had resulted in her making decisions she'd never have made as a human.

I'm going to Masada?

It was madness.

As she worked on seeing more clearly she found herself borrowing from the analyst, almost, but not quite, unconsciously. The predator was the rabid animal, now drugged and dopey, and she was leashing it and fitting the muzzle. Even so, she understood that these bonds could never be enough and moved to the next stage, which was to incorporate it back into herself and try to dominate it. It began to meld easily with her, and she understood why when she viewed the links between them. It had previously incorporated part of her into itself: the murderer, the villain, the killer without conscience . . .

I am going to Masada.

Yes, that decision had been a kind of madness—but now, with her new abilities, with the war mind . . .

She turned towards that analytical being; that war mind. She felt stronger with the predator leashed and now part of her. First she slid into its identification routines and tried to subvert them, but they were hard-wired and heavily defended. The war mind knew what its masters were and she wasn't one of them. Why, then, that vagueness? Why had it not immediately rejected and suppressed her? Why was it still fixed in some vague way on the same purpose as she?

Orders.

It came down simply to that. This thing was bigger than her: a complex, multifaceted being. It controlled internal weaponry and energies on levels only accessible to planetary AIs in the Polity. But that was not how it had started out. It was a new being and had grown within her from Penny Royal's genetic manipulations. It had started out as something small—with Isobel being part of it throughout, even though dominated by the predator. Had it been combined with Isobel alone, it would have recognized her as alien, but it knew the predator as part of itself so she'd escaped notice. She had, in fact, been consigned to that small part of itself reserved to receive orders from its masters. It did not see her as a being, just instructions.

Isobel moved quickly to affirm that, concealing those parts of her human self that had blunted its purpose. She clarified her intentions—or orders—then enforced them through her link to it via the predator. She would be in control . . .

I am Isobel.

She was instantly and utterly absorbed. She was at once predator, war machine and Isobel Satomi. Her orders were firm, her purpose was abso-lute, and now she was impatient to act.

TRENT

The screaming and sounds of weapons fire had finished long ago. And, really, if any of that started up again he didn't need to listen to it to know what had been going on aboard the *Caligula*. Trent turned the volume down, and again studied the single video clip he had obtained before the *Caligula*'s cam system went down. Isobel had come out of the hold fast and simply ripped Morgan and those others apart before moving on. Then there was just screaming—sound only available via a laser bounce detector Trent had focused on that ship's hull.

There had been a couple of atmosphere breaches over there too and a couple of escape attempts. The two in space suits had been hit by something that smeared them across space like bugs against a glass window. The shuttle, leaving some while after the last screams died away, managed to get nearly as far as the *Glory* before a missile blew it to pieces. Trent supposed that last action was Isobel recovering her senses, and deciding she didn't want those aboard the *Glory* knowing what had actually happened aboard the *Caligula*. They would doubtless get her story instead, something about a mutiny being put down. They would hear nothing about her overpowering need to rip people apart and eat them. He tried communications again, and this time Isobel responded, her image coming clear on the screen.

"So you just couldn't control yourself," he said. He had to suppress his urge to flinch back from the image of her spread right across the screen before him, her manipulators and other nasty protrusions framed by her hood.

"There was danger," she intoned.

"That why your Golem killed the captain of the *Glory*?"

After a long pause, as if this was some incident she'd not recollected, she replied, "He was slow."

"What the hell happened there, Isobel?"

"We cannot trade in virus-infected humans anymore."

Right, Trent thought. He'd seen the cargo being ejected from the *Glory*, but had assumed Isobel was abandoning evidence of their crimes before they headed to Masada. It would make sense if she'd intended to retrieve it after her supposed success on that world. However, when she steadily destroyed them with the *Caligula*'s weapons, he saw that as confirmation of her lost grip on reality. That cargo was a massive investment in time and money—the kind of investment the former Isobel would never have dispensed with so casually.

"So why is that?" he asked.

"The enemy is there, in the virus. It's dormant, but it's possible it could be inadvertently activated. The Jain are there in the virus."

Trent sat back. She'd finally stepped off a mental cliff, because he had no idea what she was babbling about.

"Now we go to Masada, to complete the mission," she added.

He felt the U-space engine engaging and guessed the same was happening aboard the other ships. Trent knew that it wouldn't be long now before answers to his questions would cease to matter to him at all.

SPEAR

It soon grew hot within the ATV, doubtless due to friction from the flute grasses that constantly brushed against its bodywork. I sat perfectly still for a while, half expecting us to crash into something, but I finally suppressed this instinctive fear with the knowledge we were unlikely to crash while the vehicle was controlled by Riss. I forced myself to relax, reclined my seat a little, and decided to do some investigating.

I opened up my aug to Masada's computer networks, first trying to track down the submind that had been set to watch us. I could make no connection with it—I next tried Amistad himself and was again disappointed.

"You won't get much there," said Riss, obviously keeping a watch on me in more than just the physical world. "Amistad just discovered he was penetrated by Penny Royal. All the other AIs in the Masadan system just dropped him like the proverbial hot potato."

"What?" I asked, wondering whether a proverbial hot potato was somehow hotter than the common kind.

"He's quarantined, isolated, his warden status on hold. He won't be making any big decisions here until a forensic AI has taken him apart and scrutinized those parts—if he allows that."

"In what way is he compromised?"

"No real details, but it seems his memories were interfered with."

"A common complaint around here," I observed.

Bouncing off Riss's announcement that Amistad was under quarantine, I checked the status of our destination. Annoyingly the quarantine there still applied, despite the initial order having come from a now "compromised" AI. Even while I was performing my checks, I was surprised to be contacted by a human rather than another AI.

"You're heading towards an interdicted zone, buddy, and we can't allow that."

The identification package attached to this communication told me that Leif Grant, the human ambassador of this world, was speaking to me. I'd always wondered about human ambassadors. They'd been used in all sorts of odd and quite critical situations, like first contact with the prador and in communications with the trans-stellar entity Dragon. They were often used on worlds that were just beyond the Line and about to be subsumed by the Polity. With the latter, I understood the reasoning—how humans on out-Polity worlds might be somewhat suspicious of AIs. But in the former two cases things hadn't gone so well. Were human ambassadors used because of some odd AI attempt to be inclusive; to not leave out their inferior organic kin? Perhaps they were deployed as just another tool, through which the AIs could gather more data.

"Who can't allow that?" I asked. "As I understand it Amistad has been isolated, so shouldn't you be questioning his previous decisions?"

"Amistad is good," said Grant, "and the present situation is only due to understandable caution in the AI world."

"Still, we're not stopping and we intend to enter that area," I said. "Amistad was being just a little too cautious, and he hasn't got all the facts."

"Like what?"

I really wished he hadn't asked that.

"It's complicated," I said.

"Isn't it always? But the quarantine still stands," Grant paused for a moment, as if checking something. "Apparently your war drone associate assaulted a couple of police officers."

"Rubbish," Riss interjected. "I merely defended myself. It wasn't my fault they fired stunners straight at hardfields and got caught in the back blast."

"Mmm, debatable. Here's how it will run. I've got a couple of assets moving to intercept you. The moment you enter the zone's half-mile border, your vehicle will be disabled. If you proceed on foot . . . or by other means, to enter the zone, you yourselves will be disabled and carted back here."

"Whatever," said Riss, doubtless sure of her own abilities.

"Yeah, whatever," said Grant, and signed off.

Ahead, the flute grasses were getting shorter so I could occasionally see more than a few feet ahead. Riss accelerated, then shortly after that swerved to avoid something. I caught a passing glimpse of a big animal with a lot of teeth, its hide shifting like chameleoncloth to match its background. I'd just seen a siluroyne, which made me think twice about the prospect of walking across this terrain, but I had to put my confidence in Riss. As if to reaffirm just how dangerous it was, we moved into an area where the grasses were actually lower than the front screen of the ATV. And in the distance, where the grasses once again grew tall, I saw a huge birdlike creature striding along, stopping, then darting down a long spike of a beak. During the conflict here many casualties had been due to creatures such as the camouflaged one back there—and now this, this heroyne.

"Fuck," said Riss. "We've got company."

I thought the drone was referring to the distant creature, which now rose up again with something wriggling in its beak.

"Not there," Riss added, then tipped her head up.

I looked up through the cab's skylight, but couldn't see anything until I turned to peer back through the roof windows in the cargo section. Two objects were hanging in the sky behind us, matching our course. These two upright cylinders looked a little battered, though the weaponry sprouting from top and bottom ends looked perfectly functional.

"Should be no problem for you," I suggested.

"Unfortunately they are," Riss replied. "Modern security drones— sub-AI but loaded with some serious shit."

"They seem quite . . . plain."

"Just a fashion," Riss shot back.

Drones were first formed in fear-inducing shapes during the war. They'd been manufactured quickly and were a little unreliable. After the war, both the need and inclination to make independent drones like Riss had waned. Most were subsequently controlled by AIs or were installed with AI subminds, which was essentially the same thing. Even though Riss looked high-tech, modern and lethal, she was over a hundred years old.

"So we're stuck."

"One way to find out—we're coming up on that half-mile border in about ten minutes."

Those minutes dragged past, while the vista around us opened out— into low flute grasses and muddy channels dotted with islands of taller grasses. There were also occasional stands of orange and black whiptails. Perfect, I thought—no cover. But in reality, tall flute grasses couldn't hide us from the senses of the two above.

"Do you have a plan?" I asked, thinking that we'd have to abandon our destination, although I wasn't quite sure why I didn't feel much disappointment.

The ATV abruptly decelerated and, glancing at Riss, I wondered if she'd come up with a strategy. Then casting my gaze forwards, I saw why she was slowing.

It stepped out of an island of flute grass, briefly stood up on its hind legs to peer in the direction we were heading, then looked back round at us. Coming to a decision, it settled down into its seated pyramidal form and extended one of its arms. Most of the claws were folded but one protruded upwards. In a manner that any human was culturally programmed to recognize, it waved this repeatedly in the direction we were going.

The ATV kept on slowing, finally coming to a halt.

"Your mouth's open," said Riss.

I abruptly snapped it closed but, really, gaping was justified. Here, out in the wilds of the planet Masada, sat the single resurrected example of the Atheter race, the Weaver. Or, to put it another way, I was seeing a gabbleduck thumbing a lift.

ISOBEL

The new Isobel felt firmly and utterly in control, even as something violently knocked the *Caligula* and her other three ships out of U-space. Her immediate conclusion was that an enemy had deployed a USER, but subsequent analysis of the data indicated otherwise. Each of the four ships had suffered from localized effects, if such terms could possibly be used within such a continuum. That meant four targeted devices had hit, perhaps U-space missiles or mines of some kind. She processed that, considered the likelihood of other enemy elements here, but remained resolute about her mission objectives.

"Snickety snick."

The communication came from a channel under her control. She briefly queried it, vaguely concerned about such unnecessary transferences of data. Information came back from the Golem, who had moved very quickly to insert itself in the *Glory*'s old-style ejection pod.

"Sverl sends his regards," it said.

Isobel reached out for answers, clarification and obedience, but she just slid off the mind. Next it ejected the pod from the *Glory*, hurtling away under an acceleration no human occupant could have survived. She immediately targeted it with the *Caligula*'s weapons, but it had timed its ejection perfectly. For in the next instant she detected a black spike of a ship out there, splintering off missiles and launching them towards her vessels. Suddenly she had nothing to spare except for defence.

"Gloves off properly this time," said this new aggressor.

The intelligence's missiles were in pre-jump, she realized, even while targeting them with her own missiles and beam weapons across four ships. She coiled tighter, generating a subspacial twist through the extended mechanisms of her body. This manifested as a gravity wavefront ahead of the *Caligula*. Two missiles jumped just a moment before the gravity wave hit the bulk of them, before it flowed on towards that black ship. Missiles still in pre-jump shattered, igniting like small suns as the anti-matter flasks they contained breached. The twist took out a further missile, U-space disruption flinging it out into the real, where it followed its detonation program. Then one of her other ships, the *Glory*, disappeared in a massive flash. Nothing material of it remaining as it was instantly transformed into light-speed plasma.

Necessary sacrifice.

More missiles splintered towards her, beam weapons webbing space. Throwing her remaining ships into a massive fusion-drive acceleration towards the centre of this system, Isobel then shut off all safety limiters. She generated a twist in all their drives and micro U-jumped them a hundred thousand miles. Immediately the *Nasturtium* came under fire, hardfields snapping on around it to deflect particle beams—but pseudo FTL matter twists in the beams themselves chewed into those protective fields. And the black ship was still with them.

"Not that fucking easy, Satomi," said the *Garrotte*.

Next the *Nasturtium* blew a hardfield generator, which exited that ship's hull as glowing wreckage. It crashed through the craft on the opposite side to a beam strike. Her *Moray Firth* wasn't being hit so hard, but soon would be targeted more fiercely. The seemingly endless supply of U-jump missiles from that black ship had simply to complete their microseconds-long warm-ups. The *Caligula* now began taking more fire, just to keep its defences occupied, Isobel felt—the black ship was just ridding itself of the irrelevancies before fully concentrating on her.

A second micro U-jump brought them within a hundred thousand kilometres of Masada. Enemy weapons revealed themselves there as a whole spectrum of energies howled out from orbital installations. The *Nasturtium* fell next, a final hardfield collapsing and a particle beam sectioning it from end to end like some hellish milling tool. It peeled open like a banana, then one of the U-jump missiles annihilated it. Isobel sent a twist towards her antagonist, but the black ship micro-jumped itself. Microseconds dragged as slow as days, then years, as a gravity wave weapon fired from Masada's orbit. Isobel saw her choices abruptly whittled down to one and something inside her hurt at the sacrifice she had to make.

She made the *Moray Firth* micro-jump at precisely the same moment as she reached out again to try and *twist* that black ship. She plotted U-space as she jumped the *Caligula* too, a large percentage of her war mind running the calculations, and they were at once close to Masada. The black ship and the *Moray Firth* surfaced behind her, just outside the gravity well while she was within it. They didn't surface in precisely the same place, but close enough. They fused and hull melded into hull. But, as they were travelling under differential vectors, they at once tore apart again. This ripped open the hulls of both ships, strewing debris across vacuum. Within that cloud, anti-matter flasks breached and the two ships were lost in multiple detonations—even as the *Caligula* hurtled down into the atmosphere of Masada.

Trent gone, thought the human part of Isobel. *All three ships gone.* Her organization was all but dead now because, despite her bases on various Graveyard worlds, its heart had been those ships and the people aboard them. All that remained was her and the *Caligula*.

But of course it wasn't over. Isobel uncoiled, fast, unstoppable, pink fire rippling down her length as she gripped the very fabric of space. She tore out of the *Caligula*'s side, even as an island-burner particle beam stabbed down from its orbital installation. She fell out through fire, the *Caligula* carved in half and tumbling. As the beam quickly tracked across to her she U-jumped herself, leaving twists behind her to defeat any known tracking. Isobel snapped back out of it deep within atmosphere, just twenty feet above the ground—then her initial impetus reasserted itself and flung her down at a forty-five-degree angle. She was travelling at just over two thousand miles an hour.

In the fractions of a second between surfacing into the real and impacting with the ground, she scanned and linked and sucked up data. Hood first, she hit, already knowing both Penny Royal's and Thorvald Spear's locations. The latter was heading towards the former, which was convenient. Her impact carved a slot through a foot-thick layer of the rhizome surface and punched her down a hundred feet through wet mud. That rhizome mat split open behind her following the subsequent eruption of mud. A momentary strong feeling of nostalgia stilled her for a second, then she applied herself to burrowing. Even though she'd probably defeated any tracking, those satellites above would doubtless have picked up her impact point. She needed to be deeper, so the catastrophic effects of any weapon capable of reaching her would be unconscionable for the Polity. At first she used the simple hooder method of burrowing, but then applied other forces, accelerating. A coned force-field spread ahead of her and hardfields extended from her limbs like paddles.

"Hello, Isobel," said a voice in her mind. "Do you understand now?"

She did, because now the whole pattern became clear to her. She had been tempted and lured into bringing all her forces here to inevitable annihilation. Penny Royal's manipulation had been perfectly couched to fit her personality and the changes it was undergoing, tied in with the transformation of her body. She felt sick with rage at her own gullibility, and at how easily the black AI had played her.

"Why?" she asked, clamping down on that rage.

"Because you are a problem I caused, and one I am solving."

"I'm coming to kill you," she replied. "Then I'm going to gut Spear."

"Yes, of course," said Penny Royal, "these are your intentions, but are they actually what you want? Are they what *you* want?"

"No more games, Penny Royal—this ends now, today."

"Doubtless," the black AI replied.

SPEAR

I unstrapped myself and stood up, heading back into the ATV's cargo area, where I surveyed the copious space available. Perhaps a fully grown gabbleduck would fit. But the vehicle's conveniently large size reinforced my deep distrust of reality and the workings of my own mind. As if to affirm that impulse, déjà vu engulfed me again—then someone else's memory used that moment of distraction to slide into my mind.

The cargo area shrank and was now packed with plastic crates and cylinders on pallets—a shipment of arms.

The enclosed space was lit by the fast-passing light of a moon and outside, somewhere, a gabbleduck was muttering to itself. I'd spread my

blanket between two of the pallets and was sitting on it. Having taken off
my boots, I was now proceeding to pull down my combats.

"We're good," said Slater from the cab. "No activity being picked up."

The new chameleonware on the vehicle's roof would keep us
concealed from Theocracy satellites, but only if we remained stationary.
The window in that surveillance would open in about five hours. Now it
was time to conclude something that had been growing between us for
some weeks now.

"Sure," I replied, taking off my top.

By the time Slater came back into the cargo area I was naked, lying
back, my arms above my head–

No!

Somehow I shut it down and snapped back into the moment, staggering as present reality cracked back into place around me. I wasn't a prude,
but really, right then I didn't need a memory of Renata Markham's sexual
adventures. I also had to wonder what the increasing frequency of these
flashbacks might mean. As I shook myself out of it I realized the cargo
door was opening and lowering to form a ramp and Riss was beside me.

"So what was it this time?" the snake drone asked.

"Nothing important," I said, donning my mask and heading for the
ramp.

The flute grasses outside stood as high as my waist and at the edge
of the ramp I hesitated. I remembered that mud snakes lurked underneath the rhizome and snatched down prey passing above. Then I stepped
down, the layer unsteady beneath my feet, and waded through the grasses
to bring the Weaver into sight. It still sat there, but was no longer waving
what could only inaccurately be described as its thumb. It now held a
device I recognized—the one it had used to detach penny molluscs from
a rock during our previous encounter.

"I take it you're going our way?" I suggested.

It nodded in solemn agreement, then peered up behind us. I turned to
see those two cylinders hovering about fifty feet up in the air and about
the same distance behind the ATV.

"We're right on the edge," said Riss. "Another hundred feet and they'd
have carried out their orders and fused our vehicle's drive. Luckily Leif

Grant was watching and he's now changed their orders—they are to follow and keep watch only."

However, Grant's problem was that the Weaver had other ideas. The device it held made a clicking sound, just that, nothing spectacular. The two cylinders dropped out of the sky like the heavy lumps of metal they were and thumped straight down into the boggy ground. One of them steadily sank out of sight while the other managed to keep its top end above the grass line. The barrel of a coil gun centred on us and small sensor dishes whirled. Another click ensued and the thing squawked, that barrel swung aside and its sensor dishes grew still. It too then began to sink.

I turned back in time to see the Weaver putting away its handy little device and heaving itself back into quadruped position, whereupon it ambled over to us.

"I need a ride," it said. "There is now some urgency."

"Urgency?"

"Do you feel it?" it enquired, raising a forelimb and stabbing one claw down towards the unsteady ground.

I could feel movement, like a constant earth tremor, but I'd put that down to the massive beast before me and the recent unexpected landing of two heavy drones. It then occurred to me that I'd felt this even on the ramp—before the Weaver had started moving and while the drones were still in the sky.

"The engine?" I suggested, nodding towards the ATV.

"No, something moving, down deep," said Riss. "I can only surmise that it's something big because of the soil displacement, otherwise it's impenetrable." The snake drone looked up. "Some sort of mudmarine?"

"You could say that," the Weaver replied, then proceeded towards the ramp.

I moved hastily aside, while Riss just turned and shot back up the ramp ahead of the creature. The moment the Weaver stepped on the ramp the whole ATV tipped over towards it, then automatically tried to right itself by expanding its cage wheels on this side and collapsing them on the other as the creature entered. I then climbed up to the doorway but upon peering inside felt suddenly vulnerable. Here was an intelligent being who we were giving a lift, but it now occupied most of the cargo area.

I'd have to squeeze past it to get to my seat and, intelligent or not, it was big, possessed huge black claws and very sharp teeth.

"Does human air bother you?" I asked, moving inside.

"Invigorating," said the Weaver, waving a dismissive claw that passed just a foot over my head with a sharp swishing sound.

The ramp closed up quickly and the scrubbers cleaned up the air in just a few seconds. There hadn't been much bleed-in since the ATV maintained a marginally higher internal air pressure than that outside. I squeezed past the gabbleduck, taking off my mask as I did so. Immediately my nostrils were filled with a smell akin to that of a big dog that had been chasing sticks in the sea, along with an underlying hint of reptile house. This close to the gabbleduck, I could see the elephantine wrinkles in its skin, subtle diamond patterns and what looked like multicoloured capillaries. Little nodes were scattered here and there, but I didn't know if they were part of the skin or some sort of parasite. Some areas also possessed an odd oily iridescence, while others were translucent and revealed quadrate patterns of black threads—like a form of carbon electronics. I was fascinated, and grateful not to find any familiarity here. I guess that no one in my available memories had come this close to a gabbleduck and had survived thereafter to become one of Penny Royal's victims.

"Ahem."

I looked up, nearly hitting my nose on this gabbleduck's bill, and backed off, staring into its green eyes.

"Do you mind?" the Weaver said.

"Sorry," I replied and quickly went to take my seat, even as the ATV moved off.

"It's heading in the same direction as us," said Riss, "and is now angling up to surface where *The Rose* came down."

"What?" I asked, distracted.

"That thing under the ground," Riss explained.

The ATV was just trundling along while Riss doubtless used her senses to probe the ground below us. She was also probably weighing the pros and cons of arriving before or after this unidentified object.

"Some speed would be good," said the Weaver from behind.

Riss accelerated.

20

BLITE

"You would be safer inside your ship," said Penny Royal, abruptly sucking its silver trunk inside and expanding into urchin form, a black star seemingly nailed to the air.

"Yeah, sure," said Blite, eyeing the AI then casting a glance out towards the nearest hooder.

"She comes," Penny Royal added, "faster than calculated, more capable than supposed because she has attained an unexpectedly stable unity."

"Yeah, sure," Blite said again, now actually starting to feel a bit worried. The AI had initially been a lethal threat, but proved itself otherwise. Thereafter, the threats had arisen from the situations into which it had dragged them. However, it had always appeared utterly sure and in control and Blite had come to trust it on some level. Even the encounter with that black ship, which he'd felt sure would kill them, had confirmed Penny Royal's capabilities; the black AI's superiority. Yet now it seemed unsure. Could it have miscalculated?

"How can Isobel be any more dangerous than these?" he indicated the three visible hooders. Even as he did this they all broke off from their circling patterns and began heading away. They were suddenly moving a lot faster than they had been, really motoring, leaving clouds of ripped-up grass fragments behind them.

As if they've been spooked, Blite thought, then wondered what the hell might spook such creatures—other than the AI floating above his ship. As he watched, he suddenly realized one of them was heading straight for the ship, so turned and reached down to grab up his particle cannon. But it was stuck, locked to the hull of his ship.

"No danger," said Penny Royal.

Blite glanced at Brond and Ikbal, who looked sick with fear, and noted that they hadn't raised their pulse-rifles. Sensible really, since those weapons would only succeed in pissing off the creature storming towards his ship.

Blite took a calming breath, believing in Penny Royal and sure that at any moment the creature would turn aside. It didn't. As it approached, it raised its spoon-like head from the ground and he could now see all those horrible manipulators underneath, and the two rows of glittering red eyes. It hit the side of the ship, rocking it, and scrambled up over it. Blite threw himself to one side as the thing came past him like an express train, its hard feet clattering against and actually scoring the hard hull metal. It simply kept going and, just a few seconds of thunderous noise later, the spike of its tail disappeared over the other side of the ship.

He looked at his two crewmen, who'd been on the other side of the creature from him. They were both standing up, brushing themselves off. Ikbal emitted a worryingly hysterical giggle.

"See," he said, "no danger at all."

"You would be safer inside your ship," Penny Royal repeated as it now began drifting out over the flute grasses. "In fact you can leave now, if you wish. You will find my final payment inside."

Blite wanted to return inside and check his supposed payment. He also considered leaving. Penny Royal was letting them go; it had finished with them, so surely the sensible thing to do was to get the hell out of here now, just as fast as they could.

"I want to see this through," said Brond.

"I agree," said Ikbal, grinning weirdly.

Blite felt the same. He wanted completion. However, though he was *The Rose*'s captain and an autocrat, he felt that his crew had been subjected to too much, and that they should *all* be offered choices.

"Is that the consensus of you all?" he asked on open channel.

"No it is fucking not," said Martina from inside. "And by the way, we've got seismic readings on something big travelling fast underground and heading straight for us."

"Captain," interjected Greer, "we all want to see this through, but we can do that as spectators, not participants."

Of course, he'd been mesmerized and hadn't been thinking straight. He turned to Brond and Ikbal. "Safety lines." They quickly moved to secure their lines to loops set in the hull, while Blite did the same. Once his line was on he continued, "Leven, are you still with us?" His ship's mind had grown increasingly uncommunicative since their last time here. It had been rendered redundant and quite possibly terrified in ways known only to AIs.

"I'm back," said Leven cheerily.

"Glad to hear it. Take us up, nice and easy, then to a safe distance and put us down again."

"I'm curious to know what might be a safe distance, Captain, other than say, a light century or two."

The ship began to rise on anti-grav, its feet making a sucking sound against the rhizome mat. Then it broke away with a lurch that sent Blite staggering.

"How's our hardfield projector?" he asked.

"I hardly think that—" began Leven, then fell silent. After a moment the Golem mind continued, "Oh wow."

"What is it?" Blite asked impatiently.

"Seems our defensive capability has increased."

"If you could be a bit clearer."

"Penny Royal's been playing around with the projector."

Blite felt a surge of excitement. If the AI had left them with a projector even just a little like the one it had deployed to defend Carapace City, then they just got stinking rich. Was this then the payment the AI had mentioned?

Leven took *The Rose* a few miles to one side of the building housing the Atheter AI and brought it down again. Blite unclipped his monocular from his belt and raised it to his enviro-suit's visor. He could now see Penny Royal hovering about a mile out from that building, turning and shifting; its shape constantly reforming, as if the AI was searching for the right response to . . . something. Then, only minutes later, the rhizome layer just a hundred metres from the AI bulged and burst open—and that something exploded from it in pink fire, mud and steam.

"So that's Isobel," said Brond. "She's not quite how I remember her."

Blite glanced at the other two and saw that they too had produced monoculars to watch this scene. Returning his gaze to the unfolding events he felt the urge to emit one of Ikbal's giggles. Yes, everyone had known what Penny Royal had done to Isobel. And he himself had seen some media footage of her new form when she went after some mafia boss on the Rock Pool. That had been shocking enough, because she was an almost complete, though small, hooder. Now she was a big albino hooder, pink fire caging her from end to end as she hurtled up into the sky and slowed, seemingly gripping the very air with her multitude of limbs. She hooked and halted, her hood pointed directly towards Penny Royal.

"Like the Technician?" Brond observed.

"Yes," Blite replied, "just smaller."

The story of the Technician hadn't exactly been suppressed, but it did lack detail and some data had been made difficult to obtain—supposedly because of the Weaver's ownership of it. However, he'd seen detailed pictures of the Technician, and recorded footage of it climbing into the sky. Isobel was about a third of the size. She also looked newer, whiter—fresh and youthful—while the Technician had been big and appallingly ancient, battered and stained.

Brond continued. "But the Technician was supposedly one of the Atheter's original war machines—so why does she look like one of those, and not like that hooder that just came close to smearing us?"

Penny Royal's earlier words, when they had first arrived here, about "a war mind growing inside her," abruptly clarified themselves in Blite's mind. Hooders were very devolved, distant ancestors of the Technician's kind—so it seemed Penny Royal's manipulations were more profound than they'd thought. But he had no time to think about them further. Up in the sky Penny Royal was changing, spreading out and curving into a great black satellite dish formed of translucent black plates. Isobel suddenly straightened out and streaked towards that dish, growing painfully bright as something travelled along her length and expelled itself ahead of her. The space-twisting force she produced wrenched at Blite's gut even here. Then that distortion struck the AI dead centre and bounced away in pieces, some heading up into the sky and some straight down into the ground.

The sound, like dreadnoughts sideswiping each other, reached them first, and Blite slammed his hands over his ears. Where one of those distortions hit nearby, the ground folded around it as if twisted by a fish-eye lens. A wave sped out, fast, ripping up rhizome and grasses. It reached them in seconds and flung *The Rose* upwards, sprawling Blite on his back. Then sound became muffled, the air turned to amber around them, and he felt his ship's grav-engines engage. They settled the ship back down gently rather than dropping it like a brick. As Blite staggered upright he saw that a hardfield now enclosed them, just in time to intercept and bounce away another of those fragments of distortion.

"Nice one, Leven," he said.

"Like I said," the Golem mind replied, "a couple of light centuries might be needed, if we want to observe comfortably."

Blite now took a moment to consider Penny Royal's earlier words. He at once understood that Spear and the AI itself were the lure to bring Isobel here. But why? Why couldn't the AI have completed its business with her when they last encountered the *Moray Firth*? And why, in all sanity, had it tampered with her transformation, turning her into this?

"How much guilt does an AI experience?" wondered Brond, now standing close beside him.

He'd gone right to the heart of it. It had become evident that Penny Royal was correcting past wrongs, trying to clear up the messes it made when it had not been quite so *nice*. Blite couldn't help but feel that Penny Royal had chosen Isobel—one of those transgressions—as a route to absolution. But did that mean he was now witnessing the elaborate suicide of the black AI?

SPEAR

"Fuck and damnation," I said, hanging upside down from my seat straps.

Annoyingly, Riss was still coiled in the driver's seat as if gravity had no effect on her, despite the fact that our ATV was now on its roof. I looked back to see the Weaver sprawled bill down against what was the ceiling—its rump up in the air and the very picture of indignity.

"Agreed," it said, then began to squirm round.

"A gravity shock wave," said Riss, "generated by an intricate form of U-space distortion—a rather more subtle spatial manipulation than a Polity USER." The drone looked back. "Stay where you are, I can right us."

Hydraulic motors began humming and the ATV began to tilt sideways. Glancing to the side, I could see one of the nearest cage wheels hinging down on its axle, which itself was telescoping out. In a moment the vehicle was up on its side, then tilting past that, before abruptly toppling back down the right way up.

"Umph," said the Weaver.

I looked back to see it on its rump again and looking mildly irritated, one claw supporting it against the wall because the ATV was still tilted. Gradually the wheel and axle combination that had flipped us back over retracted and aligned, bringing us level again.

"So what caused that?" I asked, probing tender flesh around my shoulder bone.

"Yes," said Riss, again turning to look at the Weaver, her third black eye now wide open, "what caused that?"

While the Weaver scratched at its rump and chewed over whether or not to reply, I tried using my aug to go after information. Surely I could get some sort of satellite image of whatever was occurring ahead? Nothing: Masada's computer networks were all down.

"Isobel Satomi caused that," the Weaver eventually replied.

"What?" I said, then grew irritated with myself. That admission of dumb ignorance had been issuing from me all too often of late.

"How the hell could she have possibly got here? The security here is massive and the Polity would have come down on her like a collapsing skyscraper the moment the *Moray Firth* surfaced."

"Isobel Satomi," said the Weaver, now taking up that handy little device of his and attaching some other horn-shaped item to it, "is now a stage one biomech and war mind instatement. Penny Royal is experiencing difficulties."

I managed to suppress the "what" before it left my mouth.

"What stage was the Technician?" Riss asked.

"Stage ten," said the Weaver, "there's nothing higher." It held the device up close to its eyes. "You may proceed now."

Riss turned to look at me and I met her unblinking gaze.

"Well, you heard the fella," I said.

Without comment, Riss faced the screen, the joystick shifted, and with a slight grating sound the ATV surged forwards again. I now noticed what looked like a thunderstorm lighting the horizon ahead—also the sky looked darker and the sun was setting behind us. We'd travelled maybe a further hundred feet when another of those waves heaved up the grasses far ahead and sped towards us. I gripped my seat arms, determined not to end up with my full weight against the straps if we were turned over again.

Click.

All around us the churned ground flattened, as if under some huge invisible arrowhead—and when I glanced back at the Weaver, it had raised its device once more. The approaching gravity wave hit the edge of this area and rode up over it. We also rolled on through the flattened area, weathering the wave, although I swore as the wrench forced my tender collarbone against my safety strap. But the ATV remained stuck to the ground and we continued on. I looked at the Weaver again, who exposed his white holly teeth in a grin.

"There are whole legions of forensic AIs who would fight each other to the death to get hold of that toy of yours," Riss noted.

"Yes," said the Weaver, "which is why I am here now."

Half an hour of travelling, four more waves, and a couple of detonations finally brought us close. The latter lit up the sky like nuclear strikes. But the ATV had obviously sustained damage, because even as it laboured to the top of a hill of newly compacted rhizome, something gave out and filled the vehicle with the smell of hot metal. I looked round as the Weaver abruptly straight-armed the cargo door, which went down with a crash. It quickly clambered out and I unstrapped and followed.

"Your mask," said Riss, who was dogging my footsteps. I donned it quickly, stopped just to breathe for a moment and clear the shadows from the periphery of my vision, then pursued the Weaver to the summit.

The vista we had hoped for now lay open before us. Far over to the right I could see *The Rose*, sitting under a hardfield dome. Far over to the left I could see the Atheter AI building, half buried on its side. In the sky, directly ahead, Penny Royal and the thing that had been Isobel Satomi were tearing at each other like angry gods. And it looked as if the black AI was losing.

We just watched. Isobel hung in the sky like burning vine, cupped by a disintegrating expanse of black edges and surfaces. Energies were flashing between these Titans as if they'd stopped sniping at each other and had now moved on to their particular form of hand-to-hand combat. This was a vicious scrabble, with armouries depleted and knives out. High above, in the darkening sky, I could see glinting shapes—doubtless every Polity asset in the system was poised up there. The Weaver now began heading down the slope, having inspected this view for a moment. I didn't really think this was a great idea but I followed. Just then, as if waiting for our arrival, Penny Royal came apart with a sound like some titanic glass bowl shattering and just dropped into thousands of pieces from the sky.

ISOBEL

She'd won, she'd destroyed Penny Royal, and now Thorvald Spear had come. Complete vengeance would be hers . . . her mission would be accomplished. Isobel released her hold and dropped down through the sky, her fires going out. She hit the ground heavily, partially sank, then scrabbled out.

The enemy?

Her war mind reacted, bringing its remaining resources to bear with enough energy remaining to obliterate Spear. She fought it. She didn't want his end to be that simple. And the war mind actually stopped, surprising her because she'd thought she wouldn't be able to hold it back. Using her many legs, she sped towards the three making their way down the distant slope. She raised her hood, shedding glassy shards as she sharpened her feeding sickles, targeting frames and complex tactical schematics blooming all over the three. The snake drone was a danger, but could be dealt with using just a small twist. As for the other creature . . .

She slammed to an involuntary halt.

"And this is what you want to be?" a familiar voice asked.

No, you're dead—I destroyed you.

Abruptly she forced herself into motion again, baffled by whatever had obstructed her. She inspected the last of the three. Why was Spear accompanied by a large gabbleduck? And why was it that she now, abruptly, felt so afraid?

The snake drone. She targeted it properly and began to generate the required shaping of U-space distortions to turn the thing inside out. But suddenly she couldn't remember how to do that, the war mind seemingly fading away from her.

No matter.

The predator was still with her and the drone simply could not stand against her present form. They were now just fifty feet away. She began to raise her hood, prepared to come down on Spear, who was now crouched down, gazing at her. She felt something then, an infrasound pulse hitting her. This was how Spear had paralysed Trent, Gabriel and herself when he had first escaped them. Elements inside her abruptly froze, but now they were irrelevant. She experienced a moment of vicious joy. She just bypassed those small points of paralysis and mapped Spear's body in intricate detail as she rose higher, determining the slowest and most agonizing way to take him apart.

"So that is all you can do?" she said. However, her translator had been destroyed, along with the two Polity weapons she'd attached to her body. She must therefore be using some more complex system inside her to speak.

Spear stood up, shrugged. "It was worth a try."

"Few of my human nerves remain, so your prion cascade was sure to fail."

"So the Weaver tells me," said Spear. "It also told me that obedience to their masters is integral to Atheter war machines. Are you feeling that love yet, Isobel?"

Enough of this. She began to move forwards. Click.

She froze. No. No! Somehow Spear's prion cascade was now working and her whole body just slid from her control. She came down like a falling redwood and hit the ground, splashing mud all around. Targeting frames, schematics, tactical calculations, they all fled. The predator relinquished her and faded too. Spear and the snake drone slid away from her perception and all she could now see was the gabbleduck, the Atheter, beckoning to her with one claw, summoning her.

She felt the love.

The war mind was now back in full control, perfectly melded with the predator, while she continued to recede. She felt the war mind's total loyalty, its absolute love of the kind that had created it which was utterly fundamental to its being. Then it expelled her into blackness.

SPEAR

The albino hooder, which had been partially controlled by Isobel Satomi's parasitic mind, now came forwards. It halted just a few feet from the gabbleduck and lowered its hood to the ground. I wasn't sure I liked that, the way it seemed to be prostrating itself. I found something distasteful about its lack of choice, even in something so lethal—but then humans fool themselves with their belief in free will. And I might well be the worst example of such self-deception. Also, such a reaction was hypocritical, when I considered my relationship with Flute . . .

"So, are they both dead now?" I asked, a hollow disappointment opening inside me.

"Isobel might have been killed by the war mind but Penny Royal certainly wasn't."

I turned to gaze enquiringly at the silver snake.

Riss continued, "The original Technician was much more powerful, yet was also incapable of destroying Penny Royal. Look." Riss flicked her tail at the scene ahead.

Translucent black octagons, each no thicker than paper, lay scattered across the darkening landscape—but even now they were changing. They were collapsing in on themselves, compressing their own substance into something darker, harder, and definitely more opaque—crystalline objects of all different shapes like the parts of a Chinese puzzle.

I felt suddenly angry. I understood that I was part of the lure to bring Isobel here, which was irritating enough, but my main anger stemmed from my failure to understand why she'd been lured here after all that. Also why she'd been turned into the thing still grovelling before the Weaver.

"Penny Royal seems loath to erase any data, no matter how despicable it might be," said a recognizable voice. "So I'm guessing Isobel Satomi is also alive, in some form, somewhere."

"Amistad," said Riss, turning. "You can move very quietly when you want to."

I turned to see the erstwhile war drone poised on the churned ground just behind us, flickers passing over his gleaming carapace as he dispelled some final chameleonware effect.

"So," I said, my anger at last finding direction, "the warden of Masada has at last seen fit to show his ugly face now the danger is over." It wasn't fair, I know—I wasn't feeling very fair.

"A questionable title," said Riss.

"A defunct title," said Amistad, "as of just a few minutes ago."

I fought the urge, but I lost: "What?"

Riss swung back towards me. "This world was under protectorate status and thus a ward of the Polity, requiring a warden with Polity military assets. While the Weaver had no way of defending itself, that's how it would have remained. And that is the situation the Polity AIs would have preferred. They supplied the Weaver with some technology, but not much in the way of particle cannons, U-jump missiles or CTDs."

"Ah," I said, the penny, at last, dropping.

"Not only was I compromised by Penny Royal, which would have put my warden status on hold until I'd been vetted," said Amistad. "But the AI has also just made me redundant."

It has to be noted that Amistad did not sound particularly unhappy about this.

I turned to look at the Weaver and the thing that had been Isobel Satomi. I auged into Masada's computer networks, relieved to find them reinstating, and felt my mind seeming to expand. I encompassed more data and considered legalities. The Atheter's greatest weapon and defence was the hooder war machine I saw before me. This had been refined over millennia in battles between themselves and predatory Jain technology. So it was understandable that the world had ceased to be a protectorate the moment Penny Royal provided the Weaver with this thing. Even now, polite demands had gone through to the Polity from the Atheter AI, reinforcing this change of status. Sure, the runcible transfer gates could stay, as could the people. But the orbital weapons platforms, the warships and the whole Polity military presence would have to go.

This was an Atheter world now and the Polity had no rights here.

BLITE

With his eyes glued to his monocular, Blite said, "Play that last bit for me again, Leven."

His ship mind obliged while he watched the Weaver moving off with the albino hooder trundling along at heel like some obedient hound. Spear and the snake drone were now awaiting the arrival of a gravcar to pick them up—the only vehicle now being allowed into the area. Amistad had his own methods of moving himself about quickly. On the horizon, other vehicles that had congregated were now moving off too—troop transports and gunships, two recognizable forensic AIs and a selection of war drones.

"I see that it's the Polity's intention to seize Penny Royal," the Weaver had said, ambling over like some big friendly bear to stand before Spear, Riss and Amistad.

"Doubtless," Amistad had replied. "It's what I would have ordered."

"Under your own laws," the Weaver had continued, "you have no right of seizure here unless I grant it. I do not."

"They were probably hoping to get it done before you had time to object," Amistad had replied, finishing with a scorpion shrug. "But I see your objection has been lodged via your AI. They'll withdraw now."

"Yes, to wait outside my territory in the hope of seizing Penny Royal there."

"Sure." Amistad hadn't been too bothered either way.

"They'll fail," were the Weaver's departing words as it turned away.

The others had been listening to the replay and now Brond said, "You have to wonder about our own position now. Legally, that is."

"In essence, we've been transporting about a glorified arms smuggler," Blite replied, now lowering his monocular. "We did so under duress so we shouldn't be in trouble."

"Yeah, sure," said Martina cynically from inside the ship.

"However," Blite continued, "it might be an idea for us to make ourselves scarce for a while until things have cooled down here. And maybe we should try to get out before the Polity prepares whatever trap it intends for Penny Royal."

He reached down and unclipped his line from the hull, heading for the ladder into *The Rose*. The other two followed him down and inside then, as the airlock closed for a final time, he said, "Take us up and away from here, Leven, and try to keep us out of trouble."

"Will do," the mind replied.

Blite was about to head for the bridge, but hesitated, heading back to the holds and Engineering. Within a few minutes he was standing before the bulkhead door, which he'd only gone through once since the black AI had been aboard. He hesitated again, realizing that what had resided beyond this door still frightened him, but he told himself not to be so stupid. Penny Royal was now on the rapidly receding ground below, still pulling itself back together. He opened the door.

When he was last in here, the back wall of the hold had been missing, along with most of one other wall. Their materials had been converted into organic-looking pillars and cross-members. He'd been able to see all the way to the U-space drive from this position. There had also been clumps of hardware sprouting from the structure of the ship like puff-balls, interlinked by a mycelium of optics and bright silver s-con wires. And Penny Royal, of course. Now the walls were back and the mycelium was gone. However, two of those puffball objects remained in the middle of the hold, their surfaces indented with lines so that they now looked like huge white pumpkins. Blite stared at these things for a long time, then walked over and studied them more closely.

A memory hit him.

He was a child gazing at his newly upgraded teacher's shimmering holo-display. All he had to do was speak and the thing would activate. He raised his hand then as an adult, in another memory, and it came down on the lid of a box. He opened this box and gazed greedily at the stack of diamond slate inside.

Then he returned abruptly to the moment, Penny Royal's mental tampering at an end. This time he didn't feel sick, and he knew what to do. He paused, remembering an old story about someone called Pandora, then berated himself for his silliness.

Really, if Penny Royal wanted to shaft him in some way it would do so and there was very little he could do about that.

"Okay," he said, "open up."

In eerie silence, the two pumpkins split down their indented lines, their radially divided sections folding down like waterlily petals. Inside were a mass of small, red, crystalline objects, packed together like pomegranate seeds. He reached down, took hold of one of these between his forefinger and thumb and tugged. It came out easily and, as he weighted the ruby in the palm of his hand, he smiled. Artificially generated rubies possessed minor value. However, gazing into the gem, he saw odd refractive layers and quadrate webworks of barely visible silvery wires, so he guessed these also contained quantum computing.

"Who are they?" he wondered aloud, waiting for more memories.

A noise issued from behind him—as if the stem of a wine glass had broken. He turned to see another gem hovering in the air, a black diamond this time. But this had oozed out from the underlying continuum and was fighting to maintain its hold here—so was shrinking and expanding.

"I recorded every individual when I killed them, but it was never enough," the AI replied. "There are always those who can never be retrieved."

So, final payment: Penny Royal had given Blite the minds of thousands of people. The thing in his palm, though of unconventional design, was a memplant. The Polity reward for such items was plenty, but multiplied by thousands . . .

"I have one final favour to ask of you," said the AI.

"Oh yeah."

"It is a favour, because you do not have to grant it."

"Tell me."

The AI told him and left the decision to him, and then the diamond winked out. Exiting the hold, still carrying the ruby in the palm of his hand so he could deliver the good news to his crew, Blite said, "Leven, slight course alteration."

SPEAR

The gravcar sent to take us back to Chattering, and perhaps thence to the space port, arrived and settled. I sat on an up-tilted chunk of rhizome and watched the scene before me. The black crystals—those Chinese puzzle pieces—seemed to be straining and twisting, yet I couldn't visibly see them moving. I wondered why, in the growing darkness, I could see them so clearly, sense them so personally.

"So do you have any answers for me?" I asked of them, but received no reply. I turned to Riss, "Anything?"

"Nothing," the snake drone replied.

"And you?" I asked Amistad.

"Nothing either," the erstwhile warden of Masada replied. "I've tried everything I can to get some answers, but it's not responding on any level." Amistad paused for a second. "I did consider giving it a nudge or two with some missiles, but just got ordered to stand down."

"By who?"

"Earth Central."

"Oh."

"Seems we're to remain hands and claws off until Penny Royal leaves the Masadan system and departs Atheter space. A reception committee is being prepared."

Whatever, I thought, pretty sure that the AI spread out on the ground before me had all its future options mapped out, including its route away from here. If, that is, its intention was to leave.

I turned back to Riss. "So what does all this mean for us?"

"We were used?" Riss suggested.

"Yes," I turned back to regard Penny Royal, "but I don't think this is the end."

Perhaps a minute or so later, one of the crystalline objects shot up to hang in the air just ten feet above the ground. Another leapt up, slapping against the first with a sound reminiscent of a domino being clacked down on a board, then came another and another. I watched them forming into a large black gem as I stood up and began walking over, Riss falling in behind me.

"Why did you alter my memories?" I asked. "Why did you give me the memories of others and torment me with their recollections? And why are you, through that spine of yours aboard my ship, still interfering with my mind?

At the last question I halted, gazing up at the AI, close.

"You made me hate you," I said, "when in reality I never knew you."

The surface of the black gem shifted; then, with a sound like a sharpening stone passing across some giant scythe, it extruded its black spines and grew, in half a second, back into its urchin form.

"Of course I can't demand answers from something as powerful as you," I continued quietly. "You're still treating other beings like toys, just as you always did."

I suddenly sensed the object hanging before me tilting in some way, as if it was paying greater attention to me. In that moment I felt like an ant falling under the regard of a passing naturalist, small, noticed but inferior, and that made me abruptly angry again.

"Are you going to fucking answer me?"

Now Penny Royal began to rise, gently, like a released balloon.

I couldn't stand it; I couldn't bear that the black AI was just going to leave me as baffled as ever. I wanted to strike at it in some way, to try to call some attack from the *Lance*, but knew I couldn't. Stupidly, I found myself looking at the ground in search of rocks, anything to throw at the enigmatic thing above.

"Answers?" Penny Royal whispered.

The connection, always there in some ghostly fashion, hardened. An avalanche came down on me, the vessel formed to receive it. The verbal answers Penny Royal might give no longer mattered, because suddenly I was remembering, and remembering far too much.

The momentary terror and brief bright pain which was the end for three of Blite's old crew was clearer in my mind than our journey here. The rage that was Isobel Satomi, and her anxiety and ambition, were all there within my grasp. The horror and the agony of a man skinned by skeletal Golem and nailed to a ceiling was clear, but then faded as other memories clamoured for my attention. I found myself down on my knees as too much input for a human mind to contain unfolded in my skull, and was contained. Then I was down on my face, experiencing thousands of lives, and deaths, all running in parallel. I remembered it all; all that was in their minds, as if the memories were my own; all the memories of Penny Royal's victims. Should I call these false memories? No, because, like those I was resurrected with, they weren't necessarily my own—but they were true.

I don't know how much time passed before I again became aware of my surroundings. Penny Royal was gone, and I was being carried gently in the claws of a giant steel scorpion. Recognizing that I had regained consciousness, Amistad put me down, feet first, on the viewing platform overlooking Masada, and dawn.

"I understand now," I said, an edge of hysteria in my voice as I staggered and managed not to fall flat on my face.

It wasn't just the dead who had clamoured for my attention—and I could still sense their muted howling in my mind. There was a piece of Captain Blite too. Perhaps Penny Royal had recorded him as some safeguard against him dying, or perhaps just for the purpose he served now—to inform me.

"Blite thought Penny Royal had come here to commit suicide," I said, then stumbled over to a nearby wall and rested my back against it.

"Suicide," Riss echoed, probably more in touch with that idea than many other AIs.

I nodded.

Gazing at me, Amistad lectured, "The AI's purpose here was to separate Isobel from what she was becoming, to reverse the changes. But it also wanted to restore balance—to take the Weaver out from under Polity oversight and to free it."

"Yes," I said.

"So what have you learned?" the scorpion drone asked.

With poetic timing the sun breached the horizon. I stared at it, fighting to pull together the disparate pieces of my mind, which now seemed as scattered as Penny Royal had been. I just shook my head. In a strange way I felt like that poor soul trapped in the pyrite of that ammonite fossil I had taken from Isobel—stripped down, incomplete, fractured and forever repeating the same actions. I couldn't find the words then to describe how things had turned full-circle. How I'd set out seeking vengeance and lost that impulse as I learned how my memories had been altered. Now that need for retribution had returned in full force, incited by the clamouring dead. A certainty was arising inside me that I was destined to kill the black AI. And this formed the core around which my mind began to reassemble itself.

TRENT

I was right about the bulkheads, thought Trent, as he gazed through the gaping hole in the side of the *Moray Firth* and looked down on the surface of Masada. He was right about many things, such as that Isobel would end up getting him killed. Sure, he was alive right now, but he wouldn't last for much longer. Despite the drugs his suit had injected, the pain from his busted ribs and broken shoulder was now considerable too—those bones doubtless cracked apart along fracture lines that had been scribed into his very being. And the manner of his demise was just a question of whether the Polity got to him before orbital decay finished the job. Both options were death sentences.

"How are you doing?" he asked.

The ship mind—a prador second-child Isobel had never bothered to name—replied with gibberish. It was screwed. Its casing had been breached, its cooling system was down and it was steadily proceeding from supercold to just very cold, which would be enough to finish it off. Anyway, what more did he need from it? Before it stopped making sense entirely, he'd managed to get it to confirm that his own course led to oblivion.

So where did you put it, Isobel?

He'd searched the storage on and about the bridge and, despite the wreckage, felt sure he'd checked every possible location. If she'd left it in Medical then that was a problem. Seeking relief from his injuries, he'd already ascertained that Medical was that object tumbling into the Masadan atmosphere about ten miles down. It had to be in her research area—the place he'd been most reluctant to search because, well, if it wasn't there then that was it, it was probably gone for good.

With infinite care, Trent made his way through the wrecked ship. The research area platform had been torn away from its mountings, but that was irrelevant now grav was down. Propelling himself across a short gap to come down feet first on to it, wincing, he looked around. The most likely place to look was a cylindrical store with drawers and cupboard doors making up its entire surface. It was where she kept various small and valuable technological items. She'd also transferred some personal items she'd wanted to keep here, with her portable wealth, after she'd dismantled her cabin.

Checking his watch, Trent saw that he had about another two hours before the *Firth* really started to fall. As he searched a series of further crates and boxes, he wondered how it would play out. Would the *Firth* burn up in such an oxygen-depleted atmosphere? Probably not, but it would still heat up, and a lot. Perhaps if he secured himself somewhere deep in the ship, away from the fucking great hole in its side, he might not get fried—but to what purpose? So he could die when the ship broke up, hitting the oceans down there, or making a deep muddy crater in some landmass? But the *Firth* would most likely not even get that far. Would the Polity allow a large chunk of life-threatening wreckage to hit the planet? No, they'd vaporize it before it got anywhere close.

There was nothing in the crates and boxes or in the caches of some wrecked robot. So, with the image of the ship at the bad end of a Polity particle beam fresh in his mind, Trent decided to search that cylindrical store. First he dealt with the locking mechanism—shooting it out with his pulse-gun was enough, since Isobel had never felt the need for heavy security while she controlled this ship. He opened a cupboard and peered in at a stack of plastic boxes, pulling one out and opening it. Then he dragged out the item inside and released it. A party dress took on a life of its own and danced away from him in vacuum. Even after the drastic physical changes she had undergone, Isobel had still felt some need to hang onto her clothing. He searched every box, every pocket and pouch, steadily going through them all and sending them spinning away from him, then he moved on to the next cupboard.

Her jewellery box! With shaking hands he drew it out and opened the hinged wooden lid. Inside he found various bangles hanging on a wooden rod, with brooches arrayed below. He checked there, but nothing. Next he worked through the drawers, one by one. Isobel possessed a fortune in gem-encrusted rings. In fact, if there had been any chance of him surviving he would have taken this box, along with the diamond slate doubtless stowed in one of these cupboards, but the wealth was irrelevant now.

The next drawer elicited more excitement, for here were her earrings, but it wasn't there either. His one connection to his sister, his purple sapphire earring, wasn't there.

Feeling a surge of disappointment, Trent dragged open one of the drawers below, and there it was. He snatched it up quickly, intent on inserting it into his belt pouch, but the gem came apart in his fingers. Glittering fragments of sapphire escaped his grasp, leaving only the pin and the jewel's setting. He stood there, stunned for a moment, and when he finally tried to reach out to collect them up it was already too late. The fragments were spreading out around him like the debris of some explosion.

Finally, he gave up, and watched those pieces escaping into the surrounding wreckage. Had Isobel done that, or was the damage the result of the ship's recent crash? Did it matter? Trent slumped, coiled in on himself bringing his knees up to his chest. He had nothing else to do now, nothing left to occupy the short remaining time he had until he died.

"Guilty, Trent Sobel, you are guilty," whispered a voice.

He looked around to try and locate the source, then felt foolish because the *Firth* was airless and sound couldn't carry in here.

"Who is that?"

He felt cruel amusement, but not his own. His mouth went abruptly dry. Burning up in atmosphere, or crashing into the planet below, he could accept. In the former case, if things got too bad, he could just stick his pulse-gun underneath his chin and pull the trigger, but this? It was so unfair. His death was a fait accompli, but now a demon had come to take that away from him and probably consign him to something worse.

"For your crimes you are sentenced to death many times over," Penny Royal continued. "But then, for my crimes, there are perhaps not enough deaths I could suffer."

Glittering objects were now flicking out of the surrounding debris to collect at a point just a few yards out from him. For a moment he couldn't quite make out what they were, then with growing puzzlement he understood: pieces of purple sapphire were gathering there.

Granting my last wish before my death?

After a short while they were all in place because movement ceased, then the collection of fragments went black before flashing, his visor darkening to protect his eyes. As that darkness faded, he now saw his purple sapphire hanging before him, complete, intact.

"I return your gem and, in time, Isobel," said Penny Royal. Trent gaped for a second then reached out and snatched the sapphire down. "Thank you." He shrugged, slipped the gem into his belt pouch beside its pin and fitting. "But why?"

"Redeem yourself, Trent Sobel."

What the hell was that supposed to mean, Trent wondered, knowing that the AI had gone and any further questions would be met with silence. However, an answer of a kind arrived as the *Moray Firth* lurched. He knew at once that this wasn't due to the ship starting to break up, or from anything else relating to its imminent crash into the planet. Something had just docked. Next, his suit radio crackled into life.

"Trent Sobel, get yourself over here," said Captain Blite. "We're getting the hell out of here."

ISOBEL

Suddenly the blackness was gone. She ran a hand down over the fabric of her loose white silk shirt before sliding it down to her tight black lizard-hide trousers. She turned, feeling good, to gaze at her room's screen. As ever, this was on its mirror setting. She was a devastatingly beautiful woman: dark, straight hair framing her Asiatic face, a perfect figure and eyes of an unusual blue-purple.

Isobel flinched at some memory. She remembered breaking something that had come to irritate her because it so closely matched the colour of her eyes . . . eyes she had lost. No, that couldn't be right. Some nightmare perhaps? These weren't uncommon, even though she was now so powerful and, aboard her very own spaceship, so safe. She studied her image further, the memory of breaking something fading, but her confusion remained. Something was missing, what was it? It was there, identified in a moment.

Where was the predatory joy she always felt at the sight of her own beauty, sure in the knowledge of how she could use it? Where was the vicious satisfaction in *having* used it so efficiently to raise herself so high? Why did she feel so sad?

Because this isn't real.

Even as she admired herself, the transformation began. These stretched her face with scabs of carapace appearing and eye-pits sinking. She shrieked as insect legs stabbed out of her shirt and her body began to writhe, wormlike, and extend. Reaching up, she took hold of a handful of her hair and it simply came out.

"The problem was separating you from what you'd become, so intricately bound were the two," said a voice she recognized but didn't want to name to herself. It continued, "The Weaver supplied the answer for its own benefit: change what you were becoming, then make the new being reject the old. Thereafter, the only remaining problem was to find the line of division. It was perfect, and restored some balance on Masada too."

Manipulators were now sprouting out down each side of her extended face. Horror filled her, and this time it wasn't blunted by a growing hooder psyche; by the predator melding with her own predatory instincts. It wasn't ameliorated by her knowledge that to survive, she must accept the changes she was undergoing. Everything that had screamed in her when Penny Royal had changed the course of her transformation was screaming again . . . or was that *still screaming*? Had it ever stopped?

"The war machine left you behind," said Penny Royal. Yes, it was the AI talking to her, the AI she had supposedly killed.

"I don't understand," Isobel managed, her voice horribly distorted by her changing mouth. "Why . . . you do this?" she tried, but knew it was not a question but a plea for mercy.

"I must unravel my past back to its beginning, and it's to the beginning I will go next," the black AI replied cryptically. "That is, when all is done here and events ordered and set on their course to conclusion."

"Why!" she shrieked.

"You wanted to tear your enemies apart, and I provided the tools," said the AI. "That was wrong of me. I have now taken all your tools away from you: your war machine body, your ships, your people, your power, and now only you remain."

Isobel wailed.

"And now you have a small chance to again be what you once were."

Isobel's wail died and the world snapped again around her. The shadow passed and aboard this ersatz version of the *Moray Firth* Isobel turned, feeling good, to gaze at her screen mirror. She was beautiful again, her mind whole, all her memories accessible.

"How can that be possible?" she asked.

"All you need to do," Penny Royal replied, "is let go."

"You mean die."

"You reside in me now, Isobel, and now it's time for you to leave."

"You promise—I have another chance?" Isobel asked, suddenly, unutterably weary.

"I always keep my promises," said Penny Royal.

Isobel trusted the black AI not at all, but certainly didn't want to spend her existence as a recording inside it, subject to its every whim. She let go, and found herself falling into blackness, but towards something that glittered. At the last, as she fell into it, she recognized the purple sapphire, even as it scribed her mind into its frozen layers.